Cara Colter shares her hor
British Columbia, Canada,
than thirty years, an ancient crabby cat and several horses. She has three grown children and two grandsons.

Michele Renae is the pseudonym of award-winning author Michele Hauf. She has published over ninety novels in historical, paranormal and contemporary romance and fantasy, as well as writing action/adventure as Alex Archer. Instead of writing 'what she knows' she prefers to write 'what she would love to know and do'. And, yes, that includes being a jewel thief and/or a brain surgeon! You can email Michele at toastfaery@gmail.com, and find her on Instagram: @MicheleHauf and Pinterest: @toastfaery.

Also by Cara Colter

Winning Over the Brooding Billionaire
Accidentally Engaged to the Billionaire

A White Christmas in Whistler miniseries

The Billionaire's Festive Reunion

Winter Escapes miniseries

The Billionaire's Festive Reunion

Also by Michele Renae

Consequence of Their Parisian Night
Two-Week Temptation in Paradise

A White Christmas in Whistler miniseries

Their Midnight Mistletoe Kiss

Art of Being a Billionaire miniseries

Faking It with the Boss

Discover more at millsandboon.co.uk.

INVITATION TO HIS BILLION-DOLLAR BALL

CARA COLTER

CINDERELLA'S ONE-NIGHT SURPRISE

MICHELE RENAE

MILLS & BOON

All rights reserved including the right of reproduction in whole or in part in any form. This edition is published by arrangement with Harlequin Enterprises ULC.

This is a work of fiction. Names, characters, places, locations and incidents are purely fictional and bear no relationship to any real life individuals, living or dead, or to any actual places, business establishments, locations, events or incidents. Any resemblance is entirely coincidental.

This book is sold subject to the condition that it shall not, by way of trade or otherwise, be lent, resold, hired out or otherwise circulated without the prior consent of the publisher in any form of binding or cover other than that in which it is published and without a similar condition including this condition being imposed on the subsequent purchaser.

® and TM are trademarks owned and used by the trademark owner and/or its licensee. Trademarks marked with ® are registered with the United Kingdom Patent Office and/or the Office for Harmonisation in the Internal Market and in other countries.

First published in Great Britain 2025
by Mills & Boon, an imprint of HarperCollins*Publishers* Ltd,
1 London Bridge Street, London, SE1 9GF

www.harpercollins.co.uk

HarperCollins*Publishers*, Macken House, 39/40 Mayor Street Upper, Dublin 1, D01 C9W8, Ireland

Invitation to His Billion-Dollar Ball © 2025 Cara Colter

Cinderella's One-Night Surprise © 2025 Michele Hauf

ISBN: 978-0-263-39678-2

05/25

MIX
Paper | Supporting responsible forestry
FSC
www.fsc.org
FSC™ C007454

This book contains FSC™ certified paper
and other controlled sources to ensure responsible forest management.

For more information visit www.harpercollins.co.uk/green.

Printed and Bound in the UK using 100% Renewable Electricity
at CPI Group (UK) Ltd, Croydon, CR0 4YY

INVITATION TO HIS BILLION-DOLLAR BALL

CARA COLTER

MILLS & BOON

With gratitude to Michele Renae,
for bringing her endless creativity, her humor, and
her easygoing ability to 'roll with it' to this project.

CHAPTER ONE

"Ms. Whitmore, I don't think we can spend seven thousand dollars on a chair."

Layne Prescott closed her eyes, held her cell phone in one hand and pinched the bridge of her nose with the other. She was at the front desk, in the lobby of Whitmore Castle.

The castle had been built in Maine by Charles Whitmore during the Second World War, on the outskirts of the town named after his family. Local historians said he had built it for a homesick bride whom he had met in England, where his company supplied the war effort.

At the moment, only the lobby and two of the castle's twelve bedrooms were completely finished. The noise of the refurbishment—hammers pounding, the whine of a circular saw—rose up around her.

She opened her eyes again and glanced over her shoulder up at the portrait that hung behind her.

The stern-faced but exceedingly handsome Charles Whitmore gazed down on her.

Though her best friend, Mabel, was more inclined to talk to the painting than she was—he seemed formidable and perhaps even cruel, though it might have been the portrait style of the day—Layne gave in on this occasion.

"Give me strength," she muttered.

"Pardon?"

"Oh, I just said something to one of the carpenters."

"If you wouldn't mind focusing? My time is limited today."

Reluctantly, Layne turned her attention back to the image Charles Whitmore's aging granddaughter had sent to her phone. Pamela, a widow, had reverted to her maiden name after the death of her husband, which always left Layne slightly uncertain how to address her. It wasn't Mrs. Whitmore, and somehow *Miss* seemed ludicrous.

But addressing her by her first name also felt uncomfortable, particularly given Pamela's style of communication, which tended to be lady-of-the-manor to incompetent serf.

Layne had settled on *Ms.* for Pamela, and used the first names of her adult daughters, Rebecca and Jessica. The three women had inherited the castle. Pamela owned half, while her daughters each held a quarter interest.

"Don't argue with me," Pamela Whitmore said. "I want that chair."

Layne bit her lip. She thought her response to acquiring the chair had been remarkably measured, since what she wanted to say was *Are you utterly insane?*

The chair was beyond hideous, a huge piece of furniture that could sit only two people and was covered in a nubby, faux leopard-skin print fabric.

"Beyond the expense," Layne offered tentatively, "I'm not sure it goes with the rest of the furnishings."

Despite the fact the castle had been closed for years, the original furnishings, many of which had come from Europe with Charles's bride, had been dustcovered and were in remarkable condition.

Layne held the phone away from her ear as Pamela Whitmore became quite shrill, reminding her that the transformation of the long-abandoned Whitmore Castle into a B and B was an investment, but more importantly, a way of honoring her grandfather Charles Whitmore's legacy in the Maine harbor community.

No matter that Ms. Whitmore and "the girls," as she called them, chose to live in New York City, about as far away from Charles's legacy as they could get.

"We'll just have to shave the budget somewhere else to accommodate the chair," Ms. Whitmore informed her.

"But where would we do that?" Layne asked, dangerously close to *arguing*, despite the fact that, to her own ears, her tone sounded faintly plaintive.

"My dear, that's your job," Ms. Whitmore declared. "Or that other girl. Martha."

"Mabel," Layne corrected her weakly.

"Oh, yes. Tell her to jiggle some numbers. I must have that chair. And I must go. Frederick is waiting. Ta."

Layne stared at the disconnected phone in her hand. Ta? Seriously? And she had no idea who Frederick was. Hairdresser? Chauffeur? Lover?

Ew to that last one.

Whoever he was, he trumped Ms. Whitmore's commitment to the castle. With each passing day since she had taken this job, Layne had become more and more aware that the castle was a toy to the mother and daughters who had inherited it. A passing fancy of wealthy dilettantes. It deserved more, and that was why Layne hung on through the whims and change orders and the impossible, daily demands.

She felt it was *she*, not the Whitmore women, who knew exactly how to honor the legacy of this place.

She and her best friend, Mabel, had grown up three doors away from each other, their neighborhood on the edge of the grounds of the boarded-up castle.

The magic had begun to unfold for them when they were eight and found, first, a hole in the fence, and then a loose board over a window on the castle. Hearts beating wildly at the audacity of their trespass, they'd pushed open the board swinging on a single nail, and let themselves in.

Each time they entered—and it was often—the trepidation about getting caught faded. In fact, as they explored the rooms, peeping under dustcovers and murmuring at the unused fine china, they discovered all of the castle's secrets and treasures. More and more, it felt as if the beautiful structure belonged to them. If pure love for a place determined ownership, that would certainly be true.

They were as different in their dreams as they were in their looks. Mabel was the all-American, blue-eyed blonde, and even as an eight-year-old, her future beauty had been evident in her exquisite bone structure and coloring.

Layne, on the other hand, had been dark-eyed, red-haired and freckled, and everyone, including herself, had been quite astonished when bright red hair turned to a deep, luminescent bronze and the freckles faded.

Throughout their growing-up years, the castle had highlighted the differences in their personalities. Layne, quiet and responsible, had let go in the castle, and danced among the dust motes in the ballroom, escaping from the reality of her constantly squabbling parents, with fantasies of a handsome prince, a world of romance and glamour and, most of all, *stability*.

Mabel, in sharp contrast, had been rocking to sleep the antique dolls she found in the nursery, a nurturer hiding just below the surface of the type A personality that had been emerging even when they were young.

The walls guarded the secrets they had told each other, the childish spells they had cast for future husbands, and now, with Layne's heart broken, and Mabel's dreams in tatters, it was as if the castle had called them back to its enchantment.

Layne had seen an ad in the local paper advertising for a project manager as the descendants of Charles Whitmore family had taken a sudden interest in the castle and decided to transform it into a bed-and-breakfast.

It felt as if it was the job she had been born to do, and it had a meant-to-be feeling to it, as Layne and her boyfriend, Brock, later her fiancé, had spent the last few years in her beloved Whitmore buying old houses and turning them into very successful vacation rentals. But then things had fallen apart with Brock...

Despite rocking babies in her younger years, Mabel had been eager to leave sleepy, lovely Whitmore in her dust. But her career in the music industry was short-lived, and had left her slightly jaundiced about life and dreams.

And then, the opportunity had come up at the castle, and Layne hired to direct the renovation and then manage the B and B when it was operational. It had quickly become evident the project needed Mabel's substantial business acumen, and so both women had ended up, serendipitously, at the castle where their hopes and dreams had once flourished.

But here was the thing that Layne should have known about life by now.

There was always a thorn hidden among the roses.

And hers and Mabel's was that the castle had come with—in the form of the Whitmore women, Pamela's daughters also preferring that name—its very own wicked stepmother and stepsisters!

Mabel was working from home today as the noise and dust from construction made it hard for her to concentrate.

Layne sent her a text with a picture of the chair.

Hey, Financial Director, here's the latest from the evil stepmother.

Mabel's official payroll title was project accountant, but she had kiddingly promoted herself in their private communications. The women took their delights, even small ones, where they could find them.

Mabel responded with an appropriate green-faced, about-to-chuck-up emoji. And then,

Seriously, seven thousand dollars?

But you can jiggle the numbers to make it work. She'll have forgotten all about it by next week when she decides that she needs three Thoroughbred horses in the front paddock to make it more *castley*.

Layne found herself laughing out loud, and let her friend know that.

LOL.

You're laughing now, but it won't be so funny when she turns your beloved carriage house back into accommodations for the horses.

Mabel knew how to tease her, because Layne loved her little house at the gate of the Whitmore Castle driveway beyond reason.

She was so grateful for her and Mabel's friendship, and for the fact the castle, despite the daily challenges from the owners, had brought them back together when they both needed it the most.

She tapped in another message.

On our budget, there's no danger of horses in residence.

Mabel responded, instantly.

Donkeys! The local animal shelter just had several surrendered to them.

Layne was pulled from the back-and-forth by the deep and unmistakable rumble of a motorcycle coming up the driveway. As the sound got closer and closer, she signed off from Mabel, and curious, went out from behind the desk to look out the lobby window over the lilac-lined curving driveway. Her cottage peeked out behind the shrubs at the very end.

An abundance of buds promised days ahead when the scent of blooming lilacs and roses intermingled and drifted through the window, just as they did at her cottage. As always, the order of the garden and the beauty of it soothed something in her and erased her doubts that maybe she had made a mistake coming here to work for the impossible Whitmores.

Honestly, some days, after dealing with one or another of the Whitmore women, she wondered if she wouldn't have been better off working the drive-through takeout window at the Loose Lobster.

Today, all that pastoral beauty had the rather jarring intrusion of a motorcycle sliding to a halt in the top of the circular driveway, just below the wide stairs.

Layne frowned. One of the Straightline Construction workers arriving late? That would be unusual, and the workers usually parked in the much larger lot at the back.

A helmet-clad man, a black leather jacket clinging to broad shoulders, was balancing a huge motorcycle between long, powerful-looking legs.

She knew next to nothing about motorcycles but she could see, on the polished chrome gas tank, the distinctive sun emblem of Sunshine and Storm Cycles, a company that had started right here in Whitmore and had become—along with this castle and lobster—one of the town's few claims to fame.

As Layne watched, the man turned off the bike with a strong flick of a square wrist, kicked down the stand, and then slid the helmet from his head, unleashing a tumble of dark, somewhat crushed curls.

Definitely not one of the workers!

She felt compelled to stare, feeling weirdly guilty, like a spy, and at the same time unable to look away.

The man ran a careless hand through those midnight-dark curls, and they sprang wildly to life under his touch. The sun caught in the tangles.

He dismounted the bike with an easy swing of a long leg, and then stretched, panther-like, the unconscious gracefulness in his movement that of a man who was very sure of himself and very comfortable with his own body.

He turned to hook his helmet off a handlebar, and Layne noted he was wearing black leather motorcycle chaps over dark denim jeans. She was shocked at how that framing of his narrow backside beneath that buckled band of leather was a look she found over-the-top sexy.

Then he turned back and looked fully at the castle, his gaze sweeping, and taking in every detail.

Layne knew exactly what he was seeing. The castle had been modeled in miniature after one in Sussex, England, called Bodiam.

The magnificent front steps led to the soaring, wooden front door, heavy and beautifully polished, with hammered iron pegs making it look regal and slightly formidable. That grand front entry was framed on either side by square turrets. The corners of the building were anchored by round turrets all topped with parapets so realistic you could almost picture soldiers in them scanning for the enemy.

Puzzled, Layne noticed the visitor's eyes were narrow, and his mouth faintly downturned.

Layne was used to curiosity and awe—even a kind of reverence—when people encountered the castle for the first time.

But the look on his face—anything but reverent, maybe even bordering on scornful—caused her a ripple of discomfort that deepened as something tickled along her spine. Recognition.

Did she know him from somewhere?

It seemed unlikely she would forget a face—or to be totally honest, a body—like his. Faintly whisker-shadowed, his face was utter male perfection, and breathtakingly chiseled.

The stranger, grace of movement in every stride, loped up the wide walk toward the front entrance.

Layne scrambled back behind her desk, opened her project book and managed what she hoped was a slightly surprised, but polite, inquisitive look as the heavy front door opened and he stepped in.

If he had seemed like masculine perfection from a distance, that impression was even more pronounced in a lobby that had seemed spacious only seconds ago.

Now it felt as if his presence, almost electrical, filled it: the aroma of leather, the unruly curls and his faint smile drawing Layne's attention, completely, to the fullness of his lips. Her eyes skittered away, taking in the whisker-shadowing of high cheekbones, the straightness of his nose, the squareness of his chin.

The scowl that he had regarded the castle with had vanished so completely that she was sure she must have imagined it, a trick of sunlight in her eyes.

His eyes were a delicious shade of brown, the exact shade of those dark, melted chocolate chips in the center of Whitmore Bakery's famous "crookies." They were lit from within, but she was not sure if it was mischief, devilment, seduction or some swoon-worthy combination of all three.

The front view of those motorcycle chaps, strapped over narrow hips, framing parts of him she absolutely had to keep her eyes off, was every bit as breath-stopping as the back view had been.

He took the lobby in with a glance, and then he looked at the portrait above her. His gaze rested there for what seemed like an endless moment. Did she detect a sudden, faint tension in the cast of his shoulders?

Those shoulders! Which was better? The wideness of his shoulders under that black leather, or the narrowness of his behind?

Oh, for heaven's sake. *Way* too focused on every detail about him. She was acting like a starving person suddenly presented with a sumptuous buffet.

Of course, her breakup with Brock was now nearly a year old. It was *normal* to start noticing again, wasn't it? Well, okay, she had vowed she was done with relationships, forever, that she would never trust or love again, but she was only looking at this stranger like an art patron admiring a piece of art she never intended to own. It wasn't as if she was posting banns at the local church.

Layne told herself, again, that it was perfectly *normal* to appreciate a man, given this was the first time she had noticed a member of the opposite sex in *that* way since the end of her engagement.

Her imploded engagement—not to mention the battlefield between her parents while she was growing up—should serve as enough deterrent to the dangers of *that way*!

On the other hand, why had this stranger captured her attention so completely? She was surrounded by the rather sumptuous men of the Straightline Construction crew almost every day.

And she could happily report, she had not felt one little

iota of interest, even when some of them flirted shamelessly with her.

"Hi, there," he said.

When his gaze settled on her, Layne saw she had been as mistaken about the tension in his shoulders as she had been about what had seemed like a scowl on his face when he regarded the castle.

In fact, Layne was not sure she had ever seen a man look more relaxed, more completely at home with himself, or radiating such a subtle confidence.

His voice was low, with a hint of gravel in it. It was as sensual as a touch, and Layne felt herself caught off-balance again by her reaction to him.

She was surrounded by gravelly-voiced men every day!

But to be honest, she had not experienced the strange strength of this kind of masculine pull, even before Brock.

To be really honest, not ever.

CHAPTER TWO

"HI, THERE." Layne echoed the stranger's greeting, grappling for composure, even as she tucked a stray strand of hair behind her ear, tried to remember if she'd applied mascara this morning—doubtful—and resisted an impulse to moisten her lips.

She mentally reviewed the outfit she had chosen for the day. Since Brock, she had not made an effort appearance-wise, and she sadly regretted her decision to go extra drab this morning. It was a reaction to one of the construction workers, Fred Hawley, whom she had gone to school with, confiding his own breakup with her yesterday.

He hadn't quite asked her for a date, but he had looked so pathetically hopeful.

She had told him, as gently and as firmly as she could, that she was not ready.

Though now it occurred to her that perhaps being ready to reenter the world of male-female relationships might not be so much a choice as a chance. As in a chance encounter.

Stop it, Layne ordered herself, super annoyed.

Still, she was only human. The man who had showed up at the castle *was* an amazing male specimen. It was like seeing a statue created by Michelangelo. You could admire the art and the beauty and perfection of the form and composition, all the while being very aware you couldn't actually *own* it.

Neither of them spoke for a second. He had cocked his

head slightly, and was regarding her with a compelling intensity.

"C-can I help you?" she finally managed to stutter.

He seemed jarred by the question, as if he, too, was caught in a spell where they could just gaze at each other all day.

He seemed to snap out of it quickly. "I was just passing through the area and caught a glimpse of the castle from the road. It's intrigued me since I was a kid."

Did that mean he had a connection to the town? That he was local? She did have that vague notion of having seen him before. In a place the size of Whitmore, you ran into just about everybody, eventually.

But surely he would have made more of an impression on her, even if she had just caught a momentary glimpse of him, in a line at the bank, walking down the street, or slipping a carton of milk into his grocery tote?

Not that he looked as if he drank anything quite so wholesome as milk.

"If I'm not interrupting your day, could you tell me what's going on here? It looks like a refurbishment."

Again she noticed the faint, entirely masculine rasp at the edge of his words. Again, Layne felt as if the words physically touched her, like a gentle scrape of fine-grit sandpaper on the back of her neck. As for interrupting her day, interruptions that distracted her from leopard-patterned chairs were nothing but welcome!

His words were accompanied by a smile of such charm Layne was pretty sure she was about to melt into a puddle of skin and bone on the floor.

And that was before he crossed the lobby in a single, long stride and held out his hand to her.

Layne looked at it for way too long, fighting a feeling, ridiculous as it was, that taking that hand could change everything forever.

"Jesse Kade," he said.

Jesse, she thought, the perfect name for an outlaw who rode into someone's life on a powerful machine, dressed in sexy black leather, both the bike and the attire beckoning her toward a world she had never experienced.

A world that suggested a walk on the wild side. A place that seemed as if it would be filled with impromptu adventure and flirtations with danger. It seemed as if Jesse Kade would live in a universe that invited excitement, rather than one where you ran from it.

She just knew taking that hand was going to change something fundamental in her. Touching would take her from a spectator to a participant.

Aside from her one transgression—trespassing in the castle—she considered herself to be *that* person: consistent, dependable, steadfast, mature. Her outfit reflected, thankfully, all those things.

She was the person who yearned for stability. One of her parents had been constantly leaving or threatening to leave the other, all through her growing-up years. And then they would kiss and make up, and it would be like a honeymoon for a while.

Layne had grown up on a roller coaster that plunged into despair, climbed slowly back up toward hope, rested for a millisecond on the peak of happiness and arrival, and then plunged back down again with terrifying swiftness.

So, every single time, she chose the safe route over the unpredictable.

But when Layne took Jesse's extended hand, she felt the sensual contact of his dry palm against her own, and the pure strength radiating from him. She could feel the power in his grip, being tempered for her benefit. Despite his control of the strength, as her hand disappeared into the fold of his, it felt as if a bolt of fire shot up from her fingertips to her elbow.

And she did feel the change in herself, instantly.

All of those things she had always prided herself on—being trustworthy and reliable, being the person you could count on—suddenly seemed to add up to the saddest thing. It matched her outfit perfectly.

Dull.

Layne Prescott was dull.

Touching this man's hand, weirdly, made her more acutely aware of that than even Brock's parting shot had.

"My God, Layne, I feel as if we've been married fifty years. I'm not ready to build a world around picket fences and prize-winning roses and rocking chairs on the front stoop."

He'd suggested they sell all the properties they'd worked so hard for. Since they had leveraged one to buy the next one, this wasn't quite the windfall he might have hoped for. But with the little cash he'd had in hand, Brock had bought himself a one-way ticket, and was currently backpacking across Thailand.

He was so insensitive to the distress he had caused her, that he sent postcards about the wonderful time he was having exploring caves and riding elephants.

Each postcard made her aware of how small her world was. It *had* been her idea, with their bed-and-breakfast holdings, to create a sensation of *home* in each of their properties, and the house they had shared together.

At the time, he'd approved of calling their company Home Sweet Home.

It was exactly as Brock had said: picket fences, flowers in border beds, swings hanging from huge trees that provided shade to deep front porches.

The problem was, until the exact moment she had touched Jesse's hand, she'd thought she was completely, one hundred percent happy with that world. Layne had a niggling awareness that, while she had been creating a perfect fairytale world for the guests, she had basically been boring her fiancé to death.

Now there was feeling of never wanting to let go of the firm grip of this hand. It was too much to read into it, that a complete stranger could deliver her to the road not taken.

Wasn't it really just more of the same? A romantic notion, a linking of your hopes and dreams to someone else's personality and plans?

No, the lesson she had to take from Brock's unexpected discontent with their lives was that she was no good at predicting where safety lay as soon as other people—men people—entered the equations. And so she needed complete independence, and that independence needed to be laced with healthy doses of cynicism.

There was no prince to go with her castle.

The castle wasn't even hers!

Unsettled, Layne countered the stunning feeling that she never wanted to let go of Jesse's hand by jerking out of his grip. She refrained, barely, from checking her hand for singe marks.

His smile deepened ever so slightly, making her sinfully aware of the plump pink of his full bottom lip, a sharp contrast to the rest of his hard lines. The wider smile revealed he had a crooked front tooth, one faintly overlapping the other one. The imperfection, oddly, made him even more attractive, the fighter pilot from that movie taking her into the danger zone.

Layne tucked her tingling hand behind her back, rethought it when his smile deepened, again, and then placed it on the desk between them, instead.

It spoke to her dull life that hand placement could be seen as an act of defiance!

As she scanned his face, it was apparent Jesse Kade knew

exactly the effect he had on women. That realization, she thought, trying for annoyance and falling far short, wasn't nearly as disturbing as it should have been.

"Layne Prescott," she introduced herself, tilting her head at him. "I have the strangest feeling of knowing you from somewhere. Is that possible?"

It was turning out to be Jesse Kade's favorite kind of day. One full of surprises.

The first surprise was finding Whitmore Castle no longer boarded up, as he remembered it from his last visit to his hometown. The once moss-covered facade had been power-washed until the sandstone glowed golden, the gardens had been coaxed back to life, and the wild hedge of lilacs that lined the driveway, to the point of nearly choking it, had been meticulously pruned. In a month or so the bloom would be spectacular.

As Jesse had entered the lobby he'd heard and smelled bustling activity—the whine of circular saws in some distant part of the castle, the smell of sawdust and adhesive and paint. He saw that the spacious front entryway, where he now stood, had been restored to what he assumed from his reading and research was its former, gracious glory.

Still, it was a shame that so much was being invested in the old castle, given his future plans for it, but if it hurt the Whitmore family *more*, it could only be a good thing.

The second surprise was the woman behind a tall, hotel-like reception desk. She looked to be in her midtwenties, dressed in a casual, white button-up shirt. He couldn't see her legs, but he guessed, from her height, that they were long. Her hair was loose and spilling over slender shoulders.

Her hair was possibly the most tantalizing color he had ever seen, the cast of the sun coming through the window burnishing it to glowing, antique bronze.

There was no identifying marker on the tall desk or pinned to her blouse to indicate who she was. She could have equally been a receptionist, someone involved in the renovations, or a member of the Whitmore family.

That final thought gave him pause. What was her connection to the Whitmores? He hoped none, because even on their very short acquaintance he did not want her to become caught up in a decades-in-the-making righting of wrongs.

He had to work very hard to not give anything away when Layne Prescott said she had the strangest feeling of knowing him from somewhere.

Because that *somewhere* was the portrait she was standing right underneath.

Jesse had always been aware of his likeness to his grandfather—that old bastard—but he had not seen that particular portrait before, and the strength of the resemblance jarred him.

Wait. His grandfather, technically, had not been the bastard. That mantle had been carried by Jesse's father—and his grandmother—in a time when such things were a disgrace, the weight of the shame carrying implications into all that followed.

"No, we haven't met," Jesse told Layne, truthfully. "I would have remembered that."

"Me, too," she said, and then the loveliest shade of pink crept up the flawlessness of her skin and made him aware of the high cheekbones, the set of wide lips, the sunlight-through-coffee color of her amazing eyes.

He needed to get something out of the way, *fast*.

"What's your connection to this place?" he asked her, his tone intentionally casual.

She glanced around with obvious affection.

"I grew up a few blocks from here. It was already boarded

up by that point. I don't think anybody's lived in here since Charles Whitmore died in the sixties.

"When we were just kids, me and my bestie found a way in. We came to regard it as ours, I'm afraid. Though I do feel my fate is intertwined with that of the castle. It's being turned into a bed-and-breakfast. An opportunity to be the project manager on the refurbishment, being done by the descendants of the original owner, came my way at the perfect time. I couldn't resist."

Jesse felt a wave of relief. She wasn't related to them. Though attached to the place, her attachment was not by tainted blood, nor did she have a financial stake in the ruin he planned for Whitmore Castle.

There was something about the way she said *perfect time* that hinted at unwanted changes in her life. A breakup? A closer look told him she had that faintly bruised look of one who'd had their life plans unexpectedly upended.

He didn't want to know. Because given her *attachment*, she was bound to hate him as his own plans unfolded. Though who knew? If she'd been dealing with Pamela Whitmore, she might enjoy seeing the legs get cut out from under the old bat, his much older cousin, who was just recently becoming aware of his existence.

"Are you just passing through Whitmore?" she asked.

The castle was hardly on the beaten path.

"I grew up in town. I'm back for a visit. I'll be here a few days."

"Ah," she said. "Maybe that's why I felt I recognized you?"

"Maybe," he agreed, fighting an overwhelming urge to look up at the portrait. He was fairly certain he was older than Layne, and she had the look of someone who was solidly middle-class, so chances of their paths crossing would have been slim.

She asked the usual question, and Jesse was annoyed to find he still dreaded it.

"What area did you grow up in?"

How could he still feel the faint stirring of shame, after all the success he had enjoyed? Maybe it wasn't shame. Maybe it was anger that his grandmother had finished out her days in that horrible shanty in Riverton, refusing to move even when he had pleaded with her.

In some way, his grandmother's bitterness had become her biggest investment, and she had not been able to leave it behind.

He was here for her, for Mary Katherine Kade, to finally have justice served.

"Here and there," he answered Layne's question, and he saw that she wanted to probe, to find a Whitmore connection, even a geographical one, between them, and so she pressed, just a little bit.

"What high school did you graduate from?"

He smiled, one hundred percent renegade charm, a look he had perfected. "You're assuming I graduated."

"Oh." She blushed. "I did assume that."

"Beware of guys on motorcycles dressed in black leather," he said, his tone teasing. The distraction worked.

"So noted," she said, but her smile said she wasn't wary of him at all, though he was aware she probably should be. "Though I'm not sure a true miscreant would be riding that particular motorcycle."

He gave her a quizzical look, even as he processed her easy use of *miscreant*. It occurred to him she reminded him of a small-town librarian. Decent. Trustworthy. Predictable. It wasn't the type he went for.

He went for the type that didn't have traditional longings written all over them. Not that he actually *went* for anybody. Success was his mistress, and he loved her with a singleness of focus and devotion that did not leave room for other pursuits.

Particularly complicated ones.

The woman in front of him would be complicated, he was pretty sure, and so he was more than a little surprised to uncover the unknown fact about himself that he had a librarian fantasy.

One that, sadly, he would have to resist.

"You're riding a Sunshine and Storm motorbike. The creator was from here."

"Mr. Poochy?" he said, raising his eyebrows in mock surprise.

She laughed. It was the nicest sound. "It's clever, isn't it? And fun? That the dog is listed as the company founder and CEO?"

He tried not to be too pleased that she got exactly what the creator of Sunshine and Storm had been doing when he had evaded personal recognition, and chosen to feature the dog instead.

He was aware that now there were two lies between them, even if they were lies of omission. She had given him opportunities, but Jesse had not revealed either his connection to the Whitmores or that he, in fact, was the founder of Sunshine and Storm.

She looked at him intently, and he had the uneasy feeling she was the kind of woman who got to the truth, whether a man wanted to reveal it or not.

So the answer to her next question should have been a no.

"Could I show you around?"

Jesse didn't want to look around Whitmore Castle, especially with a woman who looked as if she could draw his truth from him with no more effort than it took her to flip open the cover of a book.

And, impossibly, at the very same time, he wanted to see

the castle just about more than any other thing he'd ever wanted in his life.

And so he followed Layne when she beckoned him.

Her outfit, revealed when she walked out from behind the desk, was bland, a beige pencil skirt and flats in a matching shade of oatmeal. If the outfit was meant to downplay the sweetness of her curves, the length of slender legs, it succeeded, and it didn't at the same time. It was somehow at odds with the bronze of her hair, the spark in her eyes and the tilt of sensuous lips, and the end result was that it intrigued, rather than put off.

Was it her intention to put people—male people—off? She was surrounded by a construction crew. Maybe that was a wise time to downplay assets.

But there was really no hiding the fact that she could have walked with those fierce, proud, strong women that went willing with Boudicca into battle.

He wouldn't normally do that, but as he was drawn into the castle, Jesse ordered himself to focus on her rather than the surroundings that were so entwined with his family's history. So, he listened to her tour guide voice as she recited things she had probably said a thousand times.

"The castle is a replica of the fourteenth-century Bodiam Castle, only in miniature. But with no moat." Her recital of that was well rehearsed, and she paused for him to laugh at her little joke, but he found he couldn't.

Layne gave him a puzzled look, and moved on. "It originally had twelve bedrooms, a nursery, a ballroom and six indoor bathrooms, which was an unheard-of luxury in the day. We're reconfiguring a little bit so that the bedrooms have en suites, something that even the swankiest homes in the forties couldn't boast of. It is built with blocks of Maine's finest sandstone. Sandstone was also the material used for the original Sussex castle, but not from Maine, of course."

As she talked, Jesse shamelessly used the view of her backside, her legs, the sweet curve of her shoulders and spine beneath the blouse, the flow of her hair down her back, the lemon scent of her, the melodic sound of her voice, to distract himself from where he was.

"The castle," she said, not noticing, thank goodness, his deepening discomfort, "has been kept in good shape. It wasn't lived in, but that doesn't mean it had been abandoned. The Whitmore family retained ownership and the structure was regularly checked and maintained. Remarkably, given the treasures it held, it was never broken into—well, except by Mabel and I—and never vandalized."

As she spoke, her affection for the place was so obvious, and the refurbishment was nothing short of brilliant, the place being returned, room by room, with painstaking attention to detail, to its original glory. He tried to hang on to that, even as he felt darkness gathering around him.

"The entire place had to be taken down to the studs, to be rewired and have insulation brought up to snuff," Layne told him. "But we're trying to build it back as close to the original as we can. This room is basically identical to what it was after the place was built."

She held back a piece of plastic that had been put up to keep the dust from the nearly finished restoration of this room. He stepped through it into the main floor study.

Jesse felt a shiver along the back of his neck. He was certain he could smell cigar smoke. He hoped it was from one of the workers, even as he knew it was not. He glanced around, not sure what he was looking for until he saw it.

A candy dish on an elaborate side table. It was empty. He felt the faintest wave of dizziness and drew in a deep breath, feeling as if he was marshalling himself to move on, and that he did not want Layne to know.

Thankfully, she was in the thrall of the place, sharing how

it had been modeled after a real castle in Sussex, where the materials had been sourced from, the origins they had been able to trace for some of the furniture.

To his relief, they went to the kitchen next. It was in the process of being completely modernized. It had been gutted, the past erased.

But that past surged back as Layne drew Jesse out of the kitchen, deeper into the castle, and up the stairs. The guest rooms she showed him were projects unfolding, except for the final two, at the end of the hallway. Like the study, plastic protected the doors.

"These two are completely finished," Layne said, holding back the plastic so he could see better. "But with all the construction going on, I'm not accepting bookings until September."

The crew was working inside the primary suite, so they only took a quick look in there, which he was grateful for. He didn't want to linger where his grandfather had slept.

Despite that, he could feel shadows on this entire second floor. The only respite was in the bathrooms, most of them completely new, additions to the rooms carved out of a corner, or put in space stolen from the wide hallway.

Layne, glowing with pride and enthusiasm as she pointed out one feature after another, kept scanning his face for the reaction he could not give her.

For Jesse, even the unconscious sensuality of Layne's hair, her legs, her voice, her vibrancy were not enough to distract him now. She, and everything around her, were fading, like an old photograph that had been left out in too strong light.

The ghost was the most vibrant thing here, the presence that he could not ignore. In every room, in every hallway, behind every curtain and in every corner, he saw her, a young girl in her black maid's dress and ill-fitting shoes, on her knees, serving this house and its masters.

Mary Kade had fallen under the spell of this place as much as his tour guide.

In each area of the castle Jesse saw what Mary had seen, felt the ache in his heart for a long-ago young woman who had come into this place with innocence, curiosity, hopes and dreams. That part of her, somehow, was here, intact, not anything like the grandmother he had known, who had been all hard edges and cynicism, consumed by bitterness.

He had loved her madly, just as he had loved his father. But it was from these two flawed people that Jesse had learned how love could wound. Because his love had not changed his father's behavior, nor had it ever brought his grandmother happiness.

Mary Kade's happiness, he now saw, had all been left in this magnificent place. Every single drop of it.

For the first time, his commitment to destroying Whitmore castle wavered. Because it felt as if he might inadvertently destroy what had been best about his grandmother.

CHAPTER THREE

"AND THIS," LAYNE SAID, putting her hands on both the polished brass knobs of the large mahogany doors and swinging them open with flourish, "is the ballroom."

Given Jesse's lack of enthusiasm so far, she refrained—but just barely—from saying *ta-da*.

She realized she had hoped for some reaction to the first finished bedroom she had shown him. It was the one she had thrown herself into when she'd initially gotten the job. Somehow, creating the space in that room had become about leaving Brock, and the life they had shared together, behind her.

Instead of the homey theme that she had so painstakingly cultivated in the bed-and-breakfast houses, in that first castle bedroom she had layered neutrals, adding color with the paintings she chose for the wall. She had gone for a look that was sophisticated, serene and subtly sensual, and she had succeeded.

Not that Jesse had seemed to notice.

So, she had one last chance to impress. She always saved this room as the grand finale when she gave a tour of the castle.

The ballroom was huge and breathtaking, with its imported Italian marble floors, three enormous, crystal-dripping chandeliers drawing the eye naturally toward the soaring height and plaster detailing on the ceilings. At one end of it was an ornate staircase that led up to a balcony where a dozen or so people could retreat to a more intimate setting while still overlooking the festivities below them. A small walk-out from that area had a view of the sumptuous pool and patio area accessible from the floor-to-ceiling, glass-pane doors that lined the entire outer wall of the ballroom. With those doors open, the space could easily hold hundreds of people, flowing in and out.

She slid Jesse a look, to see if *finally* he had been won over.

Unlike most of the people who visited the castle for the first time, he didn't comment much. His reactions had been few and measured. No delighted *oohs* from him, no startled *ahs*, no deeply appreciative sighs.

Maybe he hadn't wanted to shout over the construction noise.

But when she had glanced at his face, trying to gauge his reaction, it had felt as his expression was...

Layne tried to label it. Not indifferent.

Guarded.

With something moody slipping by that guard.

More likely, a castle was just not to the taste of a motorcycle-riding outlaw with untamed locks and devilment dancing in his eyes.

Of course, she thought, *she could never fall in love with Jesse Kade, because what kind of prince did not love a castle?*

The thought took her aback.

Fall in love?

She didn't even know this man! And she was entertaining notions of falling in love with him? In his black leather, he was nothing like a prince!

The ballroom had always cast a spell on her, but really? She was older now. Wiser. Her longing for love, and her efforts to create a world opposite from the one of her parents, had ended with the very same result: nothing but heartache.

But now, as she slid another look toward him, trying to read if he felt anything at all about the best room in the castle, she saw she might have misread his quietness.

"Are you all right?" she asked, with sudden alarm. Jesse was pale and a fine bead of sweat had broken out over the subtle curve of his top lip.

He was obviously not feeling well, and she'd been so intent on making him love her castle that Layne hadn't even noticed.

He pressed a hand to his forehead and closed his eyes. "I'm sorry," he said, his voice strained.

She realized that he had probably not been feeling well when she'd begun showing him around, and now he might be feeling worse. No wonder he had not had anything to say. How could she have been so oblivious?

"Here," she said quickly, taking his arm, "let's go outside."

He surprised her by not pulling away but leaning into her, the brush of his muscular body hinting at a strength that was at odds with the paleness of his face.

She tucked herself under his shoulder and was engulfed in the rich scent of leather and the compelling scents of a man, soap and aftershave, and a little something else not so easily labeled.

Layne felt the sinewy power of him, and his warmth seeped through the leather and crept into her, like warm pudding being poured from a bowl.

She realized it was the first time she had touched a man so completely since Brock.

That explained the pang of pure, primal hunger, didn't it?

She also realized it was the first time she had *ever* touched a real man in the ballroom she had danced across with so many imaginary princes.

It felt absolutely wrong to feel as if that had a strange significance to it.

Layne guided Jesse across the ballroom, managed to hold him up as she released the antique lever on one of the doors.

Together they stepped through, and out onto the sunlit, topiary-dotted flagstone patio. The space flowed around the still, turquoise waters of the large pool. She felt Jesse suck in a breath, but again, it wasn't a reaction to the painting-like serenity of the pool area. It was more like a man who had been drowning suddenly finding the surface. His broad chest expanded as his lungs filled.

The patio and pool areas were completed but not yet furnished, as the Whitmore women contemplated a distressing number of options that included very expensive outdoor loungers, chairs, tables and sunshades.

The construction workers, however, had been taking breaks out here, so there were several plastic picnic tables to accommodate them. She nudged a chair out from under one with her foot, and eased him down into it.

"I'm fine," he protested.

She could tell at a glance he was not.

"I'll go get you something to drink," she offered.

"No, really, it's not necessary. I feel better already, with just the fresh air. I'll just sit for a second, then I'll go."

She cast him a look, and saw he was the kind of man who was used to pitting his strength and his will against any and all obstacles.

He was embarrassed by his weakness, but despite his protest that he felt better already, he still looked ashen.

"I think you should at least have a glass of water, first."

"No, I've taken enough of your time."

But had he, really? Despite her awareness of all the dangers it posed, she could not deny how attracted she was to him. She had a sensation that she would never feel like she'd had enough time with him. Drawn to him, she wanted more.

More of his scent, more of his conversation, more of the light that was coming back into his eyes.

He was making her feel like an infatuated schoolgirl, something she had *never* felt like before. It was silly. And yet, despite the danger—or maybe because of it—unbelievably compelling, as well. Perhaps a person should not go their whole life without feeling the mysterious and magnetic pull toward a member of the opposite sex?

"Wait right here," she said to him, hoping he understood it was not a request but an order. But was she keeping him for her benefit or his? The sweeping, rock-faced bar at the end of the patio was not yet operational, so Layne ran back through the castle to the kitchen.

By the time she returned, a tray laden with a frosted pitcher of water she had found in the fridge, glasses and her own lunch, Jesse was looking much better.

He had taken off the leather jacket and had on a T-shirt featuring a Mr. Poochy emblem over his left breast. The fabric, soft from much washing—a favorite shirt, perhaps—molded the broadness of his shoulders, the exquisite contours of his chest, the jut of his ribs and the flatness of his stomach. He had one sleekly muscled arm draped over the back of his chair, and he smiled at her, his confidence and coloring somewhat restored.

Still, Layne could see a hint of sheepishness in it, too, as if somehow he had let her—or perhaps himself—down by experiencing a moment of human weakness.

She poured him a glass of water and passed it to him, then sat down at the table.

"When's the last time you ate?" she asked.

He had to consider that, which meant it had probably been too long. She opened her brown bag lunch, considered its contents and then passed him a ham and cheese sandwich.

He held up his hand. "I'm not eating your lunch."

* * *

Jesse knew he should go. In fact, he should have slipped away as soon as she had offered him water. But somehow, he felt boneless, glued to this spot, unable to walk away from whatever was going to happen next.

Layne considered his rejection of her sandwich, then tore it in half, extending the bigger part to him.

"Sorry," she said with a small laugh when he didn't reach for her new offering, "I'm mothering you."

He felt unable to resist, but he was not sure which was irresistible. Was it the sandwich or the look that had softened her eyes? He took it. Their fingers brushed.

"A novel experience, for sure."

"What is? Sharing a sandwich?"

"Being mothered." Where had that come from? Obviously, he was still weak, not himself. Because one thing he did not do, ever? He did not share details of his personal life, and certainly not of his early life. "I didn't have a mother."

"Oh," she said, "I'm sorry."

Something in the way she said it weakened some wall around him. He suspected walking through the castle had damaged the chinking. Once the first brick fell, then what? Total collapse?

"I mean of course I had a mother. She just wasn't part of my life."

He silenced himself—and kept the brick in place—by taking a bite of the sandwich he had fully intended to refuse. He was eating her lunch. He realized he was famished. Where was his pride?

The sandwich was one of those spells some women—not generally the kind he went for—managed to weave, turning ham and cheese into a kind of ambrosia.

"What is this?" he asked.

"Oh, just ham and cheese."

"Not like any ham and cheese I've ever had."

"I like a lavender-infused cheese, a specialty of the local deli. It's unusual, isn't it?" And then, right on the heels of a question so innocuous, a sneak attack. "What happened to your mom?"

Mom. A word he had never used when referring to his mother, Millie Bishop, and those references had been rare. His father called her, without rancor, *that harlot*.

"She dumped me with my dad when I was three days old and never looked back."

Layne's eyes went wide and the sandwich paused on the way to her mouth. Which, as far as mouths went, was quite an adorable one. No, not adorable. Lush and full. Sensual.

"But who raised you?"

"My dad. And my grandmother. My dad was fifty-nine at the time he was told he was a father and a baby was laid in his arms. He'd been a lifelong bachelor who still lived at home with his mom."

So he could work less and drink more, his reaction to being an unacknowledged bastard son.

Not that the woman with the adorable/sensual mouth and the gift for making sandwiches needed to know any of that.

Though for some reason, he longed to tell her, to fall into the pool of her eyes, and tell her why he was really here.

Seeking revenge.

The longing to confide had to be fought.

"My dad, by the way, besides being a wizard at mechanics, turned out to be the world's best father. He took to it as if he'd been waiting his whole life for me."

Jesse never thought of his dad without missing him: he had treated his son the way he himself had never been treated, as if he was an unexpected treasure, and not a curse.

His grandmother, too, had given Jesse gifts she had seemed

incapable of giving his father, that relationship so tainted with resentment and the bitterness of dreams gone bad.

He polished off the sandwich and slugged back the water, suddenly knowing he *had* to go. Before any more bricks fell out of that badly weakened wall. He had to get away from Layne and shore up the fortress.

But before he got up from the table, a woman came around the corner of the castle. She was engrossed in her phone, and barely looked up.

She was absolutely gorgeous, tall, blue-eyed, blonde, and yet he was aware that in the short time he had known Layne, she had already managed to change what he thought gorgeous was.

"Layne! I'm being bombarded by the wicked stepmother. And the stepsisters! They've found a matching stool for that chair—"

She stopped suddenly and looked up. "Oh!" she said, registering that Layne was not alone.

"I'm sorry. Hello." She came forward and offered her hand, then looked quizzically between him and Layne.

He knew this must be Mabel, even before Layne introduced them. He could see the bond between the two friends.

"A castle complete with a wicked stepmother," he said, his tone deliberately light. "Do tell?"

"Oh!" Mabel said. "We have the boss from hell."

He saw Layne's warning look to her friend and appreciated that she was not going to allow her boss to be talked about behind her back. Mabel glanced at her, snapped her mouth shut, but flashed the picture on her phone at her friend.

Layne made a face that said it all, even before Mabel turned her screen to him.

"Well," Jesse said, looking at the gigantic chair and matching stool, "isn't that positively hideous?"

"Seven thousand dollars' worth of hideous for the chair. Another three for the *hassock*," Mabel filled him in.

Out of the corner of his eye, he saw Layne could not control her wince, not even out of loyalty.

"Everything you need to know about the Whitmore bunch right there," Mabel said, sliding the phone into the back pocket of her slacks.

It was. Everything he needed to know. Confirmation he was on the right path, though somehow when he glanced at Layne it didn't feel that way.

It felt as if he was being unreasonably vengeful.

And the thing about a woman like Layne? If he tangled any further with her, she would call on him to be the thing he was least interested in being, particularly when it came to the Whitmores.

A better man.

CHAPTER FOUR

Layne noticed Jesse look suddenly at his watch.

"Oh, geez," he said, scrambling to his feet. "I've lost track to time. So nice to meet both of you. Layne. Mabel."

And he was gone, striding across the patio and around the corner of the castle.

"What was that?" Mabel breathed.

A hurricane. A tornado. Layne was aware of feeling she had survived a storm, and instead of being grateful for the near miss, she was more aware of longing for all that swirling energy. Some subtle promise of excitement had evaporated with Jesse Kade's departure.

"He's forgotten his jacket," Mabel said, eyeing the black leather draped over the back of his chair. "You should bring it to him. You shouldn't just let him *go*."

"I'll put it in the lost and found," Layne said, carelessly. "He'll come back for it."

But when? When would she see him again? What if he didn't come back for it?

Mabel, of course, was not the least fooled by Layne's careless tone. "Oh, for heaven's sake," she snapped, "take charge of your own fate. Go after him."

"I'm not going to chase after him, like a puppy after a stick."

"Are you crazy? Didn't you see the way he was looking at you?"

Layne had been so busy trying to hide how *she* was looking at *him*, that that might have got by her. Or maybe she had noticed it, and ordered herself, *No. Absolutely not, no.* She'd seen sizzling attraction in her parents. It was something to run away from, not toward. Still…she hid the fact she felt wistful for what might have been.

"For someone who was supposedly looking at me that way, he seemed in a pretty big hurry to get away all of a sudden," Layne pointed out.

"Exactly," Mabel said, sagely. "Bring him his jacket. Tell him you'd like to see him again."

"I will not," Layne said, aghast.

"Okay, tell him you've never ridden on a motorcycle before, and you've always wanted to."

"Mabel! What kind of friend encourages her bestie to throw in with a stranger? One who drives a motorcycle, at that. Bad boys drive motorcycles."

"I know," Mabel said with a heartfelt sigh.

"You go after him, if you find him so irresistible," Layne suggested.

Mabel looked suddenly uncomfortable. Her eyes shifted in the direction all that construction noise was coming from. It occurred to Layne she might be missing something about her best friend.

They both heard the deep rumble of that powerful engine starting.

"If you run, I bet you can catch him," Mabel said.

Layne stubbornly held her seat, but despite the front she was putting up, her heart sank to her heels as she heard the robust sound of the engine throb, then pull away farther and farther until it was a distant hum, and then nothing at all.

She considered the possibility she might never see Jesse again. Mabel apparently did, too, because she sighed and gave Layne a pitying look.

"It's not as if he's a broke guy swilling beer at a low-life bar and playing pool for dollar bills."

"How do you know?" Layne demanded.

"Did you see that motorcycle?"

"Yes." She had to admit it was a beautiful machine. *Stunningly sexy, just like him.*

"Do you know what it's worth?"

"How would I know what a motorcycle is worth?"

"More than both our cars, combined. Did you notice his watch?"

"Why would I notice his watch?"

"Too busy looking into his eyes," Mabel teased her. "He looked like that actor to me, Lonnie Deep."

Layne considered that. Did Jesse look like the famous movie actor? Maybe that was why she had such a strong feeling of knowing him from somewhere.

"That watch?" Mable continued with a sigh. "Also worth more than both our cars. You should have gone after him."

But Mabel pointing out the expense of the watch, and Jesse's fabulous, actor-like good looks only made Layne more aware that the handsome stranger was out of her league. She didn't say that to her friend, though.

Instead she said, "Look, I'm pretty fresh off my breakup with Brock."

"Nearly a year is not *pretty fresh*," Mabel pointed out, without an ounce of sympathy. Layne had not missed how her nose had wrinkled ever so slightly at the mention of Brock's name. Mabel had done a poor job of hiding her dislike for him, even before the breakup, but her dislike had intensified after that.

Mabel had proven what friendship was when she flew home for a week after Brock's abandonment.

Her dislike of Layne's ex intensified with each postcard received.

Layne had showed her the last one. It featured a temple. On the back, Brock had scrawled, *Swam with sharks.*

Mabel, as only a true friend would, had neatly torn the postcard in two, put it in the trash and muttered, *"Too bad he didn't get eaten."*

Layne wished she could muster that kind of anger for her ex. It would be so preferable to the sense of unworthiness—of being not good enough—that Brock's desertion had triggered in her.

"The point is, the last thing I need is another relationship."

Mabel snorted. "Layne! Who said anything about a relationship?"

"Look at my parents," Layne said softly.

"Oh, your parents," Mable said with the sigh of a person who had occupied a front-row seat to the complete lack of domestic bliss three doors down.

"I bet they started with heated looks, too."

"You don't have to be so serious all the time. You don't have to turn a chance encounter into a lifetime commitment. Not every guy who waltzes into your life has to be your forever prince. What would have been wrong with going and having some fun with a handsome stranger?"

What would be wrong with that? The world suddenly tilted, shivered with possibilities Layne had never considered before.

"He didn't ask!" Layne pointed out with an indignant squeak, stung by her friend's remarks, even as she recognized the truth in them, an invitation to embrace life in a different way than she ever had before.

"And neither did you."

"Because I am not that type."

"Huh. Well, I as I've said before, *if you always do what you've always done, you'll always get what you always got.*"

"You've never said that before."

They glared at each other for a moment, in that way of really close friends.

"I thought you weren't coming in today," Layne said with a sniff.

"How could I stay away?" Mabel retorted.

Again, Layne thought there might be something she was missing. The new demand for a matching leopard-print hassock hardly merited Mabel's fifteen-minute bike ride from town.

"Do you have a crush on one of the construction workers?" Layne asked.

"Get real," Mabel said, way too quickly.

"Because if you did, you could just tell him you've never tried a hammer before, and you've always have wanted to."

"Wow," Mabel said. "That could be construed in many ways."

The tension was gone, just like that, and they were laughing hysterically, the way they once had when they were little girls dreaming impossible dreams.

It wasn't until she was back at her desk that Layne realized Mabel had totally skirted the question about a possible crush.

Layne took Jesse's jacket back inside with her, and the rest of the day she was aware that she was faintly tense, waiting for the sound of the motorcycle returning. She spent way too much time mentally rehearsing what she would say. If she was given a second chance, would she be bolder?

But four o'clock arrived and Jesse had not returned. Layne walked the short distance to the carriage house, aware she was nursing disappointment.

And hope.

Because she brought the jacket with her. Just in case he noticed it was gone and came back tonight. He'd have to drive right by the carriage house, and there was no way she would miss the sound of the motorcycle.

Her heart felt like it did the oddest little cartwheel inside her chest at the very thought of Jesse coming *here*, not to the castle, but to her home.

She stepped in the door of her sanctuary and looked around at her tiny, happy place. She waited for *that* feeling to come, of being home, but today it evaded her.

The offer of the carriage house had really sealed the deal for her taking the job with the Whitmores. It had been her soft place to fall after the split with Brock.

Like the castle, it was an enchanted space, but in a far different way. There was nothing grand about it. You'd be more likely to see seven dwarfs inhabiting it than a prince. In fact, the living room only held two reclining chairs. She put Jesse's jacket on one of them.

Layne paused to admire how the afternoon light poured in paned windows, across a hand-knotted rug she'd found in an antique store. The soft summer light painted the scarred pine floors golden. The kitchen was really part of the same room, though she had a bookshelf, filled with favorite reads, acting as a divider. The kitchen contained a two-burner stove and the world's smallest fridge, covered in magnets with silly sayings on them. She opened the door and took a cold piece of pizza from it, munching as she went through to her bedroom.

It was small space, with a fresh coat of pale pink paint on the walls. It was mostly filled with the bed, which was distinctly girly. A comforter matched the white lace curtains playing in a breeze that came through the open window, crisp in that way of late spring nights. The bed was covered in pillows, a wonderful nest for reading. Brock had hated too many pillows—*he had to move them to get into bed*—and so the extravagance of having all the pillows she wanted delighted her in some way.

This morning, as she had picked them up off the floor

and placed them, it had felt like a strong "I'm taking my life back and I like it" statement.

Now, changing out of her work attire, it seemed as if a much stronger statement would have been to chase after that stranger with his jacket and say she had never been on a motorcycle before.

Standing there in the puddle of her discarded clothes, Layne considered carefully what to put on, filtering everything through the lens of the possible return of Jesse. Even her cottage didn't seem quite the same when she wondered what he would think of such a feminine space, and what it would tell him about her.

She decided on a pair of black yoga pants that were extremely flattering but casual. It wouldn't look as if she was trying to impress at all.

Normally, she would spend the evening unwinding with a good book, maybe a walk around the grounds before she went to sleep.

But tonight the book could not hold her attention, and the thought of a walk did not appeal. Every time she heard a vehicle go by on the road outside the castle gate, some fine tension ran along her spine.

As the evening progressed, especially as the clock ticked toward ten, it was evident Jesse was not returning to claim his jacket. Layne had a cup of tea before bed. It was one of those teas with a name, Serenity, but it felt to her as if it should have been called Dull and she could taste in it the bitterness of regret.

Why hadn't she followed Mabel's advice? Why hadn't she said something? Why, for once in her life, hadn't she taken a chance and done something bold and uncharacteristic?

She didn't have to be a prisoner of her childhood forever! Instead of being here with her book, she could be having an alternate experience. When she finally gave up completely, aware she should not feel so restless and aggrieved because he had not come, she put on her pajamas, yellow cotton with a faint dandelion print, with a button-up top and baggy trousers. In other words, super-comfy.

But when she caught a glimpse of herself in the mirror, she was not at all surprised Brock had left her.

She looked, well, *frumpy*.

Impulsively, she went and grabbed the Jesse's jacket off the chair and pulled it on over her pajamas. She was enveloped with the smell of leather and the smell of man, and it made her knees feel weak with unspoken longings.

She went and looked in the mirror, again. The jacket was way too large for her. And yet wearing it made her yearn for the girl she had never been, one of those girls wearing a jacket offered to her by her boyfriend on a cool autumn night at the Friday night football game.

Her hands found the pockets and dropped into them. Maybe there would be something to identify him, so that she could make sure he got his jacket back. She was not experienced in motorcycle gear, but she was pretty sure it was not cheap.

There was nothing in the pockets. No, wait. Something crinkled. Her fingers closed around it and she pulled it out.

A candy.

It wasn't hers, she warned herself, but it felt as if it spoke to a life way too rule-bound, that taking the wrapper off that candy and popping it in her mouth felt like an act of wild defiance.

For some reason the rich butterscotch of the candy melting on her tongue felt like just about the best thing she had ever tasted.

The candy dissolved to nothingness, and Layne felt the oddest sense of dreamy contentment, with the jacket—and all its luscious scents—wrapped around her.

CHAPTER FIVE

LAYNE WOKE UP in the morning feeling far from refreshed. She realized she still had the jacket on, and as comforting as it had felt last night, in the cool clarity of the morning light it felt utterly ridiculous that she had gone to bed in a stranger's jacket.

She got up and yanked the jacket off, returning it to the living room chair. One of the buckles had left a mark, like a brand, on her skin.

Layne looked around her space and took a deep breath, waiting again for that calm feeling of *home* that the pure coziness of the carriage house usually made her feel.

Instead, she was shocked to find her space suddenly had the feeling of a trap. It was the kind of place a woman could grow old in, carefully filling her bird feeders, feeding cats and surrounded by her collection of lace doilies.

A woman who had played it safe, protected her fragile emotions at all costs, and as a result spent her life preserving a castle that wasn't even hers.

She had *liked* being that person until just yesterday. Layne glared at the jacket. She should have never brought it into her space.

Suddenly getting rid of that piece of clothing, which smelled of leather and motorcycles and pure man, felt imperative.

Layne threw on the same yoga pants and T-shirt she had

worn yesterday, tucked the jacket under her arm and headed for the castle.

She was surprised to see Mabel's bicycle at the bottom of the stairs. Even though Layne's reasons for taking the jacket home with her were completely rational, she somehow did not want her friend to know she had taken it, so she skirted the front entrance and went around the side. The lost and found box was in the side porch, and she stuffed the jacket in there beside one work glove, a pair of sunglasses and a bright yellow high-vis vest.

Then she heard Mabel in the kitchen and joined her.

"Why are you here today?" she asked her friend.

Mabel lifted her shoulder. "I just thought I'd work from here."

Layne squinted at Mabel. She sensed it wasn't all about work, and might have even asked, except at that moment they both heard it.

It was the sound of the motorcycle returning.

"That must be Jesse. I think he's just noticed he left his jacket," Mabel said, a trace of excitement in her voice. "Where is it?"

"In the lost and found."

Mabel darted to the enclosed porch, came back and thrust the black leather into Layne's hands. "You go, girl."

Layne stared down at the jacket, looked up to see the challenge in Mabel's eyes. Could she be a different person? Shouldn't she stop and consider where that could lead her? Hadn't she done that, ad nauseam, last night? And hadn't her little cozy cottage warned her where *not* going to him was going to lead her? *Cats. Birdfeeders. Doilies.*

Safety suddenly did not seem like a worthy goal, at all.

Surely taking that jacket out to Jesse couldn't lead her to any place that was worse than where her strict adherence to all her life rules had led her to. Being jilted. On her way to becoming a cat lady in a cottage that had always felt nothing but cute to her and yet suddenly felt claustrophobic.

Her hands closed around the leather. She'd slept with it! How could she be surprised, anew, by how soft and supple the leather was? She squared her shoulders, moved through the kitchen, down the hallway, and out the front doors of the castle.

She paused in the shadow of the doorway. Her heart was beating way too hard as she watched Jesse guide the powerful machine to a halt. The silence when he turned it off was startling and profound. As he threw down the kickstand and turned off the bike, she felt a ripple of pure awareness of masculine strength and his innate confidence.

Layne drew in a steadying breath. She was making way too much of this. She was returning a man's jacket, not proposing an elopement.

Her parents had eloped.

Stop it, she ordered herself. She squared her shoulders and stepped out of the shadows.

She arrived just as he was getting off the bike, and then watched him unstrap his helmet and shake loose those curls. He didn't have a jacket on at all, and the light blue T-shirt he wore was molded to the tantalizing lines of his chest.

His eyes rested on her for a moment.

Mabel was right. He could be the star of a pirate movie. There was something sizzling and sensual in those dark, dark eyes that female members of any audience would sigh over.

Layne noticed his flesh was pebbled from riding the motorcycle in the morning breeze. Now, why would that seem sexy to her? Why could she picture her lips, hot, on the coolness of his skin? That's what she got for sleeping in his jacket! A spell cast over her. A yearning for an undefined something *more*.

Wordlessly, Layne passed his jacket to him.

"Thank you." Jesse took it from her, shrugged it on. For a long moment, he paused. She could tell he caught a faint fragrance clinging to that leather. Layne ordered herself not to blush.

"I wasn't sure anyone would be here on a Saturday."

"I'm not always," she said, wanting to seem like she had another life. "I had something to do here this morning."

His mouth quirked upward in a smile. "Leather chairs?"

She'd been dealing with leather, but not chairs.

"Oh, wait," he said, snapping his fingers. "Leopard skin, not leather."

"Not that," she said, desperately and suddenly wanting to be seen as a woman who had a little more going on than dealing with a fractious boss.

His hand reached into the pocket of his jacket, searching. Surely not for the candy? But he patted each pocket and then scanned the ground.

"Is something missing?" she asked. She actually felt guilty for eating that candy.

"No, not at all," he said smoothly, though he scanned the ground one last time. Silence spread between them.

She was acutely aware of birds singing and the smell of freshly mown grass, as if her every sense was coming awake.

"Well," Jesse said after a moment. "It's been nice meeting you, Layne. Thanks for sharing your sandwich yesterday and keeping my jacket safe."

Candy-less but safe, she thought, and then she realized he was going to leave. Life as a lonely cat lady loomed before her, and made her dig deep for bravery.

"I've never been on a motorcycle before," Layne blurted out, absolutely stunned at herself. She was the least impulsive person on the face of the planet. She suddenly felt off-balance. Was it because it was so out of character, or was it because she was unveiling some part of herself that had been there all along?

Bolder.

Curious.

Willing to step into the abyss of the unknown, and see that step as exciting rather than terrifying?

His hand froze on the helmet strap he was adjusting at his chin.

"Really?" he asked, and turned the full force of that dark gaze on her. He looked at her with genuine distress, as if she had missed absolutely the best of human experience.

For a moment she didn't know what to say into the sudden silence between them. But then, as if she was reading off a script Mabel had thrust into her hands, she said, "I've always wanted to."

You really couldn't hint any more loudly than that, but she elaborated anyway.

"I wouldn't have any problem taking the day off."

The look of wild discomfort she braced herself for did not come.

Instead, Jesse looked at her steadily, narrowly, finding his way to what she meant. The question was in his eyes. Was it about riding a motorcycle, or something more?

"I'm sorry," he said, and at first she thought he meant about missing the experience, but then she realized he was refusing her. Layne felt crestfallen that her one effort at being bold had fizzled.

"That's okay," she said, with a smile she wasn't feeling. "Come to think of it, I should deal with those stupid chairs today. I was looking for an excuse, but you have let me down."

She meant for it to sound light and teasing, but the way she had finished that sentence in her head—*in every way possible*—felt as if it was written in neon between them.

He was looking at her intently, not fooled by her effort to be funny and light.

"I've been thinking of getting a cat," she blurted out. "I might go look at kittens later. Do you like cats?"

She was babbling. Unfortunately, she was laying out what her future life could look like, all because he'd said no.

"I'm kind of a dog guy."

"Nice!" she said, way too enthusiastically. So many questions. Did he have a dog? What kind? How long had he had it?

A dog? He probably had a girlfriend. A wife. Her eyes slid to his hand. No ring, but maybe people didn't wear rings to ride motorcycles.

"I'd better get on with my day," she said, but she didn't move. He didn't, either.

"I don't have any extra stuff with me," he said quietly. "I couldn't bring you for a spin without proper gear, a helmet and some leathers. Not even a quick one."

Of course, he had come out here without the jacket on, but there was no sense putting him on the spot. It would only make her seem humiliatingly desperate to argue with him about how weak his excuse was.

"Oh," she stammered, and wished the ground would open up and swallow her. "Of course it wouldn't be safe. I didn't think of that."

What she did think of was that this was where her one attempt to experiment with who she really was got her.

Rejection. A pretext for not being with her. She bet this wasn't his first time riding without a jacket. She bet he rode without a helmet and often.

She should have known. She should have known she was just not the type to do something as wild and crazy as hint to a stranger she wanted to spend more time with him.

Obviously, she was going to get what she had always got.

A life that was dull, dull, dull. Other people could flirt their way to new adventures. She could not. It wasn't her style. She shouldn't have even tried to break the mold. So embarrassing. Even he, who looked like he embraced adventure as a matter of course, could see how foolish she had just been.

"All right," she said, stepping away from him and the motorcycle, trying to keep a same light tone and not reveal she felt nearly strangled with humiliation. "Goodbye. Have a nice day. Off to leopard skin!"

She turned away from him, fighting the temptation to run away from his rejection and back to the safety of her castle.

"Hey." His voice stopped her.

he hoped he wasn't going to elaborate on his justification for not taking her.

"You don't know anything about me," he said softly. Did he deliberately insert a wicked note into that deep voice? "Didn't your mama warn you about strangers?"

Strangers? What her mother had warned her was that the most painful things lurked in your very own house.

Still, it touched her, somehow, that the wicked note was pure teasing, maybe even an attempt to hide the fact he was being protective of her, as if she would invite herself along with any person who roared up to the door on a motorcycle.

"You're not a stranger after you've shared a sandwich," she said, reaching again for lightness. The truth was, Jesse Kade did not feel like a stranger at all. That was more of what you got for sleeping in a man's jacket, stealing his candy right out of his pocket—a false sense of intimacy.

But, of course, that sense of intimacy could just be the Lonnie Deep resemblance.

"Or after you've totally jeopardized your masculinity by nearly fainting in a beautiful woman's arms," he concurred, cocking his head at her, that beautiful lopsided smile that revealed his imperfect teeth making him breathtakingly handsome.

He had called her beautiful. *But not beautiful enough.*

"Believe me, your masculinity was never jeopardized." Now, why had that popped out? She was like a gauche schoolgirl, awkward in the face of being noticed by her high school crush. She had to end this, before she embarrassed herself further.

"Be safe!" Of course. Her mantra! Hurriedly, she added, "Have a good ride! Have a great life!"

She turned away again, and his voice stopped her again. "Hey."

She turned back reluctantly. She just wanted this uncomfortable moment to be over.

He regarded her thoughtfully, apparently not feeling a need to end the moment nearly as urgently as she was. Of course, he was not the one in the position of embarrassment.

"You really want to go for a bit of a spin?" he asked softly.

CHAPTER SIX

SAVE A BIT of your pride, say no, Layne ordered herself, but she didn't. She nodded at Jesse.

"You could follow me to town in your car. We could pick up the stuff you need there from Whitmore Cycle. It's right on the outskirts of town."

Had her humiliation been that apparent? Did he feel sorry for her? A pathetic girl who had never ridden on a motorcycle, and probably just as evidently never been so forward with a man?

Her pride told her, again, to say no, it was okay. She really had too much work to do anyway.

But something overruled her pride.

They obviously weren't going to gear her out for a five-minute spin on his motorcycle.

"We could run up to Whitmore Falls," he said, as if he had read her mind. "That's a nice stretch of highway for a vir— Uh, newbie."

He had been going to say *virgin* before he stopped himself midsentence and changed direction.

Of course, she wasn't, though she suddenly felt like one, and not just to motorcycle rides, either.

Layne felt her face, of its own accord, break into a grin that probably looked way too foolishly eager.

"Okay," she said. "I'll just get my keys and my purse."

"Wait." Jesse opened up his saddlebag and took out a

slender wallet. He pulled his driver's license out. "Take this. Have your friend take a picture of it."

At first she was puzzled, and then she got it. Layne realized Jesse was making sure there was a record of whom she had gone with. He was protecting her in ways she would not have thought of protecting herself. It was such a lovely gesture.

He was reassuring her. *You're safe with me.*

Layne turned from him again. Despite Jesse's license, clutched in her hand, she didn't feel safe at all, though not in the way his giving his license to her implied.

She had to fight the urge to run, again, though this time for a totally different reason. She felt as if he wouldn't be here when she came back, if she took too long. Midnight would strike and the fairy tale would be over.

Poof.

But this was exactly the problem Mabel had pointed out earlier.

It wasn't a fairy tale. It was just an encounter. An experiment, really, with what taking life one moment at a time instead of planning every outcome could look like.

So, instead of running, Layne forced herself to go slowly. There might have even been an extra swish in her hips as she walked away from him.

Then she turned back. "If we're going to get me some gear, I want Sunshine and Storm."

Something crossed his face, she couldn't be sure what.

"Whitmore Cycle is closer," he said.

"But I want to support our local success story," she called and then turned and went up the front stairs. Mabel had been spying from the window, much as Layne had been when Jesse had first pulled up.

"Well?" she demanded, as Layne came back in the door.

"I'm not going on the motorcycle with him," Layne said, trying to look grim, and tossing her hair for good measure.

"Oh." Mabel's face fell.

"He doesn't think it's safe. Without a helmet and leathers. He doesn't have extras with him."

"Oh," Mabel said, knowing an excuse when she heard one. "He doesn't really seem like the type who would put safety first, does he?"

"Well, he does. He asked if my mama hadn't warned me about strangers."

"Oh," Mabel said again, "I guess he doesn't know all mothers aren't like that."

Of course Mabel knew Layne's mom had been so involved in her own unending chaos that most of the time Layne acted as the only responsible adult in the house. Layne didn't tell her friend that Jesse was just guessing at what mothers told their children. It felt like his own lack of a mother was a secret he had given into her care.

"And then, he gave me this," Layne said when Mabel looked totally dejected on her account.

Mabel eyed the license without comprehension.

"And said you should take a picture of it. He said if I follow him in my car, we'll pick out some gear together."

Mabel whooped as if Layne had just announced she won a zillion dollars on the Powerball.

Which was pretty much the exact way Layne felt.

"That's very sweet. The license thing."

"Isn't it?" Layne said with a sigh.

"You know, you're not going to go pick up a bunch of gear for a five-minute spin, don't you?"

"I know." She resisted hugging herself and shivering.

Mabel pulled her phone out of her back pocket, and dutifully snapped the picture of the license. It pinged simultaneously.

She frowned at her phone. "Oh, incoming. The daughters are weighing in on the leopard skin."

"And?"

"Rebecca for, Jessica against." Jessica didn't really qualify as an evil stepsister, because she had been quite nice.

"Oh, boy."

"Don't even give it another thought. I'll let Pamela know that Cinderella is on her way to the ball."

"She won't like it."

"You've been putting in ten-hour days and weekends since construction started. You're entitled to a day off. You can't make a wicked stepmother happy, anyway. It's part of the story."

Both women began to giggle, and it felt as if they were the dreaming girls they had once been, unaltered by a cruel world.

Jesse watched in his side mirror as Layne drove carefully behind him. She had exactly the kind of car he had thought a woman who had never been on a motorcycle would have: a little white subcompact that probably had a top speed of around seventy miles an hour. After that, smoke would likely start pouring from under the hood.

The last woman he had dated, Jenna, had had a Corvette with a custom candy-apple-red paint job and a glove box stuffed with unpaid speeding tickets.

She was a trust fund girl with no interest in his money, which was qualification enough for him to ask her out. She'd been fun, no-strings, high-speed, anything goes, but on their third date he'd caught a glimpse of white powder in a tiny plastic bag in her purse, and it was over. He wasn't into manufacturing adrenaline; he was quite capable of coming by it naturally. Plus, he'd been around his father's addiction his whole life, and he wasn't willing to travel down that road again.

He never touched any mind-altering substance. Not tobacco, not alcohol, not drugs. He would not even take an aspirin for a headache.

His one addiction was a powerful one. Success. Making it when the world had told him—and his father before him—that Kades could not.

He bet Layne Prescott had never had a speeding ticket in her life, which made him contemplate what had just happened.

It had started sitting out on that deck with her. Oddly weakened by the entrance into his grandmother's past, he'd still been able to sense that Layne posed some kind of danger to him. It was the soft reverence in her voice when she led the tour through the castle, it was way the way the sunlight had spun her hair to fire. It was in the look in her eyes and the tilt of her mouth.

But strangely, he'd been most aware of her danger when she had unhesitatingly broken that sandwich in two.

Decent.

Wholesome.

A nurturer, something a man who had not had a mother might find irresistible, though his ensuing feelings had nothing man-toward-mother about them.

He'd just had a creeping awareness that Layne Prescott was exactly the kind of woman to be avoided, the kind who stole a man's heart before he knew what had happened. Look at how he had told her things, already, that he had never told another soul.

After the tour of the castle it had been way too close to his own family history, to his grandmother having her heart stolen. And ruthlessly crushed, the consequences of that echoing down through generations.

Feelings of the sort Layne inspired—strange longings that led to places where there were no road maps—had to be avoided. He'd been avoiding the calamity of unruly and untamable emotions his entire life.

So he had known he had to escape—fast—and he had.

He hadn't been far when he realized he'd forgotten the jacket. He knew what a Freudian slip was, too, despite the fact, just as he'd alluded to Layne, he had never finished high school. The rational part of him said *Leave it*, even though it took a long time and a lot of miles to break in a jacket the way his had been. Still, his wallet and everything he needed was locked in a saddlebag, so he'd decided to go spend the night at his grandmother's house, and sacrifice the jacket.

He'd done as much to the house as his grandmother had allowed while she was alive. Mold had been remediated, the roof didn't leak, the siding was new, and the rats that he remembered scurrying in the roof during his childhood had long since been banished.

But no matter what he did, his grandmother's dark and broken life seemed to have seeped into every crack and crevice of that old shanty. He had come to Whitmore thinking he wanted to tear down two things: the house and that castle.

He'd been here less than twenty-four hours and now he was not at all sure what he wanted.

Tossing and turning all night, he'd found that another part of him, not rational at all but in fact downright unruly, *felt* something. That part of him had overridden his rational part with a distressing ease that was not the norm for him. He was aware his legendary determination could not even win a simple battle to leave a jacket behind.

He had been compelled to return to the castle this morning. He assumed he still was weakened, in some way, from venturing into it in the first place.

Under a spell, just as his grandmother had been, and look what had happened to her.

He kept that warning forefront in his mind.

It disappeared the minute he saw Layne coming down the walk toward him, gorgeous, with her burnished bronze hair swinging and the long legs beautifully shown off by simple yoga pants, her eyes looking at him with something shining in them that he couldn't quite put his finger on, but that nonetheless seemed exceedingly dangerous.

When he had put on the jacket she held out to him, he had caught the scent of her on it, so strong he considered the possibility she had worn it.

The idea of Layne Prescott wearing his jacket made his mouth go dry. So he'd reached for the candy he always kept in the pocket, the butterscotch that his grandmother had loved so much.

Sunshine and Storm put one of these candies—hard caramels created over a hundred years ago in some small German village—into the pocket of every single jacket they sold.

He always had one in his pocket, a good-luck charm. It made him feel vulnerable not to have it. It also made him wonder, again, if Layne had worn the jacket.

Of course she hadn't. It smelled of her because she had carried it out here. The candy probably fell out of the pocket while she was doing that.

Jesse didn't like feeling off-balance.

He didn't like it at all.

He liked control and he liked it a lot. Even on his bike, where it might seem he was pushing the edges of what was possible, he always felt one hundred percent in control.

He'd felt the same off-balance sensation yesterday when he had charged out of here so quickly he forgot the jacket.

Get away. She will make the world shift under your feet.

But then, clearly scared out of her wits at the possibility of being rejected, she'd announced that she'd never been on a motorcycle.

And his defenses had dissolved like sugar hitting hot coffee.

Wasn't it part of his mission in life to introduce the world to motorcycles? Her lack of gear, putting her safety first, was the perfect excuse to ride away, but he didn't.

Even as he was touched by her support of a local business, he wished they were going to the competition.

The people in the Whitmore store would recognize him. Part of why he had made such a hasty retreat was that he didn't want her to know who he really was.

Or maybe, to be strictly honest, he wished they weren't going to gear her up at all. Because, within an hour, she was going to be on a motorcycle with him, those long legs touching his, pulled in tight, her arms around him.

You didn't fully outfit someone to go on a motorcycle to go for a five-minute spin.

His will—his desire to see her danger and avoid it—dissolved as quickly as his defenses had.

Jesse knew himself to be a disciplined man; some might even say highly regimented despite the fact he could be a daredevil on a motorcycle. Still, he had said no to temptations that distracted him every single day of his life.

And yet he was aware that in Layne Prescott, he had just stumbled upon a temptation he could not say no to.

And he didn't like that one little bit.

He pulled the motorcycle over in front of the Whitmore location of Sunshine and Storm and watched as Layne carefully parallel parked in front of the building. It was excruciating to see, really, something like watching his grandmother park. Though Jesse had been begging her to surrender her license since she'd been eighty, she had stubbornly driven her huge old boat of a car until the day before she died at age ninety-three. She'd been just as stubborn about leaving that crumbling house in Whitmore's worst neighborhood.

Jesse saw one of the employees glance out the window and then look, again, at the bike with its chrome tank and custom paint, rising above the almost exclusively custom cycles they manufactured anyway.

Casey. It was a point of pride for him that he knew all his employees, and he raised a resigned hand when recognition crossed her face.

If he wanted to travel incognito he should have pushed harder for Whitmore Cycle. Though he personally felt the line they carried, expensive based on brand-name recognition, was absolute crap.

"Hey," he said as Layne came toward him, "before we go in there, there's something I need to tell you."

CHAPTER SEVEN

Jesse was well aware that a quick text to the store and he could have protected his anonymity a little longer, but subterfuge did not sit well with him, though he would indulge it as long as he could with the Whitmore connection.

Layne looked instantly nervous, though she tried not to. "Don't tell me you play pool for dollar bills in the bar," she said, her tone aiming for playful but not quite making it.

"I don't go to the bar."

"Never?" she asked, curious. "Like not even for Super Bowl?"

He had a memory, unwanted, of fishing his dad out of more seedy Whitmore establishments than he could count. The smell of spilled beer and old tobacco smoke made him feel much the way the castle had done.

Jesse had loved his father, but he also knew his love had made him a prisoner in ways that he never wanted to be again. They said that loving someone with an addiction was a hostage-taking, but Jesse couldn't help but wonder if love itself wasn't the hostage-taking.

"Not even for that. I don't drink."

"You're married," she guessed, her gaze sliding, a bit accusingly, to his empty ring finger, "or in a committed relationship."

"No," he said, and then more curtly than he should have, his memory of fishing his dad out of bars fresh in his mind, added, "I'm one hundred percent single and intent on keeping it that way."

Of course she took it personally, and said, a little huffily, "I am also one hundred percent single and feel the very same way, as a matter of fact. About keeping it that way."

"Oh, good," he said.

"I'm glad we got that sorted. We don't have designs on each other."

Who said something so sweetly old-fashioned? Have designs on each other? If she didn't look so darned earnest, he might have laughed.

"So, what do you have to tell me?" Layne said, tapping her foot as if she had people to see and places to go, "You're not married, and you don't hang out in bars." She snapped her fingers. She was terrible at it. Her thumb and her middle finger whispered against each other instead of snapping. "I hope you don't think I was expecting you to pay, if that's what you need to tell me. I can outfit myself."

She thought he was a guy who couldn't afford to look after her? That was quite hilarious.

"It's not that, either."

"Even so, I hope you don't think you're paying! I mean that would be ridiculous. I invited myself, after all, even though we've established I don't have designs on you. I'll take responsibility for getting what I need." She suddenly looked crestfallen. "Unless you've changed your mind."

Looking at her, he was aware, from the unguarded look on her face, that she'd experienced that. Someone changing their mind. When she'd counted on something.

Because he was the kind of guy who was single. But she didn't strike him as that kind of woman.

In fact, she struck him as the most dangerous kind of woman of all. She *wanted* things, probably starting with a family of her own, that he could never give her. She was fighting that wanting with all her might, but still, it was there, evident just below the surface.

She'd just given him the perfect out. A change of mind. And yet, he could not take the exit she had offered.

"I'm not changing my mind," he told her, surprised at how gentle a tone he was capable of. Had he used that tone—the one he'd always reserved for Mr. Poochy—since the last of their old dogs, always with the very same name, had drawn his last breath?

"Okay," she said, drawing it out...*oooh-kaaay*...and tilting her head at him.

"I need to tell you who I am."

She smiled nervously and reached for her hair, twisting its shiny bronze strands between her fingers and chewing her bottom lip. "Are you going to tell me you're on the FBI's most wanted list?"

He considered that, and how protective it made him feel of her "Ah, a question that might have been better asked before you followed me."

"We're not at the point of no return yet," she said, and then blushed wildly and charmingly that such a statement could easily be taken out of context.

"That's true," he said, even as he felt a sharp longing for the point of no return with her, and knew it had to be guarded against.

"Besides," she rushed on, "you gave me your license."

He decided not to point out to her that anyone could have a license, even, probably, someone on the FBI's most wanted list.

"I mean, I'm not on the bike with you yet, so it's good you're letting me know your deepest, darkest secrets now."

Well, not his deepest, darkest secret.

"I own it," he admitted quietly.

"The motorcycle?" she asked, baffled.

"Well, that too."

"And?"

He nodded to the business behind them. "I own that."

She turned and looked over her shoulder, and then back at him. "The building Sunshine and Storm is in?"

"Well, yes. And Sunshine and Storm."

She stared at him. "As in this outlet of Sunshine and Storm."

"This one and several others."

One hundred and thirty-three nationwide, to be exact, but he didn't want to totally overwhelm her.

She looked at him blankly "So you own some of the franchises?"

Jesse realized he was going to have to spell it out for her. "The company is not franchised. I own Sunshine and Storm. All of it."

Layne stared at Jesse Kade.

"*You* own Sunshine and Storm?" she asked him, stunned and, okay, quite skeptical, even if it did explain the expense of the watch. The exclusive motorcycle.

Mabel's instincts were always good. But even Mabel would be utterly astounded by how right she had been this time. If it were true…

It wasn't entirely impossible that Jesse owned the company. It was a well-known fact that the reclusive creator of the flourishing motorcycle empire did come from Whitmore. But somehow, she would have not pictured him so young and hip, though certainly the brand was both.

Didn't stodgy old executives run billion-dollar businesses?

"Um…yes," Jesse said, "I own it."

Layne realized she should probably be wondering if she had unwittingly followed someone who had a loose a screw, and who was trying to impress with outlandish lies.

But as she studied Jesse, she could see the truth was stamped all over him: his easy confidence, his self-assured grin, the way he carried himself.

Still, she had to ask. "*You're* Mr. Poochy?"

"Well, the man behind Mr. Poochy," he admitted, a little reluctantly.

"No wonder you're worried about people having designs on you," she said, and his mouth twitched as if he found that amusing. But she wasn't amused. "Why didn't you tell me before?"

He wagged a fiendish eyebrow at her. "Hey, I'm well-known and successful. Does that improve chances of your getting on a bike with me?"

"I asked *you* to go for the motorcycle ride," she reminded him.

Jesse's mischievous look disappeared. "I just don't usually lead with what I do for a living," he said quietly. "I kind of like it that you asked an ordinary guy for a ride on his bike and not the subject of this month's *Business Today* rags-to-riches story."

Note to self: look up current issue of Business Today.

She realized she found the *rags* part of that statement the most interesting. There was a reason Jesse seemed to lack conceit and was down-to-earth—the kind of guy a girl could risk her pride with—and she felt more intrigued by that than the fact the whole town said that Whitmore's most publicity-phobic son was a billionaire several times over.

If she had known that, she certainly would not have ever been as bold as she had been. You didn't ask billionaires for rides on their bikes. Who thought billionaires rode bikes? She would be more likely to think private jets and chauffeured limousines, even for one who owned a motorcycle company.

He was said to be reclusive. Recluses looked like this?

"Why this revelation now?" Layne asked.

"Someone in there recognized me, already. I saw her through the window." He sighed. "That's why I suggested Whitmore Cycle instead."

"Oh. So you would have kept the truth from me longer?"

He lifted a shoulder and gave her a smile Layne was pretty sure was intended to enchant. "Can you blame a guy for just wanting to see if he's liked for himself?"

She could not, actually. The statement—and maybe that dazzling smile—made her soften to him, see his vulnerability.

"I mean I could have sent a text and asked them to pretend they didn't know me, but it seemed duplicitous. I don't want to feel as if I'm hiding things. From you."

She could feel her heart pounding. That almost made it sound as if he was contemplating something *after* the motorcycle ride.

Not a one-off.

Whoa, girl, you are getting way ahead of yourself. He's made it clear he's not interested in anything further. So have you.

Jesse said, "If you're still game, should we go get you kitted?"

She was game. She could not have stopped herself from playing this game if she wanted to.

"I'm still paying my own way," she said stubbornly. Actually, she felt more firmly about that now that she knew who he was. Given his status, no doubt people expected him to pick up the tab for everything, all the time.

She would not be that person.

He studied her for a moment. Obviously that didn't happen to him very often. A slow smile spread across his lips and he lifted a shoulder. "Whatever makes you happy."

By the time they reached the door, one of the staff was holding it open, and the others were waiting, looking nervous and a little excited. It quickly became evident they adored their boss, and also evident why.

"Mr. Kade, how nice to see you," the woman who opened the door said. "A pleasant surprise. None of us were aware you were in town."

"Thanks, Casey, how are the twins?"

The woman beamed at him. "Fine, thanks for asking. The little mini motorbikes you sent for their birthdays were a real hit."

He greeted each member of the staff in turn. He knew each of their names and something about them.

Layne surreptitiously glanced at her phone, tapped in an inquiry. Sunshine and Storm had over a hundred locations. Surely Jesse didn't know all his employees? It was probably just because this one was the hometown store.

Even so, she felt awe as she watched his quick and genuine interactions with the people who worked for him. He cared about them. And deeply. And they knew it.

When he was done greeting the staff, he walked back to Layne and threw an easy arm over her shoulder, making it look—and feel—as if they had known each other for years, not less than a full day.

"This is my friend Layne," he said. "We need to get her completely kitted. She's going to have her first motorcycle ride today."

"How exciting," Casey said, and the way her eyes moved to her boss made Layne aware the employee thought it exciting in more ways than just a first-time motorcycle ride. "I'd be happy to help."

And just like that Layne found herself being shepherded toward the back of the store. She was not sure what she had expected of a store that sold motorbikes, but not *this*. The space reminded her of an upscale hotel lobby—good lighting, soft music, dark hardwoods, a feel of quiet and luxury and class.

Only instead of the art pieces that might be the focal point of a luxury hotel lobby, three motorcycles were the art, showcased on round, raised platforms, with light sweeping up them. They were utterly gorgeous, unlike any motorcycles Layne had ever seen before. All had chrome gas tanks so shiny they looked like mirrors, and all had extraordinary and unusual body colors. There was one in shades of gold, one the multicolors of a tropical sea, the other a stormy comingling of shimmering grays and pearls.

Tucked tastefully against one wall were floor-to-ceiling shelves of T-shirts, slacks and gloves; on another were displays of boots and helmets. And on round racks on the floor space between the motorbikes were uncrowded displays of leather jackets, pants, chaps.

"I never would have expected anything like this," Layne said to Casey as they paused at an industrial-style barn door into a changing area that was bridal-boutique-worthy, with its deep chairs, gilded mirrors and ultra-spacious change cubicles.

"It's all Mr. Kade," Casey said, with utter pride. "He has a vision." She tilted her head, taking in Layne. "I wonder what his vision is for you?"

Layne wondered that, too!

Casey called to Jesse, who was deep in conversation with the other staff, all of them looking at a pair of motorcycle gloves, "Any preferences, Mr. Kade?"

He looked up from the gloves, the intensity of his focus shifting to Layne He grinned at her and it was very easy to make her forget what he did and see who he was.

"I like that new line for women. *Catalyst*."

"I like cheap," Layne said in an undertone, and spied a rack near them. "That says 'Best Deals Ever.'"

"Mr. Kade has a policy that every store has to have a selection of quality items at really good prices, so that anyone who wants to wear our brand can afford something in here." Again, she had so much pride for her boss.

"Still," Casey added with a slight frown, "I don't think Mr. Kade would be pleased with me if I outfitted his girlfriend from the sale rack."

It was delightful to be mistaken for his girlfriend, especially after Layne had already established he was well out of her league, but still she couldn't allow that misconception to ride.

"I'm not his girlfriend."

CHAPTER EIGHT

"You're not his girlfriend?" Casey asked.

"No," Layne said.

Casey contemplated that, then said brightly, "Well, every outfit I'm going to pick is going to be chosen as if you want to be. I'm a happily married woman, a mother of three, and I *want* to be his girlfriend. Don't worry," Casey laughed, "my husband knows all about my boss crush."

Layne opened her mouth to protest—it made it sound an awfully lot as if she had *designs*—and then she closed it again. She wanted to be someone different today, didn't she? Bolder? Someone who took chances?

Making herself attractive to Jesse seemed exceedingly dangerous and also irresistibly enticing.

Take that, Mr. Single-With-No-Intention-of-Changing-Relationship-Status.

Besides, Casey was reminding her she was only joining a long, long line of women with the very same weakness. It didn't need to go anywhere.

She didn't have to think of that today. Of intentions or designs or where things went. She was just going along for the ride, literally and figuratively. Besides, it would be unnecessarily churlish to not to let someone like Casey, who knew what they were doing in terms of motorcycle garb, make these decisions for her.

Stubborn was one thing. Stupidly stubborn was another.

"Okay," the new her—*if you always do what you've always done*—said to Casey.

She soon found herself trying on Mr. Poochy T-shirts and fragrant black leather jackets.

"They're so stiff," Layne said of the jacket.

"It's wear that makes them soft," Casey told her, and Layne thought of the softness of that jacket she had worn to bed last night. It felt, suddenly, like an act of intimacy that Jesse had not given his consent to.

She was brought extraordinarily sexy leather chaps and leather pants to choose between. Strangely, surrounded by a sea of black leather instead of frills and silk, Layne felt more feminine than she had felt in a long time. In fact, she felt more like a princess getting ready for a ball than a woman about to go on her first motorbike ride.

Layne was amazed by how this kind of clothing transformed her. Slipping on a black leather jacket and cinching up chaps over her new leggings made her feel exquisitely bold and beautiful. It didn't feel as if she was *creating* a wild side, but, instead, coaxing one that had already existed to the surface. Unleashing some part of herself.

"Definitely that," Casey said, eyeing Layne in the Catalyst jacket and chaps.

Of course, Layne thought weakly. She had caught a glimpse of the tags. This last ensemble was the most expensive of anything she had tried on.

"And I think the pink Mr. Poochy T-shirt suits you the best. A nice feminine touch among all that black leather."

At least the shirt was somewhat affordable, and beautifully comfortable, something Layne could wear again after this extravagant excursion was over.

Casey fanned herself playfully. "That jacket is smokin' on you. No! Leave the zipper right there."

The zipper was a little lower than Layne was usually comfortable with but, on the other hand, why not?

Casey regarded her, tapping her lip. "Leave all that on and I'll go find you the perfect boots and a helmet."

Layne turned and looked in the mirror, shocked and delighted by the transformation the jacket made. She smoothed it over and felt something in the pocket.

She reached in and found a butterscotch candy, just like the one she had found in Jesse's pocket yesterday.

"What's with this?" she asked Casey, who had arrived back with several pairs of motorcycle boots for Layne try on.

"We put one in every jacket pocket. It was Mr. Kade's idea. Just a small thing, but a little reminder that both big things and small things can bring moments of pleasure. Our unique touches add up, and set us apart. What do you think of these boots?"

Layne felt a moment's panic when she looked at the price of them. "Haven't you got anything a little less pricey?"

"The footwear is not where you want to spare expense, believe me. Look, I know you want to pay, but that's not exactly his style."

"He's not paying for me!" Even if the boots did represent a week's wages.

Casey tilted her head and regarded Layne. "You know what? I can respect that. But would you be okay if I asked him about the staff discount for you?"

"Okay."

"Good, because look what I found. Gorgeous, but not cheap."

She held out a pink helmet, powder coated in candy-floss-pink. An abstract of a joyous Mr. Poochy raced across the side of it.

Layne noticed the price with a gulp. Twelve hundred dollars?

"Why so much?" she asked, trying not to wail.

"It's a smart helmet, with Bluetooth. You and the driver can talk back and forth and you can listen to music, send texts and make phone calls all hands-off."

"Oh."

"Plus, this helmet is a limited edition. There's only two dozen of them worldwide. Even though we're a relatively small outlet, Mr. Kade always makes sure we get one of the helmets collectors go crazy for."

Twelve hundred dollars? It was absurd. She couldn't do it. Not for one ride.

"If you decide you don't want it—in fact, if you decided you don't want any of this stuff, you can resell it. On eBay. You'd get your money back, and probably then some."

Ah, Layne tried to console herself, it wasn't a silly extravagance for a one-off adventure. It was an *investment*.

She stood patiently while Casey instructed her what to do with her hair, then popped the helmet on and made sure it fit.

"All ready," Casey finally declared, stepping back from Layne, one hundred percent satisfied.

Layne turned and looked at herself in the mirror, one last time. She'd been feeling uncharacteristically sexy until the addition of the helmet. The big, pink bulb made her feel like a Martian. She took it off and tucked it under her arm, aware her hair was hissing with static as she left the change room.

Awkward in the boots, and even without the helmet on, Layne still had the feeling of being an alien from another planet. She was tempted to hail Jesse with the Vulcan salute and call out, *Greetings, earthling*.

But when Jesse caught sight of her, his eyes widened, and there was unmistakable and deep male appreciation in the steadiness of his dark gaze. An approving smile tickled the sensual line of his lips, and she wasn't an alien at all.

Someone had waved the magic wand. She was a completely different person than she had been half an hour ago. Strangely euphoric, immersed in the pure magic of the moment, her worries far behind her.

No surviving childhood battles.

No failed relationship.

No evil stepmother.

No concern for the arrival of the credit card bill.

Suddenly not worrying—about anything, even the impression she was making—felt like the best mind-altering drug she had ever experienced.

Or maybe this sudden infusion of pure euphoria running through Layne's veins was almost entirely because of that look that darkened Jesse's eyes as he took her in with frank and unapologetic appreciation.

She was in his world, and in that world and in his view, she was wearing a ball gown.

"Wow," Jesse said, a faint hoarseness in his voice. Maybe it was even more meaningful because he had made it pretty clear he didn't intend to see her in *that* way. But whatever caused that light in his eyes and croak in his voice, it was a balm to the part of her that had been so bruised by Brock's sudden thirst for adventure. "You look stunning."

All dressed in black leather, a bowling ball of a pink helmet stuffed under her arm, knowing full well he had said he was single forever, and she had said the same thing, how could Layne possibly feel something she had always secretly wanted to feel?

As if she was a princess crossing a ballroom toward her prince.

CHAPTER NINE

CAREFUL, JESSE WARNED HIMSELF, aware that despite all his intentions, he was being swept away by some odd enchantment. Layne, coming across the room toward him, all decked out in black leather, looked as if she had been born to wear those clothes.

His fantasy—librarian transformed, let loose—was walking toward him. And it was a cautionary tale in *be careful what you wish for*. Because he was not at all sure of his ability to handle this.

But her eyes, soft and a little nervous, the self-consciousness she was trying to hide, reminded him what was required. Be a decent guy.

The problem with librarians, he reminded himself, was that he was pretty sure they adhered to traditional lifestyles.

Puppies. Babies. Those kinds of terrifying things.

"Thank you," she said softly to his compliment that she looked stunning. Honestly, despite his inner warnings for caution, he had to resist a ridiculous temptation to bend over her hand and kiss it.

He said, a bit gruffly, "Do you feel one hundred percent ready?"

She considered that—see the studious librarian still very much there—thoughtfully calculating percentages.

"Ninety-nine," she decided.

"Let's go, then," he said, "before that one percent gains any traction."

"I'll just pay for all this first."

"Ninety-nine percent stubborn," he said, faintly exasperated.

She grinned. "Absolutely," and then tentatively, "Casey said she thought I could have the staff discount. Is that okay?"

There was a sense of wanting to give her a little shake.

"It's okay to accept things when life offers them to you," he said. The statement was really much deeper than he usually was, or even wanted it to be.

She squared up on her purchases, and even though she was trying not to show it, he could tell she was shocked by the total.

Now the pressure was on him to give her a ride worth every penny of what she had just invested. He did a quick tally in his head. Could he do that in just one outing?

Well, he had to, otherwise he'd be tangling with her further, and he was already aware there were too many moving pieces here challenging his enjoyment of complete control.

He made himself stop probing around in the future. It had never been a fruitful undertaking, as far as he was concerned.

Jesse led her out to the bike, slid her helmet out from under her arm for her. Layne held her hair up and he pulled the helmet down over her head, tucking the stray strands of hair up under it. Her hair felt exactly as he had known it would, as beautifully silky as gossamer. His fingers found the strap, and he fumbled a bit trying to do it up under her chin.

He turned from her quickly, took his seat, but his effort to disengage was completely undermined when she slid onto the bike behind him, tentative, trying very hard not to touch him.

He turned on the helmet microphone that linked with hers. "Okay?" he asked her.

"I'm having butterflies," she said, her voice lovely and light through the stereo sound of the helmet.

Butterflies. Exactly the sensation in the pit of his own stomach.

"Normal for your first time," he told her.

What was weird was that it felt as if it was his first time, too, when he'd been on a motorcycle nearly every single day since he'd turned fourteen. But it was his first time with her on a motorcycle with him! When Layne pulled in a little closer, Jesse felt a belly-dropping overload of sensation as those long legs fit themselves perfectly to his legs, and her lower body formed an intimate V around his.

Focus, Jesse ordered himself.

"A couple of things to remember," he told her, his voice not betraying those *butterflies* at all, or so he hoped. "Use the passenger footrests. Don't take your feet off them, even if we're stopped."

He could feel the moment her feet found the footrests. He lifted the kickstand, and was aware of holding both their weights on his braced legs.

"Okay." She hesitated. "What do I hold on to?"

"You can use the handholds beside you." Don't say anything else, he ordered himself. "Or you can put your arms around my waist or hold on to my hips."

She opted instantly—thankfully—for the handholds.

"Just relax," he said, feeling her tension even though she was not touching him.

Sure. Relax. Despite the small space she was keeping between them, Jesse wondered if her every muscle and cell was zinging with the same energy and awareness as his was?

He did his very best to strip all of that from his voice as he spoke to her.

"Do what I do. If you feel me leaning, lean with me, not away from me."

"Got it. With you, not away from you."

Most bikes nowadays, particularly ones of the size and expense of Jesse's, were electric-start only. But there was something about kick-starting he was unable give up.

He turned the key, lifted himself up, then thrust down on the kick start. Satisfyingly, the engine roared to life on his first try. Starting the bike like that was an intensely masculine use of force, what a cowboy must feel wrestling a steer, a powerlifter hefting a weight, a carpenter lifting a wall.

He saw his own weakness in his hope that Layne was impressed.

He saw it also in how he deeply wanted her to absorb the intimacy of being on a machine like this. He wanted her to sense the thrum, the heartbeat of the bike going through her body; he needed her to understand this was not something you *did*. It was something you were, the energy surging into every part of you, until you were one with it.

He piloted the powerful machine smoothly into traffic, his legs bracing with ease again, holding both of their weights when they stopped at traffic lights.

When the light changed, he might have used just a little too much throttle, because Layne abandoned the handholds and her arms went around his waist. Tightly.

He went a little faster. She tightened her hold even more, so close to him now that even through leather barriers, he could feel her heat rising and the beat of her heart.

They left Whitmore behind them, taking a coastal highway. The roadway twisted, rock faces on one side, the ocean on the other.

He could feel the tension leaving her.

And leaving him, too.

"Any preferences for music?" he asked.

"I don't want anything. I've never experienced traveling like this, rocketing through reality but without barriers. Even the air is changed, sweet, fresh and sea-scented. The sensations are amazing. I feel a connection to the bike. To the road. To the sea. To the sky."

There was pure exhilaration in Layne's tone, and it delighted him that she got it. They were not just becoming one with the motorcycle, but with each other.

Despite how he knew he needed to fight this very thing, Jesse felt something inside of him sigh with surrender.

"You're a natural," Jesse told her as the highway hummed beneath them, and the thrumming of the bike filled Layne. His voice, coming through the helmet speaker, was masculine and warm, completely relaxed and confidence-inspiring.

Natural. That was exactly how Layne felt, as if riding behind Jesse Kade on his motorcycle was the most natural thing she had ever done. She felt exhilaratingly in sync with his energy, even as the total sensuality of the experience took her by storm.

The minutes melted and the miles zipped by.

Jesse pulled over at a tiny, roadside restaurant perched on a cliff, looking like it was going to tumble into the sea.

"I thought we were going to Whitmore Falls," she said as he turned off the engine. She dismounted from behind him, and felt an unexpected wobbliness in her legs, which he turned just in time to see.

"We are," he said. "Eventually."

And then he did the sweetest thing. He pretended the stop had nothing to do with the fact he probably knew her legs were wobbling from the unfamiliar position of being a passenger on a motorbike.

"I'm famished," he said.

She realized, startled, that she had not had breakfast and was also ravenous. Still, she cast a doubtful glance at the restaurant. "Sea Biscuit," she said. "That was the name of a horse. It's not very appetizing."

Jesse threw back his head and laughed. It was a sound a woman could live for.

"I take it you haven't been here?" he asked, his eyes dancing.

"No," she said, amused—and just a little enchanted—that this was where the billionaire would stop to eat.

"Best lobster po'boys in Maine."

"For breakfast?" she asked.

He slid back his leather and looked at his watch. It was a very nice watch, not that she would have even noticed it if Mabel hadn't pointed it out.

Actually, maybe it wasn't the watch that she found so nice, but the squareness of his wrist, her awareness of somehow having surrendered her life to the competency of those hands.

"It's not breakfast time. It's lunchtime."

Layne was utterly amazed at how time had simply evaporated since the moment she had handed him that jacket this morning.

"Po'boys it is," she said, "though nobody makes better lobster po'boys than the Loose Lobster."

"I'll bet you," he said, his mouth tilting up with mischief.

Layne was aware of feeling a tickle of delight. Twenty-four hours ago, could she have even pictured a scenario like this one? When was the last time she had found life delightfully surprising?

That, she realized, was the price of playing it safe. It left no room for the unexpected—but pure—bliss of spontaneity.

"You're on," she told Jesse. "I'll bet the Loose Lobster has the better po'boy. What are we betting?"

"You're supposed to ask what the bet is *before* you accept."

Did his eyes actually linger on her lips? Was he going to bet for a kiss? Impossible. He'd made it abundantly clear he was not going in that direction. Still, the awareness that life's surprises could be utterly joyous blossomed more deeply within her.

"I feel up to living dangerously today," she said, and she was. "What's the bet?"

"If I win, we go for a dip below Whitmore Falls."

"It's the end of May! It'll be freezing."

He cocked his head thoughtfully. "Okay, *you'll* go for a dip below the falls."

"Since it seems I'm unlikely to lose, I'll accept that."

"Okay. If you win?"

"Aha! You were supposed to ask first!"

They were both laughing. Layne tried to remember the last time she had felt like this: carefree, *fun*, flirty.

Had she ever felt like this?

"You'll go for a dip at the falls. With nothing on."

"What have I done?" he teased. "One ride on a bike, and we've unleashed your devilish side, completely."

"Completely," she agreed, and something smoldered in his eyes that could burn them both to the ground.

They stepped up to the window that took orders. The menu was painted on a faded sign screwed to the building beside it. They both scanned it, even though they knew what they were ordering.

"Any allergies?" the guy behind the counter asked.

"Love," Jesse said, and she realized it was his stock answer. And also a reiteration of what he had said earlier. It was intended to be light, but it might have had a warning threaded through it.

"Me too," she said, matching his playful tone, even though she was a bit stung that he felt it necessary to remind her how content he was in his single state.

It *was* just a motorcycle ride, she reminded herself.

"Hey, I'm referring to shellfish," the counter guy said,

"but whatever." He cocked his head at them. "If you two are allergic to love, maybe you shouldn't be glued together on that bike. Which, by the way? Is awesome."

Which was awesome? Layne wondered as the guy turned away, being glued together or the motorcycle?

Both!

Jesse was avoiding her eyes. They took seats on either side of a worn picnic table on a creaky deck that somehow clung to the side of a cliff. Jesse looked pointedly out over the vista, which was admittedly one of the best views she had ever seen.

The lobster po'boys were delivered to their table.

Jesse picked his up, met her eyes for the first time since the "glued together" comment and tilted the sandwich at her. "Cheers," he said. "Here's to winning."

They both bit into the crispy French bread sandwiches at the same time. The flavors were extraordinary. It felt as if each ingredient separated in her mind: fresh lobster, dry white wine, coriander, lemon, celery, Cajun seasoning. And then came back together in a blend of flavors that couldn't have been more perfect.

"Oh, my," she breathed, pretty sure she had just lost the bet.

She looked into his eyes. And was lost in another way. Or could have been if he wasn't *allergic*.

She reminded herself that she was, too.

"Well?"

"I'd concede that it's the best I've ever tasted, *but* I'm not sure if maybe the whole new experience of being on the bike—" *with my arms wrapped around the world's most attractive man* "—isn't just making me feel incredibly sensitive. From my taste buds to my toes."

She wouldn't even mention the sensitivity between her legs, where the heat from the small of his back had caused an alarming, delightful tingle of pure awareness.

"How do we resolve that?" he asked. She suddenly wasn't sure if he was talking about the po'boy bet or satiation hungers of a completely different variety.

She forced herself to stick to po'boys.

"I think we'll have to try the Loose Lobster before we know who has won," Layne said, aware it was bold in the same way hinting she wanted to ride with him had been bold. It was tying them together *for longer* and it was deliberate, despite the stated allergies.

There were all kinds of allergies, after all, ranging from mild hay fever to anaphylactic reactions. Maybe it was important to know everything you could about your allergy, including whether it could be overcome.

Wasn't there a new therapy that exposed people to their allergies in very small doses until they developed immunity?

Not that wrapping her legs around him on a motorcycle for a second day would be considered a small dose.

On the other hand, *if you always do what you've always done…*

Layne held her breath, waiting for his response.

She could see a range of emotions flit across Jesse's face.

"What are you doing for lunch tomorrow?" he asked her, finally.

CHAPTER TEN

Layne felt Jesse's surrender and her own, as they both stopped fighting the power of this wave they were riding, and danced with it instead. The surrender didn't feel like any kind of defeat, as surrenders so often did. In fact, the taste was as sweet—maybe sweeter—than the taste of the po'boy on her tongue.

"I happen to be available for lunch tomorrow."

He grinned at her.

In the interest of testing her allergic reaction, only, Layne reached across the table and touched his lip with her finger.

"You have just a hint of mayo, right here."

It felt like just about the boldest—and most beautiful—thing she had ever done. His tongue came out and flicked the mayo. And her finger.

"Better?" he asked huskily.

"Oh," she said, her voice also husky, "so much better."

In a day full of surprises, a simple lunch was turning sexy.

With a small smile tickling the delectable curve of the lip she had touched, he turned in his seat to scan the menu posted on the outside of the building.

"Do you want dessert?" he asked. "We could share."

As tempting as it was to order something that required a shared spoon, she was aware of feeling that nothing could be sweeter than the feel of his lush lip beneath her finger, so she shook her head. "I'm good."

"I have a sweet tooth," he admitted.

She pulled the candy out of her jacket pocket. "Is that the reason for one of these in every pocket?"

He looked at the candy, and something faintly guarded came up in his expression.

"That's the reason," he said lightly, but when he met her eyes again, his look did not match his tone. Layne was aware of the most subtle of shifts between them.

His phone rang suddenly, jarring them both. He took it out of an inside pocket of his jacket and looked at the screen. "I wouldn't normally take this, but do you mind?"

"Of course not."

He got up from the table and went around the corner of the restaurant. "Kade," she heard him answer, and then he went out of earshot.

Kade. A business call, then. Despite the fact he had said he was *one hundred percent single,* Layne had seen firsthand the effect he had on women.

Casey had kiddingly referred to her boss crush, but Jesse, with his success and his looks and that killer grin, probably had groupies chasing him. He probably had to fight off interested women with a stick. No wonder he was allergic.

She'd been relieved that it was a business call, until the realization hit. The man ran an empire. She had totally forgotten he was Whitmore's best success story when she touched her finger to his lip.

Unless she was mistaken, Jesse had seemed relieved when his cell rang, as if a break from the intensity building between them was welcome.

When he came back, he apologized.

"Look, I'm sorry," he said. "Something has come up. Are you okay with taking a rain check on Whitmore Falls?"

He had come to his senses, and she should, too. Still, she wanted to press him about their plans for lunch tomorrow, but she managed to scrounge up a shred or two of pride before she made a complete fool of herself.

She had gone too far when she had touched his lip. He had warned her, after all. Was she giving off the vibe of someone who wanted way more than he was willing to give?

Especially now that he had revealed his status in life?

While he thought he was doing something nice for a pathetic soul who had never experienced a motorcycle ride, had it been obvious she had been conjuring up smoldering looks and chemistry, as if he wasn't totally out of her league.

In a different stratosphere, in fact.

"You know what?" she said. "Let's just forget the whole bet. You're probably too busy for lunch tomorrow, anyway."

She waited for him to protest. He didn't. She got up from the table and marched back out to the motorcycle with her chin held high. She slammed on her helmet and pulled down the visor so he couldn't see her eyes.

As they left Sea Biscuit and turned back toward Whitmore, Jesse contemplated how the briefest touch of Layne's finger had felt on his lips.

Just like her, he felt exquisitely sensitive, from his taste buds—and now lips—to his toes. But unlike her, he could not blame his heightened awareness of all things on the brand-new experience of being on the bike.

There was nothing brand-new about that experience for him.

What was brand-new was her. Layne, her leather-clad body pressed into his, the beat of her heart through leather, the heat of her rising up to meet his own heat, the way her hair had spilled out from under that helmet when they'd stopped, the smile dancing across her lips as they'd made bets, the light smoking in her eyes when she'd touched his lip with her finger.

It felt as if he was on a runaway train. Her pulling out that candy had been like a flashing red warning light. The call he had just taken from his legal team had made him realize he had to pull the emergency brake, before they crashed.

Because this was heading one place, and it was heading there at breakneck speed.

And despite her leathers and her new-found boldness, she was not that kind of woman. She was the kind of woman who had fairy-tale dreams. That had been written all over her during the tour of the castle yesterday.

He could not be part of anyone's forever fantasy.

Instead of turning toward Whitmore Falls, Jesse turned back toward town, aware his relief and his regret were in about equal measure, especially when Layne chose the handholds instead of his waist.

She was insulted, and she was angry that he had changed plans. Good. It was for her own good. In fact, he felt like Sir Galahad, mounting his steed to protect the maiden.

Against himself.

"Maybe you could put on some music now," she said, her tone cold and proud.

But the husky note that still clung to the edges of her words confirmed that he was going the right way.

It was for the best that she had called off a visit to the Loose Lobster to compare po'boys. One of them was going to lose that bet.

One touch of Layne's finger had practically undone him. What on earth would playing around in the falls—possibly with one of them naked—do to him?

He was going to *hurt* her, he reminded himself. She loved that castle as much as he hated it.

Despite a bit of uncertainty yesterday, Layne producing that candy that honored the grandmother he was seeking to avenge being followed very closely from a call from his legal team, had reminded Jesse of his mission here and cemented his resolve.

After the chat with the lawyer, he felt more inclined to follow through with his master plan than ever.

A meeting had been arranged with the Whitmore women for early next week, at the offices of a Whitmore law firm that was associated with his own.

Jesse was going to confront the Whitmores with their sordid past. He was going to end up with his name on the title to Whitmore Castle. It belonged to him on moral grounds, if not legal ones.

Jesse's team of lawyers had been putting the chess pieces in place for months. The laws around illegitimate children and their rights in Maine were archaic, but the lawyers said his case was strong because of advances in genetic testing and anecdotal evidence.

Jesse, using extreme privacy measures, had submitted his DNA to one of those ancestry sites. Pamela Whitmore and her daughters had also submitted, without the caution of privacy settings.

He had been informed he had cousins, and who they were. The certainty of the relationship was one hundred percent.

And he was going to meet them next week.

This was the deal he intended to present: no civil suit, no threat to any of the Whitmores' billion-dollar business holdings, or to Charles's stellar reputation in the history of Maine and the community of Whitmore.

What Jesse wanted from the Whitmores, the only thing he wanted, was the castle and the grounds.

He wouldn't stoop to blackmail. He was willing to pay market value for it. More, if they were reluctant.

They would either see the advantages of giving in to him without a fight, or he could see them in court. He didn't care if the legal battles lasted years, but he had a feeling he was going to prevail sooner rather than later.

What he had not the slightest doubt about, in this particular war, was that he would win. And then he would knock that castle—and all it stood for—down to a pile of rubble. The property, sitting as it was on the very edge of Whitmore, was worth a fortune.

The subdivision potential was prime right now, and that would only increase if the legal wrangling went on at length.

The thing was, when he was a kid, he had seen, in his mind, the motorcycle that he wanted to build with his dad long before they had ever started on it.

And it was the same with this: Jesse could already see the houses there, right where the castle now stood. He could see the gently curving streets, the leafy trees, the backyards with swing sets.

He could see kids having the childhood he had never had, running through sprinklers on lush green lawns, having to pull down their nets to let the odd car through as they played street hockey.

He was going to erase that castle and replace it with something else.

Only one thing would remain of its history. His grandmother would be the triumphant one, though he was sorry she had not lived to see it.

Jesse could envision a sign at the entrance to the new neighborhood, right where the carriage house currently stood.

In small letters, Welcome.

And in bigger, gleaming copper letters lit up softly at night: Mary Kade Meadows.

He knew from the tour yesterday that Layne would hate every single bit of his plan. She would probably chain herself to the castle door in the face of bulldozers.

So, allowing their lives to intertwine even more was only going to make everything worse.

This was what he could not forget. He was in a battle. It was a righting-past-wrongs kind of battle. It was a give-his-grandmother-the-honor-she-deserved kind of battle. It was a take-no-prisoners kind of battle. He now saw that tangling with Layne Prescott had been a mistake that would lead to complications.

She was an impulse in Jesse's world. He'd always been impulsive about some things, the renegade who did not follow the rules, but this time there was no room for impulses. Complications were detours to his formidable will.

But when they stopped in front of Sunshine and Storm, and she took off the helmet and shook her hair, it cascaded around her in a hissing wave.

His eyes found her lips.

He wished he had touched them. With his fingertip.

With his own lips.

Some primal awareness leaped in him that was astounding in its strength.

And he knew his will, no matter how formidable, was no kind of contender against that. Maybe another night at his grandmother's house would help him gird his loins for the battles ahead.

The battle, he saw now, was not so much with the Whitmores.

But with himself.

CHAPTER ELEVEN

Layne pulled into her parking spot in front of the carriage house, walked up to it and let herself in. She slammed the door so hard that the ancient panes rattled.

Get a grip, she told herself. You barely know the man. Better to find out now that he's too important and too busy than to kid yourself... Though what was she kidding herself about, exactly? He'd made it plain he wasn't looking for a relationship.

And she'd made it plain she wasn't looking for one, either.

But there had been undertows between them that gave lie to all of that.

"Layne?"

Mabel had arrived in record time. She must have practically flown down the driveway on her bicycle.

"How was it?" she breathed, coming through the door without knocking. "You know how you left me his license? I looked him up. It's hard to find stuff about him. I think he must have a full-time staff member scrubbing the internet of his name.

"But I found it. You know me. Internet sleuth extraordinaire. He owns Sunshine and Storm," Mabel announced dreamily. "Look at this." She held up her phone.

It had a grainy photo on it of Jesse, dressed casually in jeans and a button-down shirt, going up the stairs of a private jet. The distinctive Mr. Poochy emblem was painted on the tail of it. Jesse was scowling at whoever was taking the picture, with an expression that reminded Layne of his unguarded look when he had first gotten off the motorcycle and looked toward the castle.

Just yesterday.

Why did that feel as if it was a million years ago? Why did it already feel as if a world that did not hold him in it would be stripped of color and laughter?

"And look at this one. He's on a yacht—" Mabel stopped. And tilted her head. "What's wrong?"

"I know perfectly well who he is," Layne said stiffly.

"You do? He told you?"

"Under pressure. We went to the Sunshine and Storm outlet in Whitmore. Of course, they knew him there."

Mable invited herself to flop down on one of Layne's two chairs. She patted the other one invitingly, as if it was her place and not the other way around.

"Tell me everything."

"I'll just skip to the important part. I won't be seeing him again."

Mabel's eyes went very wide. "What? Why? Please don't tell me he tried something."

"He was a perfect gentleman."

Mabel looked relieved, so Layne didn't elaborate that maybe he was too much of a perfect gentleman. Geez, one little fingertip to his lips and he was gone like a rabbit in front of a fox.

"Then why?"

"Isn't it obvious? He's one hundred percent out of my league."

"That's not what I saw on his face yesterday."

"Well, it was a repeat of yesterday. Exactly. One minute

everything seemed to be going great, and then the next, he suddenly had business that couldn't wait."

"In other words," Mabel said, "he's quite scared of how attractive he finds you."

"Don't be ridiculous."

"I'm not being. I saw how he looked at you. And that was before you had *this* on. I could not have seen this one coming. Layne in black leather. I have to say I've never seen you look so utterly gorgeous. It's like another side of you has surfaced. No wonder he's terrified."

"He's not terrified. He told me before we even got on the motorcycle that he's single and intends to stay that way."

"And that's not terrified?" Mabel inserted dryly.

"I told him I felt exactly the same way."

Mabel rolled her eyes. "Both of you: *thou dost protest too much*."

"Anyway, he got a call and all of a sudden he had to go. We were supposed to go to Whitmore Falls, but we didn't. We were supposed to go for lunch tomorrow. We made a stupid bet about who had the best lobster po'boys, the place we stopped at, or the Loose Lobster."

"Did you bet on the Loose Lobster?"

"Of course!"

"What was the bet?"

They might be best friends, but she wasn't revealing that! "It doesn't matter, because I read the writing on the wall, and I canceled the lunch for tomorrow."

"*You* canceled?" Mabel breathed.

"On a point of pride."

"Pride?" Mabel considered her, and then a small smile tickled her lips. "You're both terrified of each other."

Layne somehow doubted that Jesse Kade was terrified of her, but she could not deny her own sense of terror. She had never really felt physical sensations as strong as the ones she had felt on that motorcycle, her legs wrapped around the small of his back.

She hoped she wasn't blushing. Mabel would be all over that!

"Go after him, Layne."

"I will not. And if you say *if you always do what you've always done,* I'm going to kill you."

"See?" Mabel said, sagely. "A different side of you is coming out. Even I'm a little bit terrified. You actually look angry."

"Well, you know, jilted by the billionaire."

"*You* canceled lunch."

"Before he could!"

"You never looked that angry when Brock jilted you."

Stunned, Layne realized that was true. It occurred to her she had never been able to muster any anger toward Brock, because their relationship had never been deep enough, or passionate enough.

She had *settled*. Wanting her dream of family and stability so badly. Wanting desperately *not* to have what her parents had. Had she really looked at Brock and thought, *You'll do*. Had she sent him that message, in one way or another, every day?

No wonder he had left.

"Since we're on the topic of Brock—"

"We aren't!" Layne told Mabel.

"Did you at least take some pictures?"

"Of what?" Layne asked.

"Jesse Kade! The motorcycle. You could send them to Brock."

It occurred to Layne that Brock had not entered her mind, not even once, until Mabel had brought him up.

"Brock is address unknown," she reminded her friend.

"Huh, you know where his mother lives. You could send them there. Believe me, he'd get them."

Her nearly mother-in-law had been as devastated by her son's uncharacteristic behavior as Layne had been.

"I'm not interested in him knowing one single thing about my life," Layne said. She was surprised to find this was a hundred percent true.

"Well, I'd like him to know that you are dating a billionaire."

"I am not dating him!"

Mabel sighed. "Can I at least see the pictures?"

"I didn't take any pictures." Layne considered how she had been so in the moment it had not even occurred to her to take out her phone and snap a few photos.

Now she wished she had. Evidence of her one-day walk on the wild side.

"Make a move, Layne."

"I'm not in his league."

Mabel yawned. "You said that already. Leagues are in baseball."

"I couldn't ever," she whispered. Maybe being the one to make a move was in Mabel's type A makeup, but it wasn't in hers.

Mabel sighed heavily. "You know, it's pretty early for both of you to be hung up on never wanting a relationship again. I'm assuming he's also been burned."

"I don't know his history," she said.

"Don't even try to tell me you're not curious. The thing is, even if he doesn't want to have a girlfriend and eventually settle down and have three kids and a dog, why can't you just have some fun together?"

The idea of just having some fun with him, no strings attached, sounded…well, fun.

"Even if I liked that idea," Layne said, not admitting that

she did, "I would not know where to find him. I can't just drive through Whitmore looking for his motorcycle."

Layne realized this was a serious backing down from *I couldn't ever*.

Mabel pounced on it. "He owns a place here."

"How do you know that?" Layne felt her heart pick up tempo a bit.

Could she possibly? Just have fun?

Mabel lifted a shoulder. "I told you, internet sleuth. Once I had a copy of his license, anything was possible."

"You're wasting yourself as Financial Director of Whitmore Castle." Layne felt lighter somehow. Was it *possibility* doing that, or was it because there was nothing better in the world than your friend believing in you, even when you didn't believe in yourself?

Especially when you didn't believe in yourself?

"Where's his house?" Layne bet it was in one of those big, gated subdivisions with a guard at the gate. A guard who would take one snooty look at her little car and turn her away immediately.

"That's the weird part. It's in Riverton."

From buying houses to turn into bed-and-breakfasts, Layne knew that many of the neighborhoods in Whitmore that had been run-down and neglected—especially those close to the downtown core—were being revitalized. Riverton was not one of them.

"I mean, I have no idea if he lives there," Mabel said. "I'm just saying he owns it. It wouldn't hurt you to go have a look."

Layne considered that. She could feel curiosity pulling at her.

"With a picnic basket with some Loose Lobster po'boys in it," Mabel finished softly.

Layne considered the life she might have had if she had said *I can* more often than she had said *I can't*.

She also considered the fact that with the exception of Brock's defection, she had never really considered her life unsatisfactory.

Until a man on a motorcycle had pulled up and opened the doors to worlds unexplored.

"Okay," she said, screwing up her courage, "I'll do it."

Mabel gave a hoot of pure approval. "It's your second date. You could kiss."

"It wasn't a date," Layne protested. "What happened to just having fun?"

"Kissing is fun," Mabel said, and really that was an inarguable point, though the mere suggestion of a kiss made Layne think of Jesse's lips, and the way they had felt under her fingertip.

"Oh? What would you call it, if not a date?"

Layne considered everything that had happened—the shopping, the motorcycle ride, the lunch. What would you call it, if not a date?

That had ended badly, she reminded herself. Really? She was scared enough about being the instigator—for the second time—without adding the complications of whether or not it was a date.

Never mind kissing.

And yet, at the same time, the thought of kissing Jesse made her feel lightheaded. In a *fun* kind of way.

"Okay," she said, feeling as if she had just lost a game of truth or dare, "I'll see if he lives there."

"Go prepared in case he does," Mabel said.

For kisses?

"Bring a picnic basket," her friend reminded. "An ice breaker."

The next day things did not go quite according to Layne's plan. Pamela Whitmore was being particularly demanding and even hinted she might come for a visit to check on things, and to decide herself what could be sacrificed in the name of the leopard-skin chair. And matching ottoman.

Layne had talked her out of that and then gone to the Loose Lobster to see a sign on their door that they'd had an emergency and weren't open for lunch, that they would be back at suppertime.

Once, these obstacles would probably have been enough for Layne to have second thoughts and not follow through on the concession she had made to Mabel.

But that was before she had worn black leather.

And so Layne found herself in the heart of Riverton, a basket in the back seat that contained all the ingredients for a picnic, in the early evening. It was a little embarrassing how she had fretted what to bring.

Were plastic wineglasses and sparkling juice too much? What about the chocolate-covered strawberries? Her tiny car filled with the luscious scent of the po'boys she had picked up at the Loose Lobster take-out window in a neighborhood that was just a few blocks from here, but that was in a totally different world away.

Riverton was a six-block square area that Layne—like most of the good citizens of Whitmore—had always avoided. She had never actually entered the neighborhood before.

The long-closed fish and lobster canneries that Riverton's residents had once serviced loomed like ominous dark clouds over the neighborhood.

The narrow streets held a terrible collection of run-down shanties, some boarded up, shabby yards that sported discarded washing machines and engine parts, sometimes a mean-looking dog on a chain.

Her hands were sweaty on the wheel. It was one thing to find the courage to *say* you would do something. It was quite another to actually do it.

She hadn't expected it to be quite so scary. She had locked

her doors and rolled up her windows tight within two minutes of her GPS telling her where to turn.

As she drove through Riverton, looking for house number 1022, she became convinced she was on a wild-goose chase. Jesse might own property here, but it seemed inconceivable he would live here.

She realized she might have to abort the mission. That she *wanted* to abort the mission. She felt, increasingly, like a tourist in a dangerous foreign country. The few people who were out and about did not look friendly. In fact, they would stop and look at her car with something suspicious and maybe even hostile in their eyes.

Besides, some of the streets did not have signs on them, and most of the houses did not have numbers.

She looked for a place to turn around. But then, suddenly, there is was. 1022. She pulled over to the curb and looked at the house.

Though it was the same modest shape and size of every other house on the block, it stood out because it was tidy. The house had been freshly painted a dark sage green, with cream trim. There were two nice rocking chairs on the covered front porch. There was a matching shed in the backyard that was also freshly painted. The grass had been watered and mowed.

The front storm door was open behind the screen door, but there were no signs of life and there were no signs of a motorcycle.

Which meant he either wasn't there, or it wasn't his house. Or maybe it was his house, but he'd rented it out? No doubt he had real estate holdings.

She was contemplating the absolute foolishness of packing a picnic and coming here—*chasing after a man, no matter how she tried to trick herself into believing otherwise*—when a neighbor emerged from the house next door. The porch was leaning precariously. He put his hands on his hips and looked directly at her with narrowed eyes. He was in his undershirt that had a stain on the front of it.

That might or might not be blood.

She tried not to stare at him. Or let her fear show. Layne's hands tightened on the steering wheel. She caught a movement out of the corner of her eye, and turned to look. The man was moving toward her. He had a menacing look on his face. She stepped on the gas and twisted the steering wheel, but she was so nervous she dropped the clutch and stalled the car.

This was what *she* got for challenging the way she had always been. Mugged in Riverton, a neighborhood she had no business being in.

She fumbled, trying to restart the car. Her heightened senses—even through the tightly closed passenger-side window—picked up the distinctive snap of a screen door.

She glanced away from the man moving toward her, and saw Jesse step out onto the porch of the green house.

She had never felt such a total feeling of relief in her whole life. Layne didn't realize she had stopped breathing until she sucked in a great breath of air.

"Clive," Jesse called, "it's okay. I know her."

The man stopped, gave her one more look laden with suspicion, and then turned, lifted a hand to Jesse and went back toward his house.

Her fear dissolved and a sense of release flooded her. Release and something more as Jesse moved down the walkway toward her car. His feet were bare.

What she felt was approaching giddiness. Was it because she was awash in fight-or-flight adrenaline, or was it because a barefoot Jesse looked so good in an open-throated white shirt rolled up at the cuffs, dark denims clinging to the powerful muscles of his legs, his hair curling crazily, still wet from a shower?

Or because she had said yes instead of no to the great adventure of life? And survived to tell about it.

CHAPTER TWELVE

JESSE HAD SEEN the car arrive from his front window.

What was Layne doing here? How on earth had she found him and why? He'd moved to one side of the window, his intention—for her own good—to ignore her. But then Clive had decided to be protective. She, understandably terrified by a strange man approaching her car in this neighborhood, had stalled her car.

Pure instinct sent him out the door. As he walked toward the car, as soon as he laid eyes on her, it felt as if a man's intentions were a puny thing. Still, he girded his loins to find a way to send her off. He went around the car, and Layne rolled down the driver's-side window.

"Hi," she said, a little too brightly. Her cheeks were flushed and her pulse was beating wildly at the side of her neck, as if she had just run from a bear.

A reaction to Clive, or something else?

"Hi," he said. He was aware of his own pulse throbbing in his neck.

"I brought supper," she said in a rush, tripping over her own tongue. "I kind of overreacted yesterday. To your business call. I should have been more understanding about how busy you are!"

Jesse considered that. He'd been trying to protect her. Instead, he had managed to make her feel less-than.

And yet here she was.

And here he was.

"I can just leave it," she said uncertainly, when he didn't say anything, "Supper. I mean, if you're still busy."

That, of course, would be best. The noble thing to do would be to refuse her invitation, especially since it contained layers of complexity that went further than supper.

"It was going to be lunch," she said, talking too fast, "but the Loose Lobster was closed. Some kind of family emergency. It's not a date, or anything like that. You're single. I'm single. We both plan to stay that way. But that doesn't mean we can't have friends. Get to know people. Have fun!"

She was so nervous. He found he was simply incapable of hurting her. As she gazed up at him from behind her steering wheel, Layne looked ill at ease, and hopeful, and scared and adorable.

She had caught him off-guard, and he was hungry. It was a poor position for a man to raise a defense from. They could have supper together. She was right, wasn't she? Mature people could have friendships. They could get to know new people. They could have fun. It didn't have to go anywhere.

Though looking down at her glorious, burnished bronze hair pulled up in a messy bun, he felt as if those were just words. The temptations of her felt as if they could swamp the best of resolutions.

And that was before factoring in the smell of lobster wafting out that open window.

"No, no," he said, "come in. You just caught me by surprise. No one's ever found me here before."

"Oh," she said, "that's what you get for surrendering your license to Mabel. She knows everything about you now."

He doubted that.

He opened the door for her. Layne stepped out. His mouth went dry as the scent of that clean, piled-up hair tickled his nostrils. He was not sure that looked like a "just friends" outfit. It wasn't quite as sexy as black leather, but darned close.

She was wearing a light sundress, pale blue, with a small flower print. There were skinny straps over her slender shoulders, and the fabric hugged her curves, then the skirt flared out. It skimmed her thigh. When she leaned into the back seat to get—

He squinted, commanding himself to look at whatever she was reaching for, rather than the dress sliding up her leg. He realized it was a picnic basket. A real wicker basket, with leather hinges on the lid, like the kind of thing you saw in movie.

Romantic movies.

Jesse cursed his weakness in letting her get out of the car.

She'd brought a picnic to Riverton?

He shot a look at Clive's house, pretty sure his neighbor was hovering behind the door, watching.

"I thought we could eat outside," she said. "It's such a nice summer night."

Jesse took the basket from her—huge and heavy, enough food for a week—and held open the gate to his yard for her. "Sure," he said, "the backyard." *Away from Clive's prying eyes.* "You have to go through the house."

He contemplated that. Layne Prescott in his house.

Just yesterday he'd been a man who claimed he liked surprises. Today, holding open the door to his childhood home for her, he wasn't so sure.

"Will my car be okay?"

"Oh, sure, they'll probably just strip the hubcaps," he said straight-faced, but saw her alarm. "I'm kidding."

"Where's your motorcycle if it's so safe?" Her gaze slid over to Clive's house.

"He's a good guy. He looks after this place when I'm not here. He's protective of me."

Everyone in Riverton knew Jesse stayed at his grandmother's old place when he was in town.

His grandmother and his father had been fixtures in this neighborhood. His grandmother had been known as the wizard who could get a stain—even blood—out of anything. His dad, a wizard in another way, had coaxed life back into a lot of cars that should have ended up in the wrecking yard. Jesse had grown up here. The streets could be mean, yes, but this neighborhood also had a strong we're-all-in-this-together dynamic, possibly the strongest he'd ever experienced.

What people might have found most shocking about Riverton was the amount of pride here. The houses—and the way they were kept—represented multigenerational poverty. If they looked like they were falling down, it was because there was no money to fix them, or the money was used up the way their fathers and mothers had used money.

Paying too much on credit.

Using booze and drugs as an escape hatch from a life that ground a spirit down.

And yet for all that, people managed to hang on to the houses that had been in their families for generations.

And the people around him in this community—unlike most people he encountered who found out who he was—never asked him for anything. In fact, they *gave* him the most precious thing of all.

His privacy. They closed ranks around him the same way they closed ranks when the police were looking for somebody in the neighborhood.

It was unspoken, but he was *theirs*. The one who had made it, who carried their hopes and dreams, somehow. Without their ever saying they protected him, he knew he was protected. The few people who had found out he owned a place here were stonewalled by the residents of Riverton.

Layne's little white car was as out of place here as an iceberg in Africa. Clive had probably mistaken her for a reporter.

"Your car will be fine," he told her. "I park my bike in the shed over there, to protect it from weather, not crime. People here have my back."

She considered that. "That's very nice," she said, a bit surprised.

Her surprise served as a reminder that despite how far he had come, the lessons of Riverton ran through his veins.

"Oh," she said, stopping in the doorway of his house and letting her eyes adjust to the darker interior, "This is nice, too"

As if that was another big shock to her.

He looked at it through her eyes. He wasn't sure *nice* described it. It was plain, but spotlessly clean. Her eyes rested on the old stone fireplace that had once tried—mostly unsuccessfully—to heat the house and then went to the floors, dark heart pine.

"You expected piles of empty beer bottles?" he asked. He *wanted* to find barriers he could keep up between them.

"Don't be silly," she said. "You told me you don't drink."

It didn't help barriers that she remembered. But, hopefully, that meant there was nothing alcoholic in the heavy basket, because it felt as if it was going to be hard enough to keep a lid on things.

To keep his mission forefront: *Be polite, don't hurt her feelings, get rid of her.*

He led the way through the living room and the kitchen, and held open the back door.

But she paused and went over to the stove. "Is this a wood-burning oven?" she asked, running her hands over the shining white enamel. "I've never seen one in such good condition. I love it."

"You'd love it until you tried it," he said wryly, "though

it was my grandmother's pride and joy. I tried to talk her into replacing it with an electric a million times, but she wouldn't have it."

He didn't add that her house was a snapshot of a certain time that she could not let go of.

"This is where you grew up," Layne said, with sudden understanding.

"Yeah, my grandmother's house. She left it to me. She died last year. She was ninety-three."

"You miss her," she guessed softly.

Did he like it or not like it that Layne *saw* him?

He did miss her. She'd been always cantankerous, occasionally mean, and terribly set in her ways. She was like Riverton itself. She presented a hard face to the world. And yet, had anybody had his back the way she had?

"She was all I had left for family," Jesse said. "My dad predeceased her. About ten years ago."

Again, she *saw*. "You adored her."

"I did," he admitted, enough to be investing a lot of time and money into finding justice for her, giving her the honor she deserved.

The reason he had to eat whatever was in that basket and then send Miss Prescott on her way, no matter how delectable she was, and she was plenty delectable, was confirmed when he held open the back door. The doorway was very narrow, and when she passed by him, she had to turn sideways. She scraped against him, and he knew, from the look on her face, that the awareness was equally sharp between them.

Despite what she had said about just being friends, having fun.

"Oh," she said, gazing out at the backyard. "What is that? It's an enchantment."

An enchantment was the look in her eyes and the soft

summer evening light in her hair, and the swish of her skirt against him, but he followed her gaze.

The small backyard was completely enclosed with flowering hedges, making it extraordinarily private. Layne walked right over to the *enchantment*.

"It looks like a playhouse," she said, delighted, moving toward the structure. "A miniature Victorian, complete with a front porch."

She ran her fingers over the sign that hung over the rounded door. It said, in his father's handwriting, Mr. Poochy.

"Is this a doghouse?" she asked, astounded.

"It is."

"There's a real Mr. Poochy," she said, turning to him and smiling a smile that could make a man leave all reason behind, that could make his defenses crumble like a castle wall hit by a cannon ball.

"There isn't currently."

It occurred to him she was finding her way into his life, and she didn't need a cannon aimed at his walls to do it.

No, he had opened the door and invited her. But maybe this was the way to get rid of her once and for all. She thought she wanted to know him? All of him? If he told her the realities of growing up in Riverton, of his family, if she was smart, she would see he was probably unsuitable for her middle-class world.

She loved a castle. She needed a prince, even if she denied it. And she probably deserved one. Maybe she thought it was him because he had told her he owned Sunshine and Storm. But that was only part of his story.

"We always had a dog when I was growing up." He was aware of inserting a hard note into his voice. "Always named Mr. Poochy. One would die, and it would seem like the next day my dad, drunk, would wander home with a new half-starved mongrel that already adored him."

He didn't try and make her see his dad in a better light by telling her that animals could see what many people missed.

"My dad built the doghouse," Jesse told her.

She didn't seem fazed by the fact his dad had been a drunk. Instead, she was marveling at the doghouse. "His attention to detail is amazing. Look at all these fish scale shingles. Every one of them is ever so slightly different, cut out by hand. And then the paint! The peak pink and yellow stripes, and the main body purple. And the little window, with the flower box underneath it. It's all so whimsical."

"When I look at it, it's pure him," Jesse said, and then laid it bare for her. "No food on the table, bills to be paid, the house falling down, and he'd been out here planting hedges and building a palace for the current Mr. Poochy. The dog had a nicer house than us and, as you can see, was nicer than the majority of regular houses in Riverton.

"My dad said it was because he was always in the doghouse. And he was, too. He slept in here all the time. I'd come out here some mornings, even when it was cold enough that frost had painted the grass white, to find Dad passed out, curled into the current Mr. Poochy for warmth."

"He slept in the doghouse?" Her voice was incredulous. There! She was getting it. He did not come from the stuff people hung their dreams on.

"He slept out here when he came home after the bars kicked him out because he was broke or drunk. He didn't want to bring the wrath of my grandmother down on his head."

"But you said he was the world's best father," she reminded him, her voice soft and not full of any of the wariness he might have hoped for.

He sighed. "He was."

"Loving people is very complicated," she said.

Considering this brutal honesty had been intended to scare her off, Jesse was shocked by how good it felt to say those things, to release them. A weight he hadn't realized he'd carried was weirdly lifted.

She touched his arm, very briefly, and her eyes locked on his face. If he had expected recrimination—or worse, sympathy—he got neither.

Her eyes held some deep *knowing* that made him have to fight a desire to spill his entire life story into the softness he saw in her eyes, as if speaking it could heal something in him.

Heal something?

That hadn't been the point! Besides, there was nothing in him that needed to be healed! Look at the world he had created!

Thankfully, Layne didn't probe it any further. Instead, she relieved him of the picnic basket. She scanned the yard, went over to a particularly lush square of grass and set it down. She undid the leather hasp, opened the lid.

"You want to eat first or have fun first?" she asked him.

"Eat," he croaked.

On top was a plaid blanket and she took it out, gave it a shake and spread it on the ground. Next she pulled out what looked like a wine bottle. She put her thumbs expertly under the cork and pushed. It came out with a pop, like it was champagne.

She removed two plastic wineglasses, and plates attached to the lid with leather straps. It was all very old-world and classy. The picnic might have been unremarkable on the grounds of Whitmore Castle, but Jesse was fairly certain it was a first for Riverton.

"Sparkling fruit juice," she told him, filling the wineglasses and patting the place beside her.

He glanced back at the house. It was too late to run from what was unfolding here. He took the place beside her on the blanket. He felt a sensation of surrender. Something in him did the worst possible thing.

Relaxed. As Layne tucked her legs up under her, Jesse found himself stretching out, leaning up on his elbow as he accepted the wineglass from her, and then a po'boy.

He took a bite. He closed his eyes.

It was the best thing he had ever tasted, but to be honest, he wasn't sure if it was because of Layne in her sundress on the blanket with him, or if it was the po'boy, or if it was the glorious fading of a perfect summer day.

"What do you think?" she asked, taking a bite of her own sandwich.

He wasn't sure what he thought. He'd either died and gone to heaven, or the exact opposite, the dark side throwing temptations at him that he had no hope of resisting.

After they had been pretty much demolished the po'boys, they sipped the sparkling juice.

"Look, here's the fun part," she said. She pulled a small yellow bottle out of the basket and he stiffened, remembering that tiny plastic pouch in Jenna's purse.

But then Layne detached a hollow plastic circle from it, unscrewed the lid. She dipped the wand in and blew gently. A soap bubble, light and iridescent, floated between them.

He actually laughed out loud—it was so shockingly and refreshingly different than what he had expected.

She watched its flight, dipped the wand again and blew another one, bigger. This time, instead of watching the bigger bubble try to climb clumsily before falling, he stared at her lips, the sexy little bow they made when she blew.

"This is fun?" he asked her. It felt like a kind of torment.

She handed him a bottle. "It's only fun if you play. See if you can make a bigger one," she suggested. "I bet you can't."

"I bet I can't either," he said. "I've never blown a bubble in my life."

"You haven't? That's crazy."

"I'm trying to tell you I did not have a normal childhood." He was trying to give her plenty of warning he was damaged.

"Huh," she said. "Who did? Maybe it's never too late."

He unscrewed the lid from his bottle and removed the wand. He dipped it, and blew and blew and blew, watching with a competitor's glee as it became bigger than anything she had done. It popped, sending a spray of soapy water over his face before it broke free of the wand.

She laughed.

And then he found himself laughing, too, and the games began. Biggest, smallest, highest, oddest shape.

It might have just as well been champagne that they drank instead of fruit juice, because with soap bubbles floating around them, Jesse felt as if he was in an altered state.

He tried to put his finger on it, as he became aware of a startling attentiveness to the sharp trill of birds singing, the abundant, waxy green leaves of the lilac hedge against an orange and pink sky, and the spongy lushness of the grass beneath the blanket.

He was so aware of how her bare legs curled underneath her, the color of her hair highlighted by sunset hues, the way her smile made her lips look, her scent mingling with that from the hedge.

Suddenly, he pinpointed what he was feeling. Despite his awareness of her, the overriding sensation was not one of passion, though that certainly hovered at the edges.

What he was feeling now was something he had felt rarely, if at all.

Contentment.

Money and success had allowed him to experience things that most human beings never would. He had traveled by private jet, he had parachuted and bungee jumped and ziplined, he had skied from helicopters, he had vacationed on superyachts.

And yet he had never known anything quite like what he felt sitting in his grandmother's backyard, blowing bubbles.

CHAPTER THIRTEEN

CONTENTMENT.

It was an elixir for a man who had spent every single day of his life, every waking moment, driven.

By a need to prove something. To the world and himself.

There was an irony in the fact it was here in the backyard of a humble house in Riverton—the place where his need to prove himself had been born—that he felt what a warrior must feel when he finally found a place where it was safe to take off his armor.

"So," Layne said finally, when their bubble bottles were empty, "I definitely won biggest bubble."

"I was highest."

"I was oddest shape."

"I was smallest."

"So, we're tied. Unless we can decide between Sea Biscuit or Loose Lobster?"

It was all very light, fun, just as she had promised. And yet, right beneath all that the real question was crackling in the air between them. *What happens now?*

He needed her to go. He needed to get back in control of this situation. He should have never accepted the contents of that picnic basket. He certainly never should have given in to the silliness of blowing bubbles into the soft evening air.

It had cast a spell on him, a spell that asked him what kind of person would say no to her, to all that hopefulness, the bravery it had taken to come here? The fact she had not run, as he had expected—and hoped, but not really—when he had told her about his dad.

He was aware that as his head said it needed her to go, his heart was saying the exact opposite.

He needed her to stay.

Something about her was making him acutely aware that there were spaces in him that all the success and all the wealth in the world could not fill.

He had a sudden, almost desperate sense of wanting someone to know him. To know all of him.

Still, when she found out who he was—which was different than telling her who his father was—and when she found out that he was the enemy of her beloved castle, it was all going to go very wrong.

"Earth to Jesse."

"Huh? What?"

She gave him a puzzled look. "We're about to declare a winner."

He looked at her lips. So many wins in his life, so many victories, and not one thing that had filled him like her eyes, resting on his face, inviting him to tell her his secrets.

"I'm going to say it's a draw," he said.

She laughed.

Her laughter in his backyard filled something in him, a space that he had not known was empty. That acute awareness—of birdsong and evening air, warm on his skin—deepened.

"So, does a draw mean both of us are going swimming, or neither of us?" she asked.

"Neither," he said, way too quickly. "A draw means the bet is off."

"Why don't we go to the falls and decide there?" she asked softly.

He'd managed to avoid this very moment yesterday, but here they were, back at it, as if it was inevitable.

"I would," he said, looking for an escape hatch and sliding a glance to her. "You're not dressed for it."

"Oh," she said, "I guess I thought maybe tomorrow. It's going to be dark soon. We wouldn't be able to see the falls, and I didn't really think about riding at night."

Even in the fading light, he could see her blush after she said it, as if she'd invited him to join her at some kind of risqué event, like a burlesque show or an evening of naughty, adult games.

Tomorrow.

He'd tried to give her an out, but she hadn't taken it. Jesse was trying so hard not to hurt her by rejecting her, by trying to get her to take the exit door voluntarily. His rational mind tried to intervene, to explain to him if he didn't hurt her now, he was going to hurt her worse, later.

But the future—even tomorrow—seemed like a nebulous thing, faraway and unfathomable.

He just wanted this moment—of comfort, of connection—to last forever.

So, he didn't say a single thing about tomorrow. He just lay down on the blanket, bent his knees up, crossed his hands over his stomach and looked up at a sky turning indigo.

"The falls tomorrow," he agreed. "Tonight, do you want to watch the stars come out?"

Layne had been just about to bring out the chocolate-covered strawberries when Jesse asked her that.

He had relaxed as they ate their po'boys in his backyard, with the light leaching from the day, but there was an undercurrent of skittishness.

He reminded her of a nervous horse that was going to bolt if too fast a move was made. The bubbles had alleviated some of that, but the strawberries seemed a little too like a Valentine's Day offering.

She contemplated the strange juxtaposition, that she, small-town girl, was making him, successful billionaire, nervous. That she, shy and inhibited, was finding a bolder side, acting as the aggressor.

But this house, this neighborhood, the things he had confided in her, all let her know that underneath all that wealth and success, he was a guy from very humble beginnings. Maybe not really out of her league, after all.

Still, was she being too forward? Aggressor? Layne Prescott?

She could almost hear Mabel's snort of disdain. Forward? Aggressor? It wasn't a historical romance novel!

Even if Layne did feel distinctly romantic—not like just friends, at all—lying at Jesse's side, with their shoulders touching, the blanket beneath them and the stars winking on, one by one, above them.

"I didn't think they'd look so visible from anywhere in town," she said, after picking out the lights of Orion's belt and pointing them out to him.

He chuckled. "That's what you get when all the streetlights have been shot out. What part of town did you grow up in?"

"The neighborhood right next door to the castle. It's called Castleton."

"Wow. Zero imagination among the town planners. Houses next to the river? Riverton. Houses next to the castle? Castleton. What would they have called one next to the sewage plant?"

"Poopton," she said, and they were both laughing.

"Red-light district?"

"There is no red-light district!"

"Play along."

"Okay, Sexton."

"Or Luston."

Again the laughter was easy between them. But there was something subliminal going on, too. Both the words *sex* and *lust* had been introduced, and Layne was aware of primal hungers stirring within her in a way she had not quite ever experienced before, and that certainly didn't have a thing to do with friendship.

"Tell me about growing up in Castleton," Jesse invited. "Was it the American dream? Like the Cleavers, or something?"

"It was a modest, working, middle-class neighborhood. Mabel's dad and mine both worked on fishing boats. It was all very ordinary. I think that's why the castle seemed so extraordinary to us. Well, that, and it was an escape."

"An escape from what?"

He had told her things about his dad that made her feel as if she could share about her not so perfect life too.

"My parents fought almost continuously," Layne admitted slowly. "They were always breaking up, or threatening to break up, and then getting back together. After they got back together or made up, we'd all be on a pink cloud for a while, and then the cycle would repeat itself. They split up for good when I was fourteen."

"I'm sorry."

"It was better for everyone."

They were silent, but the silence was comfortable. She felt compelled to say more.

"The worst part was the hope." Had she ever said that to a single person before? Jesse's hand found hers, and he squeezed it. And then he didn't let go. The warmth radiating from him felt deliciously erotic as the night air turned cooler around them.

"Is that why you don't have a boyfriend?" he asked softly. "A significant other?"

"I did have a fiancé," Layne confided, after a moment. Wasn't there some kind of rule that you weren't supposed to talk about stuff like this on a first date? But Mabel had said it was a second date.

But somehow, in the most lovely way, it didn't feel like a date at all. It felt as if they already knew each other and were just filling in some of the blanks but in a deep way, not like a what's-your-favorite-color? way.

"We broke it off about a year ago."

She was letting Jesse know she was over it, even though less than twenty-four hours ago she had claimed to Mabel her heartbreak was still fresh.

But for the first time, she knew she was. Over it. Completely. Not only that she was over it, but that she was a different person than she had been back then.

"What happened?" he encouraged her, his voice as soft and sweet as the night air.

"I was determined I was going to get the whole relationship thing *right*," Layne told him, "I looked for the exact opposite of my mom and dad. Brock was just this nice, levelheaded guy who came from the kind of family I had always dreamed of. They had what I wanted—stability, routines, respect for each other. I don't think there had ever been a raised voice in that household. I felt it was worth forfeiting adventure and high romance for those things."

The word *passion*, as one of the things she had forfeited, blasted through her brain.

"So, Brock and I built a beautiful little business together, where we bought old houses and refurbished them and turned them into themed bed-and-breakfasts."

"The theme?" he asked quietly.

"Home Sweet Home."

"What you longed for, most of all. What happened?"

"He basically told me it was all a little too dull for him. He cashed in for a one-way ticket to Thailand."

Jesse's hand tightened more on hers, and then he said, his voice soft and full of gravel. "You know he did you a favor, right?"

"Letting me know that my dreams were hopeless fantasies? Letting me know I had more chance of having my dreams come true with a castle—a building—than a guy?"

"No," he said.

"What then?"

"Leaving you open. Because you could have died without knowing."

"Knowing what?" she whispered.

He was leaning up on his elbow, looking down at her through the darkness. He brushed a strand of hair away from her face, and then ran his thumb over the fullness of her bottom lip. He was so close she could count his lashes, one by one, see the small dent in his bottom lip, the pirate-like stubble thickening sexily on his cheeks.

"Without knowing this," he said, and he dropped his head over hers and claimed her mouth with his own.

So much for being friends, she told herself dreamily. The sensation of kissing Jesse erased every other sensation Layne had ever had.

Fun paled in comparison to this.

Gone were thrilling rides on roller coasters, the swish of snow under skis, the kiss of sun on an upturned face.

He was right. The touch of his lips had saved her from a life of not knowing what, in this instant, felt like the most important thing of all.

That you could melt.

You could melt into the stars above you and the grass beneath you. You could melt into the energy radiating from another person's body, and the scorching heat of their mouth.

You could melt into a place where there was no time. Where there was nothing.

And everything.

You could become one with it all.

All you had to do was follow that kiss to the place it led, a place as ancient, as mysterious, as unknowable as the speck of dust it had all exploded from.

Creation.

Creation was beckoning her.

Jesse pulled away from her and sat up. He ran a hand through his hair, turned and looked at her, astounded.

"Wow," he breathed.

And that was when she knew he had nearly missed that cosmic *knowing* too.

She had never felt so powerful, so beautiful, so connected, so in touch with the soul of another human being.

He had that skittish look back. "We need to slow down," he said, his voice a croak of pure need.

Layne contemplated that he wanted to slow down, while she wanted to speed up.

She stretched luxuriously, aware of what that movement did to him. There was a sense that she and Jesse had been destined to be together since the dawn of time. She felt the pure delicious exhilaration of the challenge before her.

She realized she had no intention of just being friends. She realized she intended to seduce Jesse Kade. For now, she would do it on his terms, slowly.

She reached into the picnic basket. She took out the box of chocolate strawberries. Aware of his eyes on her, she bit into it, closed her eyes, moaned ever so slightly.

And then she held that half-eaten strawberry out to him.

He hesitated and then leaned into her, biting the strawberry, his lips tickling her fingertips.

And under the starlight, they fed each other strawberries. There was an argument for slowness, after all, Layne realized dreamily. Because sharing strawberries was every bit as sensual as the kiss had been. It felt as if she had never tasted a strawberry before. Had that red fruit always hidden elements of the exotic and erotic?

"I think," Jesse said, his voice hoarse, after the last strawberry was gone, "maybe we should call it quits for tonight."

His lips were stained red from the strawberry. His breath was sweet and inviting.

Layne wanted nothing more than to capture his lips again with her own, but she ordered herself to slow down.

"Are we going on the motorcycle tomorrow?" she asked him, aware of a shockingly sultry note to her voice.

Again, she felt some kind of power she had never felt before as she saw him struggle to say no, to pull back.

She watched his battle play across the moonlit beauty of his face, and she watched, satisfied, as he lost.

"I'll pick you up at the castle at ten."

And then he helped her to her feet, picked up the basket and walked her to her car, protecting her in his neighborhood of shot-out streetlights.

He put her picnic basket in the back seat, hesitated, then kissed her. He was aiming for her cheek, but she moved.

And his lips found hers.

And even though the neighbors' porch light came on, Jesse kissed her as if no one was watching.

Or as if everyone was watching.

And he was letting them know.

Mine.

Under my protection.

Even though it was so dark as she drove away, she saw him standing in the middle of the road, his hands in his pockets, watching after her, standing like a stone, until she turned the last corner and was out of his sight.

A huge sigh escaped her.

One of pure bliss.

CHAPTER FOURTEEN

THE NEXT DAY, as she rode behind Jesse on the motorcycle, the hum of the motorcycle and their physical closeness sang of possibility, a continuation of what had started between them the night before.

Layne was shocked and delighted as the primal urges she had felt last night grew. She *wanted* Jesse Kade.

She wanted him as she had never wanted any other man.

An uncharacteristically bold thought blasted through her brain. *And by the end of the day I will have him.*

With the seduction of Jesse Kade forming the backdrop, the day became as perfect as any day Layne had ever had. By the time they parked the motorcycle at the Whitmore Falls parking lot, she already felt close to Jesse in ways far more complex than the physical closeness that the bike dictated.

They could hear the roar of the falls as soon as they removed their helmets.

A trail led through giant pines, and as they got closer the scent of those tress intensified in the air heavy with mist. The moistness made the path slippery, and when Layne's foot slid out from under her, Jesse reached for her hand and steadied her.

"Bike boots," he said, as if he needed an excuse to touch her. "Not really made for a hike."

Even when she had found her feet again, he didn't let it go. She had been squished against him in the most intimate way for the past hour, but holding his hand felt natural and sexy, as if it announced to the world and to them: *couple*.

She felt like a musical instrument, strings wound tight, his hand the bow that coaxed the music to life. Again, Layne's *wanting*, to know his touch more completely, almost took her breath away, adding a subtle layer of sizzle to their every movement and touch.

His palm was warm and dry, especially in contrast to the chilly mist, and it cupped hers perfectly as his fingers knit through her own. His grip was strong, but that strength was tempered.

Such a small thing, to hold hands with someone, and yet such a big thing, too, with its nonverbal message, a language of connection, trust, a deep enjoyment in togetherness.

Her own sensation of *intensity* was mirrored by the environment, because as they got closer to falls, the sounds grew louder. By the time they wove down the path that led to a low stone wall and a lookout, the cacophony of cascading water put thunder to shame. Probably the pure noise and the mist in the air should have forewarned them of this, that spring runoff had swollen the falls to monstrous but majestic proportions.

"Have you ever seen them like this?" she shouted at him.

"Never."

"I guess I've never been here at this time of year before," she said.

"Good thing neither of us won that bet," he said.

They stood side by side, awestruck by the gushing, foaming power of the water. His arm slipped around her waist. Again, it was protective, as if he was afraid she would slip over and fall into all that churning pool. Layne leaned into his protection, enjoying how exquisitely feminine he made her feel.

They stood there for a long time, lifting their faces to it, letting the spray of the falls anoint them.

They got back on the motorcycle and instead of turning back to Whitmore, Jesse turned the other way.

They sailed through the day. Even with few words—maybe because there were few words—the connection between them was as powerful as electricity, vibrating between them, a give-and-take of masculine and feminine energy like she had never felt. His heartbeat was her heartbeat, his strength was her strength, his warmth was her warmth.

They went through Somerset and then continued on. Time evaporated, as they experienced the majesty of the coastal highway. Being on the motorcycle created an immersion in the experience, of both their togetherness and the lush scenery around them. They weren't passing through, they were part of the great primal flow of energy that was life.

They turned back, finally, the day astoundingly almost gone. Jesse stopped for dinner at the fanciest restaurant in Somerset. Layne actually had doubts if they would be let in. As she pulled off her helmet, her hair was a mess. So was his. The way they were dressed, they could have easily been on the set of that TV show about a motorcycle gang.

But apparently that thought never even occurred to Jesse. And the maître d' seemed to recognize both power and money in the easy and confident way that Jesse carried himself.

Without asking and without a reservation they were escorted through the crowded restaurant to what had to be the best table in the house. They watched as the light of the day slowly seeped away.

There was the most beautiful exhilaration between them. They teased and laughed and sampled each other's menu choices off shared forks.

Jesse took out his phone, and for a moment, she felt insulted. *Really? Business?* This was where it had all fallen apart before.

But no, he turned the phone to her. "Weather coming," he said.

She looked at the severe thunderstorm warning flashing across his screen.

"Is that dangerous on a motorcycle?"

"It's best if we can avoid it," he said, his voice calm. "I think we have time to get back to Whitmore before the storm breaks."

He tossed down a mess of bills, rose from the table and extended his hand to her. Honestly, she could have stayed at the restaurant, gazing into his eyes and eating dessert off his spoon forever. But despite his nonchalance, she sensed a certain urgency in him, and took his hand.

Night had almost completely fallen by the time they got outside. A glance toward Whitmore showed black, ominous clouds silhouetted in the remaining light of day.

If she had thought the motorcycle ride was exhilarating before, it had been nothing compared to this, rocketing through blackness, the night air whistling around them, drawing her even closer to him.

The intensifying of the wind—howling around the bike and whistling through their helmets—warned of the storm before it hit. Layne could feel the motorcycle being buffeted by it. Even with the leathers on, and Jesse's body blocking most of the force of the wind, she started to feel cold.

And then the storm hit, furious. The wind shrieked. The first lightning bolt lit up the sky, so close there was no pause at all before a crack of thunder, followed by a deep, trembling rumble.

In seconds the sky opened up and the rain came down. It didn't come slowly, it came in in sheets. The leather offered only so much protection as water sluiced off the helmet, down the back and front of her neck.

"I'm looking for a place to pull over that has good shelter," Jesse assured her, his voice coming through the helmet speaker, soothing above the rage of the storm.

Despite the obvious danger and the growing discomfort, Layne felt exhilarated in a way she had never felt before, as if she was throwing open her arms to the elements and to life and to whatever it brought. Of course, part of that was trust in Jesse.

He radiated strength, confidence and competence, even as the roads grew slicker and the rain came harder.

As they drove on, the ocean was on one side, cliffs on the other. The ocean sounded as angry as the storm. There was no place to pull over.

But then, despite the murkiness, a world obliterated, she caught a glimpse of a landmark.

"We're two minutes from the castle," she said to him, "Take the next turn."

He had already seen it. Just as he made the turn the rain turned to hail. At first, the hailstones were tiny, pricks of white piercing a black, black sky. But then they grew marble-sized, pounding down, pinging off the helmets, bouncing off the jackets.

One minute to the castle.

Even against the storm, she could suddenly see the turrets, one shade of black darker than the sky.

She was not sure she had ever felt as connected to another person as she did to Jesse as he piloted them through the storm, their lives literally in his hands.

The shocking intention she had set earlier came back to her. *And by the end of the day I will have him.*

It felt as if nature itself was conspiring to make that happen.

Was she really going to take the chemistry between them to its conclusion? She had never been that kind of person.

And yet, what had the kind of person she had been gotten her? She and Brock had dated for four months before the first time. Everything so right, so measured, so timed, everything according to the rules.

Layne wanted something different now. She wanted to be wild. She wanted to be bold. She wanted to embrace every single sensation life was offering. She wanted to ride this wave of absolute exhilaration to the very top of where it could go.

"There," she said to Jesse, relief and anticipation flooding her. "Stop right there. At the carriage house."

CHAPTER FIFTEEN

When they arrived at the castle grounds, the only time Jesse felt as if he could truly see was when lightning briefly tore through the darkness of the night. The motorcycle headlight was being swallowed by the blackness of the storm. The hail was pelting them, unrelenting, painful. He'd been trying to balance speed with safety on the slick roads, laser-focused on protecting Layne.

And then she said, "*Stop right there. At the carriage house.*"

Her voice, sounding like a whisper in his ear, rose above the noise of the storm. It had a husky note to it, almost smoky, certainly sensual.

They were two seconds from safety, he told himself, and yet he could feel a new danger crackling on the air, tickling along the nape of his neck like a static charge from taking towels or sheets from the dryer.

Laundry. Something he knew a thing or two about since he had worked at his grandmother's laundry well before dryer sheets had been invented.

"The carriage house?" he repeated.

"I live there."

It showed how little they knew about each other. Until the moment she said that, he hadn't even known precisely where she lived. She didn't know where he lived when he wasn't in Riverton.

He had to stop this. They were caught in the thrall, their attraction to each other intensified by the invigorating thrill of being caught in circumstances that were beyond their control.

At the back of his mind he wondered if the attraction between them did not have many of the same elements as the storm.

It had come out of nowhere, and those elements seemed just as beyond their control.

One thing he did know, though, was he was not stopping at that carriage house. He was certainly not going in it.

"Why don't we go to one of the finished rooms in the castle?" he suggested. The hammering of the hail on his helmet felt as loud as Whitmore Falls. "Why don't I book it? Right now? I'm happy to pay for it."

Layne didn't get that his reluctance was tied to the carriage house.

"Oh," her voice, breathless, came through the helmet speaker, though he could barely hear it above the hail. "Such a good idea! I should have thought of that."

It only took a few seconds more to get there. He pulled up at the front door, and they got off the motorcycle. He tried to hold an arm above her head—as if his arm could do more than the helmet—to protect her from the relentless hammering. The hail was now the size of golf balls. They raced up the stairs. The front door had a keypad on it, and Jesse noticed Layne's hands were shaking as she put in the code.

And then the door blinked and beeped, and opened beneath her touch. They hurried in and he had to lean on the door to close it against the storm that tried to squeeze in with them. The deafening sound of the hail was instantly muted.

She reached for the light switch and flicked it.

"No power," she said.

"Not surprising."

"The keypad on the door worked because it's battery powered."

Their eyes adjusted to the darkness. He noticed her hands were still shaking and he closed the small distance between them, undid the snap and slid the helmet from her head. He set the helmet on the floor without ever once looking away from the hair that cascaded out from underneath it, turned to fire when it was illuminated by a sudden bolt of lightning.

She started at the thunderclap that followed instantly on the lightning's heels, shaking the foundations of the castle. She peered out the window. "Oh, Jesse, our poor bike."

Our.

She had felt everything he wished, one with the road. And the bike.

And him.

She turned back to him. She reached up for his chinstrap. Her fingers were shaking and cold as ice cubes when she grazed his chin with them. Lightning again, but it had nothing on the light in her eyes, as glorious as the storm.

She undid the strap, fumbling. His hand covered hers, and he helped her. And then he slid off the helmet and set it beside hers on the floor, where the water streamed off them.

He turned slowly back to her, like a man in a dream. Maybe if he hadn't been fighting the storm for so long he would have had the strength to fight what he felt.

And maybe not.

He unzipped his jacket, then took her cold hands between his own and guided them inside his jacket, hoping the warmth of his skin would radiate through the thin barrier of his wet shirt.

He was not sure he had ever felt anything quite that erotic.

Until her lips took his.

The tenderness was in extraordinarily beautiful contrast to the fury of the storm. The heat of her mouth was the exact opposite of the cold hands that rested so close to the fiery skin of his chest.

Without taking his lips from hers, he undid the zipper of her jacket, tugged it from her shoulders, let it slide from his hand to the floor, where it lay, a puddle of wet black leather. The fury of the storm had been such that it had penetrated the leather. Water had probably been sluicing down her neck for at least the last ten minutes.

The result was that her T-shirt was soaked. The fabric was sodden and molded to her slender form. He left his hand resting above her heart. Her skin, underneath the cold fabric, felt blistering hot.

And then, still with their lips clinging together, her hands came out from under his shirt and tugged at his zipper, peeled the wet leather from his arms.

His jacket joined hers on the floor.

He lifted his head, finally separated their lips and scanned her face for any doubt, for the smallest hesitation, but that was not what he found.

With a groan of complete surrender, Jesse scooped Layne into his arms and carried her up the curving staircase to the upper floor.

"That one," she said, motioning with the slightest tilt of her chin toward a closed door. He nudged it open with his foot, pushed back the layer of plastic that was protecting this room from construction dust.

He reached, automatically, for the light switch but, of course, nothing happened. He switched it back off. Still, his eyes had adjusted enough that he could see the exquisite beauty of the room, comparable to any of the five-star hotels he often stayed at on business.

"This one is your favorite," he remembered.

With hail pelting the windows and bombarding the roof in a cacophony of sound, Jesse set Layne on the bed. She fell gracefully backward and he felt some exquisite quiet unfold within himself as he gazed at her.

She looked back, her gaze frank, appraising, blissful and then opened her arms to him. The sound that came from her lips was as primal as the storm, invitation and hunger mingled in equal part.

He went to her, lying down carefully across the length of her, holding his weight off her with one elbow, while his other hand touched the fire of her hair, the exquisite curve of her lips, the arc of her cheekbones. And then, everywhere his hand had gone, he anointed with a kiss.

Her hand moved to tug at the hem of her shirt, but he stayed it. He worked the soaked fabric up slowly, revealing her taut stomach, her belly button, her ribs. He peeled the shirt up, traced the line of the startling white of her bra with his fingertips, and then followed again with his lips.

She leaned forward so he could pull the soaked shirt from her, and then fell back on the bed. He took it and dropped it to the floor, and then ran his hands around skin that should have been cold, but was not. He touched the delectable softness of her shoulders, the jut of her collarbone, the ridges of her rib cage, the concave of her belly.

Lightning would illuminate her and the room in blinding splendor, and then be gone, but somehow the imprint of all that energy seemed to be on her skin.

He reached for the waistband of her slacks, tugged them away from her, traced the lace edge of her panties with his fingertips.

And then dropped his head over her, loving her gasp of need, every bit as raw, as raging, as real, as the storm.

That need, Jesse knew, had been building in them all day. No, that was a lie.

That need had been building between them from the first moment they had laid eyes on each other. Layne quivered against him. Her mouth reached for him, ravenous, but he made her wait as he worshipped the lines of her body with his hands, and then his lips. As he explored the curves and swells and mysteries of her shape, he experienced full awe in the miracle that was her.

To Layne the pleasure of Jesse's exploration of her body was so deliciously slow and intense it was crossing into pain.

She wriggled out from underneath him, nudged him to turn over, then straddled him. She worked the edges of his shirt, and he helped her peel the fabric from his damp skin.

And then she did exactly as he had done. Got to know his body with her fingertips, those curls, the planes of his face, the curve of his lips. And then she dropped to the broad smoothness of his chest, the glorious satin of his skin stretched over his ribs, the hollow of his stomach.

As he had done, when she had completed following the map of his body with her fingertips, she went back over it all with her lips. And her tongue.

By the time she had tasted his toes, the inner trembling had intensified until it created a longing, a wanting, that was greater than anything she had ever felt.

The last thin barriers of clothing—her bra and panties, his boxer briefs—came off in a fury, both of their abilities to temper things dissolving at the same time.

They flipped again, and his body was on top of hers, and she was not sure she had ever felt the fit of something being so right as the hard lines of Jesse's body fitting themselves—molding—to the pliant curves of hers.

The tenderness disappeared, just as the first silver raindrops had disappeared from the sky tonight and been replaced by something far more furious.

Just as those raindrops had given way to larger ones,

harder ones, so was the sensation between them replaced with urgency, need, power.

The raindrops, whipped by wind, and the incredible chemistry of hot meeting cold had turned from liquid to solid in blink of an eye.

Such was the intensity between them. They moved into it as naturally—and as powerfully—as thunder follows lightning, as hail follows rain.

It was as if all the intensity of the storm had been absorbed in them, stored right underneath their skin. But containing it had allowed it to build pressure, and when it was released, the force was nothing less than cataclysmic.

It felt to Layne as if she exploded into fragments of the universe, silver as those raindrops, falling to earth, building in intensity and tempo until they were transformed from water to ice. Her transformation was the opposite—from solid to vapor, from cool to hot, and yet there was no doubt she was completely transformed by her inner storm.

As she came back into herself, vapor finding form once more, Layne was aware she was changed forever by what had just happened between her and Jesse.

She touched his curls, felt the heat of his breath, hard and ragged, where his head was nestled in the nape of her neck. The beat of his heart and the beat of hers were exactly the same.

She felt complete.

More.

She felt as close to love as she had ever been. She closed her eyes, and feeling safe and cherished, she slept.

Layne awoke to inky darkness. Had a noise awoken her? No, it was actually silence, the storm finally abated.

She contemplated the warmth radiating from the man beside her, the silky feeling where their skin touched. Jesse was on his belly, the broadness of his back naked, a rumpled sheet covering the curve of his backside. His arm was thrown over her midriff in a way that was delightfully intimate. Possessive.

Strange, she thought, that they had ended up here, in the room that had been her statement that there was so much more to her than Brock had ever discovered.

Now, in the circle of Jesse's arms, she felt so glad that she had kept some of her secrets to herself and not shared them with Brock.

That she had a bold side.

An irreverent side.

A playful side.

A side that did not follow the rules.

As if she had saved these things just for him, just for Jesse, the man it felt as if she had waited her whole life for.

Strange, again, that they were in the castle, the very place where her waiting had begun all those years ago when she and Mabel had danced and cast spells in the ballroom.

"Hey," he said, his voice adorably groggy with sleep, "I don't want to wake up yet."

As if, when he woke up, the dream might not be real.

"Don't, then," she said, tangling her hand in his curls.

"Are you going back to sleep?" he asked her.

"No."

He turned over, sat up, tucked the sheets, tight, around them both.

"What are you thinking?" he asked.

"That you have gorgeous eyelashes."

He looked at her. "You, too," he whispered, his voice sexy, rough edges to his whisper.

"And pretty nice lips."

He chuckled. "You have me beat in the lips department."

"That I could live to be a hundred years old and never get enough of you."

He didn't answer that one, and a doubt flitted around her, like a mosquito, annoying on a hot summer night.

He had warned her from the first moment he was not a forever kind of guy.

What was she playing at, and how badly was it going to hurt?

But as if Jesse sensed her doubt, his hand stroked her hair, then guided her head onto his shoulder, reassuring her.

"I want to know everything about you," Layne whispered to him, as if knowing could assuage that sudden fear that she was not bold at all, that she would want more of him than he was prepared to give.

"Everything?" he teased, taking a strand of her hair, and twisting it around his finger, then letting it escape, and going on to the next one.

"Everything," she said firmly. "I want to know every single thing about Sunshine and Storm, and how it came to be. Your dad. Your grandmother. And Mr. Poochy."

"That's a lot. I'm not sure I know where to start."

"Start," she said, "with the butterscotch candies."

CHAPTER SIXTEEN

IT WAS AS if by instinct, Jesse thought, that Layne had found the starting place. His grandmother, whose diary he had found after she died.

He was not even sure you would call it a diary. What he'd actually found were sheets of paper, so sporadic were the entries, so far spaced apart that he suspected most were missing. Even so, he had been able to piece together her story.

Those were the things he never talked about. And yet suddenly, it felt as if he had been waiting his whole life for this moment, as if their making love had opened him in some way he had never been open before.

He suddenly longed for someone to share it all with, but even now, in this astounding afterglow, part of him knew.

Not all of it, a voice warned him.

"My grandmother loved those candies," he said. "Her father had been killed overseas during the war, and she and her mother were really struggling. She went to work for a wealthy family as a maid. They had dishes all over the house full of candies."

Careful, he warned himself.

"How do you know that?"

"I found an old diary."

"Oh! How wonderful!"

Not really. He remembered the entry about the candy his grandmother had taken from Whitmore Castle, almost word for word.

The first time I took one of those forbidden candies, my heart nearly beat out of my chest, as if I had taken the silver platter from behind the glass of the display cabinet and tried to hide it down my dress.

I slid the candy into my pocket and waited to be discovered, waited for the wrath of Mrs. Malike, because surely she is mean-spirited enough to count every candy in every dish?

On the other hand, how would she know, if she did count, that it was I who had taken it? It could just as easily be the mistress of the house, couldn't it?

I kept it in my pocket all day, the rustle of the wrapper filling me with both dread and delight.

I unwrapped it carefully once I was nearly at home, far away from the all-seeing eyes of Mrs. Malike. Even so, I looked over my shoulder as if it was a weapon of murder I was taking out of my pocket.

The golden wrapper crinkled prettily, and I set the candy on my tongue and nearly wept for the rich intensity of the butterscotch that melted luxuriously in the heat of my mouth.

That candy was simply the most delicious thing I had ever tasted.

Still, as it disappeared, leaving only the faintest taste of wonder on my tongue, I swore I would not tempt fate by taking another.

And yet stealing a candy every day now has become part of everything I love and everything I hate about Whitmore Castle.

"I think she saw those candies as a kind of luxury that elevated her in some way," Jesse said, aware of stripping any emotion out of his voice. "There was always a fancy dish filled to overflowing with them. It was really the only fancy thing I remember about our Riverton house."

"Except the doghouse!" Layne interjected.

"Ah, yes, the doghouse. She hated it, but my dad loved to goad her. He said that if she could have a pretentious candy dish he could have a pretentious doghouse."

"Teasing each other?"

"Ah, not really. There was tension between them." What was shocking was that he *wanted* to tell her. He *wanted* to trust someone with it.

This was who he really was, a guy from a bad neighborhood and a bad family. Wasn't this why he rarely trumpeted his success, why he hid behind Mr. Poochy, instead of being the public face of Sunshine and Storm?

He didn't want to open himself up to people looking, *knowing*, about the family's dirty laundry. Literally, he was someone who had been raised among heaps of dirty clothes in a laundry, the son of the town drunk.

And success had not erased the questions.

Am I good enough? Can I ever have what other people have? How? What do I know about family? Am I really good enough to have what other people have?

But though those question could not be erased, they could be outdistanced, with drive, with unrelenting work, with achievement after achievement.

Now he wanted this gift he had been unexpectedly offered. For someone to know him completely.

Not just someone. Layne.

A family. What did he know about having a family?

"My dad," he heard himself saying, "was born in 1945, a few months before the end of World War II. My grandmother was only seventeen, and not married. Her dad had been killed in the war. Her mother died before the baby was born. So, she was an orphan and a child and about to become an unwed mother."

"Oh, my, Jesse," Layne whispered, not with sympath, but with her own aching heart so evident that it made it impossible for him to resist going on.

"She told people the baby's father had been killed in the war but it was the *not married* part that the good people of Whitmore held her in contempt for. And then, she seemed to pour all that contempt that was doled out to her onto my father.

"I don't know if it was a reaction to being a bastard in a time when that was so unacceptable, or if it was the way he was treated at home by his mother, but my dad started drinking early in his life and never quit.

"Despite a like for the drink, he was a dreamy, whimsical man, in a time that didn't really embrace that. My grandmother was the antithesis of him, hard, practical, a workhorse. When she found herself alone with a baby at seventeen, she started taking in laundry at home.

"She eventually built that into a business that could sustain her and my dad—and eventually me—but it was always a pretty hand-to-mouth existence. She was ambitious, though, and I think she held out hope my dad was going to make something of himself, and if he did he would prove something to the world.

"Maybe that the Kades were good enough. But my dad resisted ambition. He had zero interest in money. He said he had never seen a rich person who was happy. So, he never really launched. In the face of my grandmother's ambition, he had absolutely none. If his needs were met for today, he had not a single thought for tomorrow. He either couldn't hold a job or didn't want to.

"The new age gurus would have loved him. Nobody was more in the moment than he was.

"Of course, it irritated my grandmother no end, but it didn't matter how she tried to control him, or shame him, he was simply impervious to her constant nagging and barbs. Even good-humored about it, which drove her to distraction. That may have been the point, but I don't really think it was that complex.

"He was just utterly brilliant in that way that leaves some people out of touch with reality. He thought differently than other people.

"Without any formal training, that man could make any engine that was ever created, run. He could actually invent and manufacture parts. He was the best mechanic in town, but unreliable. People were scared to leave a car for repair, because he'd promise it would be fixed the next day, but it never was. Something else caught his fancy, or he scrounged up enough money to go to the bar.

"The Riverton Dog and Whistle, the place he belonged, and felt most at home in. Just like that TV show. Everybody knew his name. Of course, it embarrassed me, and I spent a lot of time trying to change him."

"When did you realize you couldn't?"

"Never, really," he said softly. "I begged him to stop drinking until the end. He was stumbling home drunk one night, and got hit by a car."

There it was. His failure, the one that no amount of success could ever take away.

"You carry it, don't you?"

"Oh, yeah. The what-ifs torment me."

She didn't try to fix it. Or change it. She just sighed against him. "Jesse, I'm so sorry."

"Don't be," he said, and meant it. "The addiction overshadowed so much of who he was, but he was an amazing man. Funny and loving. He had this wonderful kind of self-acceptance about him. *This is what I am, take it or leave it.*

"And, as I told you, despite the fact food on the table was an issue he couldn't quite get his head around, in so many ways, he was just the best dad. I told you I came along later in his life, basically dumped off with him when he was old enough to be having grandchildren, never mind facing fatherhood for the first time.

"But, oh, he took to it. It's as if he made it his mission to make me feel the way he never had.

"As if I was an absolute treasure, as if the whole universe danced in celebration of me. I'm not saying he didn't have flaws—I mean we're talking about a man who just didn't care about the mundane needs of life. It frustrated my grandmother. She tore into him about pride and ambition. But he simply didn't care.

"My grandmother gave me her work ethic. But I also picked up his passion for doing things he loved.

"I loved engines, just the way he did. I'd been handing him wrenches since I was three or four years old. When I wasn't working in Grandma Mary's laundry, or at school, if he was tinkering in the garage, I was with him.

"By the time I was eleven we were designing and building motorcycles together, scrounging parts from the wreckers, drawing prototypes, dreaming.

"That's what he gave me: the ability to dream."

"And your grandmother gave you ambition."

He didn't say anything to that. Because of course, that was the secret he needed to keep from her.

That he had never inherited a single dime from his grandfather's empire. But he wondered, sometimes, if he had not inherited other things.

Raw ambition and ferocious drive being among them.

Layne was silent for so long, he wondered if his history had given her pause about tangling with him, which he thought maybe it should have.

"I like that it's all part of you," she said. "I like it that you talk about them without blame and without bitterness. I like it that it's kept you humble and made you strong. I like who you are, Jesse Kade. I like all of you."

It was a gift, like walking out of a snowstorm into warmth. One he was too aware he did not deserve, at all.

And that he could lose that look that filled her eyes in an instant.

When the other secret came out.

Selfishly, he could not walk away from what he saw in her eyes, not just yet.

And yet, he was aware he was holding back.

"Hey," he said, suddenly feeling way more naked than his lack of clothing had ever made him feel, as if he had already said way, way too much. "Let's go try out the shower in this creaky old castle."

She gave him a searching look. But then she returned his smile. "Okay. And after that, would you like to make a girl's dreams come true?"

He pretended to sulk. "I thought I already had."

"I want to dance with you. In the ballroom."

Her voice was so shy and so hopeful—as if he'd been entrusted with a secret dream—that he could not refuse her.

He'd never been much of a dancer. But he found he couldn't say no to that, to making her dreams come true.

It felt as if he was embracing the surprises of the *now*, that space in time that his father had loved so much.

It also felt, though, as if in some way he was saying yes to the future, a topic his father had never given a single thought to.

But what about the past that he had come here to address?

CHAPTER SEVENTEEN

THEIR CLOTHES HAD been too wet to put back on, and so Layne and Jesse were in the ballroom barefoot, in the fluffy white housecoats that were already hung on the back of the bathroom door in anticipation of future guests.

Of course, it was nothing like the fantasies she and Mabel had once woven in this room. In that fantasy, there would be hundreds of people here, men in black ties, women in the most gorgeous gowns imaginable.

In that fantasy, hadn't she and Mabel stipulated that their prince *must* have Whitmore blood flowing through his veins?

In reality, the power wasn't even back on, and they were dancing, not under the sparkling lights of a million chandelier crystals, but through darkness.

But by now Layne should know that reality and fantasy were usually on a collision course. How silly it would be to think those worlds she and Mabel had spun out of dust and childish dreams could ever manifest into reality.

He had brought his phone to provide music and took it out of the pocket of his dressing gown.

"Any choice?" he asked.

He was humoring her. She knew this was not really his style. And yet she loved it that he was humoring her.

"'Unchained Melody,'" she said, without hesitation. "The Righteous Brothers version."

He found it, and the first strains of that beautiful song

filled the ballroom. It wasn't an orchestra, but the acoustics were amazing in the room. The sound of that haunting voice, that extraordinary melody, that timeless love song, filled the room.

And when Jesse's hand found hers and their fingers intertwined, when she rested her hand just below his shoulder and he put hers on the small of her back, everything else faded.

Except this.

The fairy tale of them.

They found each other's rhythm as naturally as the river in the song flowed to the sea. They swayed against each other, everything sharpened by senses that had come fully alive.

It felt as if they *were* that song: hungry for each other's touch, as if they had waited for each other and for this moment, across time.

Dawn found them still dancing, her head resting on his chest, not ever wanting these moments to end.

Jesse looked down at her and lifted her chin. "You want to make my dream come true, now?"

Layne nodded, looking up at him with pure wonder.

He went to the huge glass doors, undid the latch on one and opened it. He took her hand and led her to the edge of the pool. And then he found the knotted belt at her waist and loosened it. He put his hands to the lapels, opened them, then nudged the fabric off her shoulders.

In the sweet pink light of the dawn, she stood before him, naked.

And then he took off his own housecoat and stood before her just as naked, Adam and Eve in the garden at the dawn of time, gazing at each other. Not with shame but complete wonder.

He turned her to the pool and they slipped into the water.

They played, and then they played some more, something

joyous in the air between them. They ran naked from the hot tub back to the pool.

Finally they floated on their backs, their hands intertwined.

Layne gazed up at the sky, smudged now with dark clouds left over from the storm, the light just beginning to pierce through, promising another beautiful day.

Suddenly, the pool lights came on.

"Power's back," she told him dreamily.

And then she realized that the power *was* back on, but that someone had turned on those lights.

They were not alone.

She scrabbled out of the floating position and her feet found the bottom of the pool. Jesse found his feet as well. Suddenly he was putting his body in front of hers.

She peeped out from behind the broadness of his shoulder to see three women standing there, glaring at them.

"Oh no!" Layne said, peeping out from behind him. "Pamela Whitmore and her daughters."

"Right on cue," he said, "the wicked stepmother and the stepsisters."

Despite the horrible embarrassment of the moment, she giggled.

"Hey," he said, calling to the women, his voice edgy, annoyed, "in case you can't tell, we're having a private moment here."

"A private moment? How dare you act as if you own the place!" And then Pamela Whitmore squinted over his shoulder, and her mouth gaped open. "Layne! Is that you?"

"It's me," Layne admitted, trying to disappear even further behind Jesse.

He looked over his shoulder at her, and his eyes narrowed. "Don't you dare be embarrassed by the likes of them," he said, in a voice she did not recognize. Somehow his tone of voice suggested he knew more about the Whitmore women than a quick glance at a leopard-skin chair would account for.

He turned back to them. "I'm Jesse Kade," he said.

Layne watched something shift in Pamela and her daughters. The self-composed woman suddenly looked very flustered.

But they couldn't know who he really was, could they? The fact that Jesse Kade actually owned Sunshine and Storm, and not Mr. Poochy, seemed to be a well-cultivated secret.

"The Jesse Kade we're meeting with tomorrow?" Pamela asked sharply.

Layne stared at Jesse's broad, naked back. *What?*

Pamela's tone seemed to be covering something. Surely not fear?

"You don't have any claim to this property, Mr. Kade," Pamela said, shrilly. But Layne could not help but notice that running like a thread right alongside the fear, there was real—if reluctant—respect in her tone.

"I think I do," he said, his tone quiet and fierce and frightening. "Charles Whitmore seduced a sixteen-year-old maid here in 1943. At seventeen, she had his baby. My father."

The women's mouths fell open in unison. It would have been quite funny, if it weren't for the words Layne had just heard him speak.

"You cannot prove that!" Pamela said at the same time Rebecca spoke.

"Oh my God," the daughter breathed. "You look just like him."

That earned her a dirty look from her mother.

Meanwhile, Layne felt as if the bottom was falling out of the pool, that she could slip down and drown in waters that suddenly seemed to be swirling with darkness and danger.

She realized, sickly, why from the first moment she had felt as if she recognized Jesse.

He was the spitting image of the portrait she worked under every single day.

"What do you want with the castle?" Pamela snapped at him.

"Retribution," Jesse said, his voice soft and clear. "I won't rest until it's a pile of rubble on the ground."

Layne gasped audibly.

He seemed to remember she was there. He reached his hand behind himself, as if to make her understand, but she stepped away from his touch.

The magnitude of his betrayal swept around her. Not only had he never indicated who he *really* was, Jesse Kade's mission was to destroy the castle.

Her castle.

She needed to get out of here. How was she going to get out of here?

He solved it. He said to the Whitmores, "I am getting out of this pool now. You can watch or you can meet with me as planned, tomorrow morning."

Rebecca looked like she considered watching but then scurried after her mother and sister back through the ballroom doors.

"Layne," he said, turning and reaching again for her, but again she sidestepped him, already heading for the side of the pool farthest from him, her arms now crossed over herself.

He was meeting with them tomorrow morning, and had never breathed a word of that to her?

"Charles Whitmore was your grandfather," she said, a statement, not a question.

"Yes," Jesse said.

"And Pamela Whitmore is your cousin?" she said dully.

"Yes."

"You never thought to say a word about that to me? In

fact, there are quite a few things you never thought to say a word about."

"I'm sorry," he said.

"Did you just use me? To get information about the castle? The Whitmores?"

"No! It was complicated."

"I'll say. Your mission in life is to destroy what I love the most."

"You're in love with an illusion," he told her softly. "This is a wicked place. Charles Whitmore groomed a little girl, seduced her, and then abandoned her when she was pregnant with his child."

Those words, the truth of the castle, hit her like a wrecking ball.

"I can't wait to tear it down," he continued softly.

"You've apparently given this plenty of thought. And then what? After you've torn it down?"

"I'm going to build a subdivision here. I'm going to name it after my grandmother."

"You've been thinking about this for a long time."

"I have."

"And it never came up in conversation. Wow. Just wow."

"I honestly did not know how to broach it."

"How about just now, when you were telling me your life story?"

He was silent.

"How about," she said, her voice rising, "when I said I liked everything about you? Wouldn't that have been an opportune time to say, well, there's one more thing…"

Again, he was silent.

"Well, you're right about one thing," Layne snapped at him. "I'm in love with an illusion."

She let that sink in, saw the hurt dawn in his dark eyes. Eyes she had thought were so familiar.

She faced the truth. He was a stranger. Despite all the things he had just told her, how she had felt trusted with who he really was, it smacked her up the side of the head that she had never really known him at all.

Jesse started to come through the water toward her. It spoke to her deep love of illusions that she wanted to go toward him and not run away.

But with every drop of courage she had, she held up her hand. *Stop.* And he did.

"Don't come one step closer," she lashed out at him ferociously. And then she tossed her wet, heavy hair off her shoulder. "In fact, I don't ever want to see you again."

When the knock came at the carriage house door, Layne woke up groggily. Her hair was still damp from her and Jesse's interrupted swim.

In her haste to leave the pool—and him—she had grabbed the wrong housecoat. She had tumbled into bed in it, distraught, and sobbed herself to sleep. Sleeping in the housecoat he had used was every bit as bad as sleeping in his jacket.

His scent surrounded her. Memories washed over her.

The knock came again, harder.

Please be Jesse.

Please don't be Jesse.

She crept out of her bed and saw Mabel at the door. She went and flung it open. Mabel took her in—the castle housecoat, the wet hair, no doubt puffy eyes and smudged makeup—and shock registered on her face.

"What is going on?" she asked, taking Layne's elbow. She guided Layne back into the cottage and shut the door with a nudge from her heel. "I came in this morning to find soaked motorcycle jackets and two helmets in the lobby. Then Pamela phoned me, and I had to hang up on her. She was screaming that we were both fired."

"I'm sorry I got you fired."

"I don't care about being fired! I've had about enough of that old bat, but I need to know you're okay."

Layne opened her mouth to reassure her friend, but all that came out was a whimper that quickly turned into a wail.

"He lied to me," she managed to choke out.

"Now, now," Mabel said, and led her to the couch. "You come and sit down. I'm going to make you a cup of tea and you can tell me everything that happened."

Half an hour later, Layne felt somewhat calmer. She had finished the story with her and Jesse's skinny dip in the pool, the arrival of the Whitmore women and his astonishing revelations.

Mabel sat looking at her, wide-eyed, and stunned.

"Jesse Kade is Charles Whitmore's grandson?"

"Illegitimate."

"And he wants to destroy our castle?"

Layne hiccupped her distress and nodded.

"That bastard," Mabel sighed.

"Please don't use that word."

"I'm sorry. Given the circumstances, you're right. Layne, there is something, I don't know, *honorable* in his wanting to right the wrongs done to his grandmother."

"What about being honorable to me?" Layne demanded.

"There's that," Mabel agreed.

"What he wants to do is called revenge," Layne said stiffly. "And he lied to me."

Mable looked pensive. "Do you remember those spells we used to cast in the ballroom?"

"Like it was yesterday," Layne admitted, though she really thought this was an odd time to bring that up. "We put popsicle sticks and sea lavender into a container."

"An old, plastic, whipped cream container," Mabel remembered fondly. "There was a single white Barbie shoe."

"To represent Cinderella," Layne remembered.

"Didn't we have a worm in a bit of dirt mulch, just to make it extra witchy?"

"It's lucky we couldn't find a toad." Layne actually found herself smiling at the antics of their younger selves, which was probably Mabel's intent.

But, as it turned out, that wasn't Mable's intent at all. Her friend reminded her of the part Layne had long since forgotten.

"We cast a spell for our future husbands. Do you remember what he had to be?"

"Handsome? Rich? A prince?"

"He had to have his blood running through the castle walls," Mabel reminded her softly.

Layne felt as if her own blood was draining from her face. "Mabel! It was childish foolishness."

"And yet, here you are, head over heels for a man with his blood running through the castle walls."

She wanted to deny that she was head over heels for anyone.

But she knew it wasn't true. The reason Jesse's lies had hurt so badly was because she had met a man she could give her heart to.

A sensible woman would be nothing but grateful that it was over before it had really begun.

And if she had always been one thing, it was the sensible one. And look where her one foray away from that had gotten her. She wasn't even sure if she still had a job.

She wasn't even sure if there would be a castle to have a job at.

CHAPTER EIGHTEEN

Jesse left the conference room. It was the third day he'd spent in there. He wasn't sure if any progress was being made. He needed a break from Pamela Whitmore's shrillness. She was becoming more horrible as she realized the corner she was backed into.

She held the castle. But what he held was their shared grandfather's reputation.

He stood outside in a glassed-in hallway, looking out a bank of windows at Whitmore. Despite all Pamela's posturing, the result was inevitable. He was about to get what he always wanted.

If he had lost Layne to do it, was it worth it?

His heart answered no within him, and it did so resoundingly. But her parting words haunted him.

I'm in love with an illusion.

She had fallen in love with him. All his life, Jesse had said he was allergic to love. But maybe the truth had felt unworthy of it, because he had failed at it so spectacularly. All his love had never been able to give him a normal family. All his love had never been enough to repair the rift between his father and his grandmother. All his love, in the end, had not been able to save his father.

No, best to avoid that trickster called love at all costs. It gave a person the most dangerous thing of all.

Hope.

But all it delivered was havoc.

And yet, when he thought of Layne, and the time they had spent together, he knew another uncomfortable truth.

You could not avoid love. It had sought him and Layne out like a heat-seeking missile.

But not being able to avoid love was not the same things as being worthy of it. And what he'd been suddenly aware of, with Layne naked in the pool behind him, and the Whitmore women staring down their noses at them, was exactly how unworthy he was.

He had put Layne in a situation where her moral character could be judged, just as his grandmother's had been judged.

How much he was like his grandfather. And, in part of his heart, he'd always known it.

Because hadn't he just played out a modern version of what his grandfather had done to his grandmother?

Hadn't he been part of a seduction—a romancing—that was all fun and games, but with no commitment? No promise of the future? Had he showed one ounce of concern about whether she was protected from pregnancy?

Hadn't he lied to her by his omissions of the truth?

Jesse had been just like Charles. Ruled by passion and forget consequences that the woman—not he—would pay.

The conference door whispered open behind him, pulling him from his cloud of self-loathing. Jessica slipped out.

"You look like him."

"I'm aware." He studied her. "So do you."

"We even have similar names."

He hadn't thought of that.

"I can't believe you and Mom are first cousins. There's quite the age difference. I'm more your age."

"My dad was a late bloomer. He was in his late fifties when I came along."

"What does that make you and me? Second cousins?" she asked.

"I think so. I'm not up on the family tree thing."

"I know!" she said. "It gets so complicated. Third cousins twice removed."

They actually chuckled together.

"Tell me about your grandmother."

He sighed. "She was sixteen when she started to work at that castle."

Layne was certainly not sixteen, not that he was going to let himself off the hook that easily.

"Her dad had died in the war."

Layne's father had not died, but still, she had experienced the loss of her fiancé, and that had probably made her very vulnerable.

"Her mother was working at the Whitmore cannery. They lived in a shanty in Riverton." Jesse realized he didn't know what Layne's mother did, but that he wanted to. He wanted to know so much more about her.

"Charles Whitmore took advantage of her innocence and naivete."

Had he done that to Layne? Okay, she wasn't a naive child, but he remembered guiltily how shy she had been about being bold.

"He groomed her." This is where he parted, thank God, drastically from his grandfather. "It's my belief he had a plan for her from the moment he accidentally bumped into her on the cannery steps. What if she hadn't brought her mother lunch that day?"

"I guess you wouldn't be here," Jessica said.

He thought about that. How chance meetings, mere seconds in time, could have repercussions that reverberated through generations.

"My great-grandmother, Mary's mother, died before her

grandson—my father—was born. Mary Kade was little more than a child and she was all alone in the world."

Jesse could actually feel the emotion in his throat when he thought of the pure panic his grandmother must have felt: an orphan about to give birth to a married man's baby in a hostile world.

Jessica touched his arm. "I'm really sorry."

It unnerved him. Anger was so much easier than dealing with the deep feelings of sorrow that his grandmother's diary had caused in him.

"How do you know all that?" Jessica asked him, her tone gentle. "The details? Like that thing about him meeting her on the cannery steps?"

"I found her diary. After she died."

"I'm sorry."

He wanted to say it wasn't her fault. But if it wasn't her fault, why was he here?

"Yeah," he said. "I'm sure you are. Meanwhile, your grandfather lived like a little prince in a castle, and my grandmother was cast to the wolves. My dad grew up in poverty, under a cloud of shame because he was a bastard in a small town."

"Again, I'm sorry."

"Apologies aren't enough," Jesse said.

"I know that. You seem to have inherited his ambition," she said softly. "Wow. Sunshine and Storm!"

"I guess I have. And probably lots of his other unsavory qualities, as well."

His cousin cocked her head at him. "I don't believe that. You seem like a decent guy."

He frowned at her. "I'm going after your family."

"I find your loyalty to your grandmother, your desire to find justice for her, quite admirable actually."

"I think," he said softly, "that my grandmother wasn't the only victim. I think your great-grandmother was too."

"There was a time, wasn't there, when women were quite powerless in the world?"

"Most of history," he agreed sadly.

"You know, I'm not the least worried about his reputation. If you can get the town of Whitmore renamed because of all this, I'd be just as happy. Just think, I'd never have to hear my mother say, *'Actually, there's a city in Maine founded and named for our family'* again."

Jesse didn't say anything. Rewriting history had not even occurred to him.

After a long pause, Jessica continued, "You're lucky your dad didn't have anything to do with Charles Whitmore."

"Meaning?"

"Look at my mom. Her father, your dad's half brother, was always trying to win what it was not possible to win—Charles Whitmore's approval. He passed all that neediness on to my mom. She's so caught up in how everything looks all the time, needing to feel superior to everyone else, trying to shore up her nonexistent sense of herself.

"She needs to buy, buy, buy, to feel good. And there's always her latest project—like this castle—as if she's searching desperately for a reason, and never finds it. Her interest in this was already fizzling. After she's done posturing and protesting, you'll probably pick it up for a song."

Somehow that wouldn't be nearly as satisfying, he had thought it would be.

"I'm giving my share of it to you."

"What?"

"Mom owns half, and my sister and me each have a quarter. I'm giving mine to you."

"I don't understand."

"When you told us what had happened to your grandmother, I felt like all the pieces of the puzzle of this dysfunctional family fell into place. We've all pretended what a hero he was, but there was an undercurrent around him that no one ever spoke about. In fact, Charles Whitmore was awful and it's as if all of us are carrying little chunks of his awfulness around."

Including me, Jesse said. "So you're going to give me your little chunk of the awfulness?"

She smiled. "Absolutely, despite the fact I like you. You seem real. I like how you're going to bat for your grandmother. But more, because I hope you can make something good come from it. *Mary Kade Meadows*. I like that, too. I'm going to talk to Rebecca. I think she'll see it my way. She always referred to Charles as the old creep."

"Thanks, cuz," he said softly.

"I hope you'll trust me enough to let me read her diary one day. I'd like to know her."

Somehow the fact that Jessica wanted to know about his grandmother, and the truth about her own family's history, made it feel as if he'd accomplished something here beyond what he had hoped for.

Mary Kade, not a servant to be used and discarded, but someone who, finally, a Whitmore wanted to know.

"Does Mary talk about my great-grandmother? In her diary?"

"A bit."

"I'd like to know more about her too."

She turned and headed back to the conference room, with a roll of her eyes, but then she looked back at him. "Maybe we're all going to end up with what we least expected."

"And what's that?"

"Family," she said softly. "Poor you."

And then he laughed, and she did, too, and he had a feeling she might be right. That was followed by another feeling.

That maybe family was what he had always wanted most of all.

And really?

There was one person who had made that secret longing known to him. And it wasn't his well-meaning second cousin.

What if another chance meeting could have repercussions that reverberated through the generations to come?

And yet, Layne had been pretty clear. She never wanted to see him again.

His grandfather had just pushed his way into women's lives, without their permission. He could not be like that.

Even if it meant losing everything.

Here was the grim irony: to be the man worthy of Layne, he had to respect her wishes. Jesse Kade could not be his grandfather. This, then, was the face of temptation. He wanted to be with Layne more than he wanted to breathe. And he could not take advantage of the hunger she had shown she had for him to persuade her to give him another chance.

No matter how you cloaked it, that would be manipulation, the very thing his grandfather had been guilty of.

"Look, Layne," Mabel said hesitantly, "I'm probably the last person to give advice—"

"Well, then don't," Layne cut her off.

Mabel, of course, acted as if Layne hadn't said anything. "It's just that I don't understand how you can't see it from his perspective. I can't even walk in here anymore without thinking about his grandmother."

"I know," Layne said. "I think of her too."

"And then I think of Jesse's dad growing up in Whitmore. It was bad enough when we were growing up here. It's a very cliquey kind of place. There's an unspoken caste system here to this day. There's fishermen, merchants, businesspeople, the extraordinarily wealthy."

"And the people from Riverton in a class all by themselves."

"You *are* seeing it from his perspective!"

"How could I not?"

"Do you wish he'd come see you?"

Layne sighed. "Of course."

"The whole time, Layne, even before you knew who he was, it was evident Jesse Kade was terrified of love. And now you can clearly see why."

She was silent, her heart breaking for Jesse, because she knew even more than Mabel did about his terror, his insecurities, his feelings of having failed his dad.

"Why don't you go see him?"

"Oh." Layne blushed. "I just can't. If he wanted me, he would have made the first move. I think he's happy to leave it behind him. He told me right from the beginning that he's allergic to love. What kind of naive idiot ignores a warning like that?"

"Layne! Just stop it!"

Layne had never heard Mabel use that tone of voice on her before.

"Stop making it all about you! That man needs you to be bold, to be who you were when you invited yourself along on his motorcycle, when you took the picnic over there, when you swam naked in the swimming pool."

"That was an experiment that failed," Layne said stiffly.

"No, no, it wasn't. That was you becoming the best version of you I've ever seen. Be bold, Layne, go get him."

Her mouth opened and then closed.

Her automatic response was *I can't*, but somehow the thought never found her voice. Because suddenly she knew she could.

And what was more, she knew she had to.

CHAPTER NINETEEN

LAYNE'S HEART WAS in her throat when Jesse Kade opened the door of the Riverton house. She could feel Clive watching her. She clutched the picnic basket tighter and tried for a smile.

It was the first time she had seen Jesse in over a week. He looked quite terrible. Well, as terrible as a man that handsome could ever look. He hadn't shaved, his mop of curls was a mess, and his shirt was wrinkled.

But the worst thing was the dark shadows under his eyes—and the wall that was up in them.

Despite her heart trying to thud out of her chest, she held up the picnic basket. "I brought you something to eat."

Well, really, she had brought them both something to eat, but Jesse had that skittish-horse look again. The wrong move and he intended to bolt.

He looked at her for a long time. He didn't open the screen door between them. Finally, he said, "You made it pretty clear you didn't want to see me again. That was a good decision, on your part. What changed your mind?"

It could have felt like a slap in the face, but it didn't. Mabel had been right. Layne had been making this all about her.

Now she saw a man standing before her who had grown up with the message, that by Whitmore's standards, he was not good enough. A man who had been driven his whole life to prove that he was.

Good enough for everything.

Except love.

"I miss you," she said, quietly. "You changed my mind."

His face was cold, closed to her. "It wasn't the news?"

"What news?" she asked, genuinely baffled.

"It's mine."

"What is yours?"

"Your beloved castle belongs to me."

She let the shock of that set in. "You think I'm here on some sort of mercenary mission to get the castle from you?"

"Aren't you? Here to save it?"

"Jesse," she said quietly and firmly, "I'm here to save us."

"Uh-huh," he said, cynically. But beneath the cynicism, Layne saw he was protecting himself from his own sheer vulnerability.

"I miss you," she whispered.

He glanced over at his neighbor's porch, possibly saw the same movement behind the door that she had, and sighed. He opened his door for her.

It was a triumph, getting that door to open, but she didn't let it show on her face. His place was a disaster of empty pizza boxes, discarded socks, crushed soda cans.

He folded his arms over his chest. "What do you want?" he asked.

Never mind her fear of him bolting. What was he going to do now that he didn't have the option of slamming the door in her face?

"I want you, Jesse," she said huskily. She did not know where this bravery was coming from, but she was glad for it.

"Well, that's another mistake."

"I want to understand," she said simply. "Please help me understand."

"Why I want to destroy the castle?"

"Why you're so determined to say no to love."

He was silent.

"You told me once that you had your grandmother's diary. Do you think I could read it?"

"I don't have all of it," he said. "Just bits and pieces. Enough."

She understood, suddenly, this was the key. Even though he hadn't invited her to, she went past him, moved a pizza box, set her basket on the floor in front of her and plunked herself down on his couch.

"Is it here?" she asked.

"Yes."

"Please show it to me."

He tensed. He looked as if he planned to say no. But he didn't. He whirled and left the room. It wasn't until he left, that Layne realized she had stopped breathing, waiting for his answer.

When he came back, he set some papers on her lap. She looked up at him and saw exactly what he was trusting her with: his burden.

On the top of the papers was a picture of a young woman, big-eyed and solemn. The photo was in black-and-white, faded, and yet the loveliness of the girl—the innocence of her—shone through like a beacon.

Layne looked at the picture for a long time, then turned her attention to the papers. She ran her fingers over the childish, looping script. The pieces of paper were all different sizes, yellow with age, the ink fading on some of them and splotched on others. Layne felt a beautiful connection, a tenderness for the writer.

She began to read.

Jesse sat down on the couch beside her. She knew it was a

surrender, even before he said, "Could you read it out loud?" he asked softly.

Layne went to the top of the page.

She cleared her throat and read.

June 1943
I've had my first week of work at Whitmore Castle. Of course, we've all watched it being built for the bride Charles Whitmore brought here from England. The newspaper reported that he wishes to make her feel at home. Whitmore, Maine, has been a bit of a shock to her system, I understand.

I've only caught a glimpse of her, once. She is frail and so white-skinned she looks dead. She didn't even glance my way, as if I was invisible to her. But the surprising thing is she doesn't look much older than my own sixteen years. I hear whispering that she's with child, but, if she is, it doesn't yet show.

Mrs. Malike is the head of the household staff, and we are forbidden to wag our tongues, as she put it. I will "wag my tongue" on these pages, then. She cannot tell me what to write, and I miss school like an ache.

But school is out of the question. I feel sick to the pit of my stomach when I think of Mother and I's situation. We have not been able to hold on to the farm since Father died fighting overseas, and there are no men to work it. What would we pay them with, even if there were?

We have sold the farm. It was heavily mortgaged... an unpleasant surprise. We used the pittance to buy a small house—more like a shanty—in the deplorable Riverton district of Whitmore.

My beloved Martin died last year. We weren't officially betrothed, of course, but both of us have known since we were children we belonged together. I begged him not to go, but he lied about his age and went anyway. He was injured in battle, a minor thing, a graze to his finger. So, imagine our shock to learn he had died of an infection in a field hospital. I weep every time I think of him dying alone. I wonder if my name was on his lips as he drew his last breath?

Best not to dwell on these things, our worlds ripped apart. How much worse it could be if our fine Maine men were not sacrificing everything to stop the Hun!

Mother is working in a lobster cannery. She comes home so tired and reeking of smells she cannot wash off. I wanted to go work there, too, but despite our desperation, she said no. She won't have it.

And then into all this bad luck, a stroke of good fortune. I noticed, ten days ago, she had not brought a lunch, I think saving the little food we have for me. I scraped together a few small items, a withered winter apple and sugar on a chunk of bread, and I delivered it to her.

It had been raining and the streets were boiling with muck and stench, which got worse the closer you got to the harbor.

Then I saw him, Charles Whitmore himself. Of course, he owns the lobster plant and just about everything else in Whitmore, having spun his own father's lumber holdings into wealth beyond what any of us can even imagine, though the castle is certainly an indication of how vast it all is.

I have seen pictures of him in the paper, of course, looking very stern and dignified, but I had never seen him in person.

I was coming down the steps of the cannery, and he

was coming up them, surrounded by men in good suits and nice hats, all seeming to vie for his attention.

I was actually frightened to be in the great man's way, and tried to scurry down the steps as unobtrusively as possible. But he called, "Girl," and I was forced to stop and face him, though I wasn't sure what to do. Curtsy? I lowered my eyes, but glanced up briefly.

I was shocked that he didn't look anything like the stern man in the pictures. Younger, and debonair. With his dark curls, and dark eyes, Charles Whitmore was so handsome it drew the breath from my chest. His eyes seemed to be dancing with merriment, and I was never more aware of the frayed edges on the cuffs of my dress. The mud at least hid the scuffs I can't polish out of my shoes.

"Who are you?" he asked.

"My name's Mary Kade, sir."

"Your father died in the war," he said, and the laughter was gone from his dark eyes, instantly. "I'm very sorry for your loss."

I was surprised he knew about my father. Even though it was his company that bought the farm, I would not have thought he dealt with it directly nor was aware of the circumstances of its sale.

I bobbed my head, "Thank you, sir."

"Have you come looking for work?"

"No, sir, my mother forgot her lunch." I could scarcely tell him that my mother had said working in that factory was like walking through the gates of hell every morning. The hours are crushing, and she looks to have aged ten years since she started there.

Mr. Whitmore gave me a searching look, and then moved on.

But the next day I was summoned to the castle, told there was a position in housekeeping available to me.

"She's so young," Layne said. "And her situation is so desperate. She writes very well. I can picture it all."

"Am I wrong to think he targeted her from that first meeting on the steps?"

"I don't think so."

She looked over at him. Jesse's face was tight and pain-filled. "Do you want me to stop?"

"No," he said. "No, I don't. Unless you want to. Unless it's too much for you."

On the contrary, it felt like one of the gravest honors of her life that Jesse was trusting her with his grandmother's story.

Hours slipped away as they were transported back in time. They read about Mary Kade's innocent crush on Charles Whitmore, the theft of the candies, the desperation she was facing at home.

They read about Christmas at the castle from Mary Kade's perspective.

The whole beautiful place is suffocating. Whitmore Castle should be a happy place with an opulent Christmas to look forward to, a Christmas ball, and the Whitmore heir due any day. And yet, it is not. The perfect festive look has no feeling to it, a facade, a stage set, as is the rest of the castle.

They took a break, deep in the night, and ate from the picnic basket, poured the fizzy juice she had brought into wineglasses.

"Lobster po'boys," she said. "From both. From the Loose Lobster and Sea Biscuit. I thought we should do a side-by-side taste comparison."

In the end, they couldn't decide, maybe because side-by-side taste comparisons seemed so frivolous in the face of the story that was unfolding.

And so they read on. Jesse had come closer to her. Their shoulders were touching. Layne was exhausted, and Jesse was exhausted, but somehow they were connected, drawing strength from each other as they read about that poor young woman being drawn deeper and deeper in a web she had no hope of escaping.

"Oh no," Layne whispered when they came to the part about Charles Whitmore's dastardly conquest. "It was the carriage house. No wonder you didn't want to stop there the night of the storm."

Somehow, Jesse was holding her hand, and he squeezed it.

By the time she reached the final entry, Layne was weeping quietly as she read.

July 1950
Mrs. Whitmore died. I read her obituary, stunned, though I am not sure why I would be. She was not well from the time I first came to the castle. As I had always suspected, the dates in the obituary confirmed she was only eighteen months older than I was. She was a victim of him as much as I was.

Her children, both boys, are sickly as she was. They talk about that around town. The youngest was born prematurely.

If he had not been, I wonder if he and my son, Nathan, might not have shared a birthday.

Both those boys take after their mother. They are pale and flimsy, moving through life, ghostlike and weak.

It must stick in Charles Whitmore's craw that Nathan is the spitting image of him, sturdy, dark, curly-haired.

It sticks in my craw that all of them are his sons, but two live in the castle that I still have dreams about, while my son weaves his way through the piles of laun-

dry that await my attention. I am looking at renting a laundry space in town, so soon he will have a bedroom of his own. I have contracts now, with three restaurants and the hotel.

Nathan.

He is such a beautiful boy, dark-eyed and curly-haired. I hope he takes on Charles Whitmore, one day. I hope he eclipses the success of his father. I hope he shows his brothers who deserves a castle.

But I fear he won't.

There is nothing in the place my heart once was. I would say it was as withered up as a prune, but even a prune can offer nourishment. No, my heart is more like the dried pit of a peach, ground to that lethal dust that contains arsenic. There is nothing but poison there for the son of Charles Whitmore.

He is the child I hated in in my womb, and whose resemblance to his father, even now, makes me go cold.

He came home from his first day of school with a blackened eye and asked me what a bastard was.

I said it was a word he shouldn't use, and then probed a bit. Had somebody called him that? Who?

But he didn't say. I saw that far-off look in his eye. He went off to draw pictures in his room.

It made me angry that he didn't fight back. This boy who, by rights, should be living in that castle.

I didn't go to the funeral, of course. But I did go stand in the shadow of the huge oak tree that overlooked the graveyard.

I watched as they lowered her small coffin into the ground. I watched Charles Whitmore standing there, tearless. The resemblance to Nathan made me shiver. I watched those poor, pale little boys sobbing into their nanny's skirt.

And I realized nothing good could ever come from that castle.

I wished I had never seen it. Or Charles Whitmore. I wished it was a pile of rubble on the ground.

"Your poor father," Layne said quietly, through tears, as she carefully laid down the last sheet of paper.

"And her too," Jesse said quietly.

"Yes, they were both equally traumatized by Charles Whitmore, your grandmother directly, and your father indirectly. Did your father know he was Charles Whitmore's son?"

"He never said he did, but I remember seeing Whitmore in a car one day when I was with my dad. I was pretty little. It was a limousine, a Rolls Royce, if I recall, driven by a chauffeur. And he, Charles Whitmore, saw my dad, and well after he passed, he was craning his neck, looking back at him. I asked my dad if he knew him, and he said no, and that he didn't care to. And then he said, *'What you just saw there, son, was the poorest man in the whole world.'*"

"And he was right."

"He often was," Jesse said with a sad smile.

"When did you find this diary?"

"Not that long ago, actually. After she died, I was going through some of her boxes trying to figure out what to do with them, and I found those pages."

"You know what I find remarkable?" Layne said softly. "You've hinted that she was hard and bitter, and not a good mother to your father. And yet, you loved her anyway."

"I did," he said.

"You know what I think? I think you saw her. I think, at some instinctive level, you could see who she would have been without all the damage. What a gift you gave her, Jesse, you saw her soul.

"And the same with your father. You just *saw* him. What a gift you must have been to those two damaged people.

"In fact, Jesse, I have to say something to you. You told me you were allergic to love. That's the biggest lie you ever told. Withholding the fact you're Charles Whitmore's grandson doesn't hold a candle to it."

"I don't know what you mean."

"Let me spell it out for you. You told me your dad was the best dad ever, despite his flaws. You know what made him that? You did. Your love made him a better man, it drew things from him he would have never and could have never experienced without you loving him. You said your grandmother was hard and bitter, but you saw something else. You saw her story before you knew her story. What sees something else? Pure love does. Pure love asks the world to know what was good about her by putting a butterscotch candy in the pocket of every single leather jacket you sell.

"You're not allergic to love, Jesse Kade," she said, feeling the truth so strongly, speaking it with utter firmness, "You just won't name it, while you bring it to every single thing you do. You think the people of Riverton care so much about you for no reason? You think Clive is so protective of you for no reason?

"It's because you brought acceptance to them, you loved them when no one else did, even while you claimed to be allergic to it, even while you never said the words.

"Those people saw you.

"That passion, that love in you, goes into every single motorcycle that you design to be special, to be one of a kind, to be a gift to whoever buys it. It's in a sales rack where things are marked down so everyone who comes into one of your stores can afford something. It's in knowing your employees' names and remembering their kids' birthdays."

He was staring at her with complete astonishment. How

was it he was unable to see the thread of love that bound his life together when she saw it—and him—so completely.

And then he knew.

That she loved every single thing she saw.

She had fallen in love. Not with the billionaire who had a private jet, and who had woven an incredible company out of determination and dreams. But with Jesse Kade, the man who had used love to survive.

CHAPTER TWENTY

"It's even a measure of your love that you want to tear down the castle, the thing that hurt Mary the most. As if that can fix it all, somehow."

Jesse was not sure if anyone had ever seen him quite like this. It didn't feel nearly as terrifying as it should have.

It felt amazing, even as he knew he had to set her straight. But maybe he would just bask in her rose-colored vision of him for a little longer.

"I want you to know something," Layne said fiercely. "If you need to tear Whitmore Castle down because it hurts you, because of what happened to your grandmother there, I will stand beside you as you take the first swing of the sledgehammer."

Jesse could not resist any longer. He ran his fingers through her hair.

"Then my grandmother's story changed how you feel about Whitmore Castle?" Jesse asked her, softly.

She considered that. "No, I guess not, because I have my own history with the castle. It saved me when my home life was so chaotic. I feel as if my dreams are woven into those walls."

"And still, you'd watch me with the sledgehammer?"

"Jesse, you don't love things—a building—more than people," she said. "Your grandfather is an example of what happens when you do."

He went very still. In a side-wind kind of way, had Layne just told him that she loved him?

Was he worthy of that?

"Oh, Layne, I'm not the hero you want me to be. The furthest thing from it. I think I'm just like him in so many ways."

"Like Charles Whitmore?" she said, her tone incredulous.

"Look at the way I've treated you."

"I don't even know what you're talking about."

"It wasn't honorable to hide the whole truth from you. It was wrong not to tell you from the first moment, looking at that portrait that you worked under every single day, that I was his grandson."

"I think we've gotten by that," she said, quite mildly. "That's why I brought the picnic basket."

Jesse felt compelled to make her understand. "There are a number of ways I have acted without honor," he said doggedly. "I acted with passion, the very same way as Charles Whitmore. As if there was no future and no consequences. As if I can just take whatever I like, whenever I want."

"Oh, Jesse," she said softly. "You can lay down the burden of all of that, now. You are not your grandfather, and I am not your grandmother. I am not a sixteen-year-old girl. You are not in a position of authority over me. The most insulting thing for me would be for you to decide there's only one adult here, only one person capable of taking charge and making decisions."

He looked at her and saw something he was not sure he had ever seen before, someone accepting him totally, even with all his flaws. And he saw his equal, someone who would share burdens and responsibilities and pain, but also joy and discovery.

She would explore all the facets of love with him, the ones she had just pointed out, and ones they would discover together.

"Come home, Jesse," she whispered. "Come home to me."

Just like that, his deepest longing was laid raw. A place to call home, a place to be safe and accepted, not for what you had accomplished, but for who you were.

A place where it was okay to be one hundred percent yourself: strengths and weaknesses all welcomed.

Given that he had just decided he was ruled by passion, he probably would not have chosen that moment to kiss her.

But she, his equal in the decision-making process, took that choice from him. Layne kissed him. And he could not resist what she was offering, what he could taste on her lips and feel from her heart.

Homecoming, the sensation they had both waited their entire lives for.

Nobleness be damned. He gathered her in his arms and carried her to his bedroom. The lovemaking was soft, and slow and sweet.

Because there was not a single secret left between them, there were no barriers. Not a single one. He became who she thought he was, and maybe who he had been all along. A man with some good qualities, and plenty of bad ones, too, and who was accepted for all of it.

He felt as if beyond those barriers, those man-made constructs, was something so magnificent a man could not remain blood and bone in its presence.

It was pure love.

Jesse could feel himself fearlessly dissolving into everything that had passed before him, and everything that the future held, becoming one with all of it, with love and pain, and most especially with her.

With Layne.

It was as if, in each other's arms, every single thing that had separated them was gone. They evaporated into stardust. The universe welcomed them as they found their way to exactly where Layne had promised she could take him.

Home.

In the morning, the light streaming over them, he leaned up on one elbow and took her in, tracing the line of her shoulder with a reverent finger.

She opened one eye, looked at him sleepily. She was so utterly and simply gorgeous. Could a man hope for every day of the rest of his life to start just like this one?

"You know what I want?" he asked huskily.

"I hope it's the same things as me," she responded with a smile so sexy it made him melt.

"I'm pretty sure it is the same things as you, but not in the way you mean right now."

"Darn," she said.

"Listen," Jesse said, trying to get her to understand this was serious, even as she nipped at his earlobe. "I don't want to be like my grandfather. And I don't want it to be what your parents had, either. A grand passion. Impulses that nobody wants to control. I want what is between us to be more than chemistry.

"I want to look back on romancing you and feel as if I rose into it, into being the best man I could be, into setting an example for future generations. I want to be the one who breaks the chains of the family history. I don't want to be Charles Whitmore, who used people and then discarded them. I don't want to live forever in the bitterness of my grandmother. I want to change our family story. I want to be the one who says love doesn't destroy.

"It builds. It brings hope. It turns the mundane into the spectacular. Love is the only goal—not money, not success, not accomplishment—that is worth pursuing. I intend, from this moment forward, to behave like the man you think I am, and that you deserve. A man with honor and decency and respect for you.

"I want an old-fashioned love. Where I bring you flowers, and woo you, and send you love notes, and let you know in every way possible that I want to spend time with you and cherish you. I want to *honor* you with how I'm feeling."

"You don't think you do, already?" she chided him, but her face was alight as her fingertips traced his lips.

"I can do better," he said, his determination fierce.

She smiled at him, a smile more radiant than the sun streaming in that window. "I'd like to see you try."

He laughed. "If there's one thing you should know about me, Layne, it's that I'm fiercely competitive."

"That comes as a real surprise to me," she said dryly.

"I never walk away from a challenge."

"Okay, I'm challenging you to be better than last night."

"You're making me lose focus," he complained.

"Oh, good," she said. And then she kissed him, and nipped his ear again, and whispered huskily into it, "This way we both win."

After they made love, she teased him. She told him she couldn't decide if it was better or not, that it was like comparing the world's best lobster po'boys. Both had things about them that were so exquisite they defied rating.

Then, drowsy and adorable, she went back to sleep, while he contemplated the lovely intimacy of being teased after lovemaking.

It cemented his resolve, the decision he had made earlier.

In his mind, no matter what she said about them both being adults, he wanted moments like this one with Layne.

Forever.

It was fast, he knew that. But he didn't want an elopement. He didn't want a single thing to feel rushed between them.

With that in mind, he got up, got dressed and slipped from the room.

Hours later, Jesse stood out on the back deck of Whitmore Castle and looked over the pool, the gorgeous grounds. He could feel the castle, solid, behind him. He marveled at the fact it was his. He had won the battle. He could fulfill his grandmother's wish and have this place reduced to rubble.

But not all battles a man fought were about winning territory.

He had fought a battle within himself, and most things he once thought were true had shifted.

Loving Layne had changed the way he thought about everything.

He thought of how she had told him she would watch him tear the castle down if it was what he needed to do. She had held out what she loved to him with complete trust.

And more than anything in the world, he wanted to be a man worthy of her trust, of the love he saw shining in her eyes every time she looked at him.

Just as he thought about her, she came around the corner of the castle. The first thing he noticed about her, as always, was her hair, burnished. Bronze. Beautiful.

But then he noticed her confidence. The incredible confidence, the way of being in the world, of a woman who knew she was cherished.

He noticed the light in her eyes, the soft radiance when she looked at him, the incredible welcome.

"Hey," she said. "What's up?"

She came to him, reached up on tippy-toes and kissed him on the cheek.

He gestured toward the castle. "I just wanted to look at it with you."

"Her last wish," she said with a soft sigh. "She wished it was a pile of rubble on the ground."

He could see Layne was looking around, saying an inner goodbye. But when she looked back to him, she was smiling, bravely, saying hello to the future.

Her ability to sacrifice for him closed his throat.

Her belief in him—that he would do the right thing—made Jesse understand what power really was. And it wasn't necessarily winning.

"I think Mary Kade would have appreciated revenge," he agreed, his voice hoarse with emotion, "but I'm wondering if she wouldn't have appreciated something else more?"

Layne's eyes found his. What he loved most about what he saw in them right now, even as she stood to lose this place she had been attached to since she was a little girl, was that she trusted him. Completely.

And that she wanted what was best for him.

Just as he wanted what was best for her.

Always and forever.

"Revenge is a powerful motivator," he told her softly. "To have the ability to right past wrongs feels like something I am duty bound to do."

"I understand," she said.

He understood being with Layne Prescott would always require him to take the high road, to be the better man.

"What if there was a different way to right past wrongs?" he asked her. "What if there was something so powerful that revenge looked puny and petty in its presence?"

She was watching him so closely, calling from him a capacity that his grandmother had never had.

The capacity to forgive.

"What if," he continued, "there was a force so powerful it could transform instead of destroy?"

A smile found the edges of her lips and a light a man could live for sparked deep in her eyes.

"What if you and I finding each other," he continued

softly, "was the beginning of a belief that love would find a way—that love would insist on winning—no matter what?"

Those sparks in her eyes were turning to tears. One fell out and slid down her cheek. He reached out and caught it with his thumb.

"What if love waited patient, seeds planted long ago, in upheaved soil. Waiting. Even if it took decades, even if it took lifetimes. Love waited. For us."

She was in his arms, then, sobbing.

"You aren't going to tear it down," she managed to choke out through tears.

"No. How could I tear down the place where you danced as a little girl, where you brought your hopes and dreams and nurtured them in an upside-down world?"

"Thank you," she whispered. "Jesse, thank you."

"Still," he said, "I don't feel like I'm the right person for it. Even though I don't think destroying it is the right step, I don't think I'm the right person to finish the project. I could never erase him, the misery he caused, what this place stood for."

"Are you going to sell it?" she asked, taking a step back from him, still trusting him, still knowing that his healing was tied to this decision that he must make alone.

"No, Layne. I'm not selling it. How could I? You know my cousin Jessica saw the right thing to do, and she didn't even hesitate to do it. She gave me her portion of the title, and then talked her mother and sister into doing the same thing. She knew what was right.

"I know what is right. I think, our deepest selves, always know what is right."

Layne left his arms and turned to look at the castle. A smile of pure love crossed her lips, taking him and the castle in.

He saw that his destiny had always been tied to that place. As had hers.

"Just as it was given to me, I'm now going to give it to

the one person who always saw it as it could be. Who saw it *already* transformed by love. I'm going to give it to you."

"You're going to give me Whitmore Castle?" she breathed, stunned.

"Yes. Absolutely yes."

She came back to him, and she took his lips. The love was so tender and so raw between them that it could distract him from the one thing that was left to do. And it was the most important thing.

He put her away from him, and he reached into the inner pocket of his jacket and drew out an envelope. "This is for you."

She turned the creamy, thick envelope over in her hands. She cast him a puzzled look. "It looks like a wedding invitation."

"Open it."

Layne looked at Jesse once more, quizzically. He could see her hands trembling as she worked the seal of the envelope open.

"You're invited," she read out loud, her fingers touching the raised, black script, "to the grand opening ball of Whitmore Castle."

Her eyes flew to his.

"Not just any ball, Layne," he told her softly. "The most sumptuous event this castle has ever seen. I want it to surpass every dream you ever had when you danced across that ballroom floor as a child. I don't care if it costs a billion dollars."

Layne's gaze was so familiar on his face, earnest, honest, beloved.

"It's the most incredible gift anyone could ever receive," she stammered. "I can't believe this is happening to me."

"It is. It's happening to you."

"A billion dollars?" she teased him, after a moment. "Jesse! We could give each attendee a Sunshine and Storm motorcycle for that!"

"There's an idea!" he said, laughing. And then the laughter left his eyes, and he waited for her to discover what was on the rest of the invitation.

Her eyes dropped back to it. He knew the exact moment she came to the RSVP.

It read: *RSVP Will you marry me?*

The invitation fell from her fingers and she flew into his embrace. As her lips touched his, he could feel it.

Just as Jesse had hoped, he could feel love transforming every single terrible thing that had happened in this castle.

When Layne whispered yes, it was to so much more than marrying him.

It was to believing in the future. To children running through this place one day. It was to life.

She was saying yes to life with all its mysteries and all its power to surprise, all its glory.

And so was he.

* * * * *

*Look out for the next story in the
Fairy Tales in Maine duet*
Cinderella's One-Night Surprise
by Michele Renae

*And if you enjoyed this story,
check out these other great reads
from Cara Colter*

**Their Hawaiian Marriage Reunion
The Billionaire's Festive Reunion
Accidentally Engaged to the Billionaire**

All available now!

CINDERELLA'S ONE-NIGHT SURPRISE

MICHELE RENAE

MILLS & BOON

CHAPTER ONE

MABEL MITCHELL ADJUSTED the rhinestone tiara on her head. Long wavy blond hair spilled over her shoulders to brush her elbows. She'd nixed the idea of putting it up this evening. After a long day of overseeing the crews setting up for the event and helping her best friend and partner in crime, Layne, plunge the guest toilet that had decided to stop working at the most inconvenient moment, she had wanted to go simple with her hair for this grand opening celebration of Whitmore Castle.

Before heading back to the ballroom, she made a few adjustments to her gown in front of the guest bathroom mirror. Sky blue chiffon generously sprinkled with the tiniest sparkles. Felt like wearing a cloud. Touching her hair, she smiled. The tiara had been Layne's suggestion.

"We always dreamed of being princesses in this castle," her lifelong friend had said before they'd parted to get ready for tonight's party. "Time to start acting like them!"

The tiara did make her feel princess-ish. It was the *ish* she'd rinsed off after plunging the toilet that reminded Mabel achieving one's dream was always accompanied by struggle. And she'd started all over on that dream quest six months ago after failing on her first try at independence in the big city of New York.

"You asked for this," she said to her reflection. "Now try to enjoy it."

The party was in full force. Twenty minutes earlier, Layne had announced her engagement to Jesse Kade, a charming billionaire she'd met months earlier when he'd arrived in Whitmore to claim his family inheritance, specifically, the castle. While Jesse had returned to Whitmore with the intention to demolish the castle and put up a subdivision, his love for Layne had given him a change of heart. And put a dazzling diamond ring on Layne's finger.

Mabel once had dreams of falling in love and creating a family. Yet with her parents' divorce two years ago still so fresh, romance felt stupid and impractical to her now. Her dad had chosen more money and prestige over his wife of thirty years?

No, don't think about it, she reminded herself.

Romance was out.

Though how about a dance in the ballroom and maybe a good-night kiss from a man? Was that too much to hope for? A little connection. Her date hadn't arrived yet. Brian had been a last-minute call. Someone she'd gone out for drinks with a month after moving back home. Nothing serious. High school buddies catching up.

Walking through the crowded ballroom, Mabel spied her mom near the beverage table. Madilyn Mitchell's chin was lifted and she wore a smile. As well as a glittery cocktail dress styled à la the 1950s. The woman had always been content to be a homemaker. She'd never held a job away from home. And now she was alone.

Mabel didn't want that tragic life. She wanted to feel accomplished. Domesticity was fine, but not to the degree her mother had taken it. Mabel could be a working mom and show her children that life was exactly what you made it. It would be a balancing act. She never wanted to sway toward the side that saw her emulating her dad's work ambitions that had destroyed a perfectly good marriage.

She didn't approach her mom. She didn't know how to relate to her lately. She and Madilyn Mitchell had never related like friends. They loved one another, but they'd never learned how to laugh alongside one another or to simply talk.

The music changed from a quiet song to something jazzy.

Tonight's ball was to celebrate the castle B and B officially opening next week. The entire town had been invited. When her date arrived, Mabel intended to enjoy the evening. And as she gave another tap to the tiara, Mabel realized she wanted to feel noticed. To feel like a woman. And a man's gaze would fulfill that desire. She couldn't wear the princess tiara without having a prince on her arm!

Tonight would be magical. If it killed her.

Whitmore Castle was something to behold.

"Nice," Jamison Wright muttered. As a former country music singer, he'd attended all sorts of events, parties, ceremonies and galas. This one felt spectacular yet homey.

Yeah, homey. A feeling he'd been chasing for years. Touched the edges of it on occasion. Maybe a move back to Montana, to build his own home on his parents' land, was just the thing to finally satisfy his desire for peace, quiet and the ineffable quest for true love.

Commandeering a goblet of champagne from a passing waiter's tray, Jamison moved along the crowded edge of the ballroom floor. While working on the construction crew that had rehabbed the eighty-year-old castle, he hadn't been officially introduced to the two women who ran the castle, but he had seen them around. The red-haired one, Layne, had welcomed him to the party tonight. Pleasant, beautiful, she'd introduced him to her fiancé, the castle's new owner, and had wished him a fabulous night.

The scent of lilac drifted in as he neared the patio doors. Inhaling, he smiled, enjoying the simple moment of nature even amidst the cozy bustle of townsfolk, city officials, the mayor and newspaper personnel. Even eccentric Chester from the vinyl record shop that Jamison frequented was here in a plaid suitcoat and striped bowtie. Only Chester with his good nature and kind heart could ignore the dress code and be allowed admittance.

Leaning against the doorframe, Jamison cast his gaze around the ballroom, taking in the second-floor balcony that was just large enough to hold a dozen people, and featured a walk-out over the back patio. And there, standing at the balcony railing, stood what he thought a real princess would look like should she dance off the pages of a storybook.

Jamison swept a hand through his short silver hair and tugged at the bowtie that suddenly constricted. Why was his heart thudding as if he'd just raced along the beach?

The princess's long blond hair swept over bared shoulders and was topped with a tiara. Barest pink blushed her high cheekbones. Eyes the color of his favorite Gibson guitar searched the crowd. He knew her eyes were blue because he'd once stopped working as she'd passed by him, muttering an "excuse me" and not noticing that she'd stolen his breath in that ineffable moment.

Her name was Mabel Mitchell. The castle's bookkeeper. And her pale blue dress, a match to her eyes and his guitar, glittered like stardust.

When her gaze glanced over his, he nodded and lifted

his champagne goblet to her. Slowly, she smiled. Initially curious at his acknowledgment, and then a genuine grin that blossomed in her eyes. The moment felt surreal, as if she'd landed in his gaze and he caught her, could hold her close and...

Someone tapped her on the shoulder and she turned away.

And Jamison checked his heartbeats. Still fast.

Wasn't every day a man fell in love in a matter of heartbeats.

Mabel glided past chattering guests to the patio, which served as a second ballroom under the stars. Her mom had left a half hour earlier. It had been difficult watching her mom moving about the party unaccompanied by her dad. Happily-ever-after didn't seem possible now that her one example had literally combusted. And to top it off? Her date hadn't shown. Brian hadn't even texted her!

Stepping out onto the patio, she startled when a man bumped into her. With an apology spilling out, he gripped her gently by the shoulder and studied her gaze with brilliant blue eyes that dazzled her even as she'd settled into hating on all possibilities of romance.

"I'm good," she said. His more-salt-than-pepper coif was stunningly attractive, yet he didn't look old, perhaps a distinguished early forties? He had a trimmed beard and mustache that framed his mouth. A very nice mouth. That a girl could kiss if she were inclined... "Do I know you?"

"Maybe?" He offered his hand to shake. "Jamison Wright."

"Mr. Wright, eh?" Mabel inwardly kicked herself at the stupid comment. He probably got that all the time. But, oh, he could be right for someone. "I'm Mabel Mitchell.

The castle's financial director. That's the fancy title I give myself because accountant sounds boring."

"Yeah, I noticed you doing your thing here. I was with the construction crew."

"Oh, yes! Straightline Construction." She shook his hand, noting it was the strongest and surest clasp she'd ever held. The silver ring on his thumb slid a cool shiver against her skin. "Your crew rehabbed the castle. I recall your hair now."

"My hair?"

"It's stunning. I mean, it—well, it stands out. Makes you remarkable." *Mabel!* "I mean... Oh. I don't know what I'm saying." Two champagnes hadn't made her drunk, but she was feeling loose. Open to... His eyes were like jewels that twinkled under the overhead patio lights. "The silver suits you. But don't tell me you're old enough to claim the color naturally."

He chuckled deeply as he stroked his jaw and shook his head. "It's a family thing. We go gray as soon as we hit forty."

That made him...twelve years older than her? Well, who was counting? Not the makeshift princess who'd been stood up and given up on romance.

He was an incredibly handsome specimen. And she had lived in New York where all kinds of attractive men had crossed her path daily. Models, business execs, creatives, tourists. Had she been thinking of leaving the party? Maybe a few more minutes to chat with Mr. Right.

"Did you work on the entire castle?" she asked.

"I came in during the final phase of the remodel. I've only been in Whitmore a year. So, the financial director, eh? Here I thought you were the resident princess."

"Huh? Oh." She touched the tiara. "Just for the evening I get to play Cinderella."

"I hope you're not wearing glass slippers. That sounds uncomfortable if not downright dangerous."

She laughed and pointed out a toe. "Just flats. And I'm not a resident. I live in town."

He leaned in conspiratorially. "Will your ride turn into a pumpkin if you leave after midnight?"

"I hope not. It's only a fifteen-minute walk home. I was on my way out."

"But I haven't noticed you out on the dance floor."

"Is that a requirement?" She couldn't take her eyes from his. And the direct connection didn't feel uncomfortable, rather daring and even a little promising.

He shrugged. "Don't all princesses dance?"

"I did want to dance, but my dance card is unfortunately blank."

"We can't have that." He offered his hand. "Would you do me the honor before you leave?"

Mabel didn't have to think about her plans to go home, soak in the tub and snuggle with her cat, Mouse. Silver hair, bright blue eyes and a voice as smooth as dark chocolate? This makeshift princess wasn't stupid enough to pass up Mr. Right.

"Yes." She took his hand and they wandered onto the dance floor.

Smooth. That's the kind of dancer he was. Mabel hadn't shifted her gaze from Jamison's eyes during the entire first dance, a slow song. He held her respectfully, one hand at her hip, the other holding hers up near their shoulders. No body contact.

But, oh, did she want to melt against him. Close her

eyes as they swirled about the dance floor as if on a cloud. That's what princesses did, right? The tiara felt like a magical prop intent on making her dreams come true. A dreamy dance with a handsome man who smelled like cedar or something woodsy.

Nothing else in the world mattered.

She stepped closer to him, hugging up against his chest.

A song played in her Gibson guitar irises. Her pale pink lips smiled and parted and sighed as the night played on her face. The world dropped away, leaving only him and this beautiful magical being moving in perfect time with one another.

He wanted to hug her for a thousand minutes and remember the configuration of stars overhead to confirm the moment in his memory as if placing a pin on a map. And when he twirled her, her laughter crafted a melody that pattered his heart. It was a surreal space in time in which they danced and laughed.

How many dances had it taken to fall in love with a man she'd never met but felt as though their souls had finally found one another?

No, it wasn't love. It was lust. Desire. Want.

A crazy swirl of invigoration giddied Mabel's heart. She wanted a kiss. And though they'd barely shared more than a few words and laughter while they danced, she felt brazen enough to tilt onto her toes and kiss him.

His arm swept up her back and held her firmly. He bent slightly to meet her. One of his hands slipped through the ends of her loose hair, finding refuge.

And his kiss. Oh, this kiss.

It felt like a fairy tale she'd created as a child. The princess standing in the prince's arms before a background of fragrant lilac. But that dream had matured and now surged through her body in a dazzle of stars and heated desire. His mouth owned her. Teased her. Danced with her. She sighed into his kiss. Crushed her body against his. Surrendered to the fantasy.

"I don't want this night to end," Jamison said. The statement felt like a lyric. Heady, and urgent, and forever, and romantic, and...all those crazy girlie words that he associated with love.

But no one fell in love so quickly.

"I know exactly how you feel." She took his hand and led him away from the castle patio, aiming toward the stairs that descended to the beach. Fanciful lighting was strung along the wood railing, luring wanderers toward the moon-glittered harbor. "Want to walk under the stars?"

"I'll go wherever you ask, Cinderella."

At the bottom of the stairs, she paused to slip off her shoes before stepping onto the silty beach. Her dress trailed in the sand. With an unabashed twirl, she effusively declared, "Let's make this night last forever!"

Rushing up alongside her and taking her hand, Jamison shouldered against her and they strolled along the beach, which was lit by the stars and the moon that curled a silvery scythe in the azure sky.

"I've never danced so much," she said as they strolled along the shore. No tide this evening. The still water glittered in silver flashes.

"I don't dance at all. I'm more of a creator, I guess."

"I imagine your creativity is very satisfying? The buildings you make?"

"I like working with my hands. My dad taught me carpentry."

"Oh, that's special. You two must be close?"

"Not in distance. He lives in Montana. Got a flight out to visit my parents tomorrow morning."

"Oh?" Her tone wasn't thrilled.

Same, Cinderella. Same.

"How long will you be gone?" she asked.

"Two months."

She gasped but tried to hide it. "That's...a long time."

It would feel like two *years* separated from her for so long. How crazy was that thought? But he did have commitments.

"It's what I do every year around this season. First, I take a couple weeks to volunteer with Homes for Humans. Then, it's on to Butte, to spend some time with the parents. They live completely off the grid so I leave my phone in a drawer the whole time. It's nice to kick back, help my mom plant her garden, fix things with my dad. Just...exist."

"Wow. To go phone-free for so long? That's not something I could manage. It's difficult enough readjusting to the small-town esthetic after living in New York for years."

"You're from New York?"

"No, I grew up here. But I moved away for a job with a music label."

"Oh, yeah? Which one?"

"Xtatic. I was in the accounting department."

He'd heard of them. They were small, boutique. Handled alternative artists. Interesting. "And now you're back here to run a B and B?"

"Me and Layne—she's been my bestie since we were kids—have always dreamed of someday living in Whitmore Castle. It's been a lot of work, but I'm enjoying it.

Though the readjustment from big-city living to this harbor-town lifestyle is a slow process. Do you know the local coffee shop doesn't deliver?"

Jamison laughed. "But you have to appreciate that it's much less expensive than in New York City, yes?"

"Oh, yeah. I'm paying half the price for a decent cuppa here. I'll fit in. One way or another."

"Come on." He clasped her hand. "I don't live far away."

"You live on the harbor?"

"Yeah, I lucked out and picked it up the day it went on the market. Want to come inside for…"

"I do," Mabel said, and gave him a quick kiss. "I really do."

When Jamison reached to flick on the interior lights, Mabel caught his hand and shook her head. Moonlight shone through all the windows. She didn't want to be blasted back to reality. She wanted to stay in the fairy tale. Because tomorrow it would end. He'd said he planned to leave for two months.

Tonight was all she had. Her desire for skin-on-skin connection would happen. No commitment. No promises. Nothing would stop her from enjoying this moment.

Their kiss took them through the living room and into the bedroom surrounded by the floor-to-ceiling windows. Between kisses she caught glimpses of plants climbing up the walls. A low platform bed made up in pale earth colors. A simple rough wood bench at the end of the bed. A guitar, or three or four, propped on stands on the opposite side of the bed and some hanging on a wall. And beyond the window, stars danced in the midnight sky.

Jamison kissed her neck. Her entire body curled against his, devouring the delicious sensation. The salty air had scented their hair and skin. His soft hair glided under her fingers. His kisses tasted her chin, her cheek, her eyelid. She tugged away his tie and began to unbutton his shirt. Every touch, every kiss, felt like choreography they'd never practiced but they'd been born knowing the routine.

Touching the tiara, he whispered, "Take it off."

The request felt like a sensuous dare, an alluring tease, a kinky demand.

Mabel tugged the combs from her hair and set the tiara on the nightstand by the bed. "There," she proclaimed. "No longer a princess."

Jamison lifted her into his arms. "You'll always be my Cinderella."

Mabel slid from the king-size bed and stepped on her ball gown. She winced as her bare foot crunched a sequin. Glancing over her shoulder, she saw Jamison was still asleep, a soft almost-snore coming from him. The sheet barely covered his hip, exposing the other and the side of his leg. His body was ripped. Tight muscles and lean form. The man could not be forty.

He was a man in his prime. And he looked it. And acted like it. The sex had been earthshaking. In her entire life, she'd never had such fulfilling sex from a hookup. And a real orgasm that hadn't taken forever to achieve. It felt as though she'd been the instrument and he had pulled the song out of her with ease.

And now she intended to sneak out of the man's home and his life. Because the first thing that came to mind was that he was leaving today. For two months. No way to start a relationship. And—well, it had been a hookup. Just sex. All she'd wanted last night was a connection. And she got it.

Also, she'd promised Layne she would help her with party cleanup this morning. And she had to be there to pay the invoices for the rental companies that were all scheduled to arrive early.

Collecting her dress, she pulled it on. Spying her shoes, she picked them up and tiptoed to the front door. Pity they'd come together only for a night.

But on the other hand...she'd gotten exactly what she wanted. A night to remember.

Carefully opening the door, she closed it behind her, then pressed her shoulders to it. Was she doing the right thing? She could stay in bed, linger and wake up in the man's arms. Have sex again. Send him off to the airport with a kiss and coffee. The way normal people would say goodbye.

But this Cinderella was feeling like she'd been gifted a dream that was now being taken away. The clock had struck midnight. Nothing could come of a hookup. And, really, romance didn't exist. Her parents were an example of that.

Time to return to reality with a dash down the stairs. Good thing she hadn't worn glass slippers.

His rhinestone Cinderella hadn't stayed to wake him with kisses and snuggles.

Jamison sighed as the pilot announced they'd be taking off in a few minutes. He tilted his head back and closed the window shade. The night had been nothing less than perfect. So he couldn't understand why she'd fled without so much as a goodbye.

On the other hand, did he really want to get involved in another relationship when his immediate plans could see him moving yet again?

"Probably best she did sneak out. A woman like that is too good for a guy like me." Road-weary, unrooted and looking for a place to call home.

He'd cherish the memory of his Mabel in the moonlight.

CHAPTER TWO

Two months later, August

A REPORTER FOR the state's *Style* magazine was doing an article on Instagram-worthy Maine vacation attractions and wanted to include Whitmore Castle. Layne was out with the sniffles this morning, so Mabel volunteered to take her place and walk the reporter through the grounds and do the interview. She should be here any minute.

Gripping the railing where she stood on the balcony, overlooking the back patio festooned with fragrant English roses, Mabel blew out a breath. She had a lot on her mind. She didn't want to mess up the interview, but...

She'd taken a pregnancy test for the third time this morning.

Mabel Mitchell was going to be a mommy.

And that made her feel...she didn't know. It was difficult to wrap her head around something so big. And she'd been so busy these past two months that thinking beyond spreadsheets and the arrangements for Layne's fall wedding had left her little time to comprehend this life-changing news.

She wasn't feeling on top of the world, either. A little woozy and brain fog. Morning sickness? She hadn't tossed her cookies. Yet.

So here she stood. In a situation. One she had never expected, or imagined would happen to her.

Well. Her childhood dreams had included having a big family. Just in a different order, like saying "I do" before buying diapers.

Eight months ago, Mabel had been anxious about her current job and unsure what to do after a particularly fraught encounter with her new boss. In the three years she'd been with the label as their accountant, she'd learned a lot about the music industry. There were deals to be made but some at a tremendous cost. And her new boss had given her an ultimatum. Either have sex with him or lose her job.

He hadn't stated that ultimatum. It had come as a physical struggle.

Mabel had fled the office and gone home in tears. The next day, Layne, completely unaware of Mabel's angst, had called, pleading her to come help with the castle's messy accounting. It had felt like destiny. But also, a failure. She'd left Whitmore after college with aspirations of making it big. *Sex and the City* goals, like all the shoes, the clothes, the parties and connections, and even Mr. Big. That dream had been crushed.

But she also didn't want to be that small-town girl with no more desire than to stay at home, cook for her family and tidy the house. Like her mother did.

So, she'd taken the leap. Fled the big city and moved back home to start a new dream that she hadn't quite labeled yet. Things were moving along nicely for her as the castle's financial director. She and Layne had hit their groove. The castle was a hit!

The small town was welcoming Mabel back into it's comforting, cozy and slightly gossipy arms. And just two weekends ago, she'd begun spending some time at her mom's house, sorting around in the vegetable garden and picking up takeout so they could eat and watch *Super Homes* together. There was something different about the mom she'd once mentally labeled subservient and humble. She was…brighter. Lighter, in a manner. And she laughed at anything. It was a new Madilyn Mitchell. Mabel had expected something much different after being married thirty years and then suddenly divorcing.

Had it taken her only child moving to the big city to finally give her mom a new lease on what Mabel had always thought was domestic drudgery? That of cooking, cleaning, raising a daughter. Her mom had never worked away from the home and had never aspired for much more. She was happy as a housewife. She even pressed her cotton dresses and retro-styled her hair daily, putting forth the picture of domestic bliss.

It was a lifestyle Mabel had wanted to flee as well as the small-town esthetic. She didn't want to be like her mom, never aspiring for more. To equate family as her only happiness?

The thought used to give Mabel a shudder. Now? It made her tilt her head and wonder. What was up with Madilyn Mitchell that she was so light? How could a divorce have brought a bigger smile to her face? She'd told Mabel plainly that she loved her dad, but they'd fallen out of love for one another. When her dad's promotion to Norway had been offered, Madilyn had suggested he follow his aspirations, but she was content in Whitmore. They'd both said "divorce" at the same time, chuckled about it and realized their lives were ready for the split.

It sounded odd. What had happened to romance and happily-ever-after?

And what would her traditional mom say when her daughter announced she was going to have a baby? On her own?

This would be...a challenge. *Was* it a challenge? Felt strange to label it that. A baby wasn't a challenge. It was an innocent tiny being who would burst into her life in about seven months and change it forever.

It was the deciding-how-to-shape-her-new-family part that would be a challenge. Did she want to be married? Honestly, her gut reaction and traditionally raised values insisted she be married. But her career-girl-takes-on-the-big-city-and-becomes-fiercely-independent side insisted that single motherhood was very doable. Perhaps even preferable in lieu of the happily-ever-afters that seemed to be dying left and right of her. Half the town seemed to claim divorce. Most of her childhood friends were on marriage number two. Even Layne had broken it off with her first fiancé a year earlier.

Mabel gripped the railing and closed her eyes. Not feeling queasy, just...so unprepared. Unsure. Unexpected. Unqualified. All the *uns*.

Sure, she'd babysat as a teen. Had loved it. Could change a diaper, give a bottle and pat up a burp like a pro. When Layne had danced about the castle dreaming of a waltz with her knight, Mabel had rocked the carriage filled with dolls and the occasional stray cat. In her teen years, she'd been known around town as the girl to trust should a harried mother need a helping hand in the park to sit by her stroller while she wrangled the other rug rats. Mabel loved kids. And someday intended to have dozens.

Well, two or three. She wasn't crazy.

And she still aspired to create a family. Only, not the traditional family that Madilyn Mitchell so proudly embraced. Mabel had always thought it would be different for her. Modern and fast-paced, chauffeuring the kids to soccer and dance and keeping track of their classes, reading food labels and ensuring they ate all the right foods... Different than her traditional upbringing.

Life was definitely checking that "different" box right now.

Because right now her life was not perfect or ordered, nor did it fit into any plan, dream or design she may have had. She was in flux. Trying to fit herself back into a way of life she'd thought to escape. And now that retrofit would be accompanied by a baby.

"Miss Mitchell?"

She jerked up her head. The journalist stood below in the ballroom. And she wore a baby strapped in a carrier to her chest. A freaking *baby*. Of all the days! Was this some sort of sign? A test?

A challenge.

"You're Anabelle Hanson?" Mabel called as she made her way to the stairs that curved down to the main floor. She could not remove her gaze from the baby. Chubby, bright-eyed, kicking its legs gaily.

"Yes, Miss Mitchell." The woman shook her hand, then smoothed a palm over her son's head, which received a gurgling coo. "I'm so sorry, but my sitter is sick this morning. I was going to reschedule but my week is so busy—"

"It's not a problem." Mabel bent to look the infant in the eye. She gave his foot a little jiggle. "You are adorable! Did you come here this morning to tell me something?"

"Unless you can understand coos and goos..." The reporter laughed. "Don't worry. He's close to a nap. He likes to look around and listen and then...zonk. He's out." She tugged out a portable recorder. "So, how would you like to start?"

"I'll give you a tour while we talk. What's your son's name?"

"Avery."

"Well, Avery, nice to meet you. Come this way."

Mabel walked ahead, thinking for certain the universe had either a wicked sense of humor or this truly was a sign. She didn't believe in signs or any of that woo-woo stuff.

But every time she glanced at Avery, she could swear his smile was knowing.

Jamison walked into Whitmore Castle with tiara in hand. He'd found it on the nightstand the morning after he'd slept with Mabel. He'd considered having it sent to the castle because he didn't know where she lived.

While he'd thought of her every day over the last two months, that time apart made him leery now. Would she even remember him?

So here he stood. In Cinderella's castle. Heartbeat thundering. Hands growing a little sweaty. Holding the metaphorical missing shoe. He knew it would fit her. But he suspected happily-ever-after wouldn't be a sure thing.

Did he want that happily-ever-after? It was crazy to think it might come from a one-night stand. And hell, his heart wore armor against falling in love. Only a few years earlier, he'd been "this close" to becoming a daddy. His girlfriend at the time had announced she was having his baby. That had sent him over the moon, despite not being in love with the woman. It was hard to connect emotionally while on tour, but Jamison had been there for her whenever their schedules permitted. Until the ultimate betrayal by the baby's momma had torn his heart to pieces.

So he hadn't given it a second thought when he'd taken his parents up on their offer to move onto their land and build his own place. It felt…not necessarily right, but rather, like an exhale. A place of peace. It would bring another new beginning.

He was tired of starting over, traveling, never having a permanent bed to rest his weary head. He wanted to settle down and plant some roots. To find his place in the world.

On the other hand, he always aspired to grasp the best life could offer him. And he'd be a fool not to see what happened next with this tiara's owner. He'd enjoyed every moment he'd spent with Mabel at the ball and then later in his bed. If he hadn't been scheduled for visiting his parents, he could imagine they may have dated these past few months, grown closer. By now, they could be in a serious relationship. Talking about the future. Settling in with one another.

Planting those roots?

He smirked. So he had a wild imagination. Helped when it came to writing songs. But he wasn't a fool. It had been one night. She'd likely moved on. And he had about a month to finish a current construction job here in the city and a charity obligation, and then there was packing and severing his ties to Whitmore before moving on to Montana.

There was just this one emotional piece that needed exploration. He had to look into Mabel's Gibson guitar eyes one more time. Just…for closure.

Wandering through the castle's reception area, he nodded to the painting of the baron Charles Whitmore hung above the reception desk. The man wearing a dark suit and painted in the mid-twentieth century was handsome yet appropriately staunch. He'd heard rumors about the castle founder. Hadn't been a swell guy. Something about an affair? Jamison never thought ill of the dead. Or people he had no business judging.

He didn't see anyone around so he veered into the vast ballroom and noted the patio doors were open wide to waft in the scent of the pink roses. Out on the patio stood two women; one of them hugged a sleeping baby against her chest. The other was Mabel.

Jamison's heart flipped like a goldfish landing in a puddle. He caught himself, gave a little headshake. Really? One look at that beautiful starlight blonde sent his blood racing?

Hell, yes.

Hooking the hand in which he held the tiara in a belt loop he wandered across the ballroom floor. From his peripheral vision, he noticed another person near the doors. A gardener clipping the shrubbery.

Suddenly, Mabel and the woman with the baby looked to him. Mabel's jaw dropped open. He waved. To his side, the gardener stepped up beside him.

When Mabel put her hand to the woman's shoulder, turned her away from him and began to walk away, Jamison's heart strangled the giddy goldfish. She didn't even glance over her shoulder. No acknowledging smile?

But she had seen him.

Breath hushing out, he winced.

"Sir? Can I help you?"

The question ricocheted inside his skull, brushing roughly against the rejection that had just deflated his hope. She hadn't waved or smiled at him!

Maybe she hadn't recognized him? Doubtful. But the other woman was holding something, maybe a recorder. Sure, he'd seen those devices many times. Must be some kind of interview? Mabel was busy. That was the reason she'd not run into his arms and kissed him and declared how she'd missed him terribly over the months.

"Sir?"

"Huh? Oh." He moved the tiara behind his back and eyed the gardener. "Miss Mitchell must be busy?"

"Yes, she's in an interview. Is there something I can do for you?"

He should have called first. Let her know he was back in town. Would that have earned him a more welcoming reception?

"No. I… I'll, uh…yeah." He backed into the ballroom and as he turned, pulled the tiara around to his front so the gardener couldn't see it. He waved without turning back. "Thanks!"

Once on the road curling out from the castle, he tugged out his phone. He didn't have her number. Pausing by the mailbox at the end of the drive, he looked back to the castle.

Not even a smile? Maybe she didn't want to see him? Had it been nothing more than a hookup for her? Hell, Mabel could be dating someone. Engaged! Talk about getting closure.

Shaking his head to chase off that wild thought, Jamison tugged out a receipt from his back pocket and the small carpenter's pencil he always carried with him. He jotted a note.

Saw that you were busy. Missed you. Meet me at The Loose Lobster at seven?

It was a local taproom known for serving the best lobster roll in the state.

He shook his head, but then decided it was worth a try. He marched back to the castle and left the folded note on the reception desk with Mabel's name scrawled on it. If she didn't show tonight that would decide his future. He'd pack up and move to Montana without looking back.

CHAPTER THREE

Mabel held a soft blue baby sock in one hand and the handwritten note in the other. The sock she'd found at the edge of the ballroom after the reporter left with Avery snoring against her chest. She'd drop it in the mail tomorrow. Avery probably had hundreds and wouldn't miss one. But she knew how annoying a missing sock could be.

She read Jamison's note. He wanted to meet at the pub tonight.

She'd been utterly surprised to see him standing in the ballroom doorway. Hadn't been prepared for the sight of the silver-haired heartthrob. Her heart had leaped. Her hands had fidgeted. She hadn't known how to react. Oblivious to Mabel's moment, the reporter had asked about the events they had planned through to the end of the year.

Mable had blown her reunion with Jamison.

Her baby's father.

On the other hand, she wasn't sure she could talk to Jamison right now. She hadn't had the chance to absorb the fact she was pregnant and life would never be the same.

What did she want to do now? Did she want to marry and make it a traditional family? *Did* she want Jamison involved? Was single motherhood the wisest option? When she'd been dreaming about having dozens of kids, she always included a father in the picture.

All important questions she had to give some thought to. Only then could she tell Jamison about it. Because the man did deserve that courtesy. The idea of keeping it a secret from him did not sit well with her.

She rubbed the soft sock between her fingers. So tiny. And it probably smelled like baby. She wouldn't sniff it. That would end her. Reduce her to tears. Babies were just so lovable and perfect and... She pressed the sock to her nose. Oh...

"I can do this," she whispered.

But not without support.

And her most staunch supporter lived nearby in the carriage house, currently nursing the sniffles.

Mabel hadn't told Layne about her pregnancy tests over the last few weeks. Now, more than ever, she needed her best friend's advice.

Layne's first reaction to Mabel's news was to spread her arms for a gigantic bear hug, but then she stopped and shook her head.

They settled onto opposite ends of the couch, Layne blowing her nose intermittently and Mabel desperately wanting to hug her despite the germs. The morning after the ball, Mabel had told Layne about her night with Jamison, and how she'd been thrilled with the hookup but wondered if it could have been more if he hadn't had to leave for months.

"Go see him," Layne insisted after a sneeze. "He needs to know."

"I would never keep this a secret from the father," Mabel insisted. "But I won't shirk my responsibilities. I've a lot of paperwork to finish today. I'll see where I'm at later."

"Mabel. Work can wait for this auspicious announcement."

"I need some time to process this, Layne."

"I get it." She blew her nose. "You were there for me when Brock dumped me. That was tough." Mabel had flown home and stayed with Layne for a week after the breakup with her first fiancé. "I'm always here for you, Mabel, you know that. Have you talked to your mom about it?"

Mabel shrugged. "I'm getting there. I intend to take her out for lunch. Soon. I feel like I need to get to know her all over after living away for so long. And now with this news…"

"You two need to get real with one another. Madilyn needs to know she's going to be a grandma."

Mabel would share this pregnancy with her mom. But again, she needed to settle into knowing that this was happening to her. Right now!

"How are you feeling?" she asked Layne.

"I figure this bug will knock me down for a good day. I'll be back at work tomorrow. Promise."

"Take it easy. We never take time off. Sickness is the body's way of telling you to relax for a few days."

"Did you read that on one of those office motivational posters?"

Mabel fake-punched Layne on the shoulder. "You want to be healthy for your wedding! But speaking of motivation, I need to start a spreadsheet for the baby."

"Seriously?"

Mabel nodded. "If I'm doing this—and I am—it's not going to happen without pie charts, spreadsheets and visual aids. You know that's how I function. I'll catch you later." She tucked the tissue box within Layne's reach and filled her water pitcher on the way out the door.

"You always encouraged me to be bold, so be sure to schedule a handsome silver-haired carpenter into those visual aids!"

Rolling her eyes, Mabel left that one hanging and wandered back to the castle to immerse herself in work.

It was eight thirty. Mabel wasn't going to show.

Finishing his third craft beer—he did like the sours—Jamison laid a couple twenties on the table where he'd sat watching a sailboat with party lights skim the harbor. In that time, his ego had taken a dive. She'd rejected him. In the worst way possible. Ghosting wasn't something he was used to. Sure, women had broken it off with him throughout his dating career but they had always spoken to him, face-to-face. Except Clementine. She'd decided that a devastating phone call—*no, you're not my baby daddy*—followed by going large with an article in a major entertainment magazine was best.

He wouldn't return to that soul-destroying headspace by giving her another thought.

But Mabel. A no-show? Maybe she hadn't seen his note? He wished he had her number so he could text her. Apparently, he'd tagged her wrong. That marvelous starstruck night? She had just been in it for the sex. Had she known who he really was? Had having sex with him, a former country rock singer who had topped the music charts, been some sort of notch for her?

Maybe she knew his history. The scandal. The cancellation of his career. The almost baby.

He didn't want to go there. And she'd not indicated that she knew who he was. It didn't matter. It shouldn't. Yet, he still couldn't get the image of her Gibson guitar eyes out of his thoughts.

Damn. He'd never been so enamored by a woman. What was wrong with him? No, it wasn't love. Yet. But she'd grabbed hold of his fascination and hadn't released it. He was merely following the invisible tether that had formed between them that night. To sever it or grab hold and see where it took him?

He picked up the tiara. Win the girl and live happily-ever-after? What a dreamer. His wild imagination had served his songwriting well. Yet, this melody felt like the worst breakup song ever.

"Get over it, Wright. It was just one night."

Sliding out of the booth, he aimed for the patio behind the pub, knowing there was a stairway that led down to the beach. A quick walk to his place.

So this was what heartbreak felt like? Empty beer mugs, shadowed starlight and an abandoned rhinestone tiara? Hell. He was thinking like some kind of down-on-his-luck country singer right now.

With a smirk, Jamison wandered into the night.

Mabel walked into the taproom and up to the bar to ask if a silver-haired man had been in. She had not intended to make this date. And then she had. And then, while brushing her teeth, she'd changed her mind. And then, when deciding to stay home and watch TV with a cat curled on her lap, she'd changed her mind again.

She couldn't *not* see Jamison again. But she couldn't tell him about the baby. Not yet. She didn't have the language to put it out there and not burst into tears in front of him, or worse, run away. Or even worse, cling to him and plead him to make it feel right.

She was not that woman. She was Mabel Mitchell. Strong. Smart. Independent.

Maybe too independent. She knew she should relax more and allow others to help. To allow people to move into her world and not alongside it. Layne was the only person who inhabited her world fully, and she'd never push her out.

The bartender said a silver-haired man had been here for a while and left. He pointed to the table where he'd sat and Mabel thanked him. A glance to the table, lit by a sputtering candle, she spied something that glinted. Mabel walked over and picked up the tiara. She'd forgotten about it. Must have left it at his place the night…

"That night," she whispered.

She clutched the tiara to her chest. It reminded her of how she had danced with Jamison under the patio lights, then they had walked the moonlit beach hand in hand. Their conversation had been easy. About everything and nothing. She'd been bummed to hear he intended to fly out for two months. Yet when he'd suggested they go to his place, it had felt as if there was nowhere else in the world she should go but to his home, his bed. In his arms.

To grasp for a feeling she'd desired. A no-strings night that had satisfied beyond her wildest dreams.

She hadn't lost herself in Jamison's arms, she had found a piece of her soul that she'd abandoned when moving to the big city. And that piece had only flourished over the course of the months she had been back in Whitmore. Jamison had set that piece aflame, causing it to unfurl and…

"Don't be a silly romantic," she muttered. "He's gone. Because I couldn't get right with myself."

She'd lost him.

And that piece? It was an actual baby, not some flaming soul nonsense.

A bustle sounded at the pub doors. A large group of tourists charged in, so Mabel veered toward the back exit. Once on the patio, she had it all to herself, so she walked to the railing that overlooked the harbor. The patio was hugged by wild vines and smelled of sea salt. The air was heavy, promising rain. Below, a wooden walkway stretched along the narrow beach. Herring gulls—more like harbor rodents—wailed, and the water glittered from houselights along the opposite bank.

Leaning onto the railing, she sighed. And then she noticed movement. Someone stood below the patio. They shuffled onto the beach path to look up.

"Mabel?"

Her heart leaped to her throat. It was too dark to make out his features, but that deep silken voice transported her back to that night. If she had lingered in his arms the morning after, might it have gone differently? Might he have stayed in Whitmore? Could they have bonded and begun a relationship?

Too late to wonder. Time to move forward.

"I'm sorry I'm late," she called to him.

"Hang on! I'll be right up!"

The wood trellis that lined the brick base of the patio shuddered. He was not taking the stairs but rather...climbing up the trellis! It was a good ten feet from the ground. Mabel reached down, knowing she would be no help, but nervous he'd fall. "Careful!"

"I got this." His head leveled at the railing and, with minimal effort, he managed to scale it and land on the patio beside her.

Mabel stepped back to look at him. Torn jeans, casual shirt hugging impossible muscles, Dr. Martens and that gorgeous silver hair. A breath took in the man with whom she'd once flirtatiously suggested she could spend forever. And that forever had occurred in a few hours between the sheets of his bed.

And now she carried a piece of him inside her.

"Jamison," she said on a breath.

"Can I—" He stepped forward.

She didn't want to talk. She wanted to know him again. To remember his touch. To be reassured that it hadn't been a fluke. That there was the tiniest bit of her that existed in him.

Mabel plunged into his arms and kissed him. It was a kiss they'd known for a thousand years and yet it had been separated by time, made them strangers again. But only for a moment. She breathed him in. Pressed her body against his muscled form. Found her place.

"Oh, Mabel," he whispered. "I missed you. Thought you didn't want to see me again."

What a fool that she'd vacillated between seeing him and not! His arms felt like the only place she belonged. And while she had immense news to reveal to him, it could wait. A quick, *Hey, how's it been? Guess what? I'm pregnant!* No, no and no. She had to navigate this situation carefully and with discretion.

Get to know him, as Layne had suggested.

"Sorry." She pulled from his kiss but not his arms. "I've been busy with work at the castle. I didn't realize how late it was, so I rushed here. I'm glad I didn't miss you."

He took the tiara she still held. "May I?"

She nodded and he placed the tiara on her head. The prince claiming her with the missing tiara just like Prince Charming had done with Cinderella? That was silly romance stuff. And she was so over romance.

"That's where it belongs," he said. "It's not a glass slipper, but kind of the same thing. I found my rhinestone Cinderella."

"Oh. Uh…" Maybe a *little* romance? Couldn't hurt anybody. Could it?

"I mean, I know it's been months. And we only had that one night." He scrubbed a hand over his hair and said shyly, "That was the best night of my life."

How thrilled would he be about that night should he learn he'd created new life? She had no idea what his hopes for family were. Had he any intention of making a family? Did he want one? Perhaps he'd avoided having a family for reasons unbeknownst to her? All things she needed to learn.

"I'm not sure if you thought it was just a hookup," he said, leaving it hang for a moment. "But it didn't feel like it for me. Ah, hell, Mabel, I'd like to get to know you."

"I'd like that, too," she rushed out. "We did things a little backward." Making a baby was very out of order! "I don't know you. But I want to learn everything, like what's your favorite food, and how long do you stay in the shower, and where's the one place you'd never want to visit, and do you want to have a family or—"

"Last call, folks!" someone shouted from inside the pub. "Rain is on the way, so we're closing the patio. You can come inside."

Mabel took Jamison's hand. "I'd love to chat, but I know you've been here a while already. And…the day has been long. I didn't mean to ignore you at the castle. I was in an interview."

"I should have texted but I don't have your number. Can we go on a date? Tomorrow night?" he asked. "Get some lobster, walk along the beach and—"

"Learn who it is we've slept with? I'd like that." She

tugged out her phone. "Let's share our info." They exchanged numbers. "Should I meet you back here at eight?"

"Perfect." He leaned in to kiss her, but stopped, his face so close to nudging hers. He smelled like sea salt and cedar. "Till tomorrow night, Cinderella."

He kissed her on the forehead, adjusted her tiara slightly, then when the first raindrop splattered his cheek, he took her hand and led her inside.

"I walked here," he said.

"I rode my bike," she offered.

"If we leave now, we might not get too soaked."

"You want to walk alongside me as I bike? I guess you do live close. But I'm in the center of town. The opposite direction."

"You can bike to my place and wait out the rain?"

Mabel stopped at the doorway. Jamison opened it to reveal it misted lightly, but she'd seen the weather report. They were in for a downpour.

They'd made a date for tomorrow. Truly, the day had been long and fraught with so many emotional experiences. Crawling into bed, hugging Mouse close and processing it all felt like the best plan.

Instead, Mabel hopped on her bike and pedaled slowly as they made way to Jamison's place. And once there, his kiss dissolved all intention to leave. Bejeweled with rain, they shared a wet giggling kiss that led them to the bed where they shed their rain-drizzled clothing.

The tiara dropped to the floor as Mabel and Jamison fell in a passionate embrace onto his bed.

CHAPTER FOUR

JAMISON WOKE TO find Mabel looking at him. She smiled. Closed her eyes. Stretched like a cat. Then curled her head against his shoulder.

Now this is how a man liked to greet the day. Lying next to a woman who felt as if she'd been a part of his life forever yet was so unique and vibrant and interesting that… Well, he didn't know a thing about her. Beyond that unknowing, they certainly were matched when it came to making love. They shared a groove between the sheets.

But a guy shouldn't get lost in the feeling. Bad things happened when one handed all his trust to a woman he barely knew.

Didn't mean he couldn't enjoy the sex.

Sunlight beamed over the bed, streaking highlights in Mabel's hair and softening her skin. Faint floral perfume lingered on her skin, the sheets, his hands. She smelled like flowers and candy. Pretty, yet something he wanted to lick and taste and consume until he was drunk. He pulled her closer and reveled in their heartbeat harmony.

But—what time was it? He had a job this morning at nine o'clock. A glance to his watch showed eight thirty.

Jamison swore. And Mabel looked into his eyes.

"I have to be at work in half an hour."

With a yawn that ended on a smile, she murmured, "And

once again, we seem to ignore the linear process of dating. Doing the smexy first, get to know one another later?"

"It's working, isn't it?" He sat up and stretched out his muscles. Her fingers stroked down his back and tickled his backside, giving him a fierce erection. Did he really have to leave?

"We do have a date scheduled for tonight," she said. "I have work this morning, too, so I should be shuffling off along with you." She sat up. Unable to resist her breasts, he leaned over and kissed each one, taking his time so that she arched her back, asking for more. "Stop it," she said, but without any conviction. "We need to be adults and do the work stuff."

"Work stuff is no fun when all I want to do is smexy stuff."

She curled her fingers through his hair and purred. "Smexy stuff *is* more appealing. Never in my life have I played hooky from work."

"I have, but my current boss is a good man and I would never leave Straightline down one man." He kissed her and stood, regretting his loyalty. "Tonight?"

"I promise I won't leave you waiting in a bar like last night."

"You want to shower?"

"No, I'll bike home and get ready there."

She stood and gathered her clothes. Her hair spilled over her shoulder and danced across her breasts as if she were a goddess immortalized in a painting.

Jamison inhaled and forced himself to head to the bathroom. "Don't forget your tiara!" he called as he closed the door.

"See you tonight!"

He flicked on the shower. He'd just sent off a princess

with whom he would be cautious to move slowly. The last time he'd decided to go all in on a relationship it had burned him. To a crisp.

This was the longest day ever. Mabel had a list of cake decorators to contact for Layne's wedding. While the bakery in town made amazing treats, Layne wanted to go big, elegant, and have a castle-shaped cake. A big ask, but Mabel had already made a spreadsheet. After making the initial calls, she would pay some bills, go through the monthly statements, and once she made it to punch-out time, then she could breathe.

She didn't have set hours. She and Layne made their own schedules. But she was a nine-to-five girl at heart, so that would never change. And yet, she would never miss the 5:00 a.m. wakeups with a slogging journey to the subway to make it to work by eight that had been routine when she'd lived in New York. This job was a dream. Some summer evenings she worked until sunset, with an afternoon break for a dip in the pool if there were no guests enjoying it.

She tapped the keyboard, zoning out on the cake list. All she could think about was the second night she'd spent with Jamison Wright. Mr. Right? *Don't go there*. They'd yet to go on an official date! They were doing things backward, upside-down and out of order. Dance into one another's hearts. Sex. Repeat.

And why not toss a baby into the mix to make it really interesting?

"You thinking about your date tonight?" Layne, who had recovered from the sniffles, set down a stack of folded towels on the desk beside Mabel. "I know you are. You've got that dreamy look in your eyes you used to have when we were kids. Remember when we imagined who our future husbands would be and made that spell?"

Did she. She and Layne would spend long fantastical hours playing with their dolls in the old castle. They would sneak in through that one spot where a wide board swung freely on a single nail. It was a castle! How could they stay away? They'd dance across the dust-frosted ballroom floor. Dreams of princesses and knights and happily-ever-afters would always color their play.

One day—they must have been ten or eleven, and it was after they'd watched *Practical Magic*, a movie about witches living in a big white Victorian house on the sea—they'd decided to create their own spell for their future husbands. The perfect man possessed of something so extraordinary he would win their hearts instantly. But that spectacular thing had to be virtually unobtainable, otherwise the spell wouldn't work.

Into an old plastic whipped cream container, they'd gathered sweet-smelling sea lavender and yellow rocket from the banks along the shore. Popsicle sticks stained purple from their afternoon treat. A single white plastic Barbie shoe to represent Cinderella. And some kind of dirt mulch that had a worm squiggling in it just to make it witchy.

They'd cast a spell for their future husbands. Kind and handsome, Layne had suggested. Of course! But each required unique qualities only one man in the world might possess. He has to have his blood running through these castle walls, Layne said. Yes! And amazingly, Layne had gotten her wish when her true love appeared as the rightful heir to Whitmore castle.

Mabel had wished for… Hmm, what had she designated for her future husband? It had been something about stars and songs. She couldn't quite recall. Basket weaving? No.

"Earth to Mabel."

Shaking her head from the wondrous childhood memory, Mabel nudged the stack of towels. "Jamison and I had sex again last night."

Layne's mouth dropped open. Her eyes lit up. "Did you tell him about the baby?"

"Absolutely not. I…don't know how to do it."

"You have to tell him!"

"I know, but I'm still wrapping my head around it, Layne. And really, I need to go to the doctor first and then I'll have a better handle on it all."

"Have you made an appointment?"

"I'll…call today." Avoiding the doctor was her way of avoiding facing the immense life change. When faced with challenge? Bury her head in work and hope it'll work itself out. Or even, run away from it all, as she'd done when leaving her job in New York. "It'll probably be weeks before I can get in. That'll give me time to sit with this. But also, I want to get to know Jamison before I spring the news on him."

"You don't think doing the smexy is getting to know him?"

"Beyond the smexy. I only know he's a carpenter and that he likes rustic decorating and guitars. He's got maybe half a dozen in his bedroom. His place is so homey. Manly woods and earthy colors, yet so many plants it's like an arbor in the forest. I could live there."

Layne's smile said so much, and Mabel knew what she was thinking.

"But I don't live there."

And she wasn't that eager to dive into the fantasy. Much as the man needed to know he was going to be a daddy, if she were honest with herself, she was feeling some of that shame she'd felt when her boss harassed her. Had she done something wrong? Was *she* to blame for her condition now? How dare she do this to Jamison. To herself!

Not the best attitude to have, and she wasn't stupid—it took two to make a baby—but that weird feeling was right there at the surface. There was so much to deal with and most of it emotional.

"Tonight we will not have sex. We're going to talk. Get to know one another. It'll be good."

"If you say so."

"Oh, Layne, I do look forward to this baby."

"You have always wanted a dozen babies. Just don't do them all at one time. Pain!"

"Don't worry. One at a time is more my speed. And I've lowered my wild expectations from a dozen to two or three."

Layne blew out a breath. "Whew!"

"But I'm having weird feelings about all this. Will Jamison think I did this to him on purpose? Am I being pushed into domesticity? You know one of the reasons I fled Whitmore was because I didn't want to do the housewife thing like my mom."

"I know. But your mom has changed."

"Really? She seems like the same old crocheting, funeral-lunch-baking mom to me. Since when are you and my mom tight?"

"We're not. But have you seen her socials lately?"

"Her socials?" Mabel shook her head adamantly. "Madilyn Mitchell does not do social media. She still lives in the mid-twentieth century, a time period that is more fitting her own mom. Or my grandma!"

Layne rolled her eyes. "You really do need to talk to your mom, Mabel. Have you talked since the divorce?"

"Our chatter is about TV shows or the town gossip. I did help her weed the azaleas last weekend. I just don't know how to relate to her, Layne. Mom is *the* domestic goddess. I've always strived for modern sensibility."

"With a side of princess, right?" Layne laughed. "I do know the two of you tend to walk very different paths. I suppose she hasn't dared tell you."

"Tell me what?"

"Just look her up online. See what she's been up to. I'm going to refresh the towels in the ballroom bathroom. Will you have a chance to unpack the shipment from the grocer? The chef is running late this morning. I'd do it, but Jesse and I have a meeting with the florist this afternoon."

"I'll do it right now." Mabel stood and walked her friend out of the office. "You found a good one, Layne. I'm so happy for you."

"I'm not averse to a double wedding." She winked. "Get to know that man, Mabel. He could be the one! And make that gyno appointment. Today!"

As Layne walked off, Mabel hugged herself. Could Jamison be the one? He was already something. The father of her baby. Her lover. Some kind of knight who would scale a shaky trellis to place a tiara on her head.

A man who might not be happy if she didn't do what he expected of her.

Shaking her head, she chased off that shred of trauma that still clung to her. Jamison was different. He had to be. Not all men were like her former boss.

She had to get her life together. Her spreadsheets analyzing expenses, growth rate of the little tyke, best toddler learning experiences and maternity hacks currently did not forecast a place for the baby's father. She needed to work in some wiggle room should he be interested in having a column on that spreadsheet.

She tugged out her phone and scrolled through her contacts to the clinic number. This was the smart thing to do. Get a doctor's confirmation. Start vitamins and whatever else it was a pregnant woman was supposed to do.

Clicking Dial, she connected with a human immediately and made an appointment for…this afternoon. Hanging up and clutching the phone to her chest, Mabel shook her head. "No one ever gets an appointment that fast. What the…?"

If the reporter's cute little baby, Avery, had been anywhere in the room, he would have given her that knowing smile right now.

This was really happening. Mabel slid down against the nearest wall and closed her eyes.

Now she remembered the wish she'd made when she and Layne had created their witchy spell. She'd asked for a man who could weave stardust into her hair and sing to her a happily-ever-after. It had been the silliest thing. Something that could never happen, as per the movie girls who had made their impossible wishes.

And Mabel Mitchell had given up on happily-ever-afters.

Shrugging her fingers through her hair, she recalled Jamison's kisses along her neck, tickling tenderly along her jaw, whispering back to her ear and then his dive into her hair. He loved to play with her hair. Lost in his arms was the best place, holding him lost in her.

He seemed like a good man. Smart, skilled, no obvious addictions or weird habits. Dare she hope they could have something? Did she want a future with Jamison in it?

"He's going to be in it one way or another," she said.

CHAPTER FIVE

SUMMERY FLORAL CHIFFON sundress that billowed at her knees when she walked? Check. Nails painted pale pink with sparkly star decals on the tips? Check. Barest of makeup and perfect brows? Check. Hair loosely curled and hanging down with a few strands pulled back on each side? Check. Tiara?

"Would have been too much," Mabel whispered as she strolled to The Loose Lobster.

She'd told Jamison she'd meet him there because it was halfway between their respective homes.

She was going to be an adult tonight. Get to know the man! Learn his favorite color. Because that wasn't at all important, but it kept her mind on task. And no mention of a baby that her doctor had confirmed was nine weeks along. She'd left the doc's office with a list of supplements, links to websites about what happens every week and baby stuff to shop for. She lived in a one-bedroom apartment above an insurance office. Where was she going to put a baby? So much to think about!

"But not tonight. Tonight is about…"

A seek-and-learn mission. See what sort of man she'd gotten inextricably linked to for the rest of her life.

"Should have stayed in New York," she muttered as she walked toward the restaurant's entrance.

Then again, a big *no* to that one. She had made the right decision by fleeing a job that had asked far too much of her soul. And readjusting to small-town life was progressing. She didn't miss the traffic or pollution, or the crowded smelly subway. Workdays that ended at six o'clock but she never arrived home until after eight. Sharing a small apartment in Brooklyn with three other women who'd had the same dreams of making it so they never had time to even get to know one another. Ugh. And really, when had she ever thought leaving the harbor was smart? She didn't regret the move back to Whitmore.

And she didn't regret this surprise baby. Never. While it wasn't as though she were feeling her biological clock ticking at the ripe old age of twenty-eight, when she sat with it and really dug deep, she realized this timing was perfect for her.

It was just backward.

Because as much as she convinced herself she had so much to absorb and think about, her gut grabbed her and screamed, *You want to do this with a partner! You can do the single mother thing, but you don't want that.*

Mabel Mitchell wanted a family.

Was it because she'd been raised in a traditional household with loving parents and a mother who made her life as easy and blissful as possible? Sure, it was. Escaping that bliss had been... Well, she still stood by her decision to leave this town. To experience what her heart had needed to discover. If she had not, she might still be pining to learn what was out there for her. And sure, she had landed a job with a bad boss, and could have very well landed somewhere else that had suited her better. She could still be in New York.

She shook her head. Life happened for a reason. And

now she needed to follow life and see where it took her. Time to learn if Jamison Wright would qualify as good father material. At all costs, she wanted a kind man to be in her child's life. Whether she wanted him in *her* life was yet to be determined.

The taproom was dimly lit—bar lighting hid so many six-drinks-later sins—yet the patio lighting shone in, and in that beam she spotted Jamison sitting near a window. With a deep breath, and silent encouragement—*he is kind; he's not like your former boss; don't even bring that baggage into this situation*—she walked over to meet him. He stood and took her hand in his warm clasp and leaned in to kiss her on the cheek.

"You look stunning, as usual," he whispered against her ear. Another kiss to her neck sent a delicious shiver across her scalp. Their sensual connection was not a mistake at all. "But no tiara?"

Mabel sat across the table in the booth from him and set her purse aside. "You don't think the tiara would be too much for The Loose Lobster?"

He shrugged. "It's never too much on you, Cinderella."

She liked that he called her that. He had a bit of a twang to his voice that notched up his sex appeal exponentially.

"I ordered drinks for us." He slid a menu toward her. "Red wine?"

"Uh..." She had best call it quits on the alcohol. "How about an iced tea to start?"

"Not a problem." He signaled to the waitress and ordered the iced tea for her.

Since she knew the menu, Mabel ordered, and Jamison did as well. The waitress left them to chat.

Jamison's silver hair caught the patio lights like some kind of rock star standing under the spotlights. She couldn't imagine him with the dark hair he'd said he once had. The fact he was in his forties didn't bother her, but she still couldn't believe he was.

"What?" he said with a chuckle. "I know this shirt is kind of wrinkly, but I don't own an iron."

"The shirt is perfect on you." The blue cotton button-up fit him like a pair of old jeans and emphasized his solid pecs. She knew what was beneath the fabric. Rock-hard, and so touchable. She could climb him for days.

With a shake of her head to avert her wandering attention, she thanked the waitress who dropped off her iced tea. "Your whole style is so easy and yet remarkable with that eye-catching hair," she said to him. "It's definitely you."

"You don't feel like you're on a date with an old man?"

"Well, I am, aren't I? We are…twelve years apart in age."

"More like fourteen. I said I was in my forties. I'm forty-two."

She chuckled to briefly think when she'd been a teenager on a babysitting job, Jamison could have been the parents' age. But now? What was a little difference in age? "Doesn't bother me. And you certainly don't act like an old man between the sheets."

He winked and she fell into his smooth charm. Falling, surrendering, not caring about anything but his regard. Why was it so easy to be with him? Like he didn't require her to be anything but Mabel. Never would the man insist she put out to maintain her job or even status in his life.

"So you walked here?" he asked.

"Of course. I live in the center of town above the insurance shop. Not far from here."

"You didn't want to live in the castle?"

"No room for me. Layne was already living in the carriage house when I moved back. I had to be in the city. Even though said city is a small town with a postmaster who is pushing ninety but seems to know everyone's names."

"Right, the big-city girl come home to...what, exactly? Are you here for good?"

So the learning would begin.

Mabel sipped her tea. "I think so. Whitmore holds a lot of great childhood memories for me. And much as I love big cities, I can't disregard the simple pleasures of living on the harbor and picking blueberries and eating them until you get a stomachache."

"I've heard the blueberries are amazing."

"You haven't been to a patch? That's going to be our second date!"

"You're already in for date number two? I must be doing something right."

She reached across the table and they clasped hands. "You are. We seem to have connected. Intensely."

"I'll say."

"But it's on a physical level. I want to know who Jamison Wright is. I only know you're a carpenter who has lived here a year, and you have family in Montana."

"What else is there to know?"

"You've lived forty-two years. Lots, I suspect."

"Okay, shoot me the rapid questions for the win."

The waitress dropped off their food. Lobster rolls, fresh corn and mussels. It looked delicious, but it smelled...

Mabel gasped a breath. As a Maine native, she'd always loved lobster, but tonight the seafood odor did not sit right with her. She sipped at her tea and refocused while Jamison dug in.

"Rapid questions?" she said. "Okay. Only child?"

"Yes. Me and my dad were close. Still are. We talk on the phone a lot. He taught me carpentry."

"That's so cool." Mabel loved her dad but his distance because of his long work hours had never made for a close relationship. Now that he lived in Norway, they did email to keep each other updated on their lives. A baby news email was in her near future. "Hobbies?"

"Beachcombing, collecting guitars, songwriting and eating this lobster. Man, this stuff is amazing. You're not eating?"

"I…will. I'm not as hungry as I thought." She picked up the half corncob and tried that. Buttery and sweet and… she could not look at the seafood without feeling her stomach lurch. "Ever married?"

"Nope."

"Children?"

"Not yet." He swiped a hand along his jaw, rubbing his beard for a moment. Apprehensive? "I'd love to be a father someday. But I'd better hurry, eh? I'm not getting any younger."

Where to go with that one? One obvious place. Yet, she was feeling woozy. She set down the corn and wiped her hands on the napkin.

"Next question?" he asked.

Yes, something to swerve her out of the strange hole she toed the edge of falling into. He wanted to be a father? Good for her! But babies were off topic until she learned more. What could she ask that was mundane? "Favorite color?"

"Oh, come on, darling. You care little about that."

He wasn't wrong. Did men even care about colors?

Oh, Mabel, you have to tell him. He's given you the perfect opportunity.

Was it too late to dash? To rewind and start over? Retrace her steps back to the night of the ball and… No, she couldn't imagine having never danced under the moonlight with Jamison. And making love with him.

What were they talking about? Right. She was getting to know him.

"Do you plan to live in Whitmore for a while?"

He pushed a mussel shell on his plate with a fork, silent. Unwilling to answer? Or he knew the answer and didn't think she'd like it?

"Mabel." He set down the fork and leaned back against the booth. "My parents want me to move to Montana and build on their property."

"Build…them a house?"

"No, a house for myself. Move there permanently."

"Oh." That answered her question as to whether he could be in her child's life. And it bothered her—because how dare he not participate?

Mabel! He doesn't even know he's the father of your child.

He swiped a palm along his jaw. That was the sexiest salt-and-pepper stubble ever. Running her fingers over it was also the best thing to do. And if he moved to Montana, she'd never have a chance to do it again.

"When do you plan to move?" Her stomach performed a queasy jiggle.

"Not sure. I…uh… I'm at odds with the decision."

"Why is that?"

"Because I'm sitting across the table from a princess I'd never expected to dance into my life and turn it upside-down. Mabel, I want to get to know you with stupid questions as well. Because…can we have a thing?"

"A thing?"

"I don't know where this is going."

"Obviously nowhere if you intend to move."

And really? How could she tell him about the baby now?

She pulled the napkin from her lap and set it on the table. The world began to wobble. She would not be that woman who forced a man into anything. Not even if he was the father…

"Are you okay, Mabel? You don't look well."

"I do feel dizzy. Excuse me." She got up and rushed to the restroom.

Jamison wanted to hold Mabel's hand as they walked side by side toward her apartment that was three blocks east. But she clutched her arms across her chest and shook her head. She'd come out of the bathroom looking paler than when she'd gone in. Had said the lobster smell didn't agree with her.

Fair enough. It alleviated some of the guilt he felt at having told her he had plans to move. Already, he was beginning to question that decision. He shouldn't make a choice until he got to know Mabel better.

Because he wanted to know everything about her. And if lobster made her sick, then he'd never take her to The Loose Lobster again. He hated to see her feeling unwell. When he couldn't bear it any longer, he wrapped an arm around her shoulders. Her body melded against his as they walked slowly. It felt good to know she wanted to be close to him.

Or was it simply that she was feeling weak and needed the support?

"You going to make it?" he asked.

She nodded. "Sorry."

"Don't apologize. I get the same way if I even look at liver."

"Oh, don't talk about food, please."

"Sorry. It's just ahead, right?"

She quickened her pace. The date was ending. It hadn't even been a date. She'd gotten in a few questions for him. Nothing about who he had once been, though. Did she not know who he really was? How was that possible?

When he'd been at the height of fame, his face had been plastered on all the socials, magazines and awards shows. Of course, it could be ego expecting too much from Mabel. Sure, there were people who didn't know him. Wasn't like he could name every famous person out there.

Once in front of the insurance building, Mabel nodded toward the stairs that hugged the side of the brick facade. "I'm up there. I can't believe I'm being a date crasher."

"Don't worry about it, Cinderella. We'll have a do-over. If you want one?"

"Of course, I do. That is, if you want one."

"Couldn't keep me away from you if you tried."

Her smile was small and weak. He kissed her forehead. Oh, that flower-candy smell. "Can I help you up the stairs?"

"No, I'm good. I'll text you to go blueberry picking with me. How's that for a date redo?"

"Look forward to it."

She winced and started up the stairs slowly. "Gotta go! Try to remember me with a tiara and stars in my eyes, not ready to puke!"

"That's the most romantic thing a girl has ever said to me!" he called after her.

She laughed as she opened her door. "You're too easy! Good night!"

Her door closed and he chuckled. She was beautiful. Smart. And something he couldn't get enough of. And he...wasn't being completely honest with her. She had to know who he was. Right?

He scuffed his fingers through his hair. He had become virtually unrecognizable since he'd grayed. It was possible she didn't know. Would she be interested in a former country rock star who had hit the pinnacle and then fallen hard?

The big-city girl with dreams of finding her place in small-town America didn't strike him as someone particularly interested in the detritus of superstardom. But that wasn't him anymore.

He whistled a tune that felt new to him. Kind of crazy. He hadn't whistled in a while. His muse had fled the day he walked away from it all.

Jamison glanced up toward Mabel's apartment. One light shone through a small window.

"A crown of rhinestones dances in her hair..."

Eh. It wasn't terrible, as lyrics went.

CHAPTER SIX

WHY DID THEY call it morning sickness if it struck at night?

After a refreshing morning shower, Mabel pulled on her robe and wandered out of the bathroom. She no longer felt queasy as she had last night. What a bust that date had been! One sniff of the lobster roll and she hadn't lasted long. If Jamison had any interest in her at all, he did need to see her at her worst. And she had showed him a bit of that last night.

On the other hand, how interested could he possibly be? He was moving to Montana.

Settling onto the sofa and picking up the tea she'd set aside to cool before her shower, she sipped the spicy cinnamon and ginger brew. She smoothed a palm over her stomach. So the father of her child was taking off, never to be seen again? Might she change his mind by telling him about the baby?

Mabel sighed.

She didn't want to influence Jamison to change his life course by playing the baby card. That would be manipulative. Besides, she'd not thought it completely through. She may decide being a single mother was completely doable. Her best option.

The man had spurred into action when she'd returned to the table and stated she had to leave. Cash laid on the table, he'd offered to summon a cab but she'd protested, saying the walk home might clear her head. She hadn't wanted him to touch her. Then when he had, she couldn't believe she'd resisted his strong, protective embrace.

In that moment, she'd felt it was all going to work out. Those dreams she'd had as a kid were going to come true. The hero may possibly exist. Though all he'd done was kiss her hair and nuzzle into it. And climb a trellis to place a tiara on her head. And seduce her into his bed. Twice. And...make a baby with her.

Another sip of the spicy tea warmed her throat. Peering out the window, she followed the tree line on the opposite side of the harbor that dashed a jagged emerald under the pale sky.

"It is lovely here," she decided. Much nicer than the constant bustle of the big city. "Maybe the coffee shop will start delivering if I ask them nicely?"

A knock on her door startled her. Mabel tugged her robe sash and wandered over to answer it, which revealed a lush bouquet of pink roses. There had to be dozens!

"How you feeling?" Jamison lowered the bouquet and granted her a sexy smile that should be broadcast on billboards. Thankfully, this one was only for her.

"Much better. I...didn't expect you?"

"I texted."

She glanced to her phone on the counter behind her. "Missed it. I was in the shower. Come in. I'm not sure I have a vase big enough for these. They're so pretty!"

"Got 'em in the shop across the street. I bought all the pink ones because they're the color of your cheeks."

She found a vase to contain the three dozen roses. Jamison peeled away the plastic wrapper and set them inside, then took to filling it with water. Taking control of things? She liked it. And not red roses, which she would take as a love thing. Or white, which meant something like true love? She wasn't sure. Pink felt just right for where they were at in this relationship. Which wasn't really a relationship if he was going to move away...

You'll be connected to him for the rest of your life.

Mabel's heart wanted that connection. But her brain contained a pie chart that showed how men liked to control women. Jamison had not given her any indication that he would have such controlling tendencies but she had to be cautious.

Screw logic. All of a sudden she couldn't resist, so she swung around the counter and wrapped her arms around Jamison's neck and kissed him. "Thank you. I've never been given flowers before."

"You're kidding me? Cinderella, you deserve all the flowers in the town. Every single blossom blooming on the countryside. And even the fake ones graffitied on the side of the urgent care center."

She loved the graffiti that the town had decided not to sandblast away because the artist had painted the design after losing his new wife to cancer.

Jamison kissed her, and in the process lifted her and carried her into the living room before setting her down. She tucked her head against his shoulder and they swayed. Behind them, Mouse meowed and headed for his favorite window seat where she kept a bird feeder suctioned to the outside of the window.

"Dancing with my princess," Jamison sing-songed against her hair. "She doesn't realize her robe slipped open..."

Mabel tilted her head back to meet his dancing gaze. "Oh, yeah? I did realize that, smart guy."

"So this..." he ran his fingertips along her robe lapel,

slowing as he crested the curve of her breast "...isn't an accidental seduction?"

"I never do anything accidentally."

Well. She caught her breath at the back of her throat. Just one major thing. That they weren't going to discuss, because right now his shirtsleeve brushing her bare breasts did not preach patience.

"Do you have to work today?" she managed. A glide of his finger under her breast drew up a gasp. And when he cupped her, she almost lost it.

"Day off." He slid a hand around her back and the movement tugged the robe from her shoulder. "Are you thinking what I'm thinking?"

That they seemed to magnetically attract to one another physically despite not having connected on an emotional level? Most definitely.

Mabel had a brief thought that in her bedroom she'd left the laptop open to her spreadsheet. The baby spreadsheet.

She pushed Jamison to land on the couch. Then she dropped her robe to the floor.

His grin rivaled that of a spoiled cat. "Come here, Cinderella."

They had plans to pick blueberries today, so when a few hours later Jamison stood from the couch where they'd made love, laughed and made love again, he was about to ask to use the shower but it felt intrusive. Even though they could not keep their hands off one another, they still barely knew the other.

"I'm going to run home and shower and then pick you up for our blueberry adventure. How does that sound?"

Mabel lay on the couch, naked, looking a goddess

draped in a pink and yellow crochet blanket. "Perfect. But let's not do lunch."

"Still feeling queasy from last night?"

"No, I'm good. I just want to save room for all the blueberries on which I plan to gorge myself. Meet me out front in an hour?"

"I'm already counting the minutes." He blew her a kiss and left the goddess in repose.

An hour later, he met Mabel, kissed her soundly and they strolled hand in hand toward the blueberry field about a mile out of town. The farm was privately owned and it was peak blueberry season. If he got to spend the day with Mabel, then he was all for squatting in some random field assuming bear watch.

"They don't often get bears here," Mabel said as she unfolded and laid down the kneeling pad she'd toted along. The field had provided a basket for the berries. She began plucking the tiny blue jewels, eating them.

"What's your definition of often?" he wondered. "Once a decade?"

"Once every few weeks?"

He wasn't afraid of much in life, but turning to find a bear breathing down his neck didn't sound like an adventure. Jamison kept his stance to kneeling upright, his eyes sweeping the field dotted with dozens of pickers.

"You keeping bear watch?" she asked. It seemed 50 percent of her pick made it into the basket and the other half into her mouth. "Good man. Look!"

He sighted the swarm of dragonflies she pointed out. Their wings glinted iridescently under the sunlight. "A dazzle of dragonflies," he said. "Dancing on the sunshine."

"Have I told you how poetic you are?"

She had, and…she did need to know the truth about

him. Soon. Because he was already wondering if a move to Montana was the right thing for him. Yet if he stayed here in Whitmore, there had to be a good reason. Could he trust Mabel with his tattered heart?

"How much do we need for a pie?" he asked. The day was warm but slightly overcast. No wind, the hint of salt breezing in from the sea. Perfect.

"Are you determined to make a pie?"

"I'd try anything once to see you smile."

"I think you've already mastered that one."

"You do smile when you orgasm," he agreed.

"And you make a face." She made a funny face.

Jamison tossed a blueberry at her. And she caught it in her mouth! "That wasn't as effective an attack as I wanted it to be."

"I'm a champion blueberry catcher. The town holds a tournament for kids during the blueberry festival."

The woman was a marvel. It was so easy to be with her. But what other secret talents did she possess? "So now's my turn to ask you some questions."

"Go for it. Every one I answer, you have to toss me a blueberry."

"Deal." He picked a handful and flung them into the basket. "Favorite color?"

"Seriously?"

"We're starting out easy."

"Blue."

"I should have known the girl with the Gibson guitar eyes would love blue."

"Guitar eyes?"

"My favorite guitar is the same color as your eyes. A soft faded blue that has little flecks of mica in it that make it twinkle."

"You play guitar? I suppose. You do own a lot of them. Why is that?"

"I'm the one asking the questions."

He tossed a blueberry toward her and she caught it in her mouth again. The woman did have a talent. He wasn't sure how she'd feel about *his* talent and how that had shaped his past. He carried a lot of baggage. But he also wasn't sure how to make the big reveal because she obviously had no clue who he really was. And if he moved, well then, not even necessary.

"One book you could read over and over?"

She answered quickly, *"The Three Musketeers."*

"You like the swashbuckling stuff?"

"It's the first big novel I read when I was a kid. Might have been what fueled my fantasies about castles and heroes and all that adventure jazz."

"You've known Layne since you were kids?"

She opened her mouth and pointed to it. Jamison tossed another blueberry her way, which she caught.

"Probably since about three or four," she said. "Our dads worked together at the fishery. Our moms were never close. My mom, in particular, was a homebody. She was always satisfied to be a homemaker."

"And you…won't be?"

"I want to raise a family, for sure." She paused and jiggled some berries on her palm, teasing them with a fingertip. "But I'm not certain being *just* a mom and washing the clothes and cooking the meals will be satisfying for me. I've always wanted more."

"A career? Isn't motherhood a career in itself?"

"I suppose. But, well…" She sighed. "My parents divorced a few years ago. My dad chose a promotion at work, and moving to Norway, over mom. She told me they had fallen out of love and that they were both okay with the decision. Weird, isn't it?"

Jamison shrugged. "People fall out of love all the time." And sometimes they realize it was never even love in the first place.

"After thirty years of marriage?"

"I don't think it's my place to tell you how to feel about something so personal to you. Did it hurt you?"

"It did. More so than I believe it bothered my mom. She seems so accepting of losing a lifestyle she created over decades."

"Maybe she's more sad than she's willing to tell you?"

She stirred her fingers in the basket of blueberries. "Maybe. I still haven't worked up the courage to have a good heart-to-heart talk with her. Let's go on to the next question."

"Okay, some mommy issues there. I can relate."

"I thought you and your parents got along? If you're planning to move onto their land?"

"It's just an option at the moment."

"Oh, I thought you'd made a decision."

"That decision is not final. There's something more interesting that is attracting my focus lately." He tossed a blueberry her way, but she wasn't ready and it pinged her on the forehead.

"Hey!"

"One point for me," he declared.

"Fair enough. Our basket is almost full. I'll be eating blueberries on yogurt for a week!"

"How about pancakes with blueberry syrup?"

"Or blueberry brownies?"

Jamison screwed up his face. She laughed. "Here in Maine we make everything with blueberries, including vodka!"

"We're going to need another basket if we intend to make all that."

"Do you want to make stuff when we get back? Together?"

The innocence in that question grabbed him by the heart and squeezed. She wanted to spend time with him? Nice.

"I'll go get another basket," he said.

"Do that."

And with a periphery scan for bears, Jamison marched back to the main entrance to claim more time spent with his rhinestone Cinderella.

"Mom!"

Strolling the field in search of a new patch to plop down her kneeling pad, Mabel bumped into a woman who was filming herself with her phone. She seemed to be explaining something. And when the woman spun around, she gaped at the sight of her.

"Mabel! What are you doing here?"

"Isn't it obvious?" Mabel held up the basket of blueberries. "But what are you doing here? Alone? In a...retro dress that looks like something off the cover of an old women's magazine?"

Madilyn Mitchell smoothed her palm down the green-and-white-checked dress that flared out at the hips and was cuffed at the short sleeves. "Oh, it's just something I pulled out of the closet, dear. You know I like the vintage style."

She did. Another thing that had cemented Mabel's resentment toward her mother being content as simply a housewife. Why did she have to look like something out of an old magazine that advertised how useful women should be to their men? Had she never felt threatened by a man?

"You're here alone, too," Madilyn Mitchell noted. "Where's Layne?"

"Off with Jesse. Putting together wedding preparations."

"Oh, sweetie, do you feel neglected?"

"Not at all. Layne found her Prince Charming. I'm happy for her. But what are you doing standing in the middle of a blueberry field, in a dress, and who are you talking to?"

"Huh? Oh. It's just..." Her mom tucked the phone in a pocket of her dress. "Just taking some audio notes, dear. I've been busy. Making content."

"Making...content?" Mabel swiped a stray bit of hair over her ear. "Layne mentioned something about you having a social media page? What does that mean?"

Her mom laughed. "It's a little project. I've always followed you and your dad on the socials. After the divorce, I decided to start my own thing. It makes me happy."

Mabel tilted her head curiously. It was a stretch to consider her mom putting herself out there on social media. But a little account with family photos didn't seem so terrible. If it was something she used to help her overcome the emotional pain of the divorce, she couldn't argue that, either. That dress, though. It did work on her mom.

"You look nice today, Mom."

"Oh? Thank you, Mabel. You...never compliment me."

"I don't?"

Her mom shook her head, then patted Mabel's hand. "Are you okay? Everything working out with the castle job? How are you getting along living above the insurance building?"

"I'm good."

She should tell her about the pregnancy, but—Jamison was next in line to know. It only seemed fair.

"Settling back into Whitmore has been easier than expected. I'm not sure what I ever saw in New York."

"I blame it on that *Sex and the City* show. You loved following those women's adventures. But you had to make the leap. To discover for yourself. You've always been ambitious, dear."

"And look where that got me."

"That record label did not deserve someone so smart as you. You were wise to leave the moment that man laid a hand on you."

She had told her mom about her boss's advances. And his threats to fire her if those advances were not followed through. Not in person, but over a phone call, which was how she felt most comfortable talking to her mom.

"Thanks, Mom." Mabel glanced across the field. Jamison was nowhere in sight. He'd probably returned to their original picking spot. She didn't want to introduce her mom to him today. Her life was too disordered to add to it a worried mom. "I was just looking for a good patch," she said.

"Well, this area is picked," Madilyn said. "I'm heading home. Have to put the roast in the oven. Do you want to stop by for dinner?"

"Oh, uh…" Why was she making an entire roast for herself? But again, until she got right with this baby thing, she wasn't prepared to sit at the dinner table and keep it a secret. Besides, she intended to extend this date through the evening. "I have a thing later."

"Oh, sure, dear. You always do. Well, I'm heading out. Text me!"

Her mom took off with a basket in hand, skirts swaying above the berry patch, and a wave to a couple she knew from church.

You always do.

Guilt crushed Mabel's heart. Yes, she'd always tried to avoid spending time with her mom. Busy, independent career girl, don't you know? Can't be seen talking to the out-of-touch-with-the-times mom. Though lately, Mabel was growing comfortable sitting alongside her as they tended the garden. Or one evening, they'd shared fresh-baked muffins and laughed over an episode of *Brooklyn Housewives*.

"Text me?" Mabel muttered. When had her mom ever communicated in twenty-first-century terms? "Who stole my mom?"

"What's that?"

She turned into Jamison's arms. With a glance over her shoulder, Mabel was assured that her mom would not be looking back to see her daughter in the arms of a slightly older, incredibly sexy man.

"Uh…that woman dressed like an ad for a fifties diner was my mom. She's…different," she said with a wonder that surprised her.

"You didn't want to introduce me?"

"I…uh… Are you eager to meet my mom?"

"I don't know. I guess it makes sense since we're doing things backward. Sex, parents, get to know one another?"

"Let's keep the parents to the side for now. I spy another patch over there. We can fill this new basket, then head home for a cooking session."

"Sounds weirdly exciting."

He found the patch and began to fill the basket, while Mabel had to wonder what was wrong with the man. Seriously. He seemed too perfect. Something had to be bizarre, disturbing or downright wrong with him. Otherwise, she may have found her Mr. Right.

She had, actually, found Mr. Wright.

CHAPTER SEVEN

"I did protect you from bears," Jamison said as they scraped their plates clean of blueberry syrup, melted butter and the crumbly remnants of fluffy pancakes. "So… I guess that means you wash the dishes?"

"Seriously?" Mabel shoved her plate across the counter and turned to give him a tender punch to his bicep. "I could have taken a bear."

"Probably, with a right hook like that. Ouch."

She laughed at his mocked pain. And sure, she wouldn't dream of not washing the dishes. He had made the syrup and the pancakes. From a mix. But still.

"Don't worry, I've been commandeering Cinderella duties at the castle as we prepared to open. I can handle a few plates." She swung around the counter, but he followed. "I got this."

"I want to help."

"I thought you had plans for the rest of the berries?"

They glanced to the two baskets of berries. What they'd used for the syrup had barely made a dent. Must be over a gallon remaining.

"I think our stomachs are bigger than our cooking expertise," Jamison said. "I don't see us making blueberry comfort—what was that called?"

"Custard." They'd searched Pinterest for recipes. "And

no, I'm not a big cook. My mom would certainly know what to do with all these. I suppose we could freeze them. I've got some freezer baggies in that cupboard. Get to work!"

"Anything you desire, I will do."

"Anything?" She scrubbed a plate with the dish brush under warm water. "Practical or sexual?"

He slid up behind her, tangled his fingers in the ends of her hair and whispered at her ear, "I like both."

"Same. But not until those berries are washed and frozen."

"But, Ma, this is going to take forever," he whined like a frustrated kid.

Mabel laughed, but she couldn't ignore being called *Ma*. She had to tell him! "I'll help as soon as the dishes are clean. Why don't you flip on that old-fashioned stereo that came with the apartment and we can dance while we work?"

Jamison found a station that played '90s tunes. He performed some dance moves to a Backstreet Boys song that sent Mabel into peals of laughter.

An hour later, they'd sung favorite songs out loud, performed more than a few twirls and dips in the kitchen, and the berries had been tucked away in the freezer. They might last for years. Or for three or four pies if she could convince her mom to make some.

At that moment, thunder echoed and a streak of lightning flashed outside. The sky had darkened noticeably.

"I love a good thunderstorm." She tilted her head to catch the next song. "This is the perfect tune."

"You a Swiftie?"

"Always and forever. Mm, I love dancing with you." Their bodies hugged. Hands clasped. Her head tilted on his shoulder, his strong heartbeats echoed against her breast. "I feel like we both wanted that night of the ball to last forever."

"Forever," he said at the same time she did. "There's nothing stopping us from trying for forever."

"Yeah?" Even with an insta-baby in the mix? "What about that part where you intend to move to Montana? That kind of cuts everything abruptly short."

"Haven't made up my mind on that, Cinderella."

So there was yet hope she could snag him to stay here and start a family with her? What was she thinking? She didn't need to snag the man. And she would not play the baby card to manipulate their situation. Mabel Mitchell was perfectly capable of being a single mom. But that didn't mean she couldn't enjoy some physical contact in the process.

"You know," she said with consideration, "Cinderella should have never married the prince."

"Why do you say that?" He spun her out and then back into his arms so they swayed before the window that flashed intermittently with lightning.

"Well, the prince found her glass slipper. Then he had to run all around town, trying it on every woman to see if it would fit. I mean, didn't the guy remember what she looked like? She didn't change that much after her fairy godmother's spell fell away. Seems like the prince was a special kind of stupid."

Jamison's laughter rumbled against her body, and she pressed against him tighter, clutching his warmth and inhaling his blueberry-syrup scent.

"I suppose you're right," he said. "But just remember, I found the owner of the tiara on the first try."

"You are not a stupid man."

"Pretty sure I'm the luckiest guy on this earth right now. I'm holding you in my arms. Doesn't get much better than that."

The music changed to a bouncier tune that sounded like Elvis. Jamison nodded his head to the beat and spun her out as if to do a jive move.

"Oh, I don't know much more than slow dancing and the waltz," she protested. "But you can swivel those hips all you like. You've got rhythm."

He stopped dancing and raked his fingers through his hair. "Aw, darling, you really don't know who I am, do you?"

"What do you mean?" All of a sudden her heart pounded. Who was he supposed to be? Was he hiding something from her? Behind him, lightning flashed. This suddenly felt wrong in a weird way. "Jamison, you're freaking me. Who are you?"

He smirked and shook his head. "It's nothing to worry over, Mabel. I just… I used to be a singer."

"Oh?" That wasn't terrible or worrisome. Yet, his posture segued to a more guarded stance, thumbs hooked in his pockets and head bowed. "Like boy band stuff? You really do have some rhythm in your hips. Why does it feel like it's not something you want me to know about?"

"I don't mind you knowing. It's just…it was real nice being just Jamison with you. Not having my history hanging over me for you to judge."

"I would never…" Judge him? For what? Had he been someone famous?

Jamison's phone rang and he gestured to it.

"Yes, take it," she said, feeling the romantic mood had dissolved. What was he hiding that he hadn't wanted to reveal to her? His history? Something she would judge?

He walked into the kitchen, talking and agreeing that he could be there in fifteen minutes. After he ended the call, he turned to her and winced. "Sorry. Chester Brady, the owner of the record shop has a leak in his roof. Sounds like a downpour is coming through. He needs some help."

"But it's your day off."

"I know. And we are on a date. I shouldn't go, but… all those records."

It could prove an immense loss should the shop take on water damage. And she wouldn't keep Jamison from helping a friend. "It's not a problem. We can pick this up tomorrow night. I'll make dinner?"

"I'd like that." He kissed her and held her for a long moment. Was it possible for two people to sync heartbeats? Felt like it. "It's hard to walk away from you, Mabel."

She wanted to say, *Then don't*, but she didn't want Chester to be in the lurch with wet inventory.

"Maybe you can come back after you've helped Chester?"

"We'll see how long it takes, and if I have to fight the rain while I'm at it." He kissed her on the head and collected his phone, then walked to the door. Opening it, he paused and said, "Look up RJ Wright. That's the name I used as a singer. Then you'll learn about who I used to be. It's only fair you know everything."

"Oh? Thanks. I will." She hadn't heard that name before. Or had she? Why couldn't he just tell her now? "You make it sound dire, Jamison."

"It's not. It's just…not who I am anymore. Well. I am a songwriter. Always have been. Always will be. I'll text you later, depending on how long this takes?"

"Deal. Thanks for the blueberry date."

"Next up is sailing."

"I'm in!"

He blew her a kiss and left.

Mabel hugged herself—then went to her laptop and typed in *RJ Wright*.

It was midnight when Jamison finally had a chance to text Mabel. Standing in the front area of the record shop, he typed an apology and promised to make their sailing date tomorrow.

Behind him, Chester wrung water from a towel into a five-gallon bucket. Jamison had climbed onto the roof and secured a tarp. About all he could do in the storm. It would hold and keep the rain from seeping through. He'd return tomorrow to do the job right. A few joists may require replacement and a section of Sheetrock for sure. He'd helped Chester to move the heavy standing wood bins of records to get them out of splatter range.

Mabel hadn't texted back. It was late. But…

He winced. Had she researched RJ Wright?

He was proud of the success RJ had achieved and the music he'd put out into the world. He wasn't proud of a few of the other things the media had latched on to and blown out of proportion. They'd made it sound like his record company had given him the boot when it had been RJ who'd decided to leave after the unjust contract demands and downright skeevy expectations his manager and other industry professionals had foisted on him.

As well, RJ had had enough after the baby-daddy thing. He had been played. Would Mabel learn about that when researching him? It wasn't something he'd hidden. Though it hadn't gotten a lot of press thanks to Clementine's press agent who had kept a tight rein on the details—until she had decided to go big.

His soul had been tainted by his experience with Clementine. It hadn't taken but a few hours to accept her announcement, let it settle into his soul and realize it was something he could embrace. He'd wanted to be that baby's father. To start a family! He had begun imagining a life with that child, taking it to the park, building a swing set, teaching him or her to swim. And to sing and dance and make music.

Yet, he hadn't loved Clementine.

"I've got cash."

Jamison turned to find Chester stood beside him, sorting through his wallet. "No way, man. When I return to fix the joists and Sheetrock, then you can pay that bill. Tonight is on the house."

"That's too generous."

"Eh. You always do me good on the LPs. That Elvis vinyl was like new."

"I've got my eye out for the Pink Floyd first press you requested. I'll find it."

"I'm sure you will." He shook Chester's hand. "I'll return tomorrow afternoon to look everything over and give you an estimate. Deal?"

"You're a good man, Wright. Thanks."

"I'll talk to you later, Chester."

Jamison exited out the front entrance and Chester locked up from inside. The shop lights blinked out, leaving Jamison standing in the dull glow of a streetlight. The rain had settled to a mist and the salted air felt crisp.

Hopping in his work truck, he headed for the beach house.

How could Mabel have not known who he was?

Although, if she wasn't a country music fan, it was likely she wouldn't have a clue. Wasn't like he knew what was going on with Taylor Swift—okay, everyone knew about her. But he got it. The country rock singer RJ Wright may have never been on Mabel's radar.

Tomorrow he would be. He didn't want to scare off his Cinderella. And as much as he tried to be cautious, for his heart's sake, he wasn't sure how to hold on to something so precious as living, breathing stardust.

CHAPTER EIGHT

MABEL WOKE SPRAWLED on her bed, realizing with a yawn she'd fallen asleep last night still dressed. After the abrupt end to her and Jamison's blueberry date, she'd taken out her laptop and…

She rolled over and spied the laptop, still open, the screen dark. But she knew what she'd see if she tapped a key to wake it up: Jamison's face.

Or rather RJ Wright's face. A man who once wore his dark brown hair straight and to his elbows. No beard or moustache. But those same captivating blue eyes. Had she known the country music singer, she still may have never pinned him at the ball. The short silver hair had changed his look drastically.

His real name was Robert Jamison Wright, but in the music industry he'd simply been known as RJ. Occasionally, they'd tack the Wright onto his name. Not being a fan of country music, she hadn't heard of him, along with 95 percent of the rest of the country music singers. Though when she'd searched through some of his songs, she had recognized the chorus of one that had hit number one years ago. An anthem frequently played in bars across America. Everyone would raise their glasses and chime in on the chorus—"Cheers to all of us!"—which was a tribute to the working class, the farmers, the downtrodden and the rednecks. Anyone could relate to a song like that.

Except perhaps, a woman who at the time had been focused on rising within the ranks at a fancy record label. Who had a goal to get a swanky New York apartment like Carrie Bradshaw in *Sex and the City*. All the clothes. All the shoes. All the fun of big-city living. That had been a fiction she could never touch. Mr. Big had never shown up, either.

"You can take the girl out of the small town," she whispered, thinking about her experience in New York, "but I guess you can't take the small town out of the girl."

At least she'd tried it out. That had to count for something. Her dreams hadn't been quashed; they'd just been rerouted. Modified. She'd come to realize Mabel Mitchell wasn't cut out for the big-city life. Or more accurately, for handsy bosses.

Yet, now she found herself intermingled in an interesting blend of small town and lost superstardom. She hadn't expected the man she was dating—and the father of her child—whom she thought was a carpenter, to be an entertainer. Former entertainer.

It was a lot to take in. And she hadn't done much more research than surf a few pages when she'd dozed off. She was tiring so easily lately. To be expected.

A tap of the keys brought up a page that featured Jamison's—RJ's—bio. A carpenter, who'd had a songwriting hobby on the side. He'd posted one of his songs to SingSong and it went viral, hitting number one immediately. A record company signed him. He released an album. Toured across the world. Another album. Some videos. Mention of a paternity scandal. Then, a few years ago, he put out a song called "The Devil's Deal" on his own, posting it to SingSong just as he had with his first song. His record label had been furious and dropped him. And RJ walked away from it all.

Mabel searched for the song "The Devil's Deal." The search engine brought it up but most of the links were broken or led to a page that stated *no longer available*. As if someone had tried to erase it entirely. Certainly, things could go missing online, but completely?

She scrolled some more, thinking to find it on RJ's SingSong profile...

"Wait. Paternity scandal?"

Mabel scrolled back and reread the article on an entertainment site. Just a few paragraphs. Jamison had been involved in...

"Is he already someone's dad?"

That couldn't be right. He had said he would like to be a father *someday*, which had led her to believe he was not one already. Was that a detail he'd kept hidden from her just as his musical career?

"He wasn't hiding it," she whispered.

Just as she wanted to take her time before telling him about the baby, perhaps he had decided to take his time revealing his truths. Yet, it could have been something he slipped in along with "I'm a carpenter but used to be a singer." Right?

They were, after all, doing this dating thing backward.

The paternity detail pumped adrenaline through her veins. She searched for more info. How could someone who'd had number one songs and been a star in the music industry have so little about him online? Almost as if it had been erased. But that wasn't possible, was it? Not unless he had a very powerful PR team behind him. And it wasn't because he was not famous. After that number one hit, RJ had put out an album that went platinum.

Finally, she landed on a journalist's site that listed a short article titled "RJ Wright's Lover Gives Birth to Another Man's Child."

"What the...?"

It continued to say that RJ and Clementine Connor, a backup dancer who had toured with a hip-hop singer, were rumored to be engaged. The article was dated three years ago. And it had a link to a larger article in *People* magazine, which Mabel clicked immediately.

There were baby pictures and a photo of an elegantly styled beautiful woman with red hair and elaborate eyeshadow. It detailed that Connor had stayed out of the spotlight during her pregnancy. Paparazzi hadn't a single shot of her baby belly. It had all been very hush-hush. After she gave birth, she'd announced the baby was actually RJ's manager's child. RJ, her apparent boyfriend of almost a year, walked out on her. Or to read another take on it, Clementine had packed her things and left RJ because she'd always known it wasn't his child.

Mabel rolled to her back and stared up at the ceiling. This was unsettling information. Why hadn't she known about it...? Wait. There had been that one time early after she'd been hired at Xtatic that she'd heard something about a country singer being burned with a paternity accusation. Had that been RJ? Mabel hadn't paid much attention to the news. There were so many singers and entertainers. Every day a new scandal. A person couldn't keep track of all of it.

So Jamison had thought he was going to be a father and then...after the birth had found out it wasn't his? Had the woman, Clementine, been fooling him the entire time? According to the article, she knew who the baby's father was the whole time. Had never fooled RJ into thinking it was his.

It sounded sketchy to Mabel. A man like Jamison allowing a woman carrying another man's child to stay in a relationship with him? Didn't jibe.

On the other hand, he was very kind. Perhaps he'd wanted to ensure she had a safe and accepting place for both her and the baby?

But on the other hand… Mabel had run out of hands. Poor Jamison. To have gone through such a thing! It must have been an emotional nightmare.

And now…

Mabel did something she didn't often do, and that was to swear.

"How can I tell him now?"

Not sure how to feel about this new information, she made a sudden dash for the bathroom. This urgent-need-to-pee thing was new. She anticipated that the next months of her life would involve bathroom dashes, weird cravings and—she'd gotten pregnant by a country music singer who had trust issues because of the very same situation? No wonder he hadn't been able to come right out and tell her about it. He must feel as protective about his history as—well, as she did about telling him about the baby.

While washing her hands, she contemplated what a strange flip her life had taken since moving back home from New York. She'd gained employment at the castle of her dreams. Her best friend had found the hero of her dreams. Her mom, for some strange reason, was happy to be divorced. And Mabel had gotten knocked up after a one-night stand. And the guy was a freakin' star.

Catching her head in her palms, she shook it, unsure what her next move should be.

* * *

After she'd convinced Layne the photo she was looking at online of the man with the long hair singing to a massive crowd on the stage of the Grammys was, indeed, the silver-haired carpenter who had helped to rehab the castle—and had gotten her pregnant—her friend nodded with approval.

"He is such a talented man. And so gorgeous."

"Layne! You're missing the point here."

"I know." Layne set aside a book of fabric swatches. She was ordering curtains for the ballroom balcony. They'd decided they wanted something heavier, maybe damask, for the winter months. "That baby-daddy thing had to have messed with his mind. Do you think he left the industry for that reason?"

"I don't know. Seems like a long shot. Most of the articles point to that song he wrote about all the evil stuff going on in the industry."

"You see? You two are on the same page regarding your dislike for the music industry. The guy wrote a freakin' song about it, knowing he'd probably be dropped by his label. That's got to count for something, right?"

"It does. I think. I don't know. It just rubs me the wrong way."

Jamison didn't come off as skeezy or ego-driven or even a spoiled star. She knew those types because she'd dealt with them when she'd worked at Xtatic.

"Talk to him, Mabel. You have to give him a chance."

Did she?

She wanted to. They had started something. And she really enjoyed that something. And yet...

"I feel weird about it now. I mean, a rock star? Come on, that's as far from my comfort zone as it gets. And how many times can a man hear 'you're my baby's daddy!' before he quits everything?"

"Well. You would think rock stars hear that quite a lot, yeah?"

"Layne!"

"I know, I'm sorry. The man seems so nice. And super sexy. And he is the baby's father. Did he ask you to take a DNA test?"

"I haven't told him yet, Layne. I just want to do this right. I don't want to begin my baby's life with a struggle or angst or…media coverage. Can you imagine? I don't ever want to subject my child to such a circus. I want everything to be perfect."

"Nothing is ever perfect, sweetie."

"Your life is. Your man is!"

"I know." Layne drifted into a daydream and Mabel granted her that.

She tapped the one fabric sample she liked that had gold threading woven in elegant blue damask. "This one."

"Yes, I think so. It's ethereal."

"I was going with cheaper, but sure. Ethereal. Oh. I ran into my mom at the blueberry patch yesterday. She was filming herself. And she was wearing a dress. In a blueberry field. Something is definitely going on with her."

Layne nodded as if to say, *Girl, I told you*.

"I have to find her social media page. Is it under her name?"

"Uh…no, check Simply Madilyn."

Mabel mouthed the title in disbelief.

Layne pulled the sample from the ring binder. "She's amazing. But you don't have time to surf the socials this morning. That invoice addressed to the evil Pamela Whitmore and her gang of wicked stepsisters is a recurring thing. Ten thousand dollars for dresses?"

Even though Layne's fiancé had won legal ownership of the castle, the former owner and granddaughter of Charles Whitmore, Pamela Whitmore, was still listed on the occasional invoice. Apparently, she still had a credit card linked to the estate. Mabel was working as quickly as she could to get it all turned over with the lawyers, but it seemed something new popped up weekly.

"Mabel, you need to make it stop. That woman needs to be removed from anything and everything related to the castle."

"I'm on it. Thanks, Layne. I'll..." She tucked the laptop under her arm. "I will give Jamison a chance."

"Tonight?"

"I...think I want to get to the bottom of Madilyn Mitchell's secret life first."

"Oh, it's not a secret!" Layne called as Mabel left the carriage house.

Her mom was a social media influencer? Couldn't be. That would be even stranger than Mabel Mitchell finding herself pregnant by a country rock star.

Mabel did answer his text but pled off on their date because she was having dinner with her mom tonight. She promised to make him dinner tomorrow night and then they could talk.

"Talk," Jamison muttered. He ran his fingers through his hair. That single word did not feel promising.

Would his rhinestone Cinderella want to be involved with a former singer? Especially since she'd said something about fleeing the music industry. And had she found information about him and Clementine? At the time, Clementine had been so secretive about it, not wanting to go out in public, claiming if the media started bugging her about her pregnancy, it would affect her emotionally and that wasn't good for the baby.

Jamison had thought that attitude smart. Only after the baby had been born, and Clementine had packed her bags and moved out, had he realized she had been keeping things secret for a reason. She had known all along the baby was not his. But his manager, who had been stringing Clementine along, hadn't been a big enough fish for her, so she'd tried to hook RJ.

And RJ had fallen for it because he'd wanted to be a dad.

After it was all over, a friend had said something to him about dodging a bullet. Jamison did not feel that way. His heart had been trampled, kicked and pushed over the edge. A bullet would have been quicker, less painful. He'd left the music industry because of the dirty behind-the-scenes dealings. But as well, the whole baby thing had contributed to his fleeing. It had all been tangled into a big ugly mess that he'd wanted nothing to do with.

He'd initially moved into an RV and traveled across the upper United States for a few years, with yearly visits to his parents. It was on one of those visits he'd accompanied his dad to volunteer with Homes for Humans. It had been the perfect way to step back into carpentry, a profession he'd held for ten years before his song had gone viral. After settling in Whitmore, he'd been hired by Straightline; the owner—another person who had no clue who RJ Wright was—had been impressed with his skills, not to mention his work ethic. Not constantly checking his phone and taking a smoke break? You're hired!

Jamison had found a good headspace here in Whitmore

working as a carpenter, minding his own business, helping out neighbors when he could. It gave him a satisfaction no platinum record ever could. Or rather, it filled that need for the high he'd gotten when standing on stage before the cheering masses. It validated him.

Most of the time.

Something was still missing, though. He did not feel... rooted. Completely at ease with his place in this universe.

Some in town knew who he was. Jamison had never asked Chester, the record shop owner, not to tell others who he was, he just showed, through his actions, that he was a private man who wanted his own space. And everyone respected that. He'd only once been asked for an autograph. And that was by Chester, who had wielded a stack of RJ albums.

Yet even over this past year, he'd begun to think Montana would offer the ultimate escape. Clear skies. Vast meadows and forest. Abundant wildlife. He and his dad did like to hunt for deer. He hadn't gone hunting since that first song had hit number one, and he missed that time spent out in nature, sitting quietly beside his dad. He loved his parents and enjoyed spending time with them. He'd fully intended to return to Whitmore, finish up his contract with Straightline, volunteer with one last Homes for Humans job, then pack up and leave.

Until he'd climbed that trellis and placed the tiara on Mabel's head. And her Gibson guitar eyes had played music he wanted to sing over and over. The woman had stirred something awake inside him. And he wasn't sure if he should label it lust, needy attraction or love.

Hell, he'd not wanted to jump into another relationship. Especially one that was all about the sex and worry about figuring out the other person later. That could be the worst move ever for his heart.

And now the past was coming back to poke him in the heart, testing to see if the armor he'd carefully built around it was permeable. Mabel was trying to pry open that armor.

Wandering to the edge of the bed in the dark, he picked up the Gibson guitar and strummed a few chords. Then he sang the jumble of lyrics that had been brewing from within that armored heart of his.

CHAPTER NINE

"Mom, this dinner is..."

Mabel took in the spread before her, arranged artfully on a picture-perfect table that featured roasted game hen, onion-bejeweled peas and asparagus, and homemade rye bread with herbed butter—also homemade. The fine china that Mabel could not recall her mom ever using when she'd lived at home gleamed with gold-rimmed edges. And the place settings were the special silverware Mom only ever used on Christmas. Wine and lemonade were served in goblets and pretty pink glass tumblers, and the napkins were embroidered with silver fleurs-de-lis.

"It doesn't taste good?" her mom asked urgently.

"Oh, it's excellent. But it's so much. For just the two of us? And what's with the fancy place settings. I've never eaten off the china. This spread looks like something you'd see on Instagram."

"I photographed and posted right before you got here." Her mom patted Mabel's wrist. "I used a ring light since it's cloudy today."

Mabel followed her mom's glance to a camera on a tripod that had been set in the corner behind the hutch. Beside it on another stand lay an assortment of lights, clips and diffusers. Stuff a professional photographer would use.

"Mom, what is going on?" She had forgotten all about

looking up Simple Mom or Mothering Simply, or whatever it was Layne had told her to look up. "Are you putting your photos on social media?"

"Of course, dear. I figured after you spied me in the blueberry patch it was probably time to tell you about this. I've been an influencer for about two years now. Ever since the divorce!" she announced cheerily. "I've got a million followers."

Mabel's jaw dropped open. "Did you say a *million*? That's..." A rare few had so many followers. "Who *are* you?"

"I'm Madilyn Mitchell. Simply Madilyn." Her mom sipped the lemonade and then adjusted her apple-appliquéd apron, which she still wore. "Oh, Mabel. I know you've always looked down on me for never having a job and wanting to keep house for you and your dad. It's why I kept this venture so close."

"No, Mom, it's not like that." But it was like that.

"It's okay, dear. Being a homemaker has always been my strength. It gives me joy. And after the divorce, I realized I didn't need a husband to continue pursuing that joy. One day, your aunt Margo suggested I post some photos of the embroidery I did on the curtain hems in the bathroom, so I did. The next thing you know I'm making HomeCore videos on how to spatchcock a chicken and clean a rust-rimmed toilet!"

"Wow." Mabel set down her fork and leaned back to take in her mom.

The woman beamed. She was beautiful, always had been in Mabel's eyes. Her mom's medium-length blond hair was wet-set once a week and combed out into soft curls. Old-fashioned to the core when it came to hair, Madilyn had once said as she'd proudly displayed her mother's old curler set that she used to this day. She wore spare makeup but what she did with eyeliner and a little blush made her look much younger than her fifty-five years. Diamond earrings, a gift from Mabel's dad, glinted at her ears. She never took them off. And a pearl bracelet at her wrist featured a familiar symbol.

"Is that the HomeCore symbol?" The website was the hot spot for home-decorating influencers.

Madilyn lifted her wrist and tapped the silver plate on the pearl bracelet. "It was a gift they sent me along with my million-follower plaque."

"So you're an actual influencer?"

Her mom nodded.

"A...star?"

Another nod with a humble shrug. "It's been a boon since your dad moved out. There's not a day I've felt lonely thanks to my kindhearted followers. Though, you know, there will always be trolls."

Trolls? Her mom was dealing with trolls? How dare anyone be mean to her mom! And how dare she be so out of touch with her own mother that she had no clue what was going on in her life, and which obviously made her very happy.

"I should have visited after the divorce. I'm sorry." Mabel clasped her mom's hand and they shared a few moments of silence.

They'd only talked about the divorce over the phone. Mabel hadn't had the opportunity to fly back home to be with her mom. And when she'd come to stay with Layne she'd avoided going home also. Truthfully, she hadn't known *how* to be with her. Consoling a person came easily enough to her—she'd been there for Layne after her first engagement had gone bust—but all her life her mom had been something *other* to her. The woman who treated her as her child, and loved her, and doted on her, yet Mabel had been annoyed by her simple ways. It was an egotistic, selfish way to have viewed her mom.

She was beginning to realize that she'd been wrong about her mom all her life.

"How are you now?" Mabel asked. "With Dad gone? I haven't gotten an email from him in months."

Her dad had been promoted to head of international marketing for Fortnight Fisheries and he worked a sixty-hour week and was happy for it. Always a workaholic. And he was in line for COO. Though he did send her photos of the company fishing trips and remember her birthday. They'd never been close because he was always working, but they loved one another despite their distance.

"You know, Mabel, I thought the divorce would devastate me." Her mom set down her fork and folded her napkin neatly to place on the table. "And honestly? There are parts of me that mourn the loss of thirty years invested in your dad and the life we created together." She tilted her head, considering. "But another part of me can cherish those memories and knows this is right for me. I've moved on. I'm growing into myself, Mabel. I know that this—" she spread her arms to encompass the picture-perfect table setting "—is my joy, and I should never be ashamed to embrace that. You know?"

Mabel nodded. "I'm sorry."

"For what, dear?"

"For holding that against you."

"Oh, Mabel." Her mom rubbed her shoulder. "You've always been your own unique self. I know my lifestyle isn't for you. And I wouldn't have wanted to make you a mini version of myself. You've got to walk through life and learn and experience and find your own joy."

When put that way, so un-accusatory and so understanding, it brought tears to Mabel's eyes. "I love you, Mom."

"I love you, Mabel."

"But why did you never tell me about this amazing social media stuff? I could have followed you. This is so cool!"

"Do you really think so, dear? It's not exciting like you moving off to New York and working for a big-time record label. I hope you're getting settled back here in Whitmore. How is the job at the castle working for you?"

"It's good, Mom." Always quick to divert the topic from herself, Madilyn Mitchell was one humble chick. With a million followers? Amazing. "I'm fitting into the small-town vibe more easily than expected. I'm not sure the big city was ever for me."

"You had to learn that on your own. I'm proud that you dared to venture out."

It felt beyond good to hear that from her mom. And it alleviated some of the shame she carried with her from the experience that had caused her to flee.

"Are you dating anyone? Do you think I'll ever have grandchildren, Mabel?"

Yikes. That was a fast pivot. Her mom did have babies in her eyes. All. The. Time. Every time a baby was born in Whitmore they were gifted a hand-knit beanie and socks from Madilyn while still in the hospital.

The woman truly was a wonder. She'd been walking toward Simply Madilyn all her life. Mabel should accept it and embrace her as her mom had embraced Mabel's need to explore.

She would now.

As for a grandbaby... Mabel wanted to blurt that her

wish was going to come true very soon. But she had to tell Jamison first.

"You never know, Mom. Babies are in my future, for sure."

"You and Laynie always used to play dress-up and you'd be the mom with the baby pushing the carriage. Oh! Remember that little black kitten that would hold the bottle with its paws? So adorable. That's why I could never figure out why you were so against my ways… Well." She smiled, patted Mabel's wrist again. "It just took me a little time to bloom."

"You've always been a beautiful flower, Mom. No matter what you do, you do it with love and kindness. I'm proud of you."

"You…you are?"

"So proud. You are incredible."

She could see tears wobble in the corner of her mom's eyes. Feeling much the same, a little guilty at having judged her mom so harshly over the years, Mabel sought to alter the mood.

"Now, show me how to find you online so I can follow you!"

After washing the dishes and packing up some leftovers, Mabel and her Mom spent another hour looking through her posts and the incredible photography and talking about how she set up her shots and came up with ideas. Madilyn had received an invite to host an influencer's ball in the fall and she was eager to run with it.

Knowing that her mom was happier than ever, and doing something that gave her joy, gave Mabel renewed hope for her future.

Singing along with a Police song while he cruised home from a day at work, Jamison spied Cinderella minus her tiara biking along the road. Must be riding home from the castle. He slowed and rolled down his window.

"Want a lift?"

"You don't have room for my bike in that truck."

He did not. But he'd move all his tools and the ladders and abandon them on the side of the road if she had asked him to help her and put the bike in the back.

"You avoiding me, Cinderella?"

"No."

"You didn't answer my text."

"I saw your text."

He knew it! She was avoiding him because she'd learned he was RJ. And all that other stuff that had come with his fleeting fame.

"Sorry," she said. "I fell asleep last night still dressed. I was tired after a long afternoon of blueberry picking. And I had a lot of work today, then dinner with Mom. Did you know my mom is an influencer? Like a real one. She has a million followers."

Jamison whistled. "That's cool. It is cool, right?"

She seemed to marvel for a moment, then nodded. "It is. It was just a surprise to me. I've always thought her a plain old housewife with no ambition beyond achieving the perfect crease with her ironing."

"She sounds as special as her daughter."

"Are you trying to charm me, Mr. Wright?"

"How am I doing?"

She crinkled her face and wobbled her flat hand. "Fair."

Fair? Whew! Something had happened to knock him out of her orbit. Hell. The search on him must have been a doozy. But she hadn't fled yet.

"I suppose inviting you to dinner is out?"

"It is. I had roast game hen, potatoes, asparagus, fresh-baked bread and tiramisu for dessert."

"Your mom made you that fancy meal? I need to get on that woman's good side."

"I have leftovers. Are you hungry?" She handed him the brown paper bag that had been sitting in her bike basket. "Go home and eat. It's probably still warm. Then... how about I stop by in an hour?"

So maybe he was still in her orbit? Jamison took the bag of food and set it on the passenger seat. "I'll start a fire and we can sit outside and roast marshmallows."

"I'll bring the chocolate."

"Uh...could you maybe...?"

"Bring marshmallows and graham crackers, too?"

He nodded.

"Not a problem." She began to pedal away. "See you later!"

Jamison patted the steering wheel in time to the music, watching as Cinderella's hair fluttered behind her. That conversation had gone well. And he'd gotten a free meal out of it.

Had she not looked him up?

Hopefully, she had, and his past didn't bother her at all. But it couldn't be that easy. Could it?

His armored heart thudded in warning: *Be careful*.

CHAPTER TEN

MABEL HAD SLIPPED into a pale yellow maxi dress spattered with pink flowers that reminded her of the lush English roses blooming around the castle. The skirt dusted the grass after she'd abandoned her sandals on Jamison's rough stone patio behind his house. The area of grass before the land dropped off to shoreline was big enough for a firepit and two Adirondack chairs. She'd settled onto one and tucked her legs under her, while he had gone inside to retrieve the plate of s'mores supplies she'd brought along.

They'd kissed when she arrived, but it felt different. He felt different to her.

He was different. Maybe?

Who was Robert Jamison Wright?

Before he returned, she pulled out her phone and once again tried to locate his online socials. SingSong had a bunch of RJ Wright accounts but most looked like copycats. She couldn't find one that was starred or verified as his. Weird. But if he'd left the industry, maybe he'd closed it? When she tried Jamison Wright, it brought up dozens, and none of the profile photos looked at all like the sexy man walking toward her now. He always wore soft button-up shirts that looked old and faded. His entire esthetic was worn-yet-comfy cowboy with a side of rocker.

The silver ring on his thumb made her shiver every time it glided over her skin...

The fire snapped, startling her out of a fantasy. Jamison handed her a lap blanket. "Figured you'd need this."

"Thanks." She pulled it over her but let it fall off one shoulder because the warmth of the fire felt good on her skin.

Jamison set the plate on a flat-surfaced stone between the two chairs. He stoked the fire with a long dowel stick with a charred end, playing with the flames—as men were wont to do, she thought, remembering how her dad had done the same when she was a kid.

Jamison turned and noticed her quiet glee. With a shrug, he displayed his stick. "This is my fire stick. When a guy finds the right one, he takes care of it."

"I can see that. It's a very nice fire stick."

"I'm glad you appreciate the finer things in life." He stuck the charred tip of the stick into the grassy ground near his chair and sat. "It's a beautiful night. Almost hate for autumn to arrive. Gets cold here in the north too fast."

"Did you live in Montana before...?" she asked. "Before you started singing?"

"Yes. Not with my parents. I had a place in Butte. Worked on a local construction crew for ten years."

"So...how did your singing career start?"

He rubbed his jaw and cast her a glance. Firelight sparkled in his eyes and glinted in his silvered hair. He could have her with but one word.

"You looked me up?"

"Yes, RJ. I'm sorry, country music isn't even on my radar so I didn't know who you are. Were. Are?"

"Were. I'm not RJ anymore. Well...not completely. Songwriting is in my blood. So...no idea at all who I was?"

"Nada. It's probably the same with hip-hop or choral music or, heck, polka. If I'm not interested, it's not something I listen to, so had no clue about. But I did recognize that song about the everyman."

"'Cheers To You' is sort of an anthem."

"I liked it. It's more country rock."

"It is. I was labeled a crossover artist because some of my stuff tends toward the driving beats with heavy metal head-banging riffs mixed into the country-twanging stuff."

"Have you always been a singer?"

"I started writing songs when I was in high school. Wrote a silly love song for a girl I liked."

"Oh, yeah? I bet she swooned."

"Do girls still swoon? I think you've got some old-fashioned values, Cinderella." He winked at her.

"If I do, you can blame it on my mom." And there was nothing whatsoever wrong with that, she thought, as the image of her elated mom made her smile.

"No swooning," Jamison said. "The girl, she laughed, flipped her hair at me, then slid into the passenger seat with the guy who drove a neon yellow Porsche. I was just redneck RJ who never cut his hair and couldn't do math but always stayed late after school to play with the instruments in the band room."

"I bet she kicked herself when she saw you on the Grammys."

He smirked. The firelight danced across his face. Mabel wanted to sit on his lap, kiss him and snuggle. But she also wanted to keep her distance until she felt safe with all that he had once been.

Honestly, it wasn't about feeling safe. It was coming to a point that she felt she knew all of him. Every nuance and detail. And okay, the fact he had been some kind of superstar was daunting. She had never been a fangirl but to know she sat with a worldwide sensation now gave her some anxiety. It had been over half a year since she stood in the Xtatic offices, but the stomach-churning feeling of shame came upon her whenever she thought about anything related to the music industry.

"So it was a video you'd posted online that launched you to stardom?"

"Yeah, I started putting stuff online because I wanted feedback. I came to the music business a little late, in my early thirties. At the time, I was thinking about singing in bars but didn't know how to go about booking gigs. Then something weird happened. My song went viral. SingSong sent me all these official notices that I'd surpassed a million downloads. And then the record labels started calling. All the right people said all the right things to me. It was surreal."

"I bet. From what I read about you, it seems the overnight fame thing is real."

"Fame is a bitch." Uttered flatly and with no room for argument. "But..." he added "...I did flirt with her for a while. Probably longer than I should have."

"So, it wasn't exciting?"

"Oh, for sure. I got to travel the world. See places I'd never dreamed to see in my lifetime. Opened for some of the country music greats. Even headlined for a year myself. For six years, RJ was living the dream. It was crazy. I was making money, getting invited to all the shindigs, meeting famous people." Jamison shook his head. "It's a drug, Mabel. The adoration from fans and the butt-kissing from the industry folk? I can't lie and say it didn't seduce me."

"So is the sex, drugs, and rock 'n' roll thing real?" She knew the answer but she wanted to her his response.

"Oh, yeah. But I avoided drugs. I've never had the stomach for sticking myself with a needle or popping pills. But I did develop a liking for expensive whisky."

"Oh."

"Don't worry. I'm not an alcoholic. But had I stayed in the industry longer? You never know."

"Why did you leave?" She wanted to ask about the baby thing. But she had to be careful. "Did your label really drop you?"

"Faster than a hot potato. At least, according to the entertainment rags."

"Not true?"

He shrugged his fingers along his stubbled jaw and winced. "After all those years of drinking the Kool-Aid, I realized it was all a big club. And to stay in it, you had to sit, play along and roll over whenever they demanded. It started with the label telling me what to sing and who to hire as backup musicians. Then they were making my schedule for public appearances and setting me up on dates with movie stars I had no interest in even looking at. And there were other things. Secret parties that I knew were being recorded. Catch a guy in a compromising position? You own his ass for life."

Mabel nodded. She could relate, in a manner. She had only worked in the accounting department of a record label, but she had seen enough to know that very few in the industry left unscathed. Her included.

"I decided to record a song about the industry," he said. "Called it 'The Devil's Deal.'"

"I tried to find that one. No luck."

"Because they buried it. I didn't name names in the song, but I did make sure everyone knew I was talking about my label and a few key bigwigs. I put it up on Sing-

Song and it went viral. Within forty-eight hours it was taken down. Money talks. They have connections I could never dream to know about. The label threatened to fire me. So I walked. Without regrets."

"You didn't expect that would happen if you wrote a song about them?"

"Oh, I knew it would happen. I didn't think it would happen so fast. That cancel-culture thing? It's for real. But I was ready to walk. Because of…" He sighed heavily and looked to her. Was he thinking about the baby thing? "I don't ever want to look back, Mabel. Though I am a songwriter. It's in my blood. I'd love to write more songs. But my muse fled after I walked away from it all."

"I'm so sorry about that. Would you put a song out now as RJ?"

"I'm not that guy anymore. Not sure I ever was. If I write another song, it would be as me. Just Jamison."

"There's the title for your next album."

He smirked but didn't outright laugh. And Mabel tugged the blanket up to snuggle in and feel more secure. He sounded like one of the good ones. He'd been burned and fled. Just like her. But.

She had to ask him. She needed to hear it all.

"There was that one thing I wondered about…"

He nodded. "About me and Clementine?"

"I know it's personal and I have no right to ask, but…"

"You have the right to ask. We're doing something here, Cinderella. You should learn everything about me to know I'm being honest with you."

"Yes, I…" Needed that honesty and trust more than he could understand. "So what went on between you two?"

"Clementine was a dancer I met while on a video shoot. We dated six or seven months. A lot of that time we were apart. I was in the middle of a tour. She had a commitment to something I can't recall. We were lovers, basically. We weren't friends. Like we didn't hang out much during our off hours. She'd travel with me to concerts. Come out with me to restaurants and events. She always wanted to know if the paparazzi would be there so she could dress up. It never occurred to me that she was working the relationship for her own publicity. She was very cunning around the cameras. And the baby thing? That crushed me."

"I see." Mabel's heart dropped. "So you didn't want to have children?"

"Heck, yeah. I was more excited about being a daddy than anything."

"Really? You want to have kids?" Her heart skipped. Hope blossomed.

"I did then."

"But now?"

He shrugged, poked his stick in the fire. "Life changes a person."

Of course, he didn't want kids now. Who would after an experience that must have ripped out his heart and slammed it to the ground? And how could the man ever trust another woman who he wasn't in a long-term relationship with if she were to tell him she was pregnant and he was the father?

Mabel thought the worst swear word she'd never dared use. It didn't make her feel any better.

"So now I'm just the carpenter down the street. No one recognizes me anymore," he said. "I gotta say turning gray was the best thing to happen to me. It's freeing to walk the street and not having to dodge crazy autograph hunters or paparazzi. Though Chester has spilled the beans to some. You know that lady who's always walking that teeny dog?"

Mable nodded. "Mrs. Gunderson and her teacup poodle."

"Yep. Mrs. Gunderson, a self-declared avid country music aficionado, still doesn't believe I'm RJ. She told me that RJ was more lanky and darker than me, and he had a voice that could seduce her."

Jamison laughed. And Mabel had to smile at that one. "If she only knew, eh?"

"I'm fine with it. That woman is the biggest gossip in town."

That was true. Mabel had learned about Layne's breakup before Layne had even called her because her mom had talked to Mrs. Gunderson and texted Mabel the info immediately.

Mabel sat with all the information he'd just given her. It must have taken a lot of fortitude to put out a song that he knew would be a career-ender. Most put up with whatever the industry threw at them, knowing if they complied, they could keep their fame. And top it off with the baby thing? A lot going on in his life at the time.

"Does my past bother you?" he asked.

"Why should it?" She wasn't being truthful. She was bothered. And more worried about her truths now.

He shrugged. "I'm going to take a wild leap and call you my girlfriend, Cinderella. We've been seeing each other and doing the—what did you call it?"

She smirked. "The smexy."

"Right, the smexy. What we've got? It feels like a thing."

Yes, it did. She hadn't expected to earn the girlfriend label, but yes, she had become his girlfriend.

More like mother of his child.

Oh, Mabel, you have to tell him now!

"Can you handle dating a former rock star?" he asked.

She was doing it, like it or not. And she did like it. But also, there was a little bit of *not* in there she still needed to deal with. "Do you ever intend to return to the industry?"

"Not if I can help it. I'm happy building houses."

"But you said you'd always be a songwriter?"

"That'll never leave my blood. If my muse does return? I'd put up a song online for feedback. But probably not as RJ. Though posting certain content does bring in proceeds. I don't need the cash. I've always made a point to donate to Homes for Humans and have no plans to stop now."

"How did you get involved with the organization?"

"It's something my dad has always participated in. It's a nationwide charity, so I can do it wherever I land. Felt like a natural release for my pent-up frustration after I walked away from fame. I've been volunteering and donating to them ever since I left. Gives me a feeling of accomplishment that no platinum record can ever offer."

"I think I read on the coffee shop bulletin board that they're building one of those homes here in Whitmore?"

"We start the project in a few days. A family lost their home to a fire. It's a ten-minute walk from here. I look forward to it. And my boss at Straightline—I had put in my two weeks' notice, but…" He sighed.

He had said something about not being sure about the Montana move now. Because of her. Would a surprise baby keep him here in Whitmore or send him fleeing?

Ignoring the elephant sitting between them, she asked, "And you don't get paid for that work with the charity?"

"No, it's all volunteers. Takes a while for some of the college kids to figure out how to operate an electric drill or saw, but I like teaching them. It's good for me. Keeps me humble."

"Were you an egomaniac as RJ?"

"Eh. I hope not. But fame does have a way of tainting a man's soul. The spotlight feels good, Cinderella. I won't deny that."

"Thanks for telling me all that." Mabel stood and stretched her back. She was starting to get crampy muscles if she sat too long. A pregnancy thing? Mercy, she'd never make it the next six months if she didn't schedule a weekly massage. "It's a lot to take in. But I think, generally, I still like you."

"Generally? What the hell does that mean?"

She hadn't realized it had come out like that. It did sound dismissive. "I told you I used to work for a record label."

"Yeah, I'm familiar with the label."

"Even though I wasn't out on the stage or working closely with the talent, I can relate to you seeing the dirty dealings behind the scenes. It wasn't for me. But honestly? Now I've developed a hang-up about those in the music business."

Jamison wrapped his arms around her, clasping his hands across her stomach. She wanted to move his hands but thought that would alert him.

He kissed the side of her neck. A move that devastated. Always that touch permeated to her very bones. Warmed her like no fire ever could. "That's not me anymore, Mabel. Promise. But I understand. The industry is rough. You've had a peek inside, and whatever it was that made you run, I'm sure I can relate. We good?"

She nodded. His sure embrace softened her anxieties for now. She tilted her head against his shoulder. "We're good."

"Then how about a dance?"

Now she understood his excellent rhythm. But his innate charm wasn't because he'd stood on stage and dazzled millions. It was real. Something that only a kind and genuine person could possess.

She turned into his embrace. "Always."

CHAPTER ELEVEN

MABEL WOKE IN Jamison's bed. Again!

What was wrong with her?

Nothing whatsoever was the first thought that sprang to mind. Followed by a wagging finger that admonished, *You are not doing this right!*

She had to stop making love with the man and tell him that she carried his baby. And the longer she waited the worse it would sound coming from her to him. Why the wait? he'd rightfully wonder. Had she been leading him along?

No, it was what she had learned about him and that woman named Clementine. That experience had hurt him. And she didn't want to do that to him again. And really? Was she all in with this relationship? Good sex did not make for a happily-ever-after. A lot more was required, like understanding one another emotionally and being completely open and…

Tell him, Mabel. Don't let this turn into a big ugly secret.

Sitting up in the soft morning light, the sheet spilled to her waist and she realized she was alone. Then she heard the shower. A glance to the bedside clock confirmed she had a few hours before she needed to be at the castle.

Turning and looking out over the harbor, she couldn't

imagine a more perfect way to wake, surrounded by nature, nestled in the soft sheets of her lover's bed. She could embrace a life like this. Seemingly, without a care.

But she did have a care. A whooping one. And that care was courtesy of a former country rock singer who seemed to have left that life behind. She hoped he had.

Did it matter to her?

It did. In ways she couldn't quite define. He wasn't like her boss, the one person who had put a bad taste in her throat for an entire industry. She shouldn't hold that against Jamison. And she would not. But.

But it wasn't easy letting go of the fear and disdain she'd carried since leaving New York. The feeling that she wasn't worthy unless she succumbed to a man's wishes. It all made her indifference toward romance even stronger.

Jamison had not done a thing to make her doubt his sincerity. Maybe it was time to give him a chance? To start believing they could actually have a chance?

Rising and wandering into the kitchen, naked—she had best enjoy this opportunity for blatant nudity while her tummy was relatively flat—she opened the fridge. Nothing appealed. Save the container of leftover mashed potatoes she'd given him the other night. About a quarter remained.

Mabel took out the glass container, popped off the top and rummaged for a fork in his annoyingly disordered silverware drawer. She dug in and it hit the spot. Her mom made the best mashed potatoes, hands down.

She wondered if a shot of her downing Simply Madilyn's creation—in the nude—would suit her mom's social media page. Ha!

The things a daughter must never tell her mother.

"Whoa."

She turned to find Jamison standing in the living room,

a white towel wrapped around his hips. Pecs hard as chiseled rocks. The man's work kept him lean, muscled and, oh, so tan. His six-pack would make a twenty-year-old jealous. Age had not softened that man in any manner.

"What?" She forked another bite of potatoes into her mouth. "You've never seen a naked woman eating mashed potatoes in your kitchen before?"

"Can't say that I have."

"For my sake, I should hope not."

"Uh, are those cold?" He grimaced. "Use the microwave, woman. That's disgusting."

She hadn't considered that she was eating the leftovers cold. It sounded gross. But it satisfied a craving. Was this a pregnancy craving? Something to enter onto her spreadsheet.

She set down the container. "We have to stop doing this."

"Answering the call to devour one another with kisses and lots of…" He gave his hips a thrust. "Smex? But we are getting to know one another. You know all about me now. And I feel like I'm getting a handle on the Marvelous Mabel Mitchell. You did say you'd be my girlfriend."

Had she said that? She was pretty sure she had not but just accepted the label when he mentioned it last night. The girlfriend of a former country rock singer? Sounded glamorous and wild, and a little romantic.

But morning sickness and poopy diapers were never romantic. Down with romance! She had no intention of being left high and dry after thirty years like her mother.

"When do you have to be at work?" She strolled into the bedroom and pulled on her slipover dress. Returning to the living room, she sat on the couch and patted it for him to join her.

"About forty-five minutes. You?"

"I don't have to be in until ten. I need to tell you something. And you're going to want to sit down."

"Should I keep my towel on or...?"

If he sat naked beside her, she'd lose her cool and never get out what he deserved to hear. "Could you put on some pants?"

With a nod, he wandered into the bedroom. Had she heard him swear under his breath?

Mabel sighed. This would be the make-it-or-break-it conversation. It could chase him out of her life. It could cement their connection. Or it could turn another person's life inside out as it had hers. But it had to be done. Before they landed in bed again. And again. And again.

She was a big girl. She had this. Time to be a grown-up.

"This feels serious." With jeans hugging his long legs, Jamison sat beside her and turned to face her. The shirt was unbuttoned and—no, she would not stare at his abs. "Is it about RJ?"

"Why do you talk about yourself in the third person?"

"Like I explained to you, I no longer relate to the guy I used to be. I'm just Jamison now."

She could understand that. Anyone who stood on a stage before the masses may develop a personality for the crowd, one who could stand under the spotlight and paparazzi flashes while carefully concealing the real person beneath. Seemed like it would be a survival mechanism.

"It's about me," she said. "Us. I, uh...should have told you sooner but believe me when I say I wanted to wait for the right time. And, well, I needed to sit with this and absorb it myself before I told you. It's so big."

"Mabel, you are freaking me out. What's going on?"

"The last thing I want to do is freak you out." She took

his hand and he leaned in to kiss her. The brush of his skin against her, his mouth lightly touching hers, was an intimate language. One only the two of them could understand. And she wanted to keep it that way. She wanted him as hers.

Was she being greedy? Or foolishly desperate?

"Are you okay?" he asked. "Or is it your parents? Layne? Did I do something wrong? Are you—"

"I'm pregnant," she blurted. Then she dropped his hand and touched her lips. She'd tainted their shared language. It felt as though she'd released a secret that might burn her. "Sorry. I mean…"

She exhaled. *You can do this.*

"I missed my period a few weeks after you left for Montana. I thought it was stress with the job at the castle. It had been a lot of rush-rush to get the castle opened to the public. And then I missed it the next month. So I took a test. But I didn't believe it. Because, come on, I'm on the pill. I am. Promise. Or I was until recently. And I went to the doctor and she confirmed it. And I swear it's yours. I'm not trying to trap you. I'll do a DNA test if you want me to. And I'm not trying to make you marry me or pay child support. And then I saw the article about you and Clementine, and trust me this is not like that, but I fully expect it'll be a gut punch like that, which is another reason why I didn't tell you immediately. You just need to know. And…"

She finally took a breath, meeting his gaze. She couldn't read his reaction. It was emotionless. His eyes were narrowed and his mouth a straight line.

She'd lost him. Oh, God, she'd lost him.

"Jamison, say something, please."

He tilted his head back against the couch and raked his

fingers through the silver hair in which she loved to watch moonlight dance. "Wow."

"I'm sorry. I didn't mean to blurt it out like that. I'm nervous. I wasn't sure how you'd take it…"

"How long have you known about this? Since I returned?"

"Probably about two weeks before you returned I took the first test. Then I did another a week later. And then one the morning you showed at the castle when I had the interview. I went to the doctor for the first time a few days after you returned."

"So you've known the whole time we've been dating?"

She nodded. "I couldn't tell you right away."

"Why not?"

"Because I needed to get right with the news first. To wrap my head around the fact that I got pregnant after a one-night stand with the sexiest man I've ever known, who then disappeared from my life for two months."

He shoved his fingers into his hair again, a nervous habit, and scratched. "I get the needing-to-sort-it-out-in-your-brain thing. It's…big news."

"It is. I didn't know how else to tell you and not make it sound crazy. I'm sorry, Jamison."

"What are you sorry for?"

"I don't know. I don't want you to take this as some woman trying to trap you. I'm perfectly fine with raising this child on my own. I don't want anything from you. I—"

"Why wouldn't you want anything from me?"

She met his gaze. It was that loving soft stare he gave her so often but it felt harder, almost judging. Or hurt. She'd hurt him. "Well… I have no right to ask anything of you. This was my mistake. I was on the pill."

"Really? Then how…?"

"The doctor said it happens. Birth control is not one hundred percent effective."

He nodded. "I'm going to need to absorb this."

"Of course. And please, I don't want you to feel as though life is smacking you with the same issue twice. It is your baby. But… I don't want to be that woman who traps a man with a baby like…" Clementine. "I didn't do it on purpose. I swear to you, I did not. I have come to terms with the fact that I'll have to do this on my own. And I'm a little excited about it, actually. I've always wanted to be a mommy. To have dozens of kids."

"Dozens?" he blurted.

"That was the count when I was younger and didn't realize how much babies cost and how much work they require. But, Jamison, I'm going to have a baby." She patted her stomach.

"And I'm the daddy." He stood and paced to the kitchen. Leaned against the counter. Then wandered to the bed. Stared out the window, hands on his hips. "Can I have some time to think about this?"

"Of course."

He hadn't yelled at her. And he hadn't accused her of anything. Yet. But he hadn't kissed her or held her or reassured her that it was all right, either.

Yes, he did need some space. It was only fair. She had given herself that same time to wrap her head around the pregnancy before she'd approached him.

"I need to go home and shower for work." She stood, collected her purse in the kitchen, feeling like the task had been accomplished.

A kiss would feel so good right now. It would put her in that place of safety and comfort she always felt when in his arms. But she didn't dare ask for one. She wasn't sure if she had just become a villain in his life or...

"I'll wait to hear from you?"

He didn't reply.

"Okay, then. Uh..."

Right. So that was how the talk with her baby daddy had gone. Not resoundingly successful. But, with hope, not a complete failure. Time to focus on work. She was going to have to support her growing family. "Bye."

She exited quietly, carefully closing the door. But before she got to the end of his driveway, tears spilled down her cheeks.

Best-case scenario would have seen Jamison wrapping his arms around her and delighting in the fact that they were going to be parents. She hadn't expected that reaction.

But she would have felt much better had it gone that way.

Jamison tossed a cut piece of two-by-four into the refuse pile and wandered around to the back of the framework for the Homes for Humans house. When he pulled down his safety mask to hang around his neck, the smell of sawdust and chemically treated wood filled his nostrils. The bulk of volunteers wouldn't arrive for two days, so for now it was just he and Jeff from the Straightline crew and they liked that just fine. They could get the framework done and ensure the skeleton of the house was solid and prepared for the Sheetrock installation.

Jeff had taken off for a lunch break, promising to bring back a sandwich for Jamison. So he was alone and thankful for it. He'd nearly sawed off his thumb earlier when the image of Mabel holding a baby—his baby—had popped into his thoughts.

What a way to start the day!

In that instant when Mabel had been blabbering off the details like a nervous kitten, his brain had relived that time with Clementine when she'd convinced him her baby was his. They'd agreed to keep it as secret as possible. For the sake of the baby's privacy. No child should have to grow up under the flash and scrutiny of the paparazzi.

But not for long. Around her eighth month, Clementine went to *People* magazine with her news. Apparently, they'd made a deal: if she gave them "first look" photos of the baby, they'd pay her half a million dollars.

That deal? Jamison hadn't been aware of it until *after* the birth when it had all blown up. The baby had been born. And Jamison had not been in the hospital because he'd been on the final days of a tour. Six hours after giving birth, Clementine had called him—*called him*—and broken it off. Turned out the baby's daddy was his manager, whom she'd hooked up with before—*and during*—the time they had been dating. A DNA test confirmed it.

Jamison had been gutted. He'd been played. Hard. The heartbreak of expecting his child and then having it metaphorically ripped from his arms? It had been the worst.

The magazine article had featured photos of Clementine and baby Charlie. She'd been quoted as saying she couldn't figure out why everyone had thought it was RJ's baby. She'd known all along it was the manager's baby. RJ had simply been taking care of her, helping her.

She'd lied. RJ—hell, Jamison—had decided not to correct the article, fearing an even bigger media storm and the fallout should fans learn he hadn't known the baby wasn't his. Two months later, he released "The Devil's Deal" and then walked away for good before his label could drop him. The entire music industry canceled him. It had been a hell of a year.

He'd thought to leave that stuff in his past.

And now it was happening again.

But was it really? He wanted to believe Mabel when she said she hadn't slept with any other men. She'd never lied to him. Withholding the info about the baby until she'd felt comfortable enough to reveal it hadn't been a lie. They had hooked up after only an hour of dancing and a walk along the beach. There was no shame in that. And if she had hooked up with another man in the time he'd been in Montana...

"No," he muttered. He was going to give her the benefit of the doubt.

Just like you did with Clementine?

Maybe a baby was something he needed to welcome into his life? Honestly, he had been excited about being a father the first time around. Had looked forward to raising a child, teaching it, watching it grow and become a person. He wasn't getting any younger. He'd always thought someday he'd have a family. Figured he'd lost that chance when he'd hit his forties.

Was this God's way of saying, sorry about the first time, here's another chance?

He scrubbed a hand over his hair and shook his head. There was no reason why he couldn't embrace this news and be the best daddy ever.

Should he have pulled Mabel into his arms this morning to reassure her? He'd played that one wrong. But the news had been a shocker. He was still sorting it all out.

"Got you ham and cheese!" Jeff tossed a greasy bag toward Jamison and he caught it against his chest. "Will we get the roof trusses up by evening?"

Jamison tugged out the paper-wrapped sandwich and dug in. "Of course, but it might be a late one."

"My wife's out of town with her family. I've got all the time in the world."

Hearing Jeff say *my wife* sounded like an enchantment spell that Jamison wanted to utilize. Could he have a life with Mabel? Would she want him? Hell, they'd already made a baby together. Instant family! Welcome to the real world, Jamison Wright. You've done it again—or for the first time, actually. Now how will you react? Stand up and take responsibility? Or pack your bags and hightail it to Montana?

"Dude?"

Jamison looked up. "Huh?"

"Shove that sandwich in your pie hole and help me with the trusses!"

"Be right there."

He finished the sandwich and tossed the refuse in the dumpster. Yeah, he had to concentrate on work or he'd saw off a limb for sure. He wouldn't have time for Mabel today.

And maybe that was a good thing. His battered and bruised heart needed some time to digest this baby-daddy replay.

CHAPTER TWELVE

ON WEDNESDAY, MABEL WENT into the coffee shop for her favorite latte and just stopped herself from suggesting they start doing delivery. Fine. The walk to get her coffee was much-needed exercise. She'd looked up exercise for pregnancy and had already made a chart of essential moves to stay in shape. She intended to continue riding her bike to the castle until it was too cold and snowy, and even then she might strap on cross-country skis for the short trip there.

Tapping the app on her phone to pay for the latte, she then entered the maternity app she'd downloaded to track everything she ate, how much she exercised and even her morning sickness. She loved it. It even determined what foods were likely cravings. Cold mashed potatoes? Craving.

Right now, she really wanted one of those "crookies." That was a chocolate chip cookie baked inside a croissant. Her app didn't have an entry or calorie count for that treat, so she decided it would be a freebie.

Paying for that, and thanking the clerk, she headed out to her bike.

Sipping her latte, she maneuvered her bike to the sidewalk and stood watching the traffic buzz by. The town attracted a lot of tourists. There was a reason the castle was already booked through the middle of next year. This cozy harbor town offered outdoor activities such as hiking, sailing, shopping, berry picking, along with Insta-worthy photo opportunities.

Setting her coffee in the cup holder attached to the bike handlebars, she took a bite of the still-warm crookie.

"Mercy." She rolled her eyes in bliss. "This is not a craving. This. Is. Necessity." She wondered if it would look sus if she went back inside and bought three more.

Oh, Mabel, control yourself, she coached inwardly. While eating for two was a good excuse, she did want to stay fit during this pregnancy. She may not have abs like Jamison, but…

Pouting, she set the crookie back inside the paper bag.

She hadn't heard from Jamison for two days. While it hurt and made her question everything they had between them, she figured his silence was fair. She'd dumped a lot on him. An entire baby! Of course, he'd need time to sort it out. After all, she had needed that time.

But she wouldn't be a woman if she weren't curious and desperately in need of knowing exactly where he was at with the situation.

Tugging out her phone, she typed.

Thinking of you. Let's talk soon?

That would allow him to make the next move.
"Fair," she muttered.
He didn't respond immediately. Her heart tightened.
Had Cinderella lost her Prince Charming?
"Did I ever have him?"

Bouquet of roses in hand, Jamison exited the flower shop, which was closing for the night. They had sold him the last of their supply.

It had been days since Mabel had dropped the baby bomb on him. He'd been so busy with the Homes for Humans he hadn't a moment to contact her. He'd seen her text and could have texted back a quick, Sure, see you soon. But he'd convinced himself the first words to her should be spoken in person. Nothing so impersonal as a text. Call him old-fashioned, but words meant something and he used them to speak his heart.

But as well. A baby.

Again? Would it prove another crushing heartbreak?

He'd had some time, while showering in the morning and drifting off to sleep at night after a long day of work, to consider how welcoming a baby into his life would drastically change it. He'd been down this road before. He'd been excited when Clementine told him about the baby. And by the time she was ready to deliver, he'd been considering asking her to marry him. Even though he still hadn't felt he loved her.

Mabel's announcement had been a repeat of that emotional disaster. And...not. It felt different. Not so desperate. Or even calculated. It was...lighter. Real. He wanted to embrace it as much as he wanted to pull Mabel into his arms and never let her go.

Could he do this again? Dare to trust another woman for so many months until the baby was born and finally his heart would either shatter completely or breathe a sigh of relief.

He didn't want to put himself through that again. It wasn't fair. But he reasoned that it was all in the way he viewed it. He could make it good or bad. It was his choice. He didn't want to be a hardnose about this situation. Especially with Mabel in a delicate condition.

Damn, this was not easy. Every bit of him wanted to

grab Mabel and kiss her and ask her to marry him. But he knew that wouldn't work. Not yet. It wouldn't sit right in his heart.

Was it what she was waiting for from him? He didn't want to disappoint her.

And the fact he was thinking about her reaction meant he was deeper in this than he'd suspected. The woman had won his heart that night of the ball. And she'd handled it with care and respect so far.

He knocked on her door and she answered. She sucked on a red Popsicle. Her eyes brightened at the sight of him and she opened the door wider to welcome him in.

"Just having a snack," she said. "I'm so glad you stopped by. More roses?" She took the roses from him and buried her face in them. "They smell so good. And red this time?"

He figured that meant love, or something romantic. Better than noncommittal pink roses. Or the colorless white roses that had also been on display. But *did* he love her? Some moments he thought he did. Because, hell, he'd fallen hard for her that first night in the ballroom. Other times he wondered if he were merely reacting to the situation, feeling that he needed to love her if that's how they were going to handle this together.

He did know one thing. He felt more inclined to want to love Mabel than he had Clementine.

"The roses are red as your lips. That little Popsicle stain your lips that dark?"

She laughed. "This is my third. I wanted something sweet and cold."

"Pregnancy cravings?"

"I think so." She bowed her head and looked up at him through lush lashes, which had stolen his breath away that first night they danced under the stars. "So, you're here. Does that mean you've given my news some thought?"

"I have. I, uh...didn't mean to stay away from you so long. The Homes for Humans project is always intense when it's getting started."

"I understand. It's big news. I took my time before telling you. No reason you shouldn't have done the same."

Looking at her face, underlined by the lush roses, the only thing that could have made her more perfect was if she wore the tiara. His rhinestone Cinderella wore that crown like she'd been born with it. And he didn't ever want her to feel as though she were not supported.

He swept Mabel into his arms. Armful of roses swaying backward, and the hand holding the Popsicle also swinging out, he kissed her. Nothing wrong about this connection. It gave him hope and pushed away his past regrets. Most of them, anyway.

"That was the coldest kiss I've ever gotten."

"You warmed me up fast. I missed your kisses, Jamison. But I..."

She stepped out of his embrace, ate the last chunk of the Popsicle and tossed the stick to land on a dishcloth near the sink. Her bright gaze suddenly danced around his, unsure, and not really connecting. Nervous?

He could relate.

She set the bouquet on the counter. "I don't want to force you into anything, Jamison. We need to talk about what the arrangements will be between us."

"Arrangements?"

Arrangements sounded so...formal. Legal. Like they were drawing a contract between the two of them. Which was something to consider. Been there, done that. He had learned his lesson the first time.

Or had he?

Could they follow this to its natural development? Now that he stood but two feet from Mabel, had kissed her, could smell her flower-candy perfume, dance in her Gibson guitar irises, he no longer wanted to be staunch, so cautious.

"Are you thinking something legal? Written up?" he asked.

"It might be best. Since we're not married and I'm not sure where we'll be a month from now. Or even in a few weeks."

Wow. So she wasn't looking toward any kind of commitment from him? Jamison's heart dropped.

"Mabel, I thought we were dating?"

"We are." She settled the roses into a vase. "But what if that changes?"

He scrubbed a hand over his hair. "If you don't think this relationship has merit…"

"You want to continue to see me?"

He swung a look at her, surprised she'd even ask such a thing. "Hell, yes, Cinderella. I want to keep this going."

She bit her bottom lip and tears formed at the corners of her eyes. He'd never cried much himself, but he could feel it in his chest, loosening, wanting to be…understood. And loved for who he was as a person not for what he could give another person financially. Mabel hadn't asked for money. Yet. But he would give her all he had if she asked.

"Don't you?" he asked.

She nodded. Sniffed at a tear. "I do. I had thought our chances at any sort of relationship spoiled with the announcement of the baby."

"Mabel. I would be lying if I told you I wasn't surprised and I'm certainly unprepared. Hadn't thought it would happen to me. Again." He caught her lift of chin. Another teardrop spilled down her cheek. He should pull her into a hug. Kiss those tears away. But part of him still bore the wounds from his past. "I told you about Clementine."

She nodded. More tears. "This isn't the same," came out quietly.

The desperation in her voice reached in and punched his heart. Get it together, man! Mabel hadn't found herself in a situation and decided to use another man to ensure she landed a financially secure future. Mabel Mitchell hadn't a malicious bone in her body.

"I want to trust you, Mabel. Hell, you've worked in the music industry. You should know it's not easy to build trust and then keep it. And once burned?"

"We'll do a DNA test to put any concerns you might have to rest. It's only fair. I don't have a problem with that."

That felt wrong, insisting she go through with such a test. But it would ease his worries. Damn. Seriously? Is that how he was going to treat her? It didn't matter whose baby it was. He cared about Mabel. Just the fact he'd been thinking he could love her had to mean something.

"So, uh…can we take it day by day?" he asked. "I mean, I suppose the right thing to do would be to drop to my knee and propose—"

"Oh, no!" she rushed out. "I don't want that from you, Jamison."

"You don't?" Well, if that didn't stab him right in the heart. His emotions roller-coastered from relief to panic, to humiliation.

"Not right now." She touched his jaw, smoothed her fingers along his beard. The touch calmed some of his anxiety. "It would feel forced. I'd never know if you proposed to me to make things look right. I don't need that. I mean, I do dream of family, but..."

"I get it. I feel the same. It has to feel natural. But I won't take a proposal off the table."

Her eyes brightened as she looked over his face. No more tears. Thank goodness. "That works for me. I wouldn't be averse to creating a real family with you."

"Yeah?"

"Of course not," she said. "But I don't want to rush into something because we feel like it's what we *need* to do."

"I do want a family, Mabel."

"I'm glad to hear that. And I want that more than anything. But where would your family live? Here or in Montana?"

That was the question, wasn't it? He had another week left on the Homes for Humans project and then he was free to leave Whitmore. Make arrangements with a realtor. Pack his belongings and begin a new life in Montana.

But honestly? He hadn't been seriously walking toward that goal since the night he'd climbed the trellis to place the tiara on Cinderella's pretty head.

"My mom called this morning," he said. "She's wondering what portion of their land I want to build on."

"Oh."

"Mabel, I told her to put a pin in that plan for now. Since I set foot back in Whitmore I've been rethinking that decision. That night I climbed the trellis to put the tiara on your head? That stopped my plans to pack up my things dead in their tracks. Montana doesn't sound so appealing anymore."

"But your family is there."

"They are. And I don't mind the travel to visit them once

a year. Like I told you before, I also fit in volunteer work when I do that. That's something that will never change."

She clasped his hands and lifted them to brush against her cheek. She smelled like cherry Popsicles and flowers. And if he kissed her one more time, he'd not leave this home tonight.

"I want to do this with you," she said. "But I want it to work for both of us. I think we need to make the rules as we go along, yes? I like your idea of dating. For now."

"Yeah, for now." And then? Would he propose? It wasn't off the table. "So uh, when are you due?"

"February. Right around Valentine's Day."

He nodded. "Seems appropriate for Cinderella's baby. Do you…want to go for a walk? Maybe take out the sailboat?"

"I'd like that."

CHAPTER THIRTEEN

WHEN JAMISON PURCHASED his house, a small sailboat came with it. The previous owners intended to travel and had no storage means for it. He and Mabel sailed to the middle of the harbor. Now, with the sun set and the moon cut by a thin whisper of clouds, the stars twinkled above them as if they stood below on stage. It was a sultry night. Two lanterns placed at stern and bow beamed a soft glow across their faces. The water glittered. A salty breeze listed Mabel's hair across her neck. She tugged up her sweater and buttoned it.

They'd settled against one another on the bow seat, side by side, Mabel's head frequently resting on Jamison's shoulder. She talked about her plans for motherhood. He'd already figured out that she was precise, probably one of those Type A's. She liked spreadsheets and had apparently made one to chart her baby's growth—the size of a grape right now—and she had another for how many diapers she must buy weekly and how many trips that would require to the big-box store at the edge of the nearest town. She'd signed up for mommy yoga using an app and was tracking her exercise and everything she ate.

He listened quietly, agreeing with a nod. There wasn't much he could add. He didn't know how to do the baby stuff. As well, a part of him tugged him back from getting as excited as Mabel seemed over it all. Been there. Done that. Had his heart shredded. And it had happened at a time when he'd been utterly fed up with the music industry.

His muse had fled. He'd been *existing* for the past three years.

That sounded desolate. He'd done more than exist. He liked his job with Straightline. He enjoyed volunteering. So maybe he had started a new life, after all. Could he fit a child into that life? Was he too old to be a dad? He'd be pushing sixty by the time his kid's graduation rolled around.

But that was the kicker. It was *his* child. And sixty or not, that kid was going to graduate. With or without Jamison there to cheer him or her on.

He bowed his head against Mabel's hair. This felt unreal. She was too perfect for him. Why did she want to have a baby with a washed-up singer? A man who preferred to hermit himself away in a tiny town and spend his days pounding nails?

Not that she'd had a choice. He couldn't blame Mabel for any of this. Babies happened. Even with the best of plans and birth control.

Accept it, man. Make this as good as you can. For both of you.

"You tired?" he asked.

"Just relaxed. Reverent. Isn't the world beautiful?"

"The world reflects back what you put out so it's reflecting back your beauty."

"Where did you hear that one?"

"It's true." He sang the line that had been fluttering in his thoughts of late, "My big-city Cinderella with rhinestones in her hair. Mabel… Mabel in the moonlight."

She tilted her gaze up to him. Her eyes. They were the

cincher, weren't they? He could never refuse her Gibson guitar eyes a thing.

"Kissing you under the starlight is about the best thing ever, Mabel."

"Same." He smoothed a hand down her hair, threading his fingers into the lush softness. "Tell me truthfully... how do you *really* feel about this baby?"

His fingers began to move within her hair by rote, as he'd done so many times with his hair when it had been longer.

"Babies are special, aren't they?" he said. "And being a father would be special, too. I mean, I have an amazing dad as a role model. He taught me everything I know. Well, I think I got my musical ability from my mom. She still teaches band at the local high school. And being a dad is something I previously thought I'd have. I was excited about it. And now..."

"Now?"

He exhaled and began to weave her hair as he thought about it. Screw his age. Age meant little. It was what was in a man's heart and soul that mattered most.

"What are you doing?"

"Braiding your hair."

"You know how to do that?"

"My hair used to be down to my elbows. I'm an expert. You want me to stop?"

"No, I like it. Makes me feel...cared for."

Oh, he cared the world for her. Slipping a silken hank of hair under another, he worked absently as he spoke. "So, the baby... It feels..."

"Manipulative?"

He winced. It could be deemed as such, but he believed Mabel had not set out on that night of the ball to entrap him. She would never play him and then convince the world that he'd been in on the deception all along.

"It feels like a surprise, for sure. A baby will change my life. Your life. Our lives."

"It has already changed mine for the good. I'm feeling more settled here in Whitmore. Accepting. Ready for this big event. But I also want to give you space and time to work it out."

"I appreciate that." He entwined the last bits of her hair and then noticed the light glinting in her blond tresses. Like something out of a fairy tale. "Gorgeous."

"The sky?"

"The starlight is shining in your hair. I've braided stardust into the strands."

"You're such a romantic."

"Anything wrong with that?"

"Not at all." She swept her fingers over the side of the boat, skimming the water.

He didn't want to lose his rhinestone Cinderella. And, yes, they were being shoved into something they both hadn't asked for. Yet, he would be a fool to cling to the fine threads of resistance. He had to allow Mabel completely into his heart. Along with the baby.

Mabel turned, pressing a hand behind her head to hold the braid secure. "Just tell me you'll keep an open mind. That's all I ask. I'll keep the door open for you should you want to walk in and embrace this new family. And it'll always be open should you need to walk out."

"Don't say that, Mabel. If I walk in that door, you better believe it'll be for good."

"Thank you. I needed to hear that."

He sang a few more lyrics. "She's got stardust in her hair and Gibson guitars shimmering in her eyes."

"Stardust in my hair?" Mabel's breath hushed out. It felt to Jamison as if stardust had just misted from between her lips. "Will you ever write another song?"

"I'm writing one now. I think my muse may have returned, all dancing and pretty in her rhinestone tiara." He kissed her on the forehead.

"How'd I ever get so lucky to meet someone like you?"

"I was thinking the same. But I don't believe in fate."

"Nor do I."

"Weren't you supposed to meet some other guy that night of the ball?" And now that he thought on it...had Mabel and the no-show dated?

"He ghosted me. We met for coffee twice after I returned to Whitmore. Just chats. And he fixed me up with a local tech place that got the castle's antiquated computer system up to speed. And before you ask, because you have to be thinking it, I didn't sleep with him."

"I thought of it, but I wouldn't have asked."

"You can ask me anything, Jamison. We have to be honest with one another if whatever this is is going to work."

"I agree. Let's go back to my place. Feels like a night to stoke a fire and snuggle."

"You have the best ideas."

Later, as Mabel drifted to sleep nestled within Jamison's embrace in his bed, she smiled to think about him braiding her hair out on the boat. Sure hands, stroking her hair so lovingly. The braid had held until they'd returned to shore and she had jumped from the boat into his arms.

And then she realized something that made her heart swell and her stomach do a giddy twirl as if a ten-year-old wannabe princess were finally being granted her wish.

He'd woven stardust into her hair.

CHAPTER FOURTEEN

"Layne," Mabel said over speakerphone as she wandered out from her apartment to her bike.

She'd left Jamison too early this morning, but not without a kiss, a quickie and a promise to introduce him to the crookie later. Once home, she'd finished up the legal forms for the removal of Pamela Whitmore from the castle expense account. She'd just dropped them at the post office. "Layne! He wove stardust into my hair!"

"What?" Her friend had answered by telling her she was out back of the castle going over placement plans for her wedding reception with the caterer. "What are you talking about—oh. Wait. Stardust? In your hair? Are you serious?"

Mabel nodded, then realized she wasn't on video chat. "Can you believe it? And he sang to me."

"It's what you wished for when we were kids and we brewed up our perfect man like in that movie."

"A man who would weave stardust into my hair and sing to me about happily-ever-after," Mabel repeated. He hadn't mentioned the happily-ever-after, but that didn't matter. At all! "Oh, I don't want to get too excited about this."

"Why not? This is amazing! Wait. Is he being weird about the baby?"

"He has every right to be uncomfortable, Layne. I told

you about the woman who claimed he'd fathered her child, only to have it be his manager's child."

"That's rough. But he can't think the same of you. You would never try to deceive him like she did."

"He does understand that. I hope. I'm going to bring Jamison lunch. He's working at the Homes for Humans site today."

"Lunch is a well-planned move."

"I don't want to make any moves on him, Layne. This is not a rom-com where the heroine needs to snag her baby daddy or…or…"

"Or? Do you think you might lose him, Mabel?"

Mabel sighed. "I just want him to take me for what I am. And the baby. If he doesn't think he can love me, I… I'm not sure what I'll do. I mean, for the baby's sake, he's gotta love it. Doesn't he?"

"Do you love him?"

"Well." Did she? Yes. No? Maybe? She'd been so busy charting her pregnancy and stepping carefully to not scare Jamison away that she hadn't examined her feelings for the man that closely. "I like him. So much. But is it love? I don't want to jump into love because I feel like that's what it *should* be. And I don't want to get married *for the baby*. That never works."

"It could work. Seems like the two of you are on the same page."

"We're on the page that introduces the twist. In our case, a baby. This is so…"

"Eye-opening, life-expanding, world-shaking?"

"All of the above. I'd better go. I'll return to the castle later to help with the shower setup."

"I'll probably get to that around four. You can man the helium pump for the three hundred balloons."

"Oh, mercy, did I say I'd help? I think I have a thing."

"You have no thing, Mabel. I'll see you later!"

"Always."

She headed to the deli to pick up lunch. The bakery was a necessary stop to pick up two crookies. Cravings, don't ya know? And just to be sure... She took a bite of a still-warm crookie. Oh, yeah. That hit the spot.

Once on the side of the property where they were building, Mabel wheeled her bike behind a tall hedge. She could hear people talking and Jamison's voice rose above them all. He was explaining to someone how to connect a joist. The scent of sawdust crept over the hedge and she inhaled. That was the enticing cologne she always noticed on him. Fresh-cut wood!

Taking another bite of the crookie—it would be a crime to let it cool—she peeked through the foliage while munching. Most of the volunteers appeared younger, maybe college age, yet there was a kid who looked around sixteen. Jamison was helping him to grip what looked like an electric nail gun. He talked gently to the boy and placed his hand on the grip, then helped him to release the nail in a surprising jolt. The kid jumped. Jamison gave his shoulder a squeeze and met him eye to eye, asking him if he was all right. The boy nodded.

He was very patient and kind. It warmed Mabel's heart. Would he be a patient and kind father? What had his dad been like with a young Jamison? He'd mentioned how he'd learned carpentry skills from his dad. Had they spent a lot of time together? What childhood memories would Jamison want to instill in his child? *Their child.*

Just thinking that excited her. And recalling him braiding her hair. She wanted to go there with the silly childhood spell. To believe it could become reality. This could work. She was going to get a happily-ever-after!

She finished off the treat. That had disappeared faster than a cookie in a four-year-old's hand. "I am eating for two," she decided.

With one last peek through the hedges, she saw that the kid was triumphantly punching the air. Jamison met him with a fist bump and an encouraging, "You're so talented!"

"He's a good man. He will be a great father someday," Mabel whispered.

Thinking she didn't want to disturb him, she biked around the plot to where his truck was parked out front by the mailbox. The door wasn't locked so she set the food bag inside, along with the remaining crookie. Then she texted him that she'd stopped but didn't want the kids to see he had a great lunch. She missed him and would see him tonight.

It felt very domestic, leaving her lover a note and lunch. Mabel smiled. Yeah, she could go there.

"I could hug you for a thousand minutes..." Jamison smiled at the verse that came out between stacking lumber and sorting through a box of finish nails.

His muse had returned in the form of a rhinestone Cinderella. She inspired him. Nothing about Mabel made him frown. Even thinking about the baby made him smile.

A baby! He was going to be a daddy.

For real this time?

He swallowed, quashing a slip into doubt, and sang another verse. "My Mabel in the moonlight."

He set aside the nail box and strode over to his truck. It was lunchtime and he hadn't packed anything, so he planned to drive to the burger shop at the end of town.

His mind had been preoccupied since Mabel had told him the big news. He'd almost pounded his thumb earlier. He had to eat something. Keep his head on straight and focus.

Opening the door, he smiled at the sight of the brown paper bag on the driver's seat. His name had been written on it in black marker. And circled with a heart. He opened the bag to find a hearty sandwich from a local shop and a plastic baggie of carrot sticks. Beside that sat a bag from the pastry shop. She'd left this for him?

He looked around, up and down the tree-lined street. When had she stopped by? Must have rode over on her bike. Sneaky.

"But much appreciated."

He turned and sat on the footboard of the truck and dug into the sandwich and checked his texts to find her note. She had brought him lunch. A little surprise to brighten his day.

Had it been a guilt gift? Spring a wild announcement on him and then try to cozy up to him to lessen the blow?

No. That wasn't a Mabel ploy. She genuinely cared about him.

And he... He nodded. Yes. He was ready to embrace this baby situation. After spending the day teaching the kids on the project he'd been reminded how much he enjoyed helping others learn. And he wanted to do that with his own child. Just as his father had shown him how to use a hammer and saw, and then allowed him to help with home projects. Eventually Will Wright had allowed his son to put in new shelves in the hallway closet. Which had turned out perfect.

The father-son bond was something special. And even though Jamison didn't live near his dad now, he called him once a month and those yearly visits to Montana were not something he would ever miss.

He could create that lasting bond and good memories with his child. And he would.

Taking a bite of the cookie pastry thing, he nodded at the deliciousness. The sweet surprise from Mabel felt good. Made him feel noticed. Cared for. Not something that people wanted to get a piece of, exploit and then toss aside for the next big thing. Mabel was a small-town princess with a heart of stardust and a crown of rhinestones.

"I like that." He mentally added to the lyrics he was composing.

CHAPTER FIFTEEN

Balloon number one hundred and whatever was blown up, tied off and secured into the growing half-circle arch that would be anchored in the ballroom and twisted through with shiny Mylar ribbons. The photo of the finished project looked amazing, but after hours of snapping the rubber balloon ring to the helium machine, filling it, unsnapping and twisting, Mabel was seriously wondering if Layne would notice her escape out the back and down to the beach. Forever.

This was monotonous.

She opened the music app on her phone and before scrolling to her favs list, she decided to shuffle songs by RJ Wright. She'd never listened to any beyond the one hit she had heard while researching him. The twang of a steel guitar opened the first song and she adjusted the volume and picked up another balloon.

"Oh, I love RJ's music!"

Mabel spun, the balloon coming detached, and deflating with a blurting noise behind her. "Mom?"

"Hi, sweetie! What sort of event are you decorating for?"

"It's a shower tomorrow morning. I agreed to balloon duty before I realized what that involves. I feel as though I'll be here all night."

Mabel picked up another balloon, not wanting to lose any time.

Her mom joined her, grabbing the bag of rose and gold balloons to assist. "I thought Layne's fiancé was rich? Don't you ladies have the budget to hire help for things like this?"

"We do, but…we both enjoy doing some of the work, and the castle is still sort of our baby. Eventually we'll get to a point where we're comfortable hiring out all the work. Right now? We're just having fun with it."

"You don't look like you're having fun."

Mabel shrugged. "It's gotta be done." And really, she didn't mind the time to sit with her thoughts.

Today her mom wore a navy blue dress with a wide skirt, narrow waist and cuffs at the sleeves. Pearls at her neck. It was cute and suited her perfectly. Ever a sunny smile and bounce to her step. Mabel wondered now how she could have ever thought poorly of her mom's lifestyle. The woman was creating her own happiness. Always had.

"That dress is perfect on you," she said.

"You like it? Thanks! It was a freebie from a company I promote on my channel."

"Seriously? You get free stuff?"

"All the time. Mostly decorating or cooking stuff. But this company picked up on my love for retro fashion and sent me a few items. I either get free stuff or a company will pay me for a promotional post."

Mabel was aware influencers could make bank by promoting products. Some posts got hundreds or thousands of dollars. Celebrities earned much more.

"I made six figures last year from my advertising and marketing."

"Six figures?" Mabel released another balloon with a blurt. "Mom? Who are you?"

"We've been over this, Mabel. It's time you accept that your mother has found her niche and is riding it for what it's worth."

"I guess you are." She attached another balloon to the machine. "I'm so impressed, Mom. You've really made the most of your life. I'm proud of you."

"Thank you, Mabel. That means a lot coming from you. Here, let me man the helium for a while. You sort the balloons by color. It'll go faster that way."

They switched jobs and Mabel was glad for a chance to sit on the ballroom floor and rest her legs.

"So what brings you to the castle, Mom?"

"I'm thinking I'd like to rent it for an event."

Madilyn detached the blown-up balloon and twisted it, then expertly wove it into the display while Mabel handed her another balloon.

"An event?" She gave her mom the side-eye. "Is it to do with your social media stuff?"

"My brand, dear. Simply Madilyn."

She handed her another balloon, realizing they made a great team. Could she keep her here longer and get this project done faster? "So what's the event?"

"It's a gathering of local HomeCore and decorating influencers. A mini conference, if you will. I want to do it this fall when the pumpkins are ripe and a chill is in the air. We'll have a cider bar and s'mores, of course."

"Of course."

Mabel knew for a fact the woman was a s'mores master. It had been a while since she'd had her favorite, the peanut butter and bacon s'more. Her mom called it The

Hound Dog, which was a nod to Elvis. And the strawberry cheesecake s'more! Mercy...fall had better get here fast.

"How are you feeling, Mabel? You look a little peaked."

"I do?" And here she had been feeling as if she wore a rosy blush and a lighter step. Though, she had been at this project too long. "Maybe it's the helium."

"I hope you're not inhaling it."

"Of course not." She needed to tell her mom. Of course, she must suspect. While Mabel hadn't noticed any outer changes to her appearance—her belly was only just starting to pooch—she wouldn't be surprised if her mom could sniff out a pregnancy. "Uh...do you want to get some lemonade and sit out on the patio? Chat?"

Her mom gave her an open-mouthed gape. They chatted. Not often or about anything deep or meaningful. But they'd had dinner a few times since she'd returned to Whitmore and Mabel was slowly feeling comfortable being around her. "Yes, I'd like that."

Ten minutes later, with lemonade and leftover samples of the assorted berry tarts the caterers had delivered for the shower, Mabel set down her glass and turned to her mom. "I have something to tell you. It's...big. And it'll probably freak you out."

"Nothing can freak me, dear. Except that one time your father answered the door in the nude when I'd come home with armloads of groceries."

"What? No. I don't want to hear about it." Mabel grimaced and metaphorically girded her loins. Really? Her parents doing kinky sex play? No.

"It's okay. I only dropped one bag, and we didn't need those pickles, anyway."

Mabel rolled her eyes and shook her head vigorously.

"So what's up, Mabel?"

Inhaling deeply through her nose, Mabel settled her shoulders. And pushed the vision of her parents doing *that* aside. "It's something I've been wanting to tell you but needed to talk to Jamison about first."

"Jamison? Is he the man you've been seeing? When do I get to meet him? Is he handsome? Do you love him?"

"He is handsome. You can meet him... I don't know when. And I don't know if I'm in love."

The idea of being in love with Jamison was fabulous, heart-singing and birds-chirping kind of amazing. But was she in love with the man she had only known for a short time?

Yes.

No, you can't be! Love doesn't happen so quickly.

Anything was possible. Especially in fairy tales.

When had she become such a romantic!

"You may have heard of him." She recalled her mom's excitement over the music when she'd walked into the castle. Of course, she knew who he was. "He used to use the name RJ Wright."

"What?" Her mom set down her glass. "The 'Cheers to You' guy? The actual singer? He's so famous—oh, my gracious! He's so... Mabel, that man is sexier than Justin Timberlake during his permed hair years. How did you meet him? When? Where?"

Forcing the image of a curly-haired boy band singer from her thoughts—her mom had thought he was sexy... *the horror*—Mabel said, "Here at the castle when we had the grand opening ball. He was with the construction crew who worked on the castle rehab. He doesn't sing anymore."

"Oh." Her mother nodded. "Right, I heard something about him leaving the music business. I don't know why.

That man's voice..." She fanned her face with her hand. "Oh, mercy, it *does* things to me."

"Mom!"

"Oh? Oh, yes, he's your man. But his baritone..." She made an okay sign with her fingers. "So this is interesting, Mabel. You're dating a rock star?"

"We are dating. Have been since he returned to Whitmore a few weeks ago. But we've been doing things a little backward regarding normal dating procedures."

"Really? What's normal about dating nowadays? It's all done online and in apps and—oh. I do dread when I want to start dating again."

Mabel gaped at her mom. "You want to start dating?"

She shrugged. "Well, sure, Mabel. Someday. I like being in a relationship. Men are... Well, they're nice to have around. What's wrong with a little companionship?"

She didn't want to go to a place where she saw her mom in a relationship with a man other than her dad. But then, was her dad doing the same?

Keep on topic, Mabel. Just get it out!

"We'll table that subject for later, Mom. Right now, you need to know..."

Madilyn waited patiently. Her eager face had never let Mabel down. Whether she was standing on the stage in fifth grade singing a solo in the school recital or rising from the lake after making her first plunge from the high jump. Her mom's approval always shone in her expression.

Now to put that practiced yet genuine expression to the test.

"I'm pregnant."

Mabel forced on an awkward smile as she scanned her mother's face. In a split second, Madilyn Mitchell's shocked look segued to excitement. She set down her half-eaten tart and jumped up before Mabel. "Seriously? You're going to have a baby? I'm going to be a grandmother? Or no, maybe Glamma. No, too flashy. I'll go with G-Ma. Yes!"

Oh, dear. Had she just given her mom more fuel for her influencer lifestyle? *How to Tend the Grandbaby. Top Ten Tips for Styling Your Grandbaby. What Name to Choose as a New Grandma.*

"You're not freaked?" Mabel tried.

"Why would I be freaked about getting a grandbaby? Am I supposed to freak out?"

"No, that's great. I mean, thank you for being so accepting."

"Of course! Are you excited?"

"I am. I mean, it was a surprise. We didn't plan for it to happen. Jamison—RJ—left town the day after the ball and I didn't see him for another two months. I got pregnant that night of the ball. It was…" Her mom didn't need to know her daughter had hooked up with a stranger she'd only known a few hours. "But this baby thing, well, it's been settling into my soul and… I really am excited about it. I'm still in the first trimester. I would have told you sooner but I needed to get right with it first. And then tell Jamison."

"I understand, dear." Her mom sat again. "How does RJ feel about it?"

How did he feel about it? It seemed he was okay with it, but still cautious. Which was to be expected. "He's not angry. But he's been burned in the past by a woman who tried to trap him by claiming her baby was his, and it wasn't."

"Oh, dear. I do recall reading something about that in the tabloids. It was actually his manager's child?"

Mabel nodded.

"Oh, the poor man. That'll make him leery, for sure. Does he believe you? How did he take it?"

"He says he believes me. Though I can sense his caution. To be expected. It's an awkward situation for us both. I told him we could do a DNA test."

"I think that's becoming a standard offering with most births nowadays." Her traditional mother was really blowing the lid off every distorted belief Mabel had ever had about her. "So do you love RJ?"

"He goes by Jamison, Mom. RJ was his stage name. He sets his life now apart from when he used to be a singer. As for love? Maybe? Yes? I don't know."

"It's a new relationship. And you have a lot going on. You don't need to figure everything out all at once. Do you want him in your baby's life?"

"I do. I really do."

Her mom took her hand and patted it. "Then it'll work out. I'm sure it will."

That her mom hadn't suggested she needed to be married was remarkable. Domestic, God-fearing Madilyn Mitchell really had developed a new manner and Mabel loved her for it.

"Mabel? Are you okay?"

Mabel nodded but then shook her head and her mom sat beside her and tilted Mabel's head onto her shoulder. The hug that followed was a long time coming. Mabel turned into her and returned the generous squeeze.

"You don't have to be okay all the time," her mom said. "This sounds like quite an interesting situation for you and Jamison. I like that name. It's very alpha. Stalwart."

Mabel had to smile at that summation. The man was those things and more. Kind. Patient. Sexy. And truly, like a prince come to claim his rhinestone princess.

"I'll be here to talk whenever you need to."

"I'd like that, Mom. Thank you."

"And, of course, I am going to grandma the heck out of that baby."

Mabel laughed through tears. Of course, she would. She'd be the best darn grandma, just as she was the best mom, the best housewife, the best influencer. Madilyn Mitchell was truly a woman to look up to. And from here on, she was going to rely heavily on learning from the best.

The best place in the world was sitting with Jamison on the big sofa that faced the back windows where the bed hugged up. The surround windows looked over the harbor and beyond to the dark line of thick forest that jagged the opposite shore. Here and there within that forest, house lights dotted the darkness. The setting sun lingered in a weaving of violet and gold above those treetops. And already the big fat moon glowed as if a ball of vanilla ice cream.

Mabel laughed at her thoughts. But really, she wouldn't say no to a bowl of ice cream if offered.

The man whose arms she snuggled in on a big comfy sofa leaned back to study her face. He didn't say anything about her silly outburst. Just smiled, nodded and turned back to view the scenery. The silent exchange worked like no words could. They had developed an understanding with one another. Something that seeped through her pores and fixed into her atoms. The man had permeated her bones. Every kiss, hug, caress and, yes, sexual maneuver, further solidified his position inside her very being. She'd never felt this way about a man before. Safe and yet still a little vulnerable, in a good way. Like she could make a stupid joke or laugh to herself and that was okay if she showed him her embarrassment.

A woman should be happy enough to find someone with whom she could sit quietly.

"I'm ready," he said.

"Ready for what?" Mabel toed up the blanket that she'd laid over their bare feet a little higher over her legs. With the windows open to allow in a breeze, the night had cooled.

"For the baby." He gave her a squeeze that felt like acceptance and desire and a whole big world. "I want you in my life. And if that includes a bonus baby? My child, who I can nurture and teach and make memories with? I'm in one hundred percent."

"Are you saying that because that's what you think I want to hear?"

He shook his head. "It's what *I* want to hear. It's my truth, Mabel. We can do this. We made a baby together, now let's raise it and teach it about the world."

The way he put things was always so poetic. Set aside from harsh reality. That's why she adored him. He could make anything sound like a day at the amusement park. Or a romantic walk in the park.

Yes, romance had entered her life. Believe it or not. And she was inclined to believe.

"Thank you." She snuggled against his chest, nestling her ear over his heart. He smelled like cedar. He kissed the top of her head and they watched the sky lose its color and settle to gray speckled with a million stars and that big fat ice-cream moon.

"Mabel in the moonlight," Jamison sang quietly, then paused. "I forgot. There's something I want you to hear." He wandered over and picked up an acoustic guitar, whose wood face was worn from strumming, and sat on the edge of the bed facing her.

Mabel tucked her toes under one of his legs and pulled up the blanket to her lap.

He strummed a few chords and sang, "Mabel in the moonlight. My big-city Cinderella... With stardust in her hair and rhinestones in her heart." He glanced to her. "Not sure about that line, because you've got rhinestones in your hair, but... I like it." He strummed more and sang, "Eyes the color of my favorite Gibson guitar...that's blue." He winked at her. "She lost her crown, not her shoe. That trellis was a climb..."

Curling up against a pillow, she closed her eyes as he serenaded her with a song. About her! How many women had songs written about them by a handsome prince who would climb trellises and weave stardust into their hair? And now he was singing about blueberries and meadows beneath her swirling skirts. It was so personal. Just for her. And his raspy baritone—that her mom would swoon over—hit a deep true note that resonated within her Jamison-infused bones.

"You like it?"

"I love it."

And she loved him. Her heart reached for everything about him.

Yet a few molecules bobbling about inside her were still reluctant. And she could place the reason for that but didn't want to voice it. His past was his past. He'd not given her reason to mistrust him. Hell, if anything, he should be leery of her after what Clementine had put him through.

But he wasn't. He accepted her with open arms.

CHAPTER SIXTEEN

MADILYN STOPPED BY the castle as Mabel was getting off work. Her mom told her the local maternity clothing shop was having a clearance sale on their winter items. And Mabel needed to stock up to see her through the season. It was a fun way to spend some time with her mom.

"That green sweater is adorable," Madilyn said as she handed Mabel a stack of items she'd culled from the clearance rack.

"Do I really need all these clothes, Mom? I'm only going to need the stretchy stuff for a few months."

"But they're on sale and that one with the stripes is fun. I'm buying. And don't say no."

With a protest on her tongue, Mabel decided to concede. If her mom wanted to treat her, she'd let her. She'd buy dinner to say thank-you after they were done shopping.

"I can't really try these on. They'll all look too big now."

"Of course they are, dear. You should start showing soon, though. Oh! This is so exciting. What do you think it will be? Boy or girl?"

"I haven't even thought about it."

"I hope it's one of each."

"What? Mom!" Mabel gave the clerk a nod after her outburst. "It's just one. Okay?"

"Just teasing, Mabel. Though I do recall you wanting a whole baseball team at one point in your childhood."

"Or dance troop," Mabel modified. "I've gotten smarter. I'm going to aim for two or three."

"I can't wait!" Madilyn announced elatedly. Mabel suspected her grandma mode had already activated. "So let's get this stack, yes?"

After her mom swiped her card, they strolled toward Madilyn's SUV to unload their shopping haul. A motorcycle zoomed slowly by on the street and they both waved to Jesse, Layne's fiancé. The man owned a motorcycle company called Sunshine and Storm.

"He's such a cutie," her mom said and then she walked ahead to open the back door.

A truck pulled up to the curb and out hopped Jamison. The sexy silver-haired heartthrob strode up to Mabel, put an arm around her back and pulled her into a kiss. A commanding I-got-you-and-will-protect-you kind of kiss. Never would she tire of tasting this man, feeling his body hug against hers, his breath mingle with hers, his heartbeats dance with hers. As he had a habit, his fingers tickled in the ends of her hair. She loved every moment of Jamison Wright.

When they parted, Mabel noticed her mom standing behind Jamison with a gleeful look in her eyes.

"Jamison. Uh… I suppose now is as good a time as any to introduce you to my mom."

"Your mom?" He winced and whispered quickly to her, "Sorry about the PDA, Cinderella."

"That's okay." Madilyn stepped forward. "Public displays of affection are warranted when you've knocked up my daughter."

"Mom!"

Jamison offered his hand to shake. "Nice to meet you, Mrs. Mitchell. I'm Jamison Wright."

"You don't use RJ?"

"Nope, that's the other guy who used to sing for a living. I'm just a carpenter now."

"An amazing master of all things tool-like," Mabel said as she threaded an arm with his. "He's working on the Homes for Humans house on Nightingale Street."

"Oh, I heard about that poor family. The church ladies are putting together a welcome surprise for when the house is finished."

"That's so thoughtful of you, Mom. I told Jamison you're a big-time influencer."

"Well." Her mom fluffed her skirt and performed a twist of her waist, always an expert at being humble, but Mabel suspected she thrived on every compliment she got. "So you two are going to make me a nana? I'm thinking that's what I'll go with instead of G-Ma. You like it?"

"Nana it is," Jamison said with a grin at Mabel. "I think I'm interrupting something between you two, so I should be going. I just couldn't drive by my Cinderella without stopping."

"Cinderella?" Her mom's smiling perusal said so much.

"Yeah, because I met her in a castle and she did leave a tiara behind the night we—er…"

"I'll tell you about it over dinner, Mom."

"Maybe Jamison wants to have dinner with us? We're just going down to the deli. Are you done for the day?"

"Headed to the next town to pick up some lumber. I'd love to sit and chat but I have to make it before the lumberyard closes."

"Oh, I understand. It was nice to meet you, Mr. Jamison—er, Wright. But you'll not get by without coming to dinner one night. I'll make my famous everything meat loaf and gratin potatoes."

"I'm in." Jamison nodded to her and as he walked backward to his truck, he winked at Mabel. "I'll call you after work."

Mabel watched his truck drive off, aware her mother stood very close. *Nana* probably had a lot of questions for her baby daddy.

"He's so handsome," her mom finally said. "How much older is he than you?"

"Fourteen years. Does that bug you?"

"No. Does it bug you?"

"The age thing doesn't even come up. He's fit and healthy and, should it even matter?"

"He'll be...almost sixty when your child graduates?"

"Mom, stop working the math. We've just begun to figure all this stuff out. Don't have us married and in wheelchairs before we make it to the deli."

"Do you plan to marry?"

The question she suspected her mother needed an answer to. Marriage hadn't come up between she and Jamison, beyond that they'd agreed a proposal would feel forced. They'd only just gotten to the point where they were both all in. And she sensed Jamison was still harboring an ineffable sliver of reluctance, as was she.

"Mabel?"

They paused to wait for a stoplight. A horn honked and Madilyn waved but her attention stayed on Mabel.

"Marriage isn't on the table yet," she offered.

"But you do want to be married if you're having a child?"

It wouldn't help to explain to Simply Madilyn that today a woman could have a baby on her own and that was perfectly fine. Her mom was from a traditional upbringing and that was fine, too. Mabel followed her mom's beliefs more than wanting to plunge into the unknown all on her own.

"Let's just see how things go," she finally said. "It's still so new to me. I'm processing and making spreadsheets and trying to get a handle on everything."

"You and your spreadsheets." Madilyn laughed as they crossed the street. "You know the first one you ever made was for family chores? You'd assigned your dad toilet cleaning duty once a week! Not that he ever did it. He's never touched a toilet brush in his life, I'm sure."

"He did concede to handle the outdoor tasks like taking out the garbage and trimming the hedges," Mabel recalled.

"Have you talked to your father lately? Does he know he's going to be a grandpa?"

"I'll call him. We usually touch base every few months. You know we've never been close."

"I know, dear. He's always been focused on his work. And now he's happy in Sweden."

"I thought it was Norway."

"Sweden. Norway. One of those Scandinavian countries with lutefisk and wool sweaters." Madilyn laughed unabashedly and the twosome strolled hand in hand into the deli.

Mabel landed at Jamison's place around nine in the evening. It had been a great day shopping with her mom. Watching her get recognized and pose for selfies with a couple of women who loved her home tips and videos on creating a cozy nest.

She had promised Mabel she would never put the baby's image online. That was a no-no. That child would grow up without a social media account and wait until he or she was eighteen to drive and have a phone, Mabel decided along with her mom. It was realistic to wait that long for a driver's license, and smart, but perhaps she'd give in to a phone a few years earlier. As long as her kid paid their own bill. Mabel hadn't been allowed a cell phone until she could afford to buy her own with her babysitting money and pay the monthly bill. It was a wise way to teach a kid responsibility.

Now she set a bakery bag of crookies on Jamison's counter and kissed him deeply.

"What was that for?" he asked.

"For being so adorable and sexy and... I may have eaten a crookie on the way here so it was an apology kiss. Which means we'll have to split the remaining one."

"You can have it all, Cinderella."

"Don't say that!"

He mocked shock. "What?"

"All that sugar will give the baby the jitters! You eat it." She shoved the bag at him and he eyed her nervously. Then she realized she'd yelled at him for no reason. "Sorry. It's... I've developed an intense taste for sweets lately. And it's not so much that it'll affect the baby..." She sighed. "There's no way I can stay in shape through this pregnancy if I'm munching crookies every day."

"Don't be so hard on yourself. Our little crookie will appreciate you indulging yourself once in a while."

"Our crookie? Is that what you're calling the baby?"

He laughed and pulled her to him. "Do you want a boy or a girl?"

"I honestly don't have a preference. I just want a sweet little baby to rock in my arms. Will you sing to him or her?"

"Of course. So we said we were going to make some rules? About this situation?"

"Yes. I think it's wise if we get it all worked out now so there won't be concerns later. What will we do about time with the baby?"

"Time with the baby?"

"Yes, like who is going to be the principal caregiver. Well, me, obviously. But I want you to share in this, too."

"Share in it? Aren't we going to parent our crookie together?"

"Oh. Like…live together?"

"Yes, live together. Raise the baby together. Be…parents. Together."

Mabel had only dreamed that the perfect family could be baby, mommy and daddy. But she hadn't placed mommy and daddy in the same home yet. Much as she wanted that very situation. "Do you want that?"

"I do. What about you?"

"Of course, but… Jamison, I feel like you're mine but not mine. And then I think why do I need him to be mine? That feels so selfish. And then I think that every child should be raised by two parents. If it's possible. But I don't want to claim you. If you're not really mine."

He twisted his lips and made a face as if working out what she'd just said. Yes, it had been confusing. If he'd simply tell her he loved her, that would change everything. But since he didn't volunteer that declaration, Mabel held back. And she hadn't said it to him. Because she was still unsure if she said it, it would be because that was expected.

"I want to be yours." He slid a hand along her waist and up her back, stroking the ends of her hair. "But only if that would make you happy."

It would be the happily-ever-after she had craved since childhood. But what had become of her giving up on romance? It had snuck up on her, that was for sure.

"There are days being with you makes me happy," she said. "Other days, when I'm by myself or working on a baby spreadsheet, I'm just trying to hold on and not have the world explode in my face. There have been a lot of changes in my life since I returned to Whitmore. I got the job at the castle. I'm adjusting to small-town life."

"Having to walk into the coffee shop and actually buy your own coffee."

"I know! It's crazy!" She punched his bicep lightly. "And me and my mom are coming to a new understanding of one another. It's really special for me, Jamison, that we've been bonding lately. I judged my mom too harshly when I was a teenager and that attitude sort of stuck with me as I became my own person. But I've seen her in a new light. Her light. And she's an amazing woman. I can only hope to be as awesome a mom to our child as she is to me."

"I will want to get in on some of that meat loaf action she mentioned earlier."

Mabel laughed and gave him a quick kiss, holding his gaze for a long moment. What he seemed to see in her eyes that he said resembled the color of a guitar reflected back to her in soft admiration.

"And another big change was that I met you," she said, "and we jumped right to making a baby before we knew more than what sexual position we liked best."

"I do like it when you snuggle this sweet little behind up against me."

"Mm, we are very sexually compatible."

"That we are."

"But will that compatibility make for a trusting and healthy relationship?"

He hugged her against his chest and nodded. "Listen,

Mabel, it's obvious we both want to raise this child, make it happy, healthy and safe."

"Agreed."

"Let's proceed as a couple. This is our baby. We're going to take care of it. Together."

"Together," she mouthed. It was an immense declaration. One that would change her life even more amidst this upheaval she'd been experiencing. She did want it. So desperately. Why couldn't she just grasp it?

When Jamison touched her chin, she moved back into his soft unjudging gaze and it overwhelmed any doubts she was having.

"I'm never going to do wrong by you, Cinderella. Promise."

"That's a big promise to make."

"It is. But I do tend to stand by my word."

"You won't want to move with the baby to Montana?"

"Wherever you are? That's where I am." He took her hand and kissed the back of her fingers. "I love you."

"You…you do?"

He smirked. "I did just say that, didn't I? I meant it. But I don't need you to say it back to me."

"Why not?"

"Because you're still processing. And I want to give you that mental headspace." He glanced out the window. The waning moon was still nearly full. "Want to dance in the moonlight?"

"Always."

CHAPTER SEVENTEEN

MABEL HADN'T TALKED to her best friend in days, so as she rode her bike up the castle drive, she dialed Layne and put her on speaker.

"Layne, I'm just getting in."

"I'm at the caterers right now, waiting to taste wedding cake!"

"Oh, I won't bother you then, but you have to know... Jamison wrote me a song!"

"I know. It's so romantic."

"What?" Mabel wobbled to a stop before the castle entrance steps. The lush roses and boxwood shrubs provided a perfect spot for wedding photos. "How do you know? He just sang it to me the other night."

"Yeah? Well, it's blowing up on SingSong."

"He...uploaded it online?"

She supposed that made sense. The man was a songwriter. But instead of being happy about that information, her heart plunged. He'd put a personal song he'd written for her out there for...everyone?

"It's just a verse and the chorus," Layne reported. "It's almost got a million views and it hasn't even been up for twenty-four hours. Everyone is screaming for him to post the rest of it."

"Oh." She rarely used SingSong, finding her own playlist more appealing. "I'll have to check the app."

"You're at the castle? I thought you had another doctor's appointment?"

"I did, but the doc canceled. I'm going in next week."

"Oh, I gotta go. We're up!"

"Say hi to Jesse for me. Love you!"

Mabel tossed the phone into her purse and sighed. She supposed she shouldn't be upset that Jamison was sharing his song with the world—something he'd pined to do once again after losing his muse. But could he have asked her first? Had he posted it as RJ or Jamison? Did it matter? This was troubling in ways she couldn't quite pinpoint. Now the whole world would be privy to their relationship. Had he mentioned a baby in the song? She couldn't recall.

On the other hand, it was only one verse.

Still. It felt as if he'd exposed a part of her for millions to see. She couldn't help but be annoyed. But also...happy for him. And yet...

She did not want a public life. She didn't want followers like her mom or screaming fans like RJ Wright. And she'd thought Jamison had left that need in his past. They'd just come to terms that they would raise the baby together. And though it hadn't come up in their conversation, the last thing she wanted to do was raise a child that may be exposed to paparazzi or any of the stuff in the music business that had sent her fleeing.

She hooked her bag over a shoulder and put down the bike kickstand. She hadn't thought to tell Jamison there was a no-going-back-to-being-a-superstar rule if they were to be involved in creating a family. It wasn't a rule she'd thought she had to make.

Did she have any right to demand such of him? Certainly not. Jamison was a grown man. He could live his life the way he wanted to live it. Could she endure his returning to that lifestyle and still allow him to be a part of the life she was creating?

"I don't know."

Mostly because she was blindly wandering into that new life herself. There were no guidelines, no rights or wrongs. Everything was in test phase.

Taking out her phone again, she opened the SingSong app, which gave her a spinning icon as it updated.

Gazing up at the castle facade, she felt her heart flutter like that pre-tween girl who had once stolen inside and played princesses and dragons with her best friend. Then, she had created a man who couldn't possibly exist. A man who would weave stardust into her hair. Sing to her of love and happily-ever-afters.

Turns out, he did exist. But he came with a dark curse she wasn't sure this rhinestone Cinderella wanted shadowing her life.

Jamison waved goodbye to his work mates as he left the Homes for Humans site. They'd put up the roof today and a pallet of shingles had arrived to keep them busy tomorrow. Windows were due in a few days. He liked when a project went smoothly.

He approached his truck, and before opening the door, did his usual jump in place. One good jump, or two, and the sawdust rained from his shoulders and head and everywhere else it had landed during the day. He shuffled his hands vigorously over his hair, dispersing more dust.

"Good enough."

The shower was always his first destination after a long day at work.

He was thankful for this work. And much as it was a complete one-eighty from singing on stage and writing songs, he got an immense feeling of pride working with his hands and creating homes for people. A house provided shelter, protected, offered a child a place to sleep in peace and a family to share a meal together. And that warmed his heart.

Setting his tool belt on the floor of the passenger side, he started the truck and rolled out onto the street. Tapping the radio, he tuned the sound up for a Hardy song. He'd been compared to the country rocker. Best comparison a guy could get.

At a stop sign, he glanced to his phone, which he kept in the holder while on the job. The notifications flashed with...

"Two thousand?" he muttered.

Driving through the intersection, he navigated the short distance to his harborside home, following his rule of never texting while driving. Once in his driveway, he grabbed the phone and opened the SingSong app. The notifications were for the song snippet he'd posted after sending Mabel off with their plans to raise the child together. She'd been so happy. And he had been feeling as though the future looked very bright.

That good feeling had given him the crazy idea to post a verse for the song to RJ's dwindling followers just to show them he still had it, and that songwriting would never leave his blood. It was just him singing and strumming guitar for about a minute.

The comments on the audio post were mostly excited, congratulatory, many handclap emoji, lots of hearts and music notes. Some sighs, a lot of It's about time and We've been waiting to hear more from you. Overwhelmingly, they wanted him to post the entire song.

He'd only recorded one verse.

He read a few more comments.

There was a Give it up, buddy; you had your shot and blew it.

To be expected. It would be weird if they all responded positively. Though that last one did hit him like a gut punch. He'd taken that shot, ridden the entertainment rocket into the stratosphere and then jumped without a parachute, landing hard. His record company had successfully managed to remove "The Devil's Deal" from any online music site—yes, even though he'd self-published it—and they'd quickly pulled all media and promotion for his albums, effectively canceling him. Following that, RJ had been sought for interviews for about half a year, but he'd refused, stating he'd said it all in that song.

These comments made him feel noticed again. That maybe he did still have it. And he couldn't believe that he missed that feeling. There was something about a crowd cheering and clapping and hooting for him that injected that energy directly into his veins. It was like a drug.

One he hadn't tasted in a long time.

A call notification popped onto the screen. Cole Callahan? The one music producer Jamison had wanted to work with but had never been able to juggle his commitments to make it work. And the one time it had happened, his record label had throttled that collaboration because they wouldn't have received a cut. Callahan had mastered tracks for some of country music's greats.

Why was he calling?

Did it matter? He answered and Cole said, "Hey, RJ, do you think it's finally time for us to connect?"

"Cole, good to hear from you." After three years? And

him wielding a hammer and saw with no real interest in ever holding a microphone again. Or did he? "What's up?"

"What's up with you, man? You trying to go independent now? Who is Mabel? Please tell me she's a real person. That'll make the song even more popular."

"She's someone I know."

"Someone who has stolen your heart, eh? The song is incredible. What you posted of it. Is it finished? What's going on with you, man?"

Wild, weird and crazy stuff, and all of it labeled Mabel.

When he'd posted, he thought to get a few comments. Maybe he'd produce the whole song and put it out there for the few who still followed him.

"It was just a one-off," he said. "Something I wrote because…"

His muse had returned! And he couldn't have *not* written that song for Mabel. That's how he showed people his heart. What meant most to him.

Like Mabel.

And now there was a baby. *Their* baby.

"You need to release the whole song," Cole said. "And I want to make that happen. No low-production social media blip. Let's get in the studio and bring RJ Wright back to the world. Yeah?"

Getting back in the studio felt…

He'd left the industry because of a moral decision. He'd seen the drugs, the slave-like contract requirements, the creepy parties involving sex and extortion. It wasn't his style. He couldn't blame the baby-daddy thing with Clementine on the industry, though it had been interwoven so deeply into that time of his life when he'd been questioning everything that it was difficult not to. He didn't need that headache again.

"RJ?"

And yet, adrenaline bubbled in his veins after seeing the reaction to the song snippet. He was a songwriter before a carpenter. Words meant something to him. And to pair them with music was his way of putting his heart out there. To put out another song would fulfill a deep inner desire for attention and validation. To know that others enjoyed his music. And to verify that he still had that creative spark.

It was a heady thrill.

"Can I think about it?" he asked Cole.

"Sure, man, but don't think too long. You know how this works. Hot one day. Colder than the devil's toenails the next. It doesn't have to be a full plunge back into the cauldron, man. Let's put this song out, sit back and see what happens. Yes?"

Sounded good. In theory.

He would be a fool to say no to such an incredible producer. "I'll call you later. Thanks, Cole. I do want to work with you. And this may be the perfect time."

"I'll be waiting. Talk later, man." Cole disconnected.

Jamison set his phone aside and stared at it. Then he picked it up and switched to the music app. The likes had increased by hundreds in the time he'd been talking to Cole. Insane!

"It is a hell of a song," he rationalized with the part of him that was tugging to stay the course. He'd chosen to walk away for a reason.

Putting that song out there could also bring in some cash. Not that he needed that. But it could be the start to a college fund for his child.

Nodding, he decided the only person he wanted to share this great news with was the one person who meant more to him than anything.

CHAPTER EIGHTEEN

AFTER A SHOWER, Jamison texted Mabel but she didn't reply. She was likely at work. He decided to surprise her so stopped into the flower shop. But as he was eyeing the red roses, a glance landed on a little green stuffed bear with embroidered hearts for eyes.

Something was happening in the vicinity of his heart. His Cinderella had captured his heart and—a man should be married, in love and have a decent job in order to care for his family. He had a good income. He'd set aside a chunk of his song royalties in a retirement account. He wasn't worried about living on the streets. He could make a good life for his family and that college fund could become reality. He knew Mabel would not want to move to Montana. Her home was here in Whitmore. And he did love the small-town vibe. Hell, his house was a perfect nest perched on the beach and overlooking the harbor. And the bedroom on the lower level could be turned into a nursery.

What would happen if he put out more songs? Could he return to the industry on his own terms? As an independent? He knew singers and bands who had done so and with success. Doing so would feed that creative side of him that he never wanted to lose. It would validate him in ways that a relationship could not. Because love and sex and happiness were great. But someone telling him something he'd created made them happy? That meant the world to him.

Yet, he had created something. Something amazing, that would come into his life in a little over half a year. The baby should be all he required for that peace and happiness he desired.

Right?

There was a lot to consider before he called Cole back. And he wanted to make that call with Mabel's blessing.

Dare he put down roots here? He'd been a vagabond since his teen years. Had moved out of his parents' house at sixteen to live above the welding shop where he'd gotten his first job. After graduating, he worked as a roadie for a local band for a couple years. Then he'd settled into carpentry, taking jobs in towns across the upper States because he liked to move around and see new places.

He didn't know what it felt like to be still, to stay in one place. That's why the rock 'n' roll lifestyle had suited him so well. Touring had been a release of his energy, both physical and mental. On stage had been where he'd felt most real. Most at home.

The parties and media blitzes had not been home. Those had been necessary evils that had finally pushed him over the edge.

He gave the little bear a squeeze.

So what was keeping him from fully embracing fatherhood and proposing to Mabel?

He stepped off the curb and quickly stepped back as a motorcycle zoomed by, beeping its horn to alert him. Heartbeats thundering, Jamison shook his head. He wasn't in his right mind when he thought about Mabel. And if he were going to make the right decision about his future, he had to do it rationally and…

"Who are you kidding?" he muttered as he strolled across the street toward the castle. "You've never used logic your entire life. You live for the moment."

And the cheering fans. The validation of a stadium filled with people who sang along with the songs and knew every single word.

"Will Cinderella accept this rock star?"

Mabel opened her door to a cute stuffed bear.

The man holding the bear was just as cute, so she kissed him, crushing the bear between them. Kissing Jamison was the best thing besides a slice of fresh-out-of-the-oven homemade bread.

Wrong. It was better.

She pulled back and said, "But I do crave bread."

Jamison quirked a brow. "You okay, Cinderella?"

"Your kiss made me think of homemade bread. You and the bear come on in."

She studied the bear and gave it a hug as he wandered over to the window overlooking the main street.

"I stopped by the castle but Layne said I just missed you, so here I am. Uh…there's the bread shop down the street," he said. "Want me to run and get you some? Is this a pregnancy craving?"

"It could be. I put a bread maker on my online shopping list earlier. Weird, huh?"

"It's kind of cute."

"Yeah?" She set the bear on the counter. "Are you going to put that online, too? My list of cravings for the world to see?"

Jamison's jaw dropped open and Mabel realized she'd just snapped at him. And while she had good reason, the sneak attack didn't feel fair. "Sorry."

"Don't apologize for speaking your mind, Mabel. So you know about the song? Just a verse, actually."

"Why didn't you tell me about it? Layne was the one to tell me it was getting attention. I just thought…"

"You thought?"

She shrugged. Of course, the man was a musician first. And he had every right to do what he pleased with the songs he wrote. And yet. "I thought it was a gift for me. Something you wanted me to have."

"Oh, Mabel."

He kissed her. Sweetly, and then not so sweetly. Claiming her. Making her want to crawl inside him, to find a safe space. She clung to his shirt and bowed her head against his neck. Sawdust and cedar. That smell would undo her.

"I did write that song for you. It was my heart speaking to you."

"It felt like that when you sang it to me. But now that it's online, it feels…like you're giving a part of what we have away to the world. I suppose I have no right to tell you what to do with something you've created. It is your song. You can do with it as you wish."

"Please don't be angry with me, Mabel. It was a spur-of-the-moment thing. I started recording the song because I wanted to play with the guitar melody and… I posted it for some feedback. I thought maybe a few of RJ's fans might comment. I never thought it would blow up the way it has."

It made sense. He hadn't been trying to exploit the beautiful romance they were developing with the song. But it hurt her heart in a way she couldn't define. Her name was in that song.

"It got a lot of views." She stepped from his arms and wandered back to the soft bear. That he had been thinking of the baby and bought the toy was thoughtful. Something a loving dad would do. "I am thankful it wasn't the whole song. Because you did mention family in one of the verses you sang to me."

"I wasn't trying to suggest anything with that verse," he said. "But…it does feel right. And we did come to terms that we would raise the baby together."

"We did. I just never thought…" The whole world would suddenly be invited into their private lives. That was one step away from paparazzi and tabloid headlines.

Oh, Mabel! Was she doing the right thing by allowing this to bother her? It had been one verse.

"Cole said we should put the whole thing out."

She turned her attention from the bear. "Cole?"

Jamison slid onto a stool before the counter. "Cole Callahan is a producer. I've always wanted to work with him, but we never found the right time. He called earlier."

"Oh."

Something inside Mabel shivered. Was it the baby? Did it sense that this situation didn't feel quite right? That something was being forced on her? It felt akin to when her boss at the record label had harassed her. Not safe. Shameful.

"Yeah." Jamison ran his fingers along his beard. A move that always drew her like a bee to honey, but…not now. The bear between them felt like a protective barrier she needed. "He wants to produce the song. I told him I'd consider it."

"Oh." Another lurch inside her chest made her wince. "But I thought you left the music industry for a reason? I did find lyrics for that song, 'The Devil's Deal.' It was…" Right on, pointing the finger at every evil practice the industry tried to keep hidden in plain sight. "I thought it was brave, and honest, and… Why would you go back to that?"

"Now, Mabel, I'm not slipping on the spandex and renting out the tour bus again. Hell, I never wore spandex."

He waited for her response with a bemused gaze, but she wasn't in the mood for humor right now.

"It's just one song," he added. "I kind of thought you might be happy about it. It's your song. And everyone will get to hear it. I don't need the money, but if Cole and I did produce it and make it available for sale, I was thinking it would make a nice college fund for our kid."

A truly thoughtful gesture. And yet, he'd already considered putting out the whole song? *And* selling it?

Pressing a hand over her heart where the ache had risen, Mabel couldn't force herself beyond the bad taste in her mouth that lingered after her stint in the music industry. She'd thought to keep her distance from Jamison after learning he was in that same field, but it had been impossible. He wasn't like the one man who had made her flee for the protection of her hometown. And she wouldn't stop him from doing what made him happy. To judge his posture and smile, this was exciting news.

"I'm happy for you," she offered. It wasn't so much a lie as a polite acceptance on his behalf.

"Mabel." He moved aside the bear, effectively breaking down her protective barrier. "What's going on in that pretty head of yours? I feel like your tiara isn't sparkling so much today."

A glance across the room spied the tiara she'd set on the mantel above the gas fireplace. When in Jamison's arms, she really did feel like the princess she'd dreamed of becoming when she and Layne had played in the castle as kids. Safe, protected. Loved.

"I've told you how I feel about the industry," she said.

"You told me you had a bad experience. But…you didn't give me details. I'd like you to share with me. I want to understand all of you if we're going to…"

If they were going to have a baby together? She wanted that. But she didn't want it with a man who would be traveling the world, standing on the stage, singing about their personal lives to the masses.

But who was she to stop him from taking back his dreams?

"Mabel? What happened to you? Tell me?"

"It's nothing." She crossed her arms over her chest.

Jamison slid off the stool and moved around the counter, slowly, pausing to meet her eyes for a moment before pulling her in for a hug. A hug she wasn't sure about. Yet, she couldn't not embrace him. She always fit perfectly against him. As if they'd been made for one another.

Why couldn't she tell him? Right after it had happened, she'd told her mom over the phone during a tearful conversation. Of all people, Jamison should be able to understand and relate the most.

"It's just…" She sniffed back tears, surprised that the emotions emerged so quickly and without her being able to fight them back.

"Did someone hurt you, Mabel?"

She shook her head. "It didn't go that far."

"That far? Mabel." His voice ached when he spoke her name. And hugged her even closer.

Oh, to fall into him and never find her way back. His strong yet gentle presence was like nothing she'd ever had in her life. And she never wanted it to go away.

"It was…" She exhaled. "I told you I worked in accounting. I was never out in the action, not in a recording studio. I didn't have regular contact with the talent. Occasionally, I was invited to attend a release party. But I did see a lot. The label was small and so was the office. I could hear more than see some days. I witnessed the sexual harassment. The expectations, most often put out there by men toward the women, both aspiring singers and those who were established. It was disheartening."

He nodded. "Stuff like that is rampant. But it's not all bad."

"Oh, I know. Every industry has its goods and bads, but...it's certain people that can give a nasty smear to an entire industry. At least from my viewpoint. After I'd been there almost three years, our boss retired and his son took his place. He came in to shake up the label. He was younger than me by a few years. Very touchy. He would brush up against me. Say things. Sexual things. One day he implied that if I didn't have sex with him, I'd lose my job."

"Oh, Mabel."

Jamison's comforting hug was something she'd craved since walking away from her job. A safe place to feel protected, blocked from those terrible memories and emotions. From the wondering if she had done something wrong. If perhaps she had overblown the situation and should have stuck it out. Always blaming herself. Never the perpetrator. She knew in her heart she was the victim, but society made it difficult to speak up about it, to claim that mistreatment. She must have misinterpreted it. She was blowing things out of proportion. She was crying wolf. Which could have been part of the reason why she'd been so reluctant to tell Jamison about the baby.

Wow. She hadn't thought of it that way until now. She'd been protecting herself from another man misinterpreting her actions once again.

Her body stepped out of Jamison's embrace. Even as her brain wondered why she was making such a move. She clasped her arms across her chest.

"I had to leave," she said, not meeting his gaze. "My

dreams of making it in the big city came crashing down around me. I ran back to mommy and daddy like a little girl. Well, metaphorically. They were divorced by the time I returned to Whitmore. But, Jamison, I couldn't hack it. And it makes me feel so ashamed."

"No, Mabel, you did nothing wrong."

"But I feel that way, Jamison. I couldn't hack it in the big city. I hadn't the fortitude to make it with the entertainment crowd. What's wrong with me?"

"Not a damn thing. It's all on that bastard who thought he could control you."

"You believe me?"

"Of course, I do. And like you said, it's not the whole industry but specific people. Some people are entitled, pompous, egotistic assholes. If they can manipulate a person into doing something, they'll do it. Trust me, I know. I'm so sorry you went through that." He stepped forward and pulled her to him. "I'll just hold you."

She wanted to melt against him but she kept her arms crossed. Tears flowed down her cheeks. Usually, in Jamison's arms she felt safe, but right now…

If he were to step back into the role of singer, he would have to reenter that world that had sent her fleeing. And she didn't want to have a connection to that awful feeling. To any of the people who had made her feel *less than*.

And her child would never be put in a position, or be around people, who would make him or her feel inferior, or that they were required to participate in something that made them feel uncomfortable. Not on her watch.

"I can't do this." She pushed out of his embrace. "I… don't want to raise my child anywhere close to the industry that made me feel like I wasn't worthy unless I submitted to some man's expectations. Please understand,

Jamison. I certainly don't want to stop you from working with Cole and producing the song that means so much to you." She swallowed. "I love that song. You won my heart with that song."

"Mabel..."

"And it would be good if you could get back some of that validation you still seem to need. But I can't have a relationship with a man, something stable, something real, if money and fame is more important to you." Just as it had torn her dad away from her mom. "I know that's a big ask, but it's how I feel."

"The validation means—I'll pull the deal. Hell, we haven't even made a deal yet."

"No, don't lay that on me. I don't want to be the one who influenced you to miss out on an opportunity that could be so great. Please, Jamison. We need to...step away." She walked to the door and opened it for him. "I need some space."

As tears welled in her eyes, she fought for a brave stance. This felt insane. She was asking him to leave. Her life? She wasn't sure! The feelings she'd had when she'd been harassed at work had risen, and while his hug should have countered those feelings, now she was confused and—maybe it was the pregnancy. She needed some space to breathe. To process.

Jamison stood on the threshold. "Mabel," he said on a husky rasp, as if a verse to a song.

It broke her heart.

"Just give me time," she said. She turned her back and the door closed. His footsteps taking the stairs to the street level pounded in her veins.

How could she have thought a happily-ever-after could be hers?

CHAPTER NINETEEN

Jamison threw a flat rock across the water's surface. It didn't skip. He needed to fling something hard. He picked up another stone, and another, and moved his frustrations through the toss.

Splash.

Bruised and messy. That was what his heart felt like after Mabel had asked him to leave.

He hadn't expected Mabel to take his posting the song verse so harshly. But after she'd explained exactly what had made her flee the industry, he understood. Even if it wasn't at all related to him producing a song, she did not want to be connected to that which had hurt her. Had made her feel *less than*. Had destroyed her dreams.

He wandered along the sandy scruff where the beach segued into brushy grass and rock. The *shush* of water against the beach didn't calm him tonight. A dried starfish lay in a tangle of seaweed and he picked it up and shook off the sand. He'd walked down a public access to get to the beach instead of heading straight to his home. He needed to stand out in the salted air, the sky darkening and the stars twinkling above. To find his place.

Did he have a place?

Jamison loved his parents. And he loved Montana. The land was beautiful, from vast meadows and cattle ranges to soaring mountain ranges and rushing rivers that defied clarity. A person could watch the northern lights, dive into a turquoise blue lake, dream to touch the low-hanging clouds embracing Grand Teton, or walk a field in sight of a majestic moose. As a young man, he had easily placed himself there for the rest of his life. Even traveling for gigs and singing for thousands, he'd held a special place in his heart for his homeland. It had been something to return to.

And when he'd landed in Whitmore, much as he had found a great home and job, there had always been that missing piece. Something to return to.

Until his one-night stand with the rhinestone Cinderella. Mabel had been a flash in his unmoored life that burst like fireworks. The best stage pyrotechnics. Those stars in the sky.

And every time he looked at the stars—at this starfish—he was reminded of Mabel and how she made him feel. Better than settling in a cozy little cabin in Montana. Better than helping others by donating his time to build houses. Better even than singing and songwriting.

If he could have Mabel, he didn't require anything else to feel satisfied. Forget the applause and adulation. Mabel was that something he wanted to return to.

"I do love her," he muttered to the glitter of moonlight on the sea surface.

But could she love him, was the question. And could she love him if he chose to reach for something that gave him joy and a feeling of accomplishment like producing and putting out the song?

I can't have a relationship with a man who values money and fame more than family.

He didn't need the money. But did he need fame? The fact he was even considering producing the song must mean he did. Else he would have said no to Cole and that was it.

If he put out that song, then he would lose Mabel. And his baby. The choice should be an easy one.

So why did he feel as though he had to touch fame one last time?

Tugging out his phone, he dialed his parents' number. When his dad answered, he told him the whole situation. And it came down to one thing: what sort of memories did he want to leave for his child?

Mabel helped her mom pull green fabric over a frame, which she explained she was going to film in front of and then later replace with different backgrounds. Backup for days she couldn't film outside. It was a marvelous thing her mom had going.

After telling her about her talk with Jamison, and the song, she then explained how it felt like all the bad emotions from her New York job were being dredged back up. She wanted to trust Jamison. She *did* trust him. But his need to post that song for anyone to listen to bothered her.

"I wish you wouldn't have had to go through that with your boss," Madilyn said. Project completed, she sat before the dinner table across from Mabel and pushed a plate of pistachio chocolate chip cookies toward her. "Maybe you should talk to someone about it?"

"You mean like a psychiatrist? No. I'm leaving that in my past. I'll get over it."

"But you're not over it. Else you'd have no problem letting RJ—er… Jamison into your life."

"Do you think so?"

"Sweetie, he's a creative man. He's the opposite of your logical self. Creativity fuels him. Songwriting is probably his way of putting things out there that he wouldn't normally be able to discuss with others."

"He did say that's how he spoke from his heart."

"And it sounds like he doesn't want to do the rock-star thing again?"

"He just wants to put out the one song. Our song."

Her mom patted her hand. "It's a special thing to have a song written for you. I can understand you wanting to keep that private."

"It's not so much that. Mom, I don't want to raise a child around the music industry."

"You won't be, Mabel. I understand your fear. But you are a smart woman. And Jamison seems like a kind man. He's been through an accusation and had his heart ripped out when he learned the child wasn't his. And now he's willing to do it all over again? He must really love you."

"He did tell me that."

"Do you love him?"

Mabel closed her eyes and settled deeper into the padded chair. She wanted to love him.

"What will allow you to accept him into your life, dear? Him never writing a song again?"

"I don't want him to stop writing. It's the way he communicates his emotions. It's him. He's so poetic."

"Then there must be something else that you need from him beyond that?"

Not really. She could be happy in Jamison's arms. Raising their child. As long as he wasn't touring and leaving her alone to raise their child, life could be good.

She was happy here in Whitmore. She'd escaped to the big city, gotten her feet wet in the industry and decided it wasn't the job or the environment for her. How could she have ever enjoyed riding the subway? The constant push and shove of the crowded sidewalks? The smell of gasoline and worse? And never home in time to relax and enjoy herself? Sure, New York had a lot going for it. She'd miss living so close to the theaters, the access to tons of fabulous restaurants and the high-end shopping.

But if she really needed that, she could hop in the car and drive forty-five minutes to Somerset. And had she pined for any of it in the months since she'd been back in Whitmore? Not a bit.

"His parents want him to move to Montana. He was intent on doing just that. Seems like I'm the only thing keeping him here."

"Isn't a baby a good reason for him to stay? Especially if he loves you."

Mable spread a hand over her stomach. She had begun to sense the other being. The life within. And it made her proud and happy and so ready to be a mom.

"I guess I'm afraid to take another chance," she confessed. "The big-city thing didn't work out. What if this doesn't work out?"

"This? You mean bringing up a child alongside a man who loves you?"

"You make it sound so simple, Mom."

"Maybe it is."

It could be. If she weren't sabotaging that simple with irrational beliefs.

"Mom, you and Dad were married thirty years! And now what do you have to show for it?"

"I have years of wondrous memories, dear. Good, funny, happy, some fights, some downright angry moments. But I wouldn't trade it for a redo. I'm right where I belong. I'm in a good place. And I want you to find that same place. Life changes. It can't be good all the time. Struggles and challenges are what give life spice, make us stronger." Her mom shook her head. "I sound like a self-help book. Just follow your heart, Mabel. It'll lead you where you need to be in the moment."

"Thanks, Mom. I..."

She loved Jamison. But was it too late? She'd sent him away. Told him she didn't think it could work between them. And it had been a day since she'd last seen him.

She had to go to him.

"Are you sure about this photo shoot?" Mabel asked Layne, as her friend sorted through Mabel's closet for a suitable dress. "It's so late in the day."

"It's called the golden hour and this was the only time we could get this photographer. Jesse says he's the best. Bailey Marks is on his way to Somerset for a magazine layout assignment. We've only got half an hour to get the shoot done before he needs to hit the road again. Here. This is the one."

Right after talking to her mom, Layne had called Mabel and told her about the opportunity to have some promo shots of the two of them taken for the castle. They wanted to convey the summery romanticism of the place. Layne wore a floral sundress with fluttery layers that floated with every turn. Her hair was up and she'd pinned a few rhinestone barrettes here and there. She looked like a princess.

Mabel slipped on the blue dress she'd worn the night of the ball. "This might be too fancy."

"No, it's perfect. It matches your eyes."

Jamison had said much the same that first night they'd met. Gibson guitar eyes? Mabel clutched the skirt, her other hand over her heart. It ached for him. She should have never said those things to him. She wanted him. She wanted whatever messy future they could create together. Including diapers.

"Sweetie?" Layne walked over to study her face. "Are you crying?"

Mabel shook her head. "It's just hormones. This pregnancy is going to work a number on me, for sure."

"Aw. I know you love him. You two will talk. And it'll be good."

"Promise?"

Layne nodded, then swung out her hand from behind her back. "This, too. That'll make the look."

"I think a tiara is a bit too much for promo shots."

"Uh...we are the resident Cinderellas, are we not?" She waggled the tiara and Mabel snatched it. "Great. Now, do your hair in five minutes. We gotta go!"

Mabel rushed into the bathroom to comb through her hair, pin it back and tuck in the tiara.

She did love Jamison. And it was time she told him that. But first, work called.

The photographer was curt, knew exactly where to position the two women for the best shots and how to direct their movements. After only twenty minutes of shooting outside on the patio, he announced he had to go. They hadn't gotten any inside shots!

"We really need to do some inside," Mabel said to Layne as the man took off toward the ballroom, camera in hand. "We're paying him!"

"I got this. You wait here." Layne rushed off after the photographer.

Mabel understood the man was pressed for time, but really, he was being rude.

Blowing out a breath, she turned to face the harbor. The

horizon-level sunlight cast a golden glow over everything and it shimmered on the water. She tugged off the tiara. Leaning her elbows onto the railing, she sighed.

Something wonderful had begun right here on this outdoor patio/dance floor. She and Jamison had fallen in lust. It may even have been love. She wasn't afraid to go there. Then, only hours later, they'd made a baby. It was as though the universe had been privy to her childhood dreams and granted them, only out of order.

"Wouldn't change a thing," she whispered. "I got my wish granted. If only...for a little while."

The thought that she may have pushed Jamison away brought a tear to her eye. And she couldn't even blame that on hormones. But the talk with her mom had made her see through her doubts and fears. Jamison would never hurt her. She knew that in her heart.

A staticky buzz sounded over the loudspeakers and suddenly a slow song lilted out. The overhead lights strung across the patio flickered on. And when Mabel turned, she saw Jamison standing in the center of the patio. Jeans, a rustic shirt, Dr. Martens and that sexy smile that said things she would never share with anyone else.

"Jamison?"

He held out his hand. The sunlight glinted on his silver ring. "Can I have this dance?"

Walking quickly toward him, she landed in his arms. But she didn't want to dance. And the kiss was everything she wanted to say to him. An apology, a love letter, a promise for their future. In his kiss, she felt safe and loved. No matter what.

He took the tiara from her and placed it on her head. His eyes met hers. Words weren't necessary. She saw everything she needed to know in his gaze.

Snugging his hand at her hip, they started to sway to the music. Just over Jamison's shoulder Mabel spied Layne, who stood in the ballroom doorway giving her a thumbs-up, a blown kiss, and then she scampered off. Had she…?

"How did you know I'd be here?" Mabel asked, her suspicions growing. Her body hugged his gentle yet secure power, knowing its home.

"After you asked me to leave last night I didn't sleep a wink. And I couldn't let another day go by without making sure we were right with one another. I called Layne this morning and planned this all out with her."

"What? But the photo shoot…?"

"A friend from town. There's no fancy photographer. It was Layne's idea to get you here so I could tell you something."

"That sneaky…"

But it didn't matter. She was here. In the arms of the man she loved. And nothing mattered, no angry words, no unsure misgivings. Not even that song.

"You can do what you want with the song," she said. "I don't want to keep the world from hearing another RJ song."

He nuzzled up alongside her cheek and said in her ear, "It's Jamison's song. And I'm not going to do the deal with Cole."

"But you have to. It's your creative outlet. You love songwriting."

"I'm not going to do anything that frightens you away from me. If you don't want me involved with anything to do with music, I'm fine with that. Professionally, that is. I don't ever want to stop writing songs and singing to my girl. All I want to do is create great memories with you and our child. I'd do anything for you Mabel."

"That's too extreme." She paused, still holding his hand. The overhead lights caught in his silver hair, his smile. "I know you won't go all rock star on me. You can put out the song like you did that first time you went big. Doesn't mean you have to start touring again."

"Touring is the last thing I want to do if I'm going to raise a family."

"Really?"

He nodded. "My dad once told me home is where the heart always lands. I have a tendency to fall, Cinderella. Hard. Not always a good fall, either. But falling for you? It was the best fall I've ever made."

"Is that what you came here to tell me?"

He took her hand and spun her, releasing her hand. When Mabel swirled back around she saw Jamison down on one knee before her.

"You're my rhinestone Cinderella, my moonlight Mabel. And I love you with all my heart. I know you've had some misgivings…"

"They're all gone. Promise." She crossed her heart.

He tugged out a piece of paper from a back jean pocket and handed it to her.

Mabel unfolded it and smiled at the simple hand-drawn graph showing a line for her and another line for Jamison, which intersected. And in the middle was a line labeled Baby.

"I know how much you like spreadsheets. Figured it was time to draw myself onto one of them."

"It's perfect," she said. "You belong on all my spreadsheets."

"That makes my heart happy. Mabel, will you do me the honor of being my bride? I want our child to come into this world with two parents who want the best for him or her."

She'd not expected this. But what a perfect moment. And her best friend had made it happen. Jamison loved her. She loved him. It would all work out. He could put the song out there, share it with the world and not invite in something they both had had enough of. And she trusted him to keep that promise.

"Almost forgot." He stood and shuffled in his front shirt pocket to pull out a ring. "The jeweler said this was an antique, once belonging to the original woman of this castle, Charles Whitmore's wife. It's pretty. I hope you like it."

He stood and placed it on her finger. The diamonds caught the sunlight in a golden dazzle. "Will you marry me, Mabel?"

She hadn't answered him? "Of course!"

She flung herself into his arms and they swirled across the patio dance floor. And at that moment, the music changed to a familiar song.

"I told Layne to play this if it looked like you said yes." He winked and embraced her for a swaying dance. Singing along with the lyrics that he had written just for her. "My Mabel in the moonlight…"

EPILOGUE

THE FOLLOWING SUMMER, Jamison Wright married Mabel Mitchell. Their daughter, Juniper, was strolled down the aisle by Nana Madilyn, who flung rose petals in lieu of the flower girl, who wanted to chew on them.

The patio dance floor dazzled with the strung lighting, and as soon as the guests finished eating, they'd have the first dance. Jamison had promised he'd sing their song. One that Mabel had asked him to produce and release independently. The producer he'd wanted to work with understood Jamison's desire to stay away from the industry that burned him, so he'd traveled to Whitmore and they put it out together. It hit number one within a week. At Mabel's suggestion, half the proceeds had gone to Homes for Humans. The other half was sitting in a college fund.

Mabel's mom took a sleepy Juniper from her arms and kissed her sweet kitten-soft dark hair. "I'll put her down before the dancing begins."

"Thanks, Mom."

Her mother wandered inside the castle where they'd designated a room for the newlyweds. Simply Madilyn had blown up this past Valentine's Day with a post about Finding Your Mister Right in all the Wrong Places. Some subtle references to Mabel and Jamison's story had been woven in. Madilyn had reached top-influencer status and been invited to speak at an international event next month. She was thriving and loving every minute of her superbly simple life.

Mabel caught Layne's attention, and her friend, who had married last fall, dropped her hubby's hand and joined her. They walked to the railing overlooking the harbor and leaned on it, side by side.

"You got the guy whose metaphorical blood runs through these castle walls," Mabel said.

"And you found a man to weave stardust into your hair and sing to you happily-ever-after. Are we the luckiest women in the world?"

"We are," Mabel said, with a glance back to the dance floor where her new husband chatted with the DJ. He paused, met her gaze and winked. "Yes, we are."

* * * * *

*If you missed the previous story in the
Fairy Tales in Maine duet,
then check out*
Invitation to His Billion-Dollar Ball
by Cara Colter

*And if you enjoyed this story,
check out these other great reads from
Michele Renae*

Faking It with the Boss
Their Midnight Mistletoe Kiss
Two-Week Temptation in Paradise

All available now!

MILLS & BOON®

Coming next month

THEIR MAURITIUS WEDDING RUSE
Nina Milne

'If you agreed we would go to Mauritius and plan a small low-key ceremony, lie low somewhere on the beach.'

Images streamed her mind. Lying stretched out on golden sand, side by side with Logan. So close that if she reached out she'd be able to touch him. Long cool drinks sipped by a pool. Walks through the fabulous scenery of Mauritius, dinners for two at little local restaurants. Watching the sun set over a deep blue sea, turning to each other later in the moonlight, tipping her face upward and…

Jeez. Snap out of it. What was wrong with her? That was not a scenario that could play for her - not with Logan, not with anyone. And she understood that, was good with that. Unfortunately, her hormones clearly weren't.

Continue reading

THEIR MAURITIUS WEDDING RUSE
Nina Milne

Available next month
millsandboon.co.uk

Copyright © 2025 Nina Milne

COMING SOON!

We really hope you enjoyed reading this book.
If you're looking for more romance
be sure to head to the shops when
new books are available on

Thursday 19th June

To see which titles are coming soon, please visit
millsandboon.co.uk/nextmonth

MILLS & BOON

afterglow BOOKS

Afterglow Books is a trend-led, trope-filled list of books with diverse, authentic and relatable characters, a wide array of voices and representations, plus real world trials and tribulations. Featuring all the tropes you could possibly want (think small-town settings, fake relationships, grumpy vs sunshine, enemies to lovers) and all with a generous dose of spice in every story.

♪ @millsandboonuk
◉ @millsandboonuk
afterglowbooks.co.uk

#AfterglowBooks

For all the latest book news, exclusive content and giveaways scan the QR code below to sign up to the Afterglow newsletter:

SCAN ME

afterglow BOOKS

- Sports romance
- Enemies to lovers
- Spicy

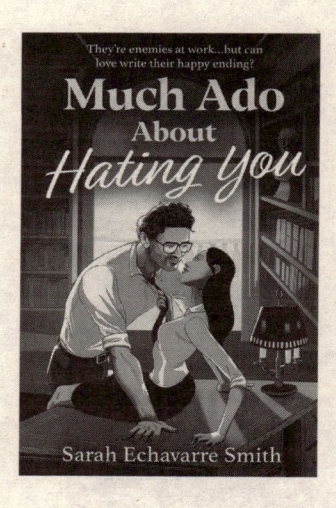

- Workplace romance
- Forbidden love
- Opposites attract

OUT NOW

Two stories published every month. Discover more at:
Afterglowbooks.co.uk

FOUR BRAND NEW BOOKS FROM
MILLS & BOON MODERN

The same great stories you love, a stylish new look!

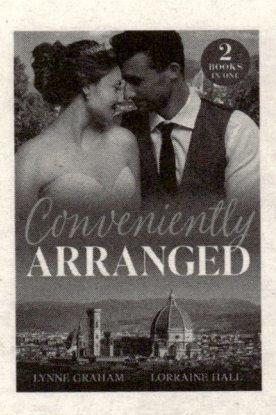

OUT NOW

Eight Modern stories published every month, find them all at:
millsandboon.co.uk

OUT NOW!

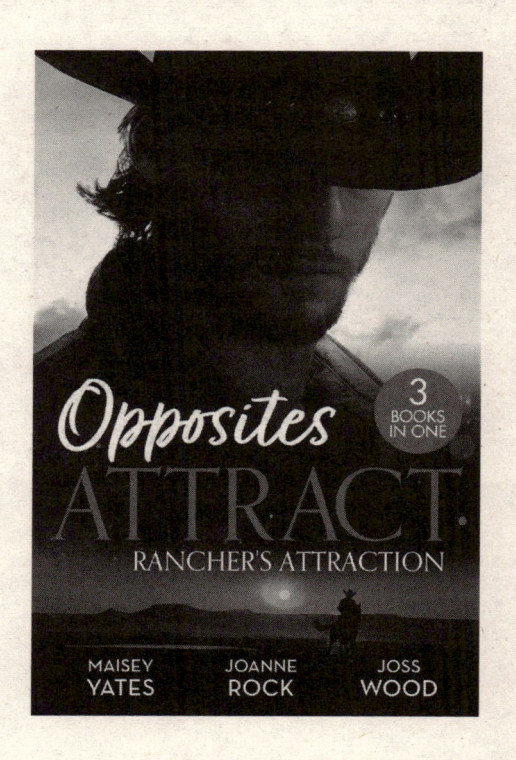

Opposites Attract: Rancher's Attraction

3 BOOKS IN ONE

MAISEY YATES · JOANNE ROCK · JOSS WOOD

Available at
millsandboon.co.uk

MILLS & BOON

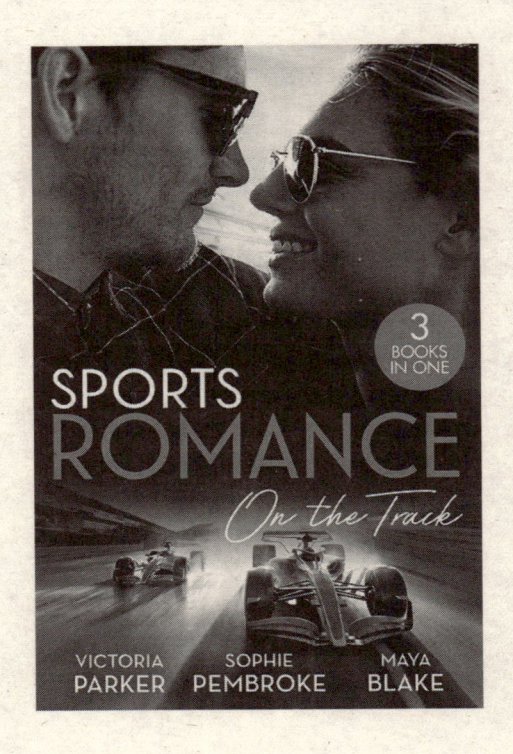

OUT NOW!

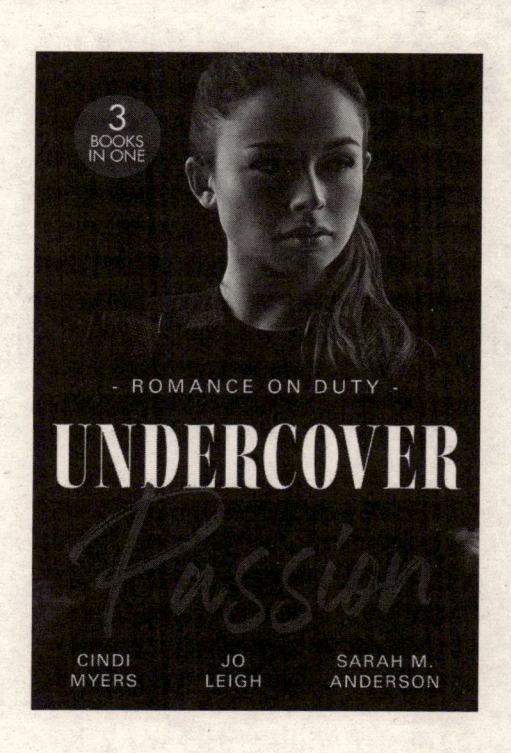

3 BOOKS IN ONE

- ROMANCE ON DUTY -

UNDERCOVER
Passion

CINDI MYERS · JO LEIGH · SARAH M. ANDERSON

Available at
millsandboon.co.uk

MILLS & BOON

LET'S TALK
Romance

For exclusive extracts, competitions and special offers, find us online:

- **f** MillsandBoon
- **X** @MillsandBoon
- **◯** @MillsandBoonUK
- **♪** @MillsandBoonUK

Get in touch on 01413 063 232

For all the latest titles coming soon, visit millsandboon.co.uk/nextmonth